**Praise for
Olivia Drake's Cinderella Sisterhood series**

"Drake proves the right pair of shoes can change your life—especially if they're red and belong to the Cinderella Sisterhood."

—*RT Book Reviews* on *Bella and the Beast*

"Lush historical romance, complete with all the sprinklings of a fairy tale. Olivia Drake is an excellent writer, and this story knows how to submerge readers completely."

—*Fresh Fiction*

"Breathtaking."

—*Night Owl Reviews* on *Abducted by a Prince*

"A compelling romance filled with intrigue."

—*Affaire de Coeur* on *Stroke of Midnight*

"Cinderella knew it was all about the shoes, and so does master storyteller Drake as she kicks off the Cinderella Sisterhood with a tale filled with gothic overtones, sensuality, sprightly dialogue, emotion, an engaging cast, and a beautiful pair of perfectly fitting slippers."

—*RT Book Reviews* (4 stars) on *If the Slipper Fits*

THE
Duke I
ONCE KNEW

OLIVIA DRAKE

St. Martin's Paperbacks

This is a work of fiction. All of the characters, organizations, and events portrayed in this novel are either products of the author's imagination or are used fictitiously.

THE DUKE I ONCE KNEW

Copyright © 2019 by Barbara Dawson Smith.

All rights reserved.

For information address St. Martin's Press, 175 Fifth Avenue, New York, NY 10010.

ISBN: 978-1-250-17437-6

Our books may be purchased in bulk for promotional, educational, or business use. Please contact your local bookseller or the Macmillan Corporate and Premium Sales Department at 1-800-221-7945, ext. 5442, or by e-mail at MacmillanSpecialMarkets@macmillan.com.

Printed in the United States of America

St. Martin's Paperbacks edition / January 2019

St. Martin's Paperbacks are published by St. Martin's Press, 175 Fifth Avenue, New York, NY 10010.

10 9 8 7 6 5 4 3 2 1

Chapter 1

If they didn't stop rearranging her life, she would shriek at them—all of them. Right here, right now, in the midst of a family party.

The tide of anger caught Abigail Linton by surprise, and she drew a deep breath in an effort to dispel it. It wasn't like her to feel such resentment toward those most dear to her. Or to be tempted to rant at them like an escapee from Bedlam. Especially not when she cuddled her infant nephew.

Standing near the open window, she gently rocked Freddie in her arms. Looking at his sweet little face helped to calm her. He'd fallen into a fretful sleep, thank goodness, after an eventful morning in which he'd suffered the indignity of having cold water poured over his brow at the baptismal font.

Abby, her four siblings, and their spouses had gathered in the drawing room to celebrate his christening. The newborn's father, Abby's brother James, was vicar of the village church. Since the rectory was cramped, the extended family had proceeded to their childhood home a mile away. Linton Manor now belonged to her eldest brother,

Clifford, upon the death of their elderly parents the previous autumn.

The youngest of the five, Abby had enjoyed exchanging news with her two sisters and two brothers. She had relished visiting with a throng of nieces and nephews. She had loved hearing the laughter of the younger children playing outdoors on this pleasant summer afternoon, and she'd smiled at the older ones who were gathered around the pianoforte while seventeen-year-old Valerie practiced her playing.

Abby had felt enveloped by a warm sense of family. At least until a moment ago when the conversation had turned to her future.

"It is only fitting that Abby remain here in her childhood home," Clifford proclaimed from his stance by the hearth. A portly man in his early fifties, he presided over the gathering as head of the family. "Now that our children are married, Lucille needs a companion."

"Indeed," his stout wife murmured, taking up the silver pot to refresh his tea. "You've so many duties since inheriting the estate, my dear, and it's pleasant to have someone with me during the day while you're out."

Abby's middle sibling, Rosalind, set down her cup with a rattle. At forty, she had retained her girlish figure, though strands of silver glinted in the signature copper hair of the Lintons. "But Abby *must* come back to Kent with me. I'm counting on her!"

"Whatever for?" Clifford asked testily.

"Valerie will be making her bows soon, and you *know* how lively the dear girl can be." Rosalind cast a fond glance at the strawberry-blond beauty flirting at the pianoforte with her older male cousins. "I daresay she'll be the toast of the season. It shall take two of us to properly chaperone her."

"For pity's sake, it's merely August." Mary, the second oldest, bestirred herself from a scrutiny of the cake plate in order to address her younger sister. "You shan't be departing for London until February at the earliest."

"But there is her trousseau to prepare! Her dancing and curtsies to practice!"

"Bah," Mary said dismissingly. "Rather, *I* should find it extremely helpful to have Abby with *me*. The twins will soon be coming for an extended visit while George and Caroline holiday in Italy. Poor Caro cannot find a nanny who can stop them from running wild. Isn't that so, Ronald?"

"What's that?" Her balding husband glanced up from where he and Peter, Rosalind's husband, were studying the latest racing form. "Yes, darling, whatever you say."

"There, you see?" Mary said, regarding her siblings with a superior air. "Abby is much needed in Suffolk. I am the wife of a baronet, after all. I cannot be chasing after a pair of three-year-old boys. It isn't dignified."

"Oh, pooh!" Rosalind waved her hand. "A title doesn't make you any better than the rest of us. Nor should your wishes take precedence over mine."

Clifford frowned. "Nevertheless, Mary is right, you've no need of Abby until spring. As for you, Mary, you ought to hire an extra nanny for a few months rather than drag Abby halfway across the country. *This* is her home, after all. She ought to remain right here."

"Hire an extra nanny!" Mary looked aghast at the prospect. She could be pleasant company except in matters of money, when her skinflint nature rose to the fore. "Only think of the expense—"

"I must concur with Clifford," James said. He was a slim man in a clerical collar who exuded a gentle demeanor that helped him to shepherd his flock. "There are needs greater than yours, I'm afraid. Now that the new baby has arrived, it has been a blessing to have Abby so close to the village. Daphne can scarcely find time to breathe between caring for our other three children and fulfilling the duties of a vicar's wife."

"It has indeed been difficult," Daphne said, languidly waving an ivory fan at her pretty face. "There are times when I am quite overwhelmed, and Abby's help has been a godsend. Heaven knows, Freddie is very blessed to have the loving care of his aunt."

At the sound of his mama's voice, the baby stirred restlessly in his sleep, and Abby walked back and forth to settle him. She told herself to be grateful that she was needed. Grateful that her siblings desired her assistance. Grateful that she would always have a home with one of them.

Nevertheless, a rare knot of resentment tightened inside her.

They were speaking of her future. Yet she might as well be invisible for as much as they consulted *her* wishes on where she preferred to live.

Perhaps it was her looming birthday that made her feel so prickly. In a fortnight, she would turn thirty years of age. Thirty! With no husband or children to call her own.

The youngest by seven years, she'd been the surprise child born when their mother had been in her middle forties. While her siblings had wed and started families, the task of caring for their aging parents had fallen to Abby. In her youth, when she ought to have enjoyed a season in London, being courted by a bevy of eligible gentlemen, she had remained here in Hampshire because Mama had broken her hip in a tumble from a horse and had never regained complete mobility. As well, Papa had come to depend on Abby to help with the research for his book on medieval history. Her twenties had slipped away as she'd busied herself with tending to their needs. Then, less than a year ago, both her parents had fallen ill with influenza.

Their deaths had been a shock. She had spent her entire life in their company and for months afterward she had grieved. Today, in deference to the happy occasion, she'd put off her blacks for a gown of dove gray. The rest of the family had donned brighter colors weeks ago. Of course, none of her siblings had had such a special closeness to their parents as she'd had.

Nor did they quite understand the sacrifices she'd made.

Not that she had *minded*. Certainly not! She'd dearly loved Mama and Papa. Their care had never been a burden. Yet now, contemplating the rest of her life, Abby felt a disquiet that bordered on panic.

Was this to be her future? Was she doomed to be shuttled among her siblings, never having a place to call her own? When she grew old and gray, would there come a time when her nieces and nephews squabbled over who must take her in?

Running a fingertip over the baby's soft cheek, Abby knew with a pang that life had passed her by. The romantic dreams of her youth had burned to ashes. She was a spinster. In all likelihood, she would never know marriage or motherhood.

Oh, she'd had a few suitors over the years, one quite recently. Mr. Babcock, a gentleman farmer, had offered for her this past spring, but she had put him off with a polite refusal. Nevertheless, he'd declared his intention to ask again once her full year of mourning was over.

Abby toyed with the notion of accepting him. Mr. Babcock was a decent man, solid and respectable, but she would have to share the same house with his henpecking mother and strict Calvinistic father. Was she truly so desperate as to wed someone whose sole interests were cows and sheep, anyway? Who failed to stir even the smallest spark of fire in her blood? Could she endure his dull company day after day, month after month, year after year, for the chance to avoid being a vagabond who moved from relative to relative?

A deep-seated resistance in her balked at taking that drastic step. Yet she did not relish the notion of spending the rest of her life as the family's unpaid servant, either.

Perhaps there was another answer.

Just that morning, she'd learned an interesting tidbit of news from her best friend in the village. Lizzie Pentwater had whispered it in her ear during the christening at church. An idea had crept into the back of Abby's mind. An idea that was appealing and audacious. An idea that would most definitely put her at odds with her siblings.

Clutching the swaddled baby, she started toward the door of the drawing room. She needed to be alone to think. To consider all the consequences.

"Abby! Where are you taking my son?"

She turned to face her sister-in-law. Daphne lounged in her chair in a place of honor at the center of the gathering. Since her papa owned the draper's shop in the village, she always dressed like an illustration out of *La Belle Assemblée,* despite being the vicar's wife. Today, a gown of shell-pink India muslin swathed her dainty form and a gold comb secured her sable curls.

"I'm going to the nursery," Abby murmured over the music of the pianoforte and the laughter of the children. "The noise is disturbing Freddie."

"Oh, but my little darling *must* stay. It is his day, after all, so why should he be put upstairs?" Daphne turned a winsome smile toward her husband. "Do tell her, James."

"Babies need their naps," he said, though his face softened as he gazed at his wife. "Nevertheless, this *is* a special occasion, so I'm agreeable to making an exception."

"Perhaps you should hold him, then," Abby said.

Stepping forward, she placed the sleeping child in her brother's arms. His brown eyes widened. Although an otherwise affectionate father, James, like most men, was accustomed to leaving the care of infants to the women.

He gingerly clutched the bundle against his black clerical suit. "Er . . . I'm not certain this is wise. What if he should awaken? He might howl!" He glanced rather desperately at Daphne, who in her finery looked equally unwilling to take the baby, then turned his gaze back up at Abby. "Perchance you'll be so kind as to have him back?"

"No. I won't."

The words spilled from Abby's lips without conscious thought. Nor had she planned to shove the baby at him like that. It wasn't like her to be rude. Or to refuse to do what was expected of her.

Yet her tongue seemed incapable of voicing a retraction.

Everyone gaped at her. Clifford paused with his teacup half raised to his mouth. Lucille clutched a plate of cakes. Rosalind's eyebrows winged upward. James and Daphne wore identical frowns as if Abby had just uttered a salty expletive. Even Ronald and Peter glanced up from their study of the races.

They all appeared so shocked, Abby had to swallow a mad laugh that bubbled up from nowhere. There was nothing remotely amusing about the situation. It was just that she'd always acquiesced to their wishes.

And it felt incredibly liberating to utter a refusal for once.

Mary huffed out a breath. "Abigail Jane Linton! That is most ill-mannered. Do take the child and apologize at once."

By way of reply, Abby crossed her arms. Her slippers felt glued to the ancient rug with its cabbage-rose pattern that had been worn threadbare by generations of Linton feet. An inner voice whispered that if she conceded now, she might never again find the courage to stand up for herself.

"Well!" Rosalind said in a perky tone. "One can scarcely blame our sister for rebelling at being treated like a nurse-maid. That's all the more reason for her to come home with me. Together, we can plan Valerie's wardrobe and study *Burke's* to make a list of the most eligible bachelors. It shall be a treat for Abby."

"That matter is already settled," Clifford declared. "Since both James and I have need of her, she must remain right here for the near future."

"Ever since we lost our parents, you've had Abby at your beck and call," Rosalind countered. "You haven't stopped to consider that the rest of us might appreciate her company, too. Why, she has never even traveled to Kent to visit me!"

"Enough." He slashed his hand downward. "There is nothing more to discuss. She *will* stay here."

"No," Abby said. "I most certainly will not."

Again, everyone turned to stare. It was as if, in the midst of their bickering, they'd forgotten her presence again. Was she merely a wallflower to fade into the woodwork except when they needed something from her? Or worse, a com-modity to be traded back and forth between them, depend-ing upon who complained the loudest?

She loved them all dearly—they and their children, her nieces and nephews. Family had always been her entire world, the very center of her existence. But it was time to break free of their stifling demands. Her siblings must be made to understand that she wanted to set her own path for once.

At least for a time. At least until she'd experienced a little of life outside the sphere of their influence.

She was nearly *thirty*, after all, and she had never ventured farther than twenty miles from home. She had never lived anywhere but right here in this old manor house with its ancient wallpaper and the chipped porcelain dogs on the mantelpiece that had been there for as long as she could remember.

Clifford stared at her with a hint of bewilderment. "I cannot fathom this sudden defiance in you. Is our company so abhorrent to you?"

"Of course not!" Abby said. "You mustn't think such a thing—"

"What else am I to conclude when you seem so eager to leave my home and my protection?"

She nearly quailed under the force of that piercing look. Because of their age difference, she and her eldest brother had never been close. He'd married Lucille the year before Abby had been born. At fifty-three, he was old enough to be her father.

Nevertheless, she must not allow him to dictate to her.

"You may conclude," she said firmly, "that what I do should not be decided by anyone but myself. And no one here has bothered to inquire as to my thoughts on the matter."

Lucille wrung her hands as she glanced at her husband, then back at Abby. "Does your head ache, darling? I daresay it's this changeable weather, chilly one day and scorching the next. Perhaps you would care to go upstairs and have a lie-down?"

"Thank you, but I'm perfectly fine. It is only that I should like to have a say in my own future."

Rosalind jumped up, looped her arm through Abby's,

and smirked at Clifford. "There, you see? Our sister doesn't wish to be the subject of your decrees. She must be allowed to make her own choice and enjoy a holiday in Kent with me."

Abby slipped her arm free. "That is *your* choice, Rosie, not mine. And what *I* choose to do is to apply for the post of governess to Lady Gwendolyn Bryce at Rothwell Court."

For a moment, the only sounds were the tinkle of the pianoforte and the shriek of children engaged in a raucous game of blindman's buff outside the open windows of the drawing room. Then a clamor of adult voices broke out.

"A governess?" Clifford said in astonishment. "Whatever put such a wild notion in your mind? Your place is with your family!"

"Oh, dear," Lucille murmured, looking scandalized, "you cannot *labor* for a living. Whatever will the neighbors think?"

"You've never even had a season," Mary added bluntly. "Lady Gwendolyn must be close to an age to make her debut. What training do you have for preparing the sister of a duke for presentation at court?"

Abby had wondered that herself. But she chose to sidestep the question. "Lady Gwendolyn has just turned fifteen. She won't be entering society for another three years."

"Never mind all that," Rosalind said, her brown eyes bright with interest. "Did no one *think* to tell me that the Duke of Rothwell is in residence? Valerie and I must pay a neighborly call on him tomorrow. Why, he is the most eligible bachelor in England!"

"He is also England's most infamous libertine," Clifford said curtly, pacing back and forth. "Lechery, fighting, gambling—he is the master of vices. You would scarce believe the stories that circulate in London! I cannot—I *will* not—permit any sister of mine to venture within a mile of his house."

"His Grace isn't at Rothwell Court," Abby pointed out. "You know as well as I that he hasn't come in many years."

Fifteen, to be precise. Not since his late father had whisked the family away upon the death of the duchess, the present duke's mother. She had died of childbed fever shortly after Lady Gwendolyn's birth.

The duke's vast acreage adjoined Linton land and dwarfed all other holdings in this part of rural Hampshire. Wicked reputation or not, Rothwell would have stirred excitement with a visit to his ducal seat. The village and its surrounds would have been abuzz with excitement.

Except for Abby. If it was up to her, Maxwell Bryce, the Duke of Rothwell, need never again sully the neighborhood with his beastly presence.

Rosalind plopped back down in her chair. "I don't understand. Why would His Grace's sister live there without him?"

"She's made her home at the Court for the past few years," Lucille said, moving around the room to refresh everyone's teacup. "I believe His Grace's aunt, Lady Hester, has a particular fondness for the gardens."

"Then let Lady Hester see to the girl," Clifford burst out in irritation. "There is no reason why Abby should seek employment there!"

The baby in James's lap let out a whimper. "Do keep your voices down," James hissed. "You needn't shout."

"Doesn't Lady Gwendolyn already have a governess?" Daphne asked in a loud whisper. "Miss Herrington, I believe is her name. The two of them sometimes attend church on Sundays."

Abby had found Miss Herrington to be remarkably young and pretty, though they'd never exchanged more than an occasional greeting. "Lizzie Pentwater told me that Miss Herrington departed suddenly due to a family illness. And I intend to apply for the vacant post."

Lucille set down the teapot. "But why, darling? Have we made you feel unwelcome here? Oh, I know it must be difficult when a woman is unattached. But I assure you, we *want* you to make your home with us."

"And here is where she must stay," Clifford insisted. "No sister of mine will be employed. People will say that I'm impoverished, sending her out to earn her own keep."

"There will indeed be a great deal of unpleasant gossip," Mary added, casting a shrewd glance at Abby. "It won't do for the Linton name to be tainted by rumors and innuendos. The chinwags will whisper that our family is on the brink of disaster."

Rosalind's eyes widened. "Why, I hadn't considered that. The scandal is bound to harm Valerie's chance to make a brilliant match. Many gentlemen will disdain to wed a girl with a host of penniless relations!"

"More importantly, Abby, you're our dear sister," James said as he awkwardly attempted to jiggle his fussing son back to sleep. "We need you to remain right here with us."

They all gazed at Abby as if her departure would cause them desperate sorrow and grave ruination. The infant echoed the sentiment with a series of peevish cries.

For a moment, her resolve wavered. She felt horribly selfish for abandoning her family in order to venture out on her own. It would be so easy to say that she was wrong and to bow to their wishes. To subdue her longing to experience something more of life beyond these familiar walls.

Yet Abby knew she was being maneuvered.

Their arguments were flimsy. They had to realize that any gossip about a minor family of the gentry wouldn't cause much of a stir as far away as London, and it likely wouldn't hurt her niece's marital prospects, either. No, her siblings wanted her to stay in order to serve their own purposes.

"I'm sorry," Abby said firmly. "I love all of you, but I have made up my mind. I'm walking over to Rothwell Court at once to speak with Lady Hester."

Turning on her heel, she departed the drawing room.

The squalling of the baby followed Abby down the corridor and into the entry hall with its ticking casement clock and the ancient umbrella stand in the corner. She half expected one or another of her siblings to come scurrying to stop her. But no one did. They likely were banking on the hope that she would be turned down for the post.

And she might well be. But a lack of experience wasn't what worried her.

Rather, she feared that Lady Hester would seek the duke's permission before hiring a new governess for his sister. Somehow, she would have to convince his aunt not to contact him, for he undoubtedly would deny her application. In truth, had she known of any suitable employment other than at the Court, she would have vastly preferred it.

Lifting her straw bonnet from a hook on the wall, Abby tied the blue ribbons beneath her chin. Never in her life had she taken such a bold step. Never had she abandoned her role of caregiver to the family. Never had she indulged her desire to earn a wage of her own. The prospect of leaving the confines of her childhood home felt both exhilarating and terrifying.

But her family could have no inkling of her true misgivings. They didn't know that fifteen years ago, she and Maxwell Bryce had shared a clandestine romance. Or that he had abandoned her for the pleasures of London.

Chapter 2

No one observing His Grace, the Duke of Rothwell, would have noticed the slightest hint of tension in him—or seen the unease that increased in him with each passing mile. Rather, he was the image of aristocratic indolence.

Like an invitation to sin, Max lounged against the plush blue squabs of his traveling coach. His eyes were half closed as he watched the rain spatter the window. He wore a claret cutaway coat with a burnished gold waistcoat, and buckskins with a pair of polished black Hessians. A pearl stickpin glinted in the starched folds of his cravat. The dark hair that brushed his collar was artfully disheveled in such a manner as to stir in a woman the hope of waking up in bed to find him eyeing her from the adjacent pillow.

At present, however, the woman beside him appeared more disgruntled than lusty.

"*Must* you take up so much space?" Elise, Lady Desmond, inquired crossly of the third occupant of the ducal coach. "Your monstrous shoes are crushing my hem."

On the opposite seat sat a hulking man clad in a garish

imitation of the gentry. His garb included a checkered coat in a hideous combination of orange and brown, a lime-green stock tied beneath his square jaw, and matching green trousers specially tailored to accommodate his gigantic proportions. A porkpie hat perched at a jaunty angle atop his massive shaved skull. His rough countenance featured a jagged scar across one cheek, squinty blue eyes, and a misshapen nose.

Goliath peeled back his lips in a grin that revealed a gap where his front teeth had been knocked out in a brawl the previous year. He shifted his feet closer to the door and away from Lady Desmond's fine muslin gown. "Beggin' yer pardon, milady. Me mum always grumbled about these clodhoppers, too."

"Well, see to it that it doesn't happen again." She twitched her cream skirt away from his offending presence. "I still contend you should have ridden in the baggage cart with the other servants."

"Now, see 'ere! Oi ain't the 'ired 'elp! Oi'm England's champ, that Oi am!"

Disliking to see his pugilist insulted, Max bestirred himself from his contemplation of the drenched scenery. "Quite so, which is why I won't have you catching a chill in this rain. You must be in prime form for the mill with Wolfman."

"I'll thrash 'im," Goliath vowed, brandishing a pair of ham fists. "Ye can stake all yer riches on it, Yer Grace."

"I trust so. Wagering *is* the point, after all."

"Why, the prizefight is not until the end of the week," Elise said. "I very much doubt a little summer drizzle would harm the man."

"Nevertheless, he will remain right here. Should you find him offensive, perhaps you'd prefer to ride with the others in Pettibone's carriage." Max reached for his ebony cane as if to rap on the upper panel and signal the coachman to stop.

Elise's expression underwent a miraculous transformation from disdainful glare to winsome smile. "Certainly not! You *know* that I vastly prefer your company to anyone else's."

Max tucked the cane beneath his booted feet. He was not a man to abide having his decisions challenged. Nor did he do the bidding of any woman. He had been too long his own master. In fact, had he not been determined to seduce Elise, he would never have allowed her in his coach at all.

He valued his prizefighter more than any female, no matter how lush a figure she possessed.

She placed her dainty gloved hand on his arm. "Pray don't be angry with me, Your Grace," she murmured. "It's just that I find it rather maddening we cannot engage in . . . a more private conversation."

Her suggestive manner stirred his blood. She was a truly ravishing morsel from her pouty pink lips and green-gold eyes framed by soft flaxen curls, to her hourglass form with its extravagant bosom and slender waist. Her charms, he judged, outweighed a tendency toward petulance. One expected a bit of sulkiness in one's mistress, after all. He was well acquainted with the way women wheedled jewelry and other favors from a man.

No, the fly in the ointment was that Lady Desmond desired more from him than covert visits to her bedchamber. For the past month, she had teased and tempted, only to deny him the ultimate prize. Instead of lifting her skirts, she had played the coy maiden. The former actress had been plucked from the stage by an ancient baronet who had promptly expired of a heart seizure on their honeymoon.

Now she sought to become a duchess.

Max had no intention of being enticed to the altar. Duty did not oblige him to sire an heir, for he had a sober-minded cousin who sufficed in that role. He had no elderly relations, either, to bedevil him into a leg shackle. At one-and-thirty, he was quite comfortable in his bachelorhood. He had seen in his own father's case that having a wife only made a man weak and wretched.

He had always known he would never marry.

Well, perhaps not *always*. There had been that one brief interlude in his callow youth. Thankfully, he had escaped to London where he'd soothed his bruised heart with a boundless array of pretty damsels and lusty opera singers. He'd learned quite a lot about women since his salad days. In particular, that two could play Elise's cat-and-mouse game.

He rubbed his thumb across the palm of her kid glove. "Patience, my lady. We shall have ample privacy quite soon."

She leaned closer, her bosom pressed to his upper arm. With a glance at Goliath, she whispered, "That does sound enticing, my lord duke. What did you have in mind?"

"You're well aware of what I want." He kissed her fingers while gazing deeply into her eyes. "And pray know that *my* patience has its limits."

"Oh, la!" she said rather breathlessly. "We shall have an entire week at Rothwell Court in which to enjoy ourselves. I am looking very much forward to it. Are you not delighted by the change in our plans?"

The reminder of their destination dampened his ardor, and he released her hand. "Traveling an additional twenty-five miles is hardly delightful."

"Nevertheless, I should think it very comfortable to stay in a house so well appointed as Rothwell Court is reputed to be. And you must allow, it is closer to the site of the match."

Max tightened his jaw. That was a point he could not argue.

"Besides," Elise rattled on, "it was impossible to stay at Pettibone's estate when his entire staff has taken ill with the measles. Why, they were bound to be horribly infectious! How dreadful to imagine coming down with spots from head to toe!"

"Yes. The fever and itching might have felled my champion."

"Oi ain't never missed a match," Goliath bragged. "Nor lost one, neither."

Elise frowned at the giant as if to discourage his interjection into their conversation. Then her soulful gaze returned to Max. "Don't tease, Your Grace, you *know* I was referring to myself. Should I be confined to bed, it must not be due to dreadful blotches, but to . . . other pursuits."

Under different circumstances, Max would have found her innuendo arousing. He appreciated sexual byplay as much as the next man. Just not now. Today, his temper had an edge.

"We will speak of this later," he said tersely.

Her fingers toyed with the narrow ruffle that edged his cuff. "Do tell me about Rothwell Court, then. I understand you seldom entertain there."

"I prefer the amusements of London to rusticating in the country."

"But you grew up at the estate, did you not? You surely must have fond memories. The house is said to be the most magnificent edifice in all of England. If it is indeed so fine, why do you never invite your friends to visit?"

"My underage sister makes her home there with my aunt."

"Why, surely our paths need seldom cross in so large a house. There must be numerous wings and apartments. Is that not so?"

"You may form your own opinion of the place when we arrive in half an hour. That is enough chatter for now."

He fixed Elise with a hard stare. It was a look he used to silence underlings—or those who dared to probe too deeply into his private life.

Elise dropped her hand back into her lap. Her lips formed a little moue, but she said no more, apparently realizing the risk of overstepping her bounds.

Max shifted his gaze to the rain-wet window of the coach. As the vehicle swayed to avoid a pothole, his earlier tension returned, though he hid it behind a relaxed posture. There had been no time to prepare himself for this unexpected detour. Upon their arrival at Pettibone's estate earlier, Max and a small party of his friends had discovered the entire staff to be contagious with measles. Alternative accommodations had been needed on short notice, and there were no local inns large enough to hold all of them in comfort for the coming week.

Besides, Max wanted private space for Goliath to practice in an area that was shielded from prying eyes. He must take no chance of the opposition spying on the bruiser's training sessions in the hopes of spotting a weakness to exploit.

Rothwell Court had been the only feasible location. Lord Pettibone had proposed it, Lord Ambrose Hood had seconded the motion, while Elise and Mrs. Chalmers had been ecstatic at the chance to view the estate. It would have been illogical for him to refuse.

Max prided himself on his rationality. He did not allow sentiment to color his judgment. Only a man with the spine of a jellyfish made decisions based on emotion.

Nevertheless, he had to subdue a craven urge to order the coachman to turn and beat a swift retreat. Except for a brief overnight trip to bury his father in the private chapel a decade ago, it had been fifteen years since he'd last stayed at his ducal seat. Fifteen years of avoiding the site of so many unpleasant childhood memories.

In the interim, he had immersed himself in the myriad pleasures of the city. If ever he felt a hankering for rural pursuits, he owned three other estates from which to choose, his favorite being The Ridings near Oxford, where Aunt Hester and Gwen always joined him for the holidays.

His irritability eased somewhat as he thought of his sister. Though they'd exchanged letters, it had been months since they'd last met at Easter. He wanted to know how she was faring, particularly in light of the abrupt departure of her governess the previous week. Max had decided not to conduct interviews for a replacement until he returned to London after the prizefight. His sister had earned a few weeks of freedom from her studies.

As the coach descended a hill, the village of Rothcommon spread out like a jeweled necklace alongside the river. His heart lurched in spite of his outward discipline. He recognized every thicket of trees, every knoll and every vale, every bend in the road. He had roamed these woods as a boy. If truth be told, he had to restrain the impulse to throw open the door, plunge into the forest, and head straight to . . .

No. The secret glade was the last place he wished to revisit. The very thought of it made his gut churn with memories best left buried.

The coach swayed around a curve to reveal several familiar landmarks: the steeple of St. John the Baptist Church poking through the trees, a string of thatch-roofed cottages, the arch of the stone bridge across the river.

Within moments, the vehicle slowed to a more sedate pace along the high street, passing the apothecary, the black-smith, the butcher. It was the same as he remembered, as if time here had stopped.

Pedestrians stopped to stare. Shopkeepers stepped into their doorways to watch the black coach with the gold strawberry-leaf crest embellishing the door. Several urchins ran alongside the vehicle, their excited chatter blending with the rattle of the wheels over the cobble-stones.

It struck Max that they were his people, his responsi-bility. But that was absurd. These were modern times, not a medieval fiefdom.

"How quaint," Elise remarked, peering out her window. "Look at that tiny draper's shop and the haberdashery next door. It never fails to astonish me that provincials can be content with so little."

Her words hardly registered, so intense was his concen-tration. Something keen and sharp filled his chest. He felt a curious sense of homecoming. As if he belonged here.

He irritably rejected the sentiment. This Hampshire backwater was no longer his home. He had gone away from here long ago, when he was a youth on the cusp of man-hood. His bailiff handled the day-to-day operations of the farms and pasturelands. The estate meant nothing to him anymore except as a source of revenue to fund his life in the city. In fact, given the prosperity of his other holdings, he didn't even need the income. Had the property not been entailed, Max would have sold it.

Nevertheless, as the coach left the village and ap-proached the stone gatehouse that marked the entry to Rothwell land, he felt hard-pressed to maintain his devil-may-care pose.

Chapter 3

"The rain has nearly stopped, Miss Linton. Are you *quite* certain I cannot go riding today?"

Lady Gwendolyn stood at the window with her dainty nose pressed to the glass. The mint-green paneled walls of the morning room were decorated with white rococo plasterwork of delicate flowers and birds. White fluted silk draperies had been drawn back with tasseled gold cord to reveal the dismal gray sky.

Against the elegant backdrop, the duke's sister looked like the subject in a painting of the ideal young lady. Slim and willowy, she wore a gown of pale blue muslin with cap sleeves. A Brussels-lace ribbon secured her wavy chestnut tresses at the nape of her neck.

Over the course of the past week, Abby had found her new charge to be quiet and biddable and diligent at her studies. In truth, the girl was so well behaved that Abby felt almost guilty for accepting a wage as governess. If Lady Gwendolyn had any slight fault at all, it was that she was mad about horses. All of her free time was spent either sketching them, reading equine journals, or visiting the stables. Every afternoon, after completing her lessons, she went for a long ride, accompanied by one of the grooms.

Stepping to her side, Abby glanced out at the expanse of manicured greenery to the rear of the house. Since Rothwell Court sprawled on a low hill, the garden was terraced with wide steps leading down from one large section to the next. It featured stone pathways and geometric beds of pink and yellow roses, along with a variety of other blooming bushes. A fountain with the statue of a mermaid formed the centerpiece. There were arches hung with crimson roses and stone benches where one might sit and enjoy the flowers—though not today when a steady drizzle had soaked everything.

Beyond the formal gardens, mist hazed the hills of the parkland. The blue of a lake could be glimpsed past groves of beech and oak, as could the roof of a faux Greek temple beside the water. Discreetly out of sight were the many tenant farms that provided income to the estate.

A memory disturbed her. It had been on such a damp day that Mama had been thrown from her horse in the woods close to where her family's small property adjoined the vast ducal lands. The fall had left her partially crippled and dependent upon the assistance of her youngest—and only unmarried—daughter. Abby had been sixteen, barely older than Lady Gwendolyn was now. She shuddered to imagine the girl suffering such a terrible accident.

"I'm afraid your ride will have to be postponed," Abby said. "The grass looks too wet and the trails will be muddy."

"Not even if I promise to hold Pixie to a walk? And if we go only to the lake and back?"

It was the first time she had ever heard a plea from Lady

Gwendolyn. The girl usually obeyed instructions without question.

She looked so disappointed that Abby slid an arm around her shoulders. "I'm sorry, darling, but you might catch a chill—or come to other harm. I'd never forgive myself if anything happened to you."

The girl smiled uncertainly. Abby knew that an embrace—however swift it might be—was overstepping her bounds as a servant. But it seemed a foolish rule when Lady Gwendolyn was so clearly starved for affection. The girl wasn't used to being hugged by scores of nieces and nephews and other assorted relations as Abby was. Lady Gwendolyn lived virtually alone in this great house. Aside from the staff, she had only her aging aunt for company, and Lady Hester spent most of her time pottering in the garden.

Of course, the wicked Duke of Rothwell never deigned to visit his sister and aunt. The rogue was too busy with his lecheries in London.

Loath to dwell on ill thoughts, Abby said, "It's time for you to write your daily essay. Afterward, you may go down to the stables and see Pixie."

Gwendolyn went willingly to the writing desk beside the window, sat down, and reached for a quill, holding it poised over the silver ink pot. "Please, what shall my topic be?"

Since she still looked woebegone, Abby decided upon an easy assignment. "Perhaps you could write about what you see on your daily rides about the estate, including the farms."

"But I've never seen them."

"You haven't ever visited any of the tenants?"

The girl shook her head. "Miss Herrington preferred the parkland trails."

Abby found that to be remiss. Someday, when Lady Gwendolyn married, it would be her duty to provide care and comfort to all the inhabitants of her husband's estate. "Then pray write in detail about whatever else it is you see on your rides. Make sure you use specific nouns and adjectives as we discussed earlier. I shall expect a minimum of five pages."

"May I write about Pixie, too? And include the stables?"

Seeing Lady Gwendolyn's dove-gray eyes alight gave Abby the odd sense of peering through a blurry window into the past. Although softer and more delicate, the girl's features were a feminine version of her elder brother's.

Shaking off the disturbing observation, she said, "Yes, you may. In the meantime, I'll look in the library for some books on the Roman occupation of ancient Britain for our history lesson."

As the girl dipped her pen into the inkwell and began to write, Abby headed out of the morning room and walked with swift, springing steps down a long corridor. She was pleased to see Lady Gwendolyn beginning to emerge from her shell. The girl had an inquisitive mind that only wanted a bit of nurturing. Abby felt confident the girl could benefit from her instruction.

Proceeding along another passage, she absorbed the beauty of gilt and marble, the frescoes on the high ceiling. The walls featured soaring pillars, shell sconces, and classical busts on pedestals. She glided past room after room filled with exquisite fittings that were seldom used anymore. It had taken her most of the week to learn her way around the place.

On her first day here, Lady Gwendolyn had taken Abby on a tour of the mansion, which had been built by the girl's grandfather, the eighth duke. They'd spent an entire morning tramping through cavernous drawing rooms, formal

apartments, sitting rooms, and galleries. Holland cloth
swathed the furniture in dozens of bedchambers in both
wings. The ballroom was so vast that it seemed all of Linton House surely must fit into it.

In the previous duke's time, there had been frequent
parties, especially during the long summer months when
the nobility escaped the heat of London. Abby had liked
to watch from a hidden vantage point in the woods. Pur-
loining an old spyglass that had belonged to one of her
brothers, she'd gawked at the ladies and gentlemen prom-
enading in the gardens. And she had dreamed of someday
having the chance to enter the ducal palace.

Her wish had been granted, though not in quite the
manner she had envisioned as a romantic girl, when she
had known the young scion of the ducal dynasty. But there
was no sense in dwelling on regrettable ancient history
when she meant to enjoy her stay here.

Her family had been distraught when she'd returned to
gather her belongings the previous week. While packing,
she had been subjected to more pleas and scolding from
her sisters and brothers. Clifford in particular had been
critical and angry, although he could hardly forbid her.

She was, after all, fast approaching the venerable old
age of thirty.

The memory of their disapproval brought a lump to her
throat. Having always been the nurturer and peacemaker,
Abby felt uncomfortable in the role of rebel. She thought
about her family often, and wondered if Freddie had overcome his colic, if Lucille had reminded Clifford to take
his gout medication, if James had found someone else to
copy over his sermons. If only they could understand that
although she loved them dearly, she yearned to see beyond
the cloistered existence that had constituted her life until
now.

As she descended a side staircase, the air had a hushed stillness, the only sound the tapping of her shoes on the marble steps. Before going to the library, she had one detour to make in answer to a summons delivered earlier by a footman.

The rich scent of loam enveloped her as she entered the conservatory. A light rain pattered on the domed glass roof, and the fronds of several tall palm trees brushed the high panes. On this chilly day, smudge pots with glowing coals kept the large room noticeably warmer than the rest of the house. A jungle of exotic plants filled the air with their pleasant perfumes.

At the far end of the tropical paradise knelt a stooped brown figure. Abby made her way toward the gnome, who was humming tunelessly while digging in the dirt. "Good afternoon, Lady Hester."

The rotund woman swiveled on her knees, and a clod fell from her trowel onto the slate floor. A russet turban sat askew on a mop of wild gray curls. She squinted her nearsighted blue eyes. "Hallo?"

Abby dipped a curtsy. "It's the new governess, my lady."

"Ah! You're one of the Linton daughters, I recollect."

As the elderly woman struggled to her feet, Abby lent her a hand. "Yes, I'm Abby, the youngest."

"Indeed! Your mama and I were launched the same season. Margaret married, but I never did, thank goodness. I vow, I should far rather manage a garden than a husband!" Cackling, Lady Hester attempted to brush the dirt off her soiled gloves. "I must say, 'twas a gift from heaven when you arrived last week. I was at my wit's end trying to keep dear Gwen entertained. Why, the cheek of Miss Herrington, to run off on scarcely a moment's notice!"

"I daresay she had little choice since she'd received word of a family crisis."

"Crisis, bah! It was more likely she went off with her lover. She was forever with her nose poked in one of those marble-covered gothic novels—and receiving missives from who knows whom!"

"Perhaps from one of her relatives?"

"Oh, I think not. I know the look of a woman in love. These past few weeks, she was all starry eyes and silly smiles." As she spoke, Lady Hester tenderly stroked a stalk of striking purple flowers. "Now, what do you think of my most magnificent plant?"

"It's lovely." Abby spoke absently, still a bit startled by the woman's assessment of Miss Herrington's departure. "Is that a lady's slipper?"

"Oh, nothing so common! Rather, this is a dendrobium orchid from the wilds of Malaysia. It has taken me a full year to coax it into bloom. Should you ever wish to purchase one yourself, I highly recommend contacting Loddiges Nursery in London."

"Yes, my lady." Abby desired to be polite, but conscious of the time, she prompted, "You summoned me?"

"Did I? Hmm, I seem to recall there was something important I needed to tell you." Frowning, Lady Hester wiped her gloved hands on her apron, leaving dark streaks on the white linen. "Oh, fiddle, it has slipped my mind, so it cannot be of any great importance. But it shall come to me in due course, you may be sure of that!"

"Might it concern Lady Gwendolyn's studies?"

"Goodness, no. I should rather leave all that to you, my dear. I haven't the least interest in such dull faradiddle. Have you seen my trowel?"

Her gaze had been darting around in perplexity, so Abby picked up the implement from the floor. "Here it is."

"How very obliging, Miss Linton. Such a delight that

you've come to stay with us. By the way, have I mentioned
that I remember seeing you here fifteen years ago?"

"Here, my lady? I'd never been in this house until recently."

"I meant outdoors. I was in the garden tending the roses
on the day of Cordelia's funeral, and I saw you meet my
nephew at the edge of the woods. The poor lad was distraught over his mama's death, and you were patting his
hand and talking to him. You struck me as a kind, warmhearted girl."

Lady Hester turned back around to fuss with her prize
orchid. The resumption of her happy humming signaled
the end of the conversation.

Abby walked slowly out of the conservatory. She was
stunned to learn she had been spotted with Max. Except
for that one time, they'd always taken care to rendezvous
at their secret glade in the forest, away from judgmental
eyes that would disapprove of the ducal heir befriending a
provincial nobody.

Well. What did it matter, really, after all these years?

Absolutely nothing.

After the abrupt departure of Max and his family on
the day following the funeral, she had come to a slow,
painful epiphany about his true nature. The tales of his
wild debaucheries had trickled back from London. His
wicked exploits were fodder for the local gossip mill, his
sins so boundless that it was doubtful he even remembered
the girl he'd met one summer in his youth.

Nevertheless, during her interview for the post of
governess, Abby had taken care to convince Lady Hester
not to solicit his permission in writing. His aunt had been
so keen to escape back to her garden that she'd readily
agreed that he wouldn't mind his sister being tutored by a

woman who hailed from a local family of excellent re-
pute. The subterfuge was harmless, Abby reasoned. The
Duke of Rothwell probably didn't even care to know the
name of his sister's governess, anyway.

But there was no sense courting trouble.

Her confidence high, she headed down another passageway to the library. There, she stepped inside the spacious
room and breathed in the blissful scent of books. The
masculine décor featured wine-red walls, a large writing
desk, and a number of mahogany tables with cabriole legs
and ball-and-claw feet. A globe of the world sat atop a
carved pedestal.

She would have loved to curl up in one of the leather
chairs to read. But if she didn't hurry, Lady Gwendolyn
would wonder at her long absence.

The task of finding one particular work among thou-
sands of volumes was daunting. In perusing the shelves,
however, she realized that the books were arranged by subject matter. There were sections devoted to botany, phi-
losophy, mathematics, biographies, languages, poetry, and
literature.

In a far corner of the room, she discovered the history
books. The shelves at eye level abounded with familiar ti-
tles, including all thirteen volumes of Hume's *History of
England*. The lower shelves held studies of the ancient
classical world.

Given the gloominess of the day, Abby had to crouch
down in order to read the tooled-leather spines. Here were
Virgil, Cicero, Gibbon's *Rise and Fall of the Roman Em-
pire*. She was particularly thrilled to discover a new series,
*The History of England: From the First Invasion by the
Romans to the Accession of Henry VIII*. How Papa would
have loved to have read it!

Just as she pulled out volume one, the approach of

voices out in the corridor penetrated her absorption. She paid little heed at first. In so large an establishment, the servants waged an endless war against dust and tarnish. She had heard an earful of laments on the topic from the housekeeper, Mrs. Jeffries, a righteous woman who had been pleased to welcome the vicar's sister into the household and hadn't needed much coaxing to sit down for a cozy chat over a pot of tea and a plate of Cook's plum cake.

Abby had made a point to befriend her fellow employees. Although she had been born to the gentry, it was not in her nature to lord over those of lesser birth. She liked hearing their stories, learning about their lives, partaking in their joys and their sorrows. Most people just wanted someone to listen to them.

The voices grew louder. A man and a woman.

As they entered the library, the click of the closing door sharpened her attention. Servants had no need of privacy while they tended to their duties. She quickly noticed two anomalies to their conversation: the flirty tone of it and also their use of the refined speech of the upper class.

"Have we given them the slip?" It was a lady's voice, high-pitched and frolicsome. "Oh, darling, I do believe we're alone at last."

"So it would seem. Though it is hardly good manners for the host to disappear and leave his guests to fend for themselves."

"Then perhaps you should find a way to entertain at least one of your guests."

A deep chuckle resounded. "I'm always happy to oblige a lady."

That voice.

A bone-deep shiver suffused Abby. She knew that caressing male baritone. It came straight out of the vault of the past. It had figured in her dreams at a time when she had been young and vulnerable.

Max.

No. No, it could not be him. It simply was not possible. Except for a brief visit to bury his father a decade ago, Rothwell had not set foot in this house in fifteen years. Nor had anyone mentioned an imminent visit. Surely Lady Gwendolyn or his aunt would have been all atwitter over such a rare event.

Panic scrambled Abby's thoughts. Her heart thumped so hard she felt light-headed and short of breath. She was mistaken. She must have misheard an exchange between servants. Her mind was playing tricks only because she had thought of him recently for the first time in ages.

And yet . . .

Still in a crouch, she turned around only to find that a large table blocked her view. She raised her head ever so slowly to peek over the edge.

At the opposite end of the library, a couple stood locked in a passionate embrace. The woman was a ravishing creature with blond curls, a shapely figure in a cream gown, and pale arms that were entwined like twin vipers around the man's neck. His hair looked thick and dark and attractively tousled. He was facing away from Abby, so that she could see only broad shoulders in a claret-colored coat, and powerful legs in form-fitting buckskins and black boots.

She had a moment's giddy respite. It wasn't him. He was not the boy of her memory. This man looked too muscular, too self-assured, too potently masculine. *Her* Max had been gangly and awkward.

Then he turned slightly, his hand supporting the woman's back as he lowered her onto one of the library tables. Leaning over her, he traced his fingertip along the

generous bosom revealed by her scandalously low décol-
letage. He muttered something in a jesting tone, something
that made his lover playfully slap at his chest.

In that instant, Abby had a clear view of his profile. Her
brief hope shattered under a jolt of reality. She would know
those distinctively handsome features anywhere.

It *was* Max.

He was really here.

She melted back down out of sight. Another tremor rippled through her. Thank goodness for the concealment of
the table and this shadowed corner. It wouldn't do to be
spotted by him, not when her thoughts reeled in a tizzy.

What on earth had brought him back to the Court without any notice to his family or the staff?

The answer didn't signify. All that mattered was that
he had come. And he had brought one of his lightskirts
with him. Or perhaps more than one, for according to their
conversation, there were other guests in his party. Abby
envisioned a harem of trollops fluttering and fawning, fulfilling his every whim.

She shook her head to dislodge the distasteful image.
One thing was certain. He had changed utterly over the
years, in both appearance and in character. No wonder
she hadn't recognized him at first. She hadn't seen Max
since he'd been sixteen to her fifteen.

No, not Max.

He was the Duke of Rothwell now. The boy she had
once loved was gone forever. Perhaps he'd never really existed. His warmth, his tenderness, had all been a sham.
That long-ago summer, he had been practicing his wiles
on a naïve girl in preparation for the more sophisticated
temptations of London.

The sounds of cooing and kissing mortified her. Good

heavens, would they never stop? Anyone might walk into the library! They ought to have the decency to take their amorous activities upstairs to a bedchamber.

But, of course, Rothwell did not possess a shred of decency. It made her cringe to recall that she herself had once fallen prey to his allure.

She risked another look over the edge of the table. Her eyes goggled.

The duke was delving beneath the hem of his paramour's gown, sliding his hand up her ankle and out of sight. The ladybird squirmed and squealed in a frisky attempt at evasion. He leaned down and silenced her playful protests with a masterful kiss.

Abby sank back down again. Her pulse pounded and a blush heated her inside and out. She oughtn't be so scandalized. Rothwell had a reputation as a notorious rake. Over the years, she had heard many a tale whispered among the neighbors of his disgraceful doings. Yet it was one thing to listen to idle gossip and quite another to actually witness him in the throes of depravity.

And here she was, trapped. What was she to do?

If she made her presence known, the duke would find out that Miss Abigail Linton was the new governess. She could not be absolutely certain that he had forgotten her. And if he did remember, he surely would dismiss her on the spot, for he wanted nothing to do with her.

Her spirits fell into a fit of the dismals. That would mark the end of her little adventure out into the world. Oh, she could apply for a position elsewhere, but who would hire her if she'd been summarily discharged from her previous post? She would be forced to return to her brother's house and resume her predictable life as the maiden aunt, growing withered and gray, shuttled between relatives, with no real say in her future.

The very thought was suffocating.

Nevertheless, she could not continue to crouch here while the two lovers were smooching and whispering. What if their intimate activities escalated? What if they did the deed right here, right now?

The horrid prospect spurred Abby to action. She must try to sneak out of the library unobserved. It was her only hope.

Dropping to her hands and knees, she crept along the carpet, weaving a path between the tables. Her long skirts hampered her progress, forcing her to inch along at a snail's pace. Rothwell's black boots were visible through a forest of chair legs. At least he was too distracted to notice her, judging by the amorous sounds emanating from across the room. To be safe, she made a wide berth around the couple.

Feverish plans raced through her head. If only she could reach the door and slip out, then all might be well. Perhaps she could convince Lady Gwendolyn not to mention the new governess to her brother. And what of Lady Hester? Was there a chance that she could be persuaded to bide her tongue, too? Should Abby confess the truth and enlist her help? Was it possible to stay out of sight until he departed the Court?

Sweet heaven, how long *did* he intend to stay?

In the midst of her meditations, she couldn't help overhearing the syrupy drivel of their tête-à-tête.

"Your Grace, you are too bold! Such a naughty boy you are!"

"I left boyhood behind long ago. Shall I demonstrate?"

"Mm, no. You mustn't . . . ah, yes. *Yes!*"

Abby grimaced under a tide of acute embarrassment. As she crawled closer to the door, she glared in the direction of the lovers. She could just see Rothwell's legs pressed against a froth of cream skirts. Blast him and his debauchery! He was the worst of rogues, the king of scoundrels. A more wicked man had never been born—!

Too caught up in remonstrations to watch where she was going, Abby bumped her hip hard against a mahogany pedestal. A little squeak escaped before she could clap her hand to her mouth. At the same instant, a faint clanking noise drew her attention upward.

The globe atop the pedestal wobbled precariously. As she watched in horror, the sphere toppled from its perch and clunked onto the floor, where it rolled straight past the chairs and tables to land at Rothwell's heels.

"What the devil—!"

Frozen in concealment, Abby watched wide-eyed through the maze of table legs as his boots shifted around. A large male hand flashed down to stop the spinning of the globe. Any faint hope that he might assume it had fallen of its own accord vanished in a millisecond.

Rothwell strode forward, his footfalls sharp and decisive. He came straight to her. To her great consternation, she found herself gazing at the polished black leather of his boots only a few inches away.

"Who are you?" he demanded. "What are you doing in here?"

Abby raised her chin only slightly, keeping her face averted. It was best that he didn't gaze fully at her—or hear the normal pitch of her voice lest it trigger his memory. "I'm just a servant," she whispered, "tending to my duties."

"Speak up! Why did you not make your presence known at once?"

His dictatorial tone shredded her better judgment. "I was trying to leave discreetly," she flared. "It didn't strike me as wise to interrupt your tryst." She paused, then added in a more servile tone, "I do beg your pardon, Your Grace."

She felt his gaze boring down like a physical force that

threatened to smother her. She wanted badly to look up, to glare into his face and tell him in no uncertain terms exactly what she thought of him.

But that would be highly imprudent.

With lightning swiftness, he clamped his hands around her upper arms and hauled Abby to her feet. She found herself staring up into a pair of wintry gray eyes set in a face of unabashed masculinity. Although a dissipated life had hardened his expression and etched faint lines on either side of his mouth, he was more disturbingly handsome than ever. He also seemed taller and tougher, his chest broader and his shoulders wider.

She hated that he still had the power to make the breath catch in her throat. Worse, she hated that he had the authority to dismiss her with a snap of his arrogant fingers. As she racked her beleaguered brain for a way to convince him not to do so, something flickered in those icy eyes.

"Abby?"

Chapter 4

Her presence dealt Max a sharp blow to the solar plexus.

He had not set eyes on Abigail Linton in fifteen years. Not since she had scorned to answer his letters. He noticed several details in quick succession. She had lost the bloom of youth, for she must be approaching thirty. Yet her skin was still smooth and unblemished, and the maturity of her fine bone structure lent her an air of consequence. The long cinnamon hair that had once been tied back with a ribbon now was pinned up tightly beneath a lace cap as befitting a prim spinster. Yet her eyes . . . they were the same brilliant sapphire blue that had once beguiled him into surrendering his heart.

Why the hell was she lurking in his library? If he'd spared a thought for her at all, he'd have expected to catch a glimpse of her in the village, perhaps with a husband or a passel of children in tow. But certainly not here under his roof.

She gave a small tug. Realizing he still held her arms, he relaxed his grip and let go.

She took several steps back, her gaze watchful. "I am Miss Linton," she said, correcting his familiarity of address. "Your aunt has engaged me as Lady Gwendolyn's new governess. Perhaps you didn't know, but Miss Herrington had to leave unexpectedly."

Miss Linton? He was startled that she had never wed. If any female had been designed for marriage, it was Abby. Though, of course, he had been wrong about her in other matters. She had revealed her true colors after he'd departed for good.

The note of disdain in her voice irritated him. "Of course I knew," he said. "My sister's well-being is of the utmost importance to me. Though I did not give my aunt permission to hire a replacement."

Feeling a touch to his arm, he turned to see Elise appear at his side. "What is the meaning of this outrage, Your Grace? I'm astounded that your servants feel free to spy on you."

He had forgotten all about the delectable widow. Her blond curls were tousled, her lips rosy from his kisses, her eyes alert and inquisitive. Only a moment ago, he had been caught up in the throes of seduction. He had been on the brink of charming Elise into becoming his mistress. All that heat had dissipated with the discovery they were not alone.

"I wasn't *spying*," Abby said coolly. "I was on my knees, looking for a book on a lower shelf, which is why you didn't see me. I wasn't aware the duke was even expected."

"You were snooping," Elise insisted. "And no doubt you were on your way below stairs to spread gossip among the other servants." She tilted her angry face up to Max. "I will not have it, Rothwell. You must dismiss her at once."

"Pray leave us, Lady Desmond. I want a word in private with Miss Linton."

"I'm involved in this matter, too, darling, so there is no

need for me to depart. I assure you, I'm well versed in dealing with unruly servants."

"Nevertheless, I must insist." Annoyed by the way she clung to his arm in a proprietary manner, he escorted her to the door and opened it. "Proceed to the left. At the end of the corridor, you'll find the entrance hall. One of the footmen will summon Mrs. Jeffries to show you to your chambers."

Elise cast a suspicious frown at Abby; then she looked back at Max. She had very likely noticed his involuntary use of Abby's name when he had first seen her. Elise would be wondering at their past relationship. But if she had the sense of a peahen, she wouldn't probe into his private life.

Her lips parted as if to protest again. Apparently thinking better of it, she dipped a curtsy. "Until later, Your Grace."

She walked with a saucy sway of her hips down the passageway. He knew it was for his benefit, but he had no interest in her enticements just now. He shut the door and turned back toward Abby.

Miss Linton, he reminded himself. He should never have uttered *Abby* as if they were still intimates. It was a mistake he would not make again—at least not in conversation. His thoughts were another matter, he suspected grimly, for her name was too deeply ingrained in his memory.

She stood waiting, her expression composed, her hands clasped at her waist. The simple gray gown skimmed the fine curves of her figure. She had a natural elegance that hadn't been present in her as a coltish fifteen-year-old. He had to admit, though, her strict expression was that of a governess who had witnessed a wrongdoing and was prepared to issue a severe scolding.

How much had she heard—and seen?

Picking up the globe, he walked over to the pedestal to replace it on its stand. An uncomfortable sensation bedeviled him, and he realized it was embarrassment. He didn't care to think of her having witnessed his randy conduct.

Max clenched his jaw. To hell with that. He wouldn't make apologies when she had been the one eavesdropping.

"So," he said curtly, "you believe yourself to be qualified to teach my sister. Might I presume you've experience as a governess?"

She gazed steadily at him, offering no smile or artifice to cajole him. "No, Your Grace. Until recently, I devoted myself to the care of my parents. I did, however, study under my father for many years. You may recall, he was a scholar of history."

"Was?"

"Papa was taken by influenza last autumn, as was Mama."

Max had not known her parents beyond the slight acquaintance he'd had with all the villagers. But Abby had always spoken warmly of them, relating amusing little household stories, and he remembered envying her close-knit family. That had been part of the irresistible appeal of her. She had seemed to have everything that he did not, a world full of love and laughter.

"I'm sorry," he said with curt civility. "Your family has fallen on hard times, then."

"No, the estate has prospered under Clifford's guidance. Rather, I merely wished . . . to earn my own way."

He raised a skeptical eyebrow. Ladies did not leave home to seek employment except in the direst of circumstances. Had she been ill-treated? Misused in some manner? Had her father left her no means of independence at all?

Her closed features revealed no clue to enlighten him.

He suddenly knew what was so profoundly different about Abby. Her face lacked that sweetness of expression, the open warmth and guilelessness of girlhood. Now she had the chilly poise of a duchess ruling this household.

But she was not his duchess. Nor would she ever be. She had spurned his suit long ago, and he was profoundly thankful for that. Did she regret it now? Did she wish she had not been reduced to servitude when she might have shared all the glory of his rank?

He didn't care a whit one way or the other. He only wanted her banished from his sight. "You shall have to seek employment elsewhere, Miss Linton. I am hereby dismissing you."

Her eyes widened. "Because of our past? I assure you, I will never reference it. It will be as if it had never occurred."

"The past is of no consequence to me."

"Then if this is about my *spying* on you, it was wholly unintentional. Had you notified the household, I'd have been more careful not to venture into your domain."

"I did send word to my aunt by courier . . . blast it, I don't owe you any explanation."

"I spoke to Lady Hester only a short while ago and she mentioned nothing of your expected arrival . . ." Abby glanced away, adding pensively, "Oh! I wonder if *that* was the message she forgot. It must have been!" Her vivid blue gaze returned to him. "But never mind. The pertinent issue, Your Grace, is that you've brought your mistress to a house where Lady Gwendolyn is in residence. Nothing could be more improper—or more irresponsible."

"That is no concern of yours!"

"Clearly, it should be *someone*'s concern. An innocent girl must not be exposed to such vulgar company."

It galled Max to be rebuked by Abby of all people. And

to hear Elise described in so sordid a manner, especially when she was not precisely his mistress—yet. But after the lusty tableau Abby had witnessed, he had no defense to offer. Even if he'd been inclined to voice one.

Nor could he condemn her for having a desire to protect Gwen. It *was* unconscionable to expose his sister and his aunt to somewhat dubious company. For that very reason, he'd been reluctant to invite the party to Rothwell Court. Had there been any other course open to him, had the prizefight not been looming and Goliath requiring a private spot for sparring practice, Max would send the lot of them packing at once.

"I have a proposal for you, Your Grace."

His gaze sharpened on Abby. His body reacted to her words with a flare of hot desire. His mind raced with possibilities, none of them moral or decent. And all of them abhorrent in regard to this woman. "A proposal."

"So long as your guests are under this roof, Lady Gwendolyn will require a chaperone, and Lady Hester is far too busy with her gardening. Since there isn't time to apply to a London agency for my replacement, it would be wise for me to stay right here for now."

She stood with her hands tightly clasped. So tightly that he could see the whites of her dainty knuckles. This position as governess was vitally important to her. Why?

It didn't matter. He had no interest in her life anymore. But she did have a point, he grudgingly admitted. It would be irrational for him to send her away immediately. He could not risk Gwen encountering Lord Ambrose or Pettibone in a deserted corridor.

"Fine," he snapped. "You may remain for the coming week. However, when I depart, you will leave my employ. Is that clear?"

"Quite."

"Kindly inform Lady Gwendolyn that I will see her in her chambers in half an hour."

"At once, my lord duke."

Lowering her gaze, Abby swept a modest curtsy, though not before he had seen the relief in her eyes. Perplexed in spite of his irritation, he stood watching as she glided away. He didn't understand her willingness to work as a servant. It should cut her to the bone to know that she might have been mistress of Rothwell Court had she replied to his letters all those years ago.

But she'd made no attempt to use their prior closeness to wheedle him, or to apologize prettily in the hopes of making amends. Her only reference to their past had been to declare any mention of it out of bounds.

Perhaps she'd realized the danger of reminding him of how shabbily she'd treated him. So much the better. If Abby Linton knew what was best for her, she would stay out of his path. She would bide her tongue and cease to address him in this bold manner of hers.

In the next moment, she contradicted that notion.

Pausing in the doorway, she cast a backward glance at him. "By the way, your sister knew I'd gone to the library. What if she had come looking for me and found you with your mistress? Might I suggest, Your Grace, that while you're under this roof, you curtail your amorous activities!"

After informing Lady Gwendolyn of her brother's arrival, Abby made an excuse to slip away before he came upstairs. The girl had scarcely noticed, so excited had she been at the prospect of seeing him again. Abby had rung for a maid and left the pair of them to decide which gown from the crowded wardrobe Lady Gwendolyn should wear for the momentous occasion.

Brother and sister had not met since Easter. Abby found that peculiar, accustomed as she was to a big, noisy family and the prolonged visits of her siblings. Rothwell, it seemed, had little time to spare for an underage sister. His many debaucheries kept him too busy in London.

She marched down one of the narrow corridors designated for use by the servants. He had been exceedingly displeased when she had advised him to suspend such lascivious doings while at Rothwell Court. The look on his face had been cold enough to freeze flames. She had departed before he could change his mind about permitting her to stay.

Despite the risk, she didn't regret speaking out. The proprieties must be observed for Lady Gwendolyn's sake. And someone had to hold him in check!

That it was unlike her to so sharply reprove another adult, let alone a duke, did occur to Abby. She was usually the one to smooth over quarrels between her family members. Yet her memory burned with the image of him locked in an embrace with that beautiful temptress, Lady Desmond.

Was she a widow? Or a wife betraying her wedding vows?

Either way, Abby could not countenance the change in Max, that he would associate with such a female. The sweet, gawky boy she had once loved had vanished forever. Now, in the prime of his life, he had become a hardened libertine, focused only on hedonistic pleasures.

One thing was certain. Seeing him again had cured her of any long-buried vestige of heartbreak. She was now very thankful that he had abandoned her fifteen years ago. No matter how handsome he might be, no matter how much she craved a bit of adventure, she was better off without a philandering rake in her life.

And it was just as well that her identity was out in the open. There need be no more fretting about the fear of discovery. Even though he'd dismissed her, at least she did not have to pack her belongings just yet. There would be one more week to enjoy here at Rothwell Court. One more week of being independent and earning her own wage before returning home—unless she could come up with another plan for her future. In the meanwhile, she would do her best to avoid Rothwell and his cronies. She certainly would *not* cower just because *he* was here.

Considerably cheered, she proceeded to the end of the long corridor and opened the door to the servants' wing. She would take her tea in the kitchen today. The staff would provide pleasant company to pass the time while she waited for Rothwell to complete his visit with Lady Gwendolyn.

But a commotion of upraised voices greeted her ears. There seemed to be some sort of altercation going on. Following the sound of the turmoil, she hastened past the butler's pantry and the scullery and entered the kitchen.

The massive room had a high, vaulted ceiling and a hearth large enough to roast an entire ox. Scores of copper pots gleamed on shelves against the stone walls. A long table ran the length of the chamber, where two young maids sat before a mound of carrots and turnips, their peeling forgotten as they listened goggle-eyed to the heated discussion between Finchley, the butler; Mrs. Jeffries, the housekeeper; and Mrs. Beech, the cook.

Old Finchley was shaking a knobby finger at the other two gray-haired retainers. A fixture at Rothwell Court, he had worked his way up from lowly boot boy during the reign of the eighth duke, the present duke's grandfather.

"A rackety lot of blackguards, they be," he pronounced

darkly. "Raffish blades cavorting with bits o' muslin. They already demanded a deck of cards. There'll be gambling and orgies in the days to come, mark my word, unless the duke puts a stop to it!"

"It is not the fault of the master," Mrs. Jeffries said, fairly bristling with indignation. "He has been taken in by That Woman. I knew at once the sort she was, all treacle to His Grace and vinegar to the staff. The cheek of her to order me about as if she's a duchess when it's plain as the nose on my face she is nothing but a whore of Babylon!"

"And if she doesn't like what's served for dinner, then let her starve." Mrs. Beech grappled behind her thick waist to untie her apron, which she flung onto the flagstone floor. "I never cooked Frenchie and I won't start now!"

Abby hurried forward. "May I ask what is going on here? Mrs. Beech, surely you cannot be resigning!"

They opened a space to welcome her into their little circle. Upon her arrival a week ago, she had made it clear that she was not so high in the instep as to lord over them by virtue of her birth. Why would she? They all hailed from local families that Abby had known since the time she could walk. She had sung with them in church, delivered baskets to their ill and infirm, and worked alongside them at festivals and rummage sales.

Mrs. Beech planted her hands on her ample hips. "I don't know what else to do, Miss Abby! I've already planned the meals for the week and stocked the larder and now I'm to toss it all away and make some fancy-frippery recipes just delivered to my hand by Mrs. Jeffries!" She snatched up a clutch of papers from the table and vigorously rattled them. "All of these His Grace's favorites, Lady Desmond claims, when I know him to be one who likes his meat and potatoes served plain and simple!"

"You must allow that was before he went to London fifteen years ago," Abby diplomatically pointed out. "Perhaps his tastes have changed."

"Be that as it may," Mrs. Jeffries said with a sniff of her sharp nose, "I cannot think the master would be so rude as to expect Cook to prepare a seven-course dinner of peculiar new recipes on such short notice. And with only the two kitchen maids to help her!"

"Might we draft the laundry and dairy maids to aid with the chopping this evening?" Abby suggested. "Then tomorrow, you can seek temporary help from among the tenants. I can think of several wives who would be pleased to make a few extra coins."

"I suppose we have no choice," the housekeeper fretted. "But that isn't the worst of it, Miss Abby. The recipes are written in French!"

"Likely frogs and snails," Finchley uttered in his raspy voice. "'Tis food fit for traitors and turncoats, not respectable Englishmen. But I daresay that after this rain, Tom can nab some of the slimy creatures out in the garden."

"I'm sure that won't be necessary," Abby said, hiding a smile. "And I'm well versed enough in French to translate the recipes if you like."

Mrs. Beech's plump features were set in obstinate lines. "It'll be all creams and herbs and froufrou nonsense. I don't see why I should change my menus, anyhow, unless the order comes straight from the master. Her ladyship is not the mistress of this house."

"I should certainly hope not!" Mrs. Jeffries fanned her gaunt face with her apron so that her large ring of keys jingled. "Why, I had the measure of her at once. She is one of His Grace's fancy pieces, if you'll pardon my plain speaking, Miss Abby. She even had the effrontery to request chambers conveniently close to the duke's apartment.

I wouldn't be in the least surprised to hear that *she* is the ravisher of *him*!"

Abby was perfectly content to listen to their disparagement of Lady Desmond. Nothing would delight her more than to convey to them a detailed description of the sordid tryst that she had witnessed in the library. It also would serve the purpose of correcting their misapprehension about Rothwell's blamelessness in the matter. But it was not her place to spread gossip—or to disabuse their loyalty to the master whom they'd known since his boyhood.

"I daresay, Mrs. Beech, we might find some manner of compromise if only we put our heads together. Why, Lady Hester and Lady Gwendolyn would wither away without your delicious meals. Now do pick up your apron and we shall discuss the matter over a nice pot of tea."

As the grumbling cook relented and went to do Abby's bidding, Mrs. Jeffries said, "Alas, I daren't tarry here any longer. The upper maids have been changing the linens and airing out the bedchambers, and I must ascertain that they have not been set upon by this troop of sinners!"

Finchley, too, had duties to fulfill. The stooped old butler shuffled to the door, then turned around to utter forebodingly, "You mustn't allow Lady Gwen to go out to the stables alone, Miss Abby. There's a monstrous heathen bunking down with the lads there."

He vanished before Abby could query his meaning. Mrs. Beech knew only that His Grace had brought along a veritable giant in his retinue. She had glimpsed the fellow from the back door and it had been enough to make her slam it shut and turn the key in the lock. While the cook muttered about everyone in the house being murdered in their beds, Abby wondered what in the world Rothwell wanted with such a fearsome retainer. It wouldn't

shock her to learn he had gambling debts and needed a
bodyguard to ward off all the dun collectors.

Putting him out of her mind, she took a seat at the table
to translate the recipes. At home, she often had planned
the daily meals with their cook when her mother had become too infirm for the task. Now, she worked together
with Mrs. Beech to determine how the menus could be
adjusted to suit the refined tastes of the London guests.
While drinking their tea and nibbling on a plate of Mrs.
Beech's currant tarts, they discussed ways to alter the
cook's own recipes for a more sophisticated palate by adding a cream sauce in place of a plain beef gravy, or a bit of
shaved mushrooms and braised butter to the *pommes de
terre*. Since Mrs. Beech excelled at pastry, they settled on
a dinner menu for that evening that included *bouchée à la
reine* stuffed with chicken and onions, and served with a
stew of the carrots and turnips that the kitchen maids were
already peeling.

In less than an hour's time, she had sufficiently soothed
Mrs. Beech's qualms and convinced her to appreciate this
rare opportunity to show off her superior cooking skills.
As the woman hopped up to issue orders to the three additional maids who had appeared, Abby hoped the inter-
fering Lady Desmond would be satisfied with the results
and cease badgering the staff.

She herself was feeling quite pleased for having averted
disaster. There would have been an uproar had Cook
walked out on a houseful of hungry guests. Of course,
Rothwell deserved chaos for having sprung a party of his
cronies on the staff without sufficient warning. Even if he
had sent word to his aunt, a few hours' notice was scarcely
adequate to complete the necessary preparations.

But what more could one expect of a self-indulgent libertine?

She took one last swallow from her teacup, realizing it was time to head back upstairs to guard Lady Gwendolyn against the barbarian horde. The duke surely would have departed his sister's chambers by now so there was little chance of encountering him.

A movement drew her gaze to the doorway. Her eyes widened as the Duke of Rothwell strolled into the kitchen.

Chapter 5

Abby nearly choked on a mouthful of tepid tea. He must have taken a wrong turn. She couldn't imagine any other reason why he'd venture into the staff wing.

Since the kitchen was a beehive of activity, the duke didn't notice her perched on a bench near the hearth. His attention was focused toward the other end of the chamber, where several laundry and dairy maids had been enlisted as temporary helpers. The air echoed with their high-pitched chatter as they chopped and peeled, knives flashing. Pots bubbled on the Bodley Range and Mrs. Beech barked orders over her shoulder while she busied herself at a task near the stove.

It was just as well that he didn't spot Abby because the sight of him in his evening clothes held her enthralled. He had exchanged his traveling garb for a coat of midnight-blue superfine, a white silk waistcoat, and a pair of black pantaloons, all of a superior cut that emphasized his muscular form. Yet there was nothing in the least dandified about him, from the top of his neatly brushed hair to the toes of his tooled-leather shoes. Within the folds of his cravat glinted a pearl stickpin, his only jewelry except for a gold signet ring. His aura of posh sophistication made her conscious of her dowdy gray gown and spinster's cap.

She was a plain peahen compared to his peacock glory.

Not, of course, that she had the slightest interest in attracting his admiration. Rather, it was merely a natural feminine instinct for a lady to wish to look her best in the presence of a handsome gentleman. Especially when the gentleman in question had spurned her so abominably many years ago in favor of more stylish women.

Thankfully, he did not so much as flick a glance in her direction. He sauntered straight to Mrs. Beech, who was cutting butter into flour for the cream cake she was preparing to bake. With her back turned, she didn't notice the duke until he reached past her stout form and snatched a strawberry from the bowl beside her.

The cook spun around, her wooden spoon raised. "Thief! I ought to— Oh!" As she spied Rothwell, a broad smile stretched across her doughy features and she bobbed a curtsy. "Why, 'tis Master Max! Your Grace, I should say."

Bending, he planted a loud smack on her floury cheek. "Good old Beechy. I was hoping to find you still here. But it seems I must beg your forgiveness for putting you to so much trouble on my behalf."

"Oh, bosh, 'tis no trouble at all. Not a bit! The only trouble, milord, is you staying away from your home here for so many years."

Abby blinked. No one would ever have guessed Mrs. Beech to be the same irate cook who had ripped off her apron and threatened to walk out only a short while ago. And . . . *Beechy*?

"I've certainly missed your culinary delights," Rothwell said, popping the strawberry into his mouth. "What was that raspberry treat you used to make for me?"

"Jam roly-poly. Might I whip up a batch for you straight-away?"

"Tomorrow is soon enough. You appear far too busy at the moment. Though I don't suppose you've anything else lying around to feed a starving man?"

A deep belly laugh issued from her. "You always did have a hollow leg, Your Grace, and that's the truth."

While Mrs. Beech disappeared into the pantry, he stole several more berries and ate them while prowling around the kitchen, peering into the steaming copper pots on the stove and sniffing the delicious aromas. When he nodded at the maids, they blushed and twittered. All of a sudden, his gaze roved to the far end of the table and halted on Abby.

He checked his pace in mid-step. His genial expression vanished, the charming smile gone in a blink. One dark eyebrow crooked upward.

His displeasure at finding her here could not be more obvious.

Abby's heart thumped. She knew she ought to arise, to make her curtsy, and depart to her duties. She could not afford to antagonize her employer. But her limbs seemed incapable of obeying the dictates of her mind. Her lungs felt squeezed of air, rendering her giddy and light-headed. If only he were not so infernally handsome . . .

Their gazes held for one prolonged moment. Then the duke inclined his head in a cool nod.

He appeared about to speak when Mrs. Beech came bustling out of the larder with a meat pie in one hand, a wheel of cheese in the other, and a loaf of bread in the crook of her arm. She placed the items at the end of the table where Abby sat and began slicing the bread and buttering it, chattering all the while. "I daresay this ain't fancy enough fare for London folk like you are now, Your Grace.

But there's naught else in the world like good country cooking, I always say."

"What she means," Abby said, recovering her tongue, "is that Lady Desmond has been so kind as to give Mrs. Beech a number of your favorite French recipes to cook."

"Has she?" Rothwell's eyes narrowed for the briefest flash. Then he aimed a crooked smile at Mrs. Beech. "Pray do not feel obliged to follow any but your own menus. Whatever you prepare is bound to be perfectly delectable. In truth, I'd sack my French chef in an instant if I thought you might be persuaded to take over my kitchen in London."

Blushing at the extravagant compliment, the cook cut a generous slice of meat pie and arranged everything on a plate for him as if he were a little boy. "Well! My dear old father-in-law might raise a ruckus over me leaving him, so I'd best stay put." She poured a cup of tea for him and then pulled out a chair. "Now sit yourself down, milord, and don't blame me if your appetite is spoiled for dinner!"

"Make me a treacle tart for breakfast tomorrow and I'll forgive you anything."

Seeing him grin at Mrs. Beech, Abby suspected he had been closer to the servants than to his own family. No wonder the cook, the butler, and the housekeeper had taken his side during that earlier heated discussion. Having known him as a lad, they had an entrenched loyalty that made allowances for his wicked behavior. They judged Max by how he had been fifteen years ago—not by his peccadilloes as a man in his prime.

As the duke slid into his seat across from Abby, she caught a whiff of his scent, spicy and masculine and hauntingly familiar. She had a sudden clear memory of lying beside Max in the warm summer grass, gazing up at the clouds and exchanging silly little stories with him about their everyday lives. While hers had involved mostly family members, his had all been about the staff at Rothwell Court.

He had never wanted to talk about his parents. And it occurred to her now that she ought to have pressed him to do so.

It felt strangely unreal to be sitting near him again after so much time had passed. She found herself wondering if any trace of the tender boy she'd known still lurked inside him. Was it hidden behind the urbane charm that he showed the world? Or did he simply know how to maneuver gullible souls like Mrs. Beech—and unsuspecting girls as Abby had once been?

The answer didn't signify. In a week, they would part ways for good. He would go back to London, and she would return to her duties as caregiver to her siblings and their children.

As Mrs. Beech scurried off to her dinner preparations, Abby strove for levity by saying, "Treacle tarts and jam roly-poly? One would think you have the palate of a schoolboy, Your Grace."

"Even a rake has fond memories of his youth." He forked a slice of Stilton and held it out to her. "Would you care for a bite, Miss Linton?"

The question seemed imbued with hidden sensual meanings. Abby felt a tightening in her bosom, a languor in her limbs. She found the glint in his gray eyes to be particularly disquieting, for this mature version of his familiar features held an alluring sway over her senses. The notion that she might be attracted to the adult Max was far too disturbing to contemplate.

She rose to her feet. "No, thank you. With your permission, I shall return to Lady Gwendolyn."

"Permission denied." With a wave of his fork, he added,

"Sit down now, lest you force me to be a gentleman and stand up when I would rather be eating."

Abby wrestled with her pride before resuming her seat. She really had no choice. As his servant, she was obliged to obey his direct command. Yet his presence made her uncomfortable and she held her spine stiffly upright. "Should I not be with your sister? After all, my purpose in this house is to protect her from any vulgar influences."

"I've instructed Gwen not to venture from her chamber until your return." He ate a bite of meat pie before continuing. "You should know that I've decided to grant my sister a short holiday from her studies. That is why I didn't immediately send a replacement for Miss Herrington."

"A holiday?" Abby clasped her hands beneath the table. "With all due respect, how do you propose Lady Gwendolyn fill her time? It would be wiser to keep her occupied with studying in order to avoid your . . . guests."

"With all due respect, Miss Linton, filling her time is *your* province, not mine. Though I've given her permission to ride in the mornings before my . . . guests arise."

She bristled at his sardonic tone. It must be a habit he'd acquired in the city, for he had never been prone to mockery. "I'm surprised you believe riding will be safe for her, given the circumstances."

"Circumstances?"

"I understand there's a monstrous heathen residing in the stables. A giant, or so he was described to me."

"Ah, Goliath. Don't fret, he'll be busy elsewhere in the morning."

It grated on her to see Rothwell eating so nonchalantly. "Who is he? Your bodyguard? I shouldn't think you would need one. I'm certain you could ward off any dun collectors with the sheer force of your ducal glare."

She found herself subjected to that very glare as

Rothwell cocked an eyebrow at her. The silence between them pulsed louder than the clinking of dishes, the banging of pans, and the chatter of the maids at work. Then he startled her by chuckling.

"Your sharp tongue should suffice to protect Gwen from any danger. As for Goliath, his real name is Harold Jones, and he happens to be England's boxing champion. As his sponsor, I must ensure that he trains for a very important match at the end of the week."

"Prizefighting!" What little Abby knew about the bare-knuckle sport had been gleaned over the years from references made by her brothers and also from hearing occasional talk among the village men. "Isn't that illegal?"

The duke lifted one broad shoulder in a shrug. "The authorities tend to look away so long as order is maintained."

"You mean so long as you *bribe* them. I suppose there will be betting and high stakes involved, too."

"That is the general notion, yes," he said, looking sardonically amused by her prim reaction. "However, this is also a celebrated contest between Goliath and Wolfman, who hails from the wild frontiers of America. It shall be our chance as Brits to beat the tar out of the Yanks."

In spite of herself, Abby felt a tug of unholy interest. Wouldn't that be an adventure, to infiltrate the crowd, to watch the brutal match, to cheer England as the winner? She scotched the outrageous thought before it could take form. "Then I should presume all your guests are gamblers who intend to wager on the outcome of the fight."

"And you, Miss Linton, seem determined always to have the worst possible view of me." Rothwell paused to savor a drink of tea. Setting the mug back down, he continued, "But I confess you would be correct this time."

His manner had an ironic charm that was far more

polished than in his youth. She could see why he was a favorite among the ladies, for she too felt the tug of his allure. But she must not let herself be rattled by his suave style.

"Pray tell me, who are these gamester friends of yours?"

"There are two widowed ladies and two gentlemen. Besides Lady Desmond, there is Mrs. Chalmers, the Earl of Pettibone, and Lord Ambrose Hood." He dabbed his mouth with a linen serviette. "But you needn't look quite so prudish. They aren't so far beyond the pale that they will pose any threat to Gwen. They're welcome in London drawing rooms except perhaps in those belonging to the highest sticklers."

Abby remained skeptical. "Nevertheless, I will endeavor to keep Lady Gwendolyn away from them."

"They're late risers. So the two of you should be at the stables no later than nine tomorrow morning."

"I will certainly walk your sister there, of course."

His gaze sharpened. "You *do* ride with her, do you not?"

"Actually, no. I'm not much of an equestrian."

"What? You used to be the most bruising little rider I ever did see."

There was no need to squirm, Abby told herself, simply because Rothwell had fixed her with a frowning stare. "Yes, well, my mother suffered a fall from a horse fifteen years ago that fractured her hip. It never quite healed properly, and I was kept very busy caring for her. Since she grew terribly alarmed at the thought of me on horseback . . . I gave it up."

"Fifteen years? I don't recall this."

"It happened in autumn, a few months after you'd left here."

Abby already had been sunk in the blue devils by Max's abrupt departure and his failure to write after he had promised faithfully to correspond. The accident had added to her misery, for when her letters went unanswered, she'd had to face the fact that his professions of love had been nothing but a sham.

There was a hardness to his expression now, as if he scorned any reminder of their shared past. "Miss Herrington always accompanied Gwen. My sister may be gently-bred, but every now and again she takes a mind to ride neck-or-nothing."

"Perhaps she misbehaved when she was younger, but she's quite grown-up now and a groom always accompanies her. Dawkins is extremely reliable."

"So, you admit you're not as qualified as your predecessor."

Abby refused to snap at his bait. "Since you didn't intend to hire a new governess just yet, only a groom would have been riding with Lady Gwendolyn, anyway. Besides, Miss Herrington did not teach her *everything* about proper behavior."

"Oh?"

"It is the duty of a lady to visit the poor and the infirm. But your sister told me that she's never done so."

"She's been busy with her studies."

"Charitable works should be a part of every young lady's training. Only imagine how a visit would cheer a tenant who is confined to bed as an invalid. Or how a poor family would welcome a basket of food and a few kind words from the lady of the manor."

"I will not have my sister exposed to diseases."

"Any cottage harboring an infectious ailment can be avoided. And since you have charged *me* with filling her time, I would propose to take Lady Gwendolyn to visit a few of your tenants tomorrow."

He stared at her another moment with those keen gray

eyes, then gave a brusque nod. "You may do so in the afternoon. Then we shall see if you are a match for the estimable Miss Herrington."

His championing of her predecessor rubbed Abby raw. It was almost as if he'd taken a personal interest in the woman. Had there been a flirtation between them, perhaps when the pretty governess had accompanied his sister to visit him at holidays? She could think of nothing more dastardly.

Goaded, Abby leaned across the table and said in an undertone, "Yes, she was so estimable that she ran off with her lover."

His eyebrows lowered in a thunderous look. "Who told you that?"

"It is what Lady Hester believes."

"Spreading gossip, Miss Linton? I trust you will not repeat such slander to anyone—most especially not to my sister." His fierce gaze bored into her. "That would be beneath even you."

He surged to his feet and strode from the kitchen.

His harsh denouncement made Abby regret having mentioned the elopement. Why had she done so? Because he had seemed so inclined to compare her unfavorably to the young and beauteous Miss Herrington? She oughtn't have let him irk her so.

That would be beneath even you.

The vehemence of his words echoed in her head. What did he mean, *even you*? What had she ever done but love him, heart and soul? The wrongfulness of his attack threw her off-kilter.

Conscious of the curious glances from the kitchen maids, Abby left the table and went out into the corridor, heading toward the servants' staircase. She could see only the frostiness of his features, the hardness of his eyes—as if he blamed *her* for their parting. How could he possibly view himself as the injured party when it was *he* who had left and never returned? *He* who had disdained to answer any of her fervent letters?

She had no answers, but one thing was certain. The Max of her youth no longer existed. He was Rothwell now, and he had no heart, no scruples. All trace had vanished of the tender boy who had once vowed to marry her.

In an unsettled temper, Max headed straight to the conservatory to greet his aunt. He found her humming tunelessly at the spigot by the wall, her stout form bent over to fill a metal container. A smile creased her plump features, and she set down her watering can.

"Maxwell, my dear boy! Is it really you?"

His mood thawed somewhat as he leaned down to kiss her on the cheek. At times, she had been more a mother to him than his own mama. "Indeed so. I presume you received the note I sent by courier this morning."

She blinked owlishly. "Ah, yes. But do you know, I was so busy today that I believe I forgot to tell Gwen!"

"I've already seen her. Pray forgive me for bringing a party of friends here on such short notice. It couldn't be avoided."

After describing the outbreak of measles at Pettibone's manor and then warning her about Goliath's presence, Max gave voice to the subject that needled him. "I understand you've engaged a new governess for Gwen."

"After Miss Herrington left, I hired Margaret Linton's youngest daughter. A fine, cheerful girl she is, so kind and warmhearted."

Max clamped his jaw to keep from ranting. Lady Hester knew nothing of what had transpired between himself and Abby in the past, or he'd have told his aunt just how mistaken she was about Abby's character. It was bad enough having to come back to this house with all its memories, let alone to encounter Abby every time he turned around. His heart had actually skipped a beat when he'd spied her sitting at the table in the kitchen.

That would be beneath even you.

Despite his legendary coolness, he had been unable to bide his tongue in her presence. Fool! Now she would think him still wounded by her refusal to answer his letters all those years ago.

Nothing could be further from the truth.

"Pray know that I've given Miss Linton her notice," he said curtly. "She'll be departing at the end of the week."

"Departing?" Aunt Hester's blue eyes rounded. "But why?"

"Gwen needs someone familiar with society who can prepare her for her come-out. Besides, she deserves a short holiday from her schoolwork. I explained all this in the note I sent you more than a week ago."

His aunt fretfully tugged on her gardening gloves. "Yes, I do recall that. But Abigail is almost like family. I made my debut with her mother, you know. Besides, *I* would be left to entertain the girl when I've so much else to do."

"Don't trouble yourself over the matter, Auntie," he said, patting her on the shoulder. "I'll contact an employment agency for a more qualified governess when I return to London next week."

His aunt gave him a reproachful look, as she'd done when he was a naughty little boy. "Fiddle! Abigail Linton is precisely the sweet, loving companion that Gwen needs. You of all people should know that!"

"Pardon?"

She leaned forward as if to convey a confidence. "On the afternoon of your mama's funeral, Abigail was waiting for you at the edge of the woods. She held your hand and gave you comfort when you needed it the most. Surely you have not forgotten!"

Max stood stock-still. Aunt Hester had seen them together. Yet all these years she'd never breathed a word.

His mind hurtled back to that black day. He had lagged behind as the mourners had returned to the house after the burial in the private chapel. Then he had dashed across the lawn to where Abby had been waiting. He could still feel his desperation to reach the warm sanctuary of her arms . . .

The shuffle of footsteps snapped him back to the present. He turned to see a stooped figure advancing through the jungle of greenery. Finchley made a creaky bow. "A message, Your Grace. It seemed best to bring it myself."

But the butler didn't offer the scrap of folded paper that lay on a silver salver. His manner conspiratorial, he jerked his grizzled head toward the door. "Best to come at once, if you please."

Max bade a terse farewell to his aunt, who had picked up the watering can again and tipped the spout over a plant. Striding away, he joined Finchley, who was glancing up and down the corridor as if expecting a murderer to pounce at any moment.

"Good God, man. What is the point of this melodrama?"

Finchley merely nodded at the folded paper.

Max snatched the note from the tray. Upon breaking the wafer and reading the brief message, he frowned in exasperated surprise. Here was a circumstance he had not anticipated. Word of his return certainly had traveled fast, his coach having been spotted in the village.

He looked up to see Finchley observing him closely. "I presume you saw who brought this."

"A veiled lady, Your Grace, scratching on my door whilst the staff was having their tea. She knew right when to come and not be seen, that she did. Didn't fool me, not a wink. 'Twas that absconder, Miss Herrington!"

Max ignored the inflammatory description. "No one else saw her?"

"Nay, milord, but if I might ask why she's come back after leaving Lady Gwen on a moment's notice—"

"You may ask nothing," Max stated, tucking the note into an inner pocket of his coat. "Nor will you mention this encounter to anyone at all."

Chapter 6

The following morning, shortly before nine, Abby walked with Lady Gwendolyn along a graveled pathway lined by hawthorn trees. The girl had a decided spring to her steps. The day had dawned cloudless and bright, the sky washed clean by the previous afternoon's rain. Golden shafts of sunlight dried the few remaining puddles.

The stable compound was situated a discreet distance from the house. It was the very picture of bucolic prosperity, with an enormous horse barn painted red with gleaming white trim and a brick carriage house, along with outbuildings and paddocks where grooms were exercising the horses.

Nearing the open doors of the stable, Lady Gwendolyn could no longer contain herself. "May I please go ahead, Miss Linton?"

Abby smiled. "Of course."

As the girl darted inside, slim and elegant in her blue riding habit, she called over her shoulder, "Oh, do come and see! Brimstone is here to visit!"

Brimstone?

Abby stepped inside the dim interior, blinking to adjust her eyes after the brilliant sunlight. Lady Gwendolyn had rushed past Pixie, the small gray mare being saddled by a bandy-legged groom named Dawkins. She had gone straight to a stall midway down the long row. There, she fussed over a gigantic black horse with its head poked over the half-door, stroking the perked ears and patting the glossy neck.

Abby approached them, stopping a prudent distance away. Her heart beat faster and her palms felt damp, but she kept her voice steady. "I gather this is Brimstone."

"Isn't he a beauty? He belongs to my brother. But Max says he's too dangerous for any lady to ride." She dug into her pocket. "Would you like to feed him some sugar?"

"That's quite all right. You go ahead."

"How silly you are, Miss Linton." Gwendolyn giggled as Brimstone nuzzled her gloved palm for the lumps of sugar. "He won't harm you, I promise he won't."

"I'm sure you're right."

It was beyond silly; it was illogical, this wariness that she'd developed around horses. Abby didn't quite understand it, for she had ridden since she was scarcely out of leading strings. And it hadn't been she who'd taken a nasty tumble, but Mama. Yet somehow, her anxiety was all tangled up in that dreadful autumn fifteen years ago when her life had changed forever.

Lady Gwendolyn returned to her gray mare, lavishly patting Pixie to make up for not having greeted her at once. The horse was fed a share of sugar; then the groom led the animal to the mounting block for Gwendolyn to lift herself into the sidesaddle and arrange her skirts.

A few minutes later, Abby waved good-bye as the girl set off along the trail leading to the lake with Dawkins following on a chestnut gelding. In light of Rothwell's scold, she felt a little guilty not to be accompanying Lady

Gwendolyn, even though it was unnecessary. She very much disliked being made to feel she was inadequate for the post of governess.

Their conversation in the kitchen the previous afternoon had kept her tossing and turning for half the night. The wrongfulness of his criticism, the severity of his words, had played over and over in her head.

That would be beneath even you.

Nothing could be more baffling or more unmerited. Why would he lash out at her as if *she* was at fault for their parting? He was the one who had gone away, the one who had never replied to her letters, the one who'd never fulfilled the vow he had made to her on the afternoon of his mother's funeral.

She'd waited for hours at the edge of the woods, watching the stately house and hoping to catch a glimpse of Max. Much to her dismay, only close family members had been allowed to attend the burial. When at last he hurried across the lawn, he looked more dejected than she'd ever seen him.

She took his cold hands in hers, standing on tiptoes to kiss his cheek. "Oh, Max, I'm so very sorry. If only I could have been there."

"Never mind. Come, before someone sees us."

Hand in hand, they ran deep into the woods to their secret place, a glade beside a burbling stream, where a little outcropping sheltered them from view. Only then did he speak again. "I'm leaving," he said abruptly. "My father is taking Gwen and me to London tomorrow."

"To London! But when will I see you again?"

"I don't know. At the holidays, perhaps. He's keeping me out of school this term, too, so I won't be able to sneak away to visit you."

He looked so miserable that she opened her arms to him. "I'll write to you often, I promise!"

"Tell me that you love me, Abby," he whispered fiercely into her hair. "I need to hear you say it."

"I do love you, Max. I'll love you forever."

"I intend to marry you the moment I come of age. Will you wait for me?"

"Yes! Oh, yes." Though overjoyed at the prospect, concern for him made her add, "But are you sure? You've just suffered a terrible loss. You must be feeling such wretched misery over your mother—"

"I know my own mind! Please . . . just help me forget."

Drawing her down onto the grass, he began to kiss her with keen desperation. She delighted in the pressure of his mouth on hers, in knowing that he wished to spend the rest of his life with her. The desire to comfort him in his sorrow filled her with an overwhelming tenderness. They kissed with more boldness than she'd ever known, and a deep excitement swept through her as he caressed her bosom and hips. She could scarcely think or even breathe. Max. He was the one she loved with all her heart and soul . . .

All of a sudden, she experienced a shocking new sensation. His hand had delved beneath her skirts, brushing against her privates, startling her with a jolt of forbidden pleasure . . .

She pushed at him. "No! We mustn't—!"

"Please, Abby, I need you so much."

When he tried to hold on to her, she twisted away and sat up on the grass, one palm pressed to her wildly beating heart. He sat up as well and stared at her from a short distance away. He looked dazed and dreadfully unhappy, and despite her own rattled senses, she felt a rush of concern for him, realizing that he sought to forget his anguish rather than face it. "I know you're grieving for your mother," she said, "but we mustn't—"

"Don't speak of things you know nothing about!"

"Then tell me, Max. You must be hurting. It's better to talk about it than to keep it bottled up inside."

"She died. There's nothing else to say."

His surly aloofness sparked frustration in her. "Of course there's more to say, and you know it! Why will you never talk to me about your family?"

"Because there's no point."

"If you refuse to speak, then I can't help to ease your pain."

He sprang to his feet. "Fine. I'll seek my comfort elsewhere!"

Turning on his heel, he plunged away into the forest, and she felt too cross and upset to go after him . . .

A horse nickered in a nearby paddock and jolted Abby back to reality. Realizing that a groom was looking curiously at her, she started along a pathway that took her past the carriage house. Perhaps a brisk walk in the sunshine would help to disperse the cloud that dampened her spirits.

Yet that long-ago day remained seared in her mind. She blushed to recall their close embrace, though at least she'd retained the sense to refuse him the ultimate intimacy. After their brief quarrel, when he'd said *I'll seek my comfort elsewhere,* he had done just that. He'd gone off to London to live the freewheeling life of a rogue and she'd never seen or heard from him again.

Until yesterday.

No one but the two of them knew about that interlude in the woods or his marriage offer. All these years, Abby had kept the secret from her family and friends. It would have shocked her parents to know that she'd been meeting the duke's heir in the woods, that he'd proposed to her, and that she'd almost succumbed to his seduction.

Yet now Max—*Rothwell*—had had the gall to blame her for his own misdeeds. No matter how deeply he'd sunk into debauchery, he ought to be at least a trifle shamefaced over ignoring the many letters she'd written to him. Not to mention, breaking his promise to court her once he'd reached his majority. His father had been dead by then, and there had been no one to stop him from wedding whomever he'd pleased.

Back then, it had been a bitter blow to realize she had meant nothing more to him than a trifling summer fling.

Nevertheless, Abby had long since put the regrettable episode behind her. Though she failed to grasp how he could have twisted around the events of the past, she had come to one conclusion at least. She herself would never behave with such cavalier cruelty toward another human being.

For that reason, she owed Rothwell an apology for gossiping about Miss Herrington. It had been unkind to cast aspersions on her predecessor, who was unable to speak in her own defense. Lady Hester was likely wrong, and Miss Herrington had resigned in order to tend to a family crisis. Abby resolved to express her regret to the duke at the first opportunity. It was not in her nature to speak ill of people, no matter how goaded she had been by his rudeness.

The sound of jeering male voices caught her attention. She heard a taunting cry, then several dull thuds in quick succession. Intrigued, she proceeded around the back of the carriage house and stopped dead.

The sight before her could not have been more startling.

In a paddock behind the stables, two men were engaged in a bout of fisticuffs. The larger of the pair was a

baldheaded brute with an ugly, scarred face. His opponent was the Duke of Rothwell.

Both men were stripped to the waist. Sweat gleamed on
their bare torsos as they circled each other, their gazes intent. They wore padded gloves and every now and then, a
fist whipped out and a blow thumped. In between strikes,
they snapped insults at one another.

The huge one must be Goliath, England's champion pugilist. Although Rothwell had mentioned the boxer would
be training for a prizefight, Abby had never dreamed the
duke himself would act as the man's sparring partner.

She told herself to retreat. Clearly, ladies weren't meant
to witness this private training exercise back here, out of
sight of the house. There was no one else nearby except
for a few stable lads who were watching the bout, along
with a husky man in commoner's garb who observed from
a corner of the paddock.

Yet she couldn't bring herself to walk away. The fight
held her too enthralled.

Never before had she witnessed such a display of physical brawn. Until this moment, her only glimpse of the
half-nude male form had been statues of ancient Greeks
and Romans depicted in books. But those tame illustra-
tions were mere shadows of a flesh-and-blood man.

Her gaze was snared by the allure of Rothwell. His naked chest rippled with muscles, and as he moved, his back
and shoulders undulated with strength. Though tall and
powerful, he was not quite as fearsome as his burly, gargantuan opponent. Yet he was quicker on his feet and
landed his share of punches in between barrages from
Goliath. Rothwell appeared to be intent on goading the
man to try harder. The duke feinted to avoid being struck,
weaving in and out, his keen gaze never leaving the giant.

A flurry of near misses had Abby clutching her hands

to her throat. At a glancing blow to Rothwell's jaw, she cried out and took a spontaneous step toward the paddock. His concentration broke.

As the duke glanced her way, Goliath's fist caught him solidly in the gut. The savage strike caused Rothwell to stagger backward, his arms wheeling. He tumbled to the ground and lay unmoving with his face in the dirt.

"Max!"

She dashed forward before her thoughts could catch up with the advisability of her actions. How badly was he hurt? Was he only knocked out? Could a hard blow *kill* a man?

Even as she plunged through the open gate of the paddock, her imagination churning out a host of grisly possibilities, she saw Rothwell push himself up onto his elbow. He half lay there in the dust, struggling to catch his breath.

Goliath stood chortling over him. "Should Oi do the count, Yer Grace? One . . . two . . . three . . ."

In a mighty thrust, the duke surged to his feet. "Excellent knockout punch," he said, gasping for air. "But take a lesson from this, you blasted jackanapes. Never look away. Especially not at a female."

Only then did he aim a glower at Abby. "What the deuce are you doing here?"

Without allowing her to reply, Rothwell planted one gloved hand in the middle of her back and propelled her toward the gate. Abby scarcely took heed of his overbearing manner. She was too caught up in noticing the harshness of his breathing, the bronzed chest muscles glistening in the sunshine, the male scent that ought to repel her, but instead aroused the disgraceful desire to tuck her face in the crook of his neck.

Never in her life had she felt more keenly aware of any man. The fall had done its damage, and as they stepped outside the paddock, she asked, "Have you a handkerchief?"

He nodded at the garment hanging from a nearby post. "In my coat."

She dug in an inner pocket and found the folded square of linen, then turned back to him, reaching up to swab the trickle of blood at the corner of his mouth.

He jerked away. "What are you doing?"

"You're hurt."

"It's nothing."

Glowering, he peeled off his overstuffed gloves and threw them to the ground, then snatched the scrap of cloth from her. He gingerly wiped the side of his face, including a smear of dirt from his cheek. Abby knew it was highly improper to stare, yet she couldn't help herself. No matter how low her opinion of his character might be, she had to allow that in physique, Rothwell was the ideal of male perfection. He certainly was no longer the skinny, gangly Max of her memory. Now, the mere sight of him had the power to weaken her legs and hasten her heartbeat.

To hide her confusion, she picked up one of his leather gloves with its thick padding. "I thought this was to be bare-knuckle fighting."

"The mufflers protect Goliath during training."

He tossed the soiled handkerchief aside, then turned to grab his shirt from the fence post. He pulled it over his head, leaving his hair an attractive tousle of chocolate and coffee strands. Only then did he set his hands on his hips and fix her with a penetrating glare.

"Well, Miss Linton?" he demanded. "You never answered my question. Why are you here?"

His harsh tone slapped her. Striving for calm, she handed him the glove. "Your sister just departed on her ride, and I decided to take a walk. It was mere happenstance that I came upon you practicing."

"You ought to have turned around at once and gone away. That's what most ladies would have done."

It wouldn't do to admit she had been fascinated by the spectacle of his half-naked form. Or that she was sorry he'd now covered himself. She dropped a curtsy lest a blush betray her. "I was startled and forgot myself. Pray forgive me, Your Grace."

He was silent a moment, and she felt his cold stare as if it were an icicle piercing her bosom. Then he growled, "Don't ever come back here again."

Pivoting on his heel, he seized the other glove from the ground and strode back toward England's champion. A pack of goggle-eyed stable lads watched from a doorway as Goliath hopped around in the middle of the paddock while punching the air at an imaginary opponent.

Abby hastily retraced her steps. The chilliness of Rothwell's manner had magnified the coil of confusion inside her. She could think only of putting as much distance as possible between herself and the duke.

Abandoning her walk, she returned to the house and entered by a side door, then ran lightly up a staircase. She wandered through a random doorway and found herself in the Long Gallery. The stately chamber displayed portraits of past dukes, illuminated by natural light from the tall windows. It was deserted, which perfectly suited her agitated state of mind.

She sank onto the padded blue brocade of a gilt bench and rested her chin in her palms. How absurd that Rothwell could so easily shatter her equilibrium when she hadn't thought about him in years! What they had once shared had been mere puppy love. She had long ago reconciled herself to his abandonment and had found happiness by adopting a sensible outlook on life.

What, then, had brought on this mad whirl of disorder inside of her? Why was she feeling like an infatuated schoolgirl in the throes of her first romance?

Taking several deep breaths, Abby decided it was the fault of that lightning bolt of attraction that had struck her in his presence. Even now, the memory of him stripped to the waist made her pulse quicken. The man might be hostile and unprincipled, he might have crushed her youthful heart, yet he still had the power to tug at the core of her femininity.

She mustn't allow him.

Over the years, she had cultivated an aura of quiet serenity. That composure had served her well in her dealings with her family. She was the one to whom her nieces and nephews came when they'd scraped an elbow, the one who listened to confidences from her sisters and who visited infirm tenants on behalf of her brothers. Her tranquil nature had allowed her to shift smoothly into the role of governess, as well. Yet in less than twenty-four hours, her perfectly ordered existence had been turned topsy-turvy.

Because of Rothwell.

Near him, she felt all the quivering uncertainties of a girl in her first blush of youth. That fluttery awareness harkened back to a time when she'd been a green girl. But surely she'd outgrown such naïveté. Nothing could be more irrational or more ill-advised than mooning after an inveterate rogue.

It was especially ridiculous at her advanced age to succumb to romantic flights of fancy. She was, after all, on the verge of turning thirty. That fateful milestone was creeping up on her, with a mere few days to go before she would don the mantle of spinsterhood once and for all.

Unless, of course, she encouraged Mr. Babcock's suit.

She latched onto the prospect. The previous spring, the gentleman farmer had promised to renew his offer of marriage once her year of mourning was completed. He would make a steady husband, one who cared more about practical matters like raising sheep than arranging illicit prizefights. His parents might be henpecking and dogmatic, but she had a skill for soothing ill-tempered folk.

This untimely attraction to Rothwell was nothing more than the last gasp of youth. But all of that nonsense soon would be behind her. She resolved to engage Mr. Babcock in conversation after church on the coming Sunday. She would hint to him that a resumption of his courtship would be welcome.

Then her future would be settled once and for all. She need not spare another thought for the wicked Duke of Rothwell.

Her equanimity restored, Abby arose from the bench and paced to the nearest window to gaze out upon the vast expanse of lush lawn. The white marble of the Greek temple gleamed through the trees by the lake. Beyond the rolling hills lay the tenant farms with their fields of corn and rye, and farther still, the faint bluish shape of the downs. From here, she also could see the trail that meandered from the stables to the lake. This was as good a place as any to watch for Lady Gwendolyn's return.

To pass the time, Abby strolled around the gallery, stopping now and then to study the picture of a somber Cavalier in a starched ruff, or a hunter in red jacket with hounds milling at his booted feet. The Rothwell ancestors appeared to be proud aristocrats, some portrayed with wife and children, others depicted in full ducal regalia complete with ermine-trimmed cloak and gold coronet decorated by strawberry leaves.

A more modern painting brought her to an abrupt halt. She found herself staring at the image of Max sitting at his mother's side in the garden. Behind them stood the ninth duke, a man with cool gray eyes in a haughty, unsmiling face. His hand rested on his wife's shoulder. Delicately beautiful with a mass of spun-gold hair, the duchess held in her arms a swaddled infant . . . Lady Gwendolyn.

This portrait had been painted the summer that Abby had met Max. She remembered him grumbling about having to leave their secret glade in the woods in order to return to the house for a sitting. Having only glimpsed his parents from afar, she had begged him for a description. But as always, he had refused to speak of them.

He caught her close, his lips warm against her brow. "There is little enough to say. Only that I am much happier here with you, Abby."

Scrutinizing his image, she again felt the swirl of unsettled emotions. Here was the Max of her memory, preserved in oil paints at sixteen years of age. He had been lean and wiry then, and the artist had perfectly captured the hint of gawkiness in the inelegant slope of his shoulders, as if he had shot up too fast to be comfortable with his new height.

How warm and witty he had been, his only fault a sullen reluctance to discuss his family. She had believed the two of them to be kindred spirits. Why, oh why, had he never answered the *billets-doux* into which she'd poured out her heart?

Abby knew the answer. She had refused him the intimacy he'd desired at their final meeting, and so he had turned his attention to more sophisticated women. Despite the passage of years, his parting words to her still burned. *I'll seek my comfort elsewhere.*

The sound of voices penetrated her musings. Whirling around, she saw a pair of couples stroll into the gallery.

Chapter 7

Laughing and chatting, the two gentlemen and two ladies headed straight toward her. These must be the gamesters who had come to attend the prizefight, Abby realized. She schooled her features into a pleasant expression. It was too late to slip away unnoticed, and anyway, she admitted to a keen curiosity about Rothwell's friends.

Though never having enjoyed a London season, she had gleaned enough from her family members to recognize the sheen of town bronze. Her sisters, sisters-in-law, and nieces could gabble for hours about fashion, soliciting Abby's opinion on colors and fabrics, discussing how best to accessorize a gown, and poring over ladies' periodicals for the latest styles. Rothwell's guests, she judged, could have stepped right off those color-plated pages.

She recognized only one of the quartet—Max's current mistress, Lady Desmond. Looking like an ingenue in blossom pink, the dainty blonde glided forward on the arm of a gentleman. All that marred her exquisite beauty was a slightly petulant set to her rosebud lips.

"Ah, Miss Abigail Linton. Fancy seeing you here all alone."

Abby dipped the requisite curtsy. "Good morning, my lady."

"And where is Lady Gwendolyn?" Before Abby could answer, Lady Desmond turned to her escort. "Ambrose, this is the governess. She always seems to be wandering hither and yon without her charge anywhere in sight. I encountered her yesterday when Rothwell gave me a private tour of the house."

Private tour of the house, indeed! It was more of a private tour beneath the woman's skirts. The thought tickled Abby's sense of the absurd, but she mustn't laugh, for that would be out of keeping for someone of her station.

The gentleman beside Lady Desmond was a tulip of fashion, from his artfully barbered sandy hair down to his polished black Hessians. A gold watch fob dangled against his biscuit-colored silk waistcoat, and his pomona-green coat fit so flawlessly that it must have required the assistance of a valet to shoehorn him into it.

"Lord Ambrose Hood, at your service," he said, closely eyeing her as he gave a slight bow. "Dare I say you've a pretty name, Miss Abigail? It matches your remarkably pretty blue eyes."

Abby found herself the focus of a caressing smile as her fingers were clasped in a firm male grip. She wasn't so rustic as to fail to recognize an accomplished flirt. "How do you do, sir?" she said, withdrawing her hand. "It's a pleasure to make your acquaintance."

"She has the name of a servant," Lady Desmond said, clearly irked to be displaced, even for a moment. "I refer to my maid as my abigail."

"I believe that particular meaning came from a character in a popular old play, *The Scornful Lady*," Abby said. "Or so my papa told me."

"And who is your papa?"

"Was," she corrected. "He passed away last year. He was a scholar of English history, and he owned Linton Manor, the neighboring estate, which my eldest brother has inherited."

Lady Desmond's brow furrowed. "Landed gentry?"

She looked as if she'd have been happier to learn that Abby had grown up in a poorhouse. Perhaps it was understandable that the woman had taken a dislike to her, Abby mused, for she had caught Lady Desmond in an embarrassing indiscretion in the library the previous day. Yet there seemed to be something more, too. Had Lady Desmond guessed that Abby had had a past acquaintance with the duke? Was it possible she viewed her as a rival?

The notion was beyond ludicrous. Not only did Rothwell care not a jot for Abby, but there could scarcely be a sharper contrast than a spinster governess in sober slate gray and Lady Desmond's youthful perfection.

"But why are you not living with your brother, then?" Lady Desmond continued. "Why must you earn your bread—"

"Oh, bosh, Elise, don't grill her with impertinent questions," the other lady broke in. "Miss Linton, if I may present myself, I am Mrs. Chalmers. Mrs. *Sally* Chalmers, I might add. One cannot help one's birth name, and with an ordinary tag like mine, one would expect to find me not as a guest here, but churning the butter or making up the beds."

Abby appreciated the twinkle in Mrs. Chalmers's warm brown eyes. She had a lively manner, soft black hair, and a boldly stylish elegance in a peony-red muslin gown.

Her companion gave a gravelly chuckle. "Now that would be a sight to behold," he drawled. "Sally's fine posterior bent over a mattress."

The others seemed to find his outrageous comment

amusing, for they all laughed, including Mrs. Chalmers, who playfully struck his arm with her closed fan. "This naughty man, Miss Linton, is Lord Pettibone. And he is hereby ordered to bide his tongue while we're at Rothwell Court. Else you will think us all dreadfully rag-mannered!"

Abby did find them a trifle shocking, though intriguing as well, affording her a glimpse into Rothwell's life in London. "I daresay one's manners may be easier when one is among friends."

"Ah," Lord Ambrose said, "so you're a diplomat as well as a governess."

"And a dashed pretty one, too," Lord Pettibone added bluntly. "Every bit as fetching as the last one. Rothwell does know how to pick 'em."

With a languid hand, he held up a quizzing glass so that Abby found herself scrutinized by a magnified hazel eye. She took his flattery with a grain of salt and gazed levelly back at him, for she had the dubious distinction in her family of being the champion of staring contests. Lord Pettibone couldn't have been much older than herself, yet his dark hair was receding and his prominent aquiline nose kept him from true handsomeness. His foppish tastes included a wasp-waisted coat of claret superfine with collar points so high they nearly grazed his cheeks.

He lowered the glass. "By the by, Miss Linton, you never answered Elise's question. Where *is* your young charge?"

"Indeed," Lord Ambrose echoed. "We should very much like to meet Rothwell's sister."

"Lady Gwendolyn is presently out riding with a groom," Abby said. "I was watching for her return from the window here."

"How peculiar," Lady Desmond said. "I could have sworn you were ogling that portrait of Rothwell with his parents." She cast an arch look at Abby, then strolled away with Lord Pettibone to examine the painting.

The snide comment confirmed that Rothwell's mistress intended to guard against any poachers. Abby was struck by a distasteful thought. Perhaps the duke had such an incorrigibly roving eye that he kept several *chères amies* at a time, preying even upon the servants.

Her attention was pulled back by a reference to Lady Gwendolyn.

"Rothwell won't let you within a hundred yards of her," Mrs. Chalmers was telling Lord Ambrose. "Even if your pockets weren't to let, Lady Gwendolyn is only fifteen, a mere child. When she makes her bows three years from now, she is bound to command scores of brilliant offers."

"All the more reason for me to get a jump on the pack," Lord Ambrose countered with a devilish smile. "I may be a trifle in the suds at the moment, but may I remind you, my father is the Duke of Chesterton. The title is even more ancient than Rothwell's, for my family counts its lineage back to the time of the Conqueror."

"Oh, la, and I trace mine back to Adam and Eve," Mrs. Chalmers said with a merry laugh. "Do come off your high horse now. My only point is that you mustn't badger Miss Linton for an introduction."

"It isn't my decision who Lady Gwendolyn meets," Abby pointed out. "That is something you shall have to take up with His Grace."

"Where *is* the old boy?" Lord Ambrose asked. "If he's sparring with Goliath, it should be a bang-up match. Max is the best amateur heavyweight in England."

"He warned us not to disturb him," Mrs. Chalmers said. "And don't think I tumbled off the turnip cart only yesterday. I know you want an excuse to tarry around the stables and await his sister's return."

While they squabbled, Abby stepped to the window. Was Max truly a famous bruiser? No wonder he'd been so furious when she'd destroyed his concentration. Because of her, he had taken a punch that had knocked him down. She would never forget the sight of him stripped to the waist, his broad chest bathed by sunlight. He had surged toward her with swift, angry strides and pressed his gloved hand to her back, marching her out of the paddock. They'd been so close that the heat of his body had scorched her—

Abby swallowed a gasp as Lord Ambrose materialized at her side. A blush warmed her cheeks. For one mad moment, she feared he had read her lascivious thoughts.

He bestowed a charming smile on her. "Forgive me for startling you, Miss Linton. Perhaps you would care to join us for luncheon later. We're three gentlemen and only two ladies, so you would round out our numbers quite nicely."

She almost laughed to imagine Rothwell's reaction to finding her seated among his cronies at the dining table. Half of her was tempted to needle him by doing just that, but thankfully, her rational half prevailed.

She glanced out the window. "I believe I see Lady Gwendolyn in the distance. Thank you for the kind offer, sir, but duty calls."

Sketching a curtsy, she left the gallery in a whirl of skirts, her swift steps carrying her along an echoing corridor and then down a marble staircase. Abby didn't pause until she caught sight of herself in a large gilt-framed mirror.

Pinkness still tinted her face, and she hoped Lord Ambrose hadn't interpreted the blush to mean she harbored any interest in him. Both he and Lord Pettibone had been lavish in their compliments, but they were surely quizzing her, for she was mystified as to what they could see in a spinster of her advanced years.

She scrutinized her reflection. The large blue eyes were perhaps her best feature, the color enhanced today by the bluish-gray of her gown. Her skin was unblemished save for a few scattered freckles, and her eyebrows merely had a nice curve. Her mouth was a trifle generous, her nose unremarkable. Her hair was a wavy reddish brown, drawn up into a simple knot, a few wisps having escaped her lace cap to frame her face and neck.

She could spot nothing particularly noteworthy in her appearance. It was the same ordinary face she saw every day in the mirror.

Her customary levelheadedness reasserted itself. These London gentlemen must be accustomed to flirtations. It was a habit for them to use charm to ingratiate themselves with any female they met. Nevertheless, she allowed it was quite delightful to have been the subject of flattery by not one but two London dandies.

As for Rothwell, if he chose to be rude, then he could go to the devil.

Max was late for luncheon. Having sent orders for his guests not to wait, he trod downstairs to find them already seated around the linen-draped table in the dining parlor, a sunlit chamber with sea-green walls that his mother had liked to use for informal meals.

A chorus of greetings met his ears. Ambrose saluted him with a crystal goblet. "A fine French burgundy you've been hiding here, old chap. Given your long absence from the ducal seat, I was anticipating a week of swilling vinegar."

"My father laid the cellar," Max said. "One can only suppose aging did the wine a service. Now, pray forgive my tardiness in joining you."

Finchley stood waiting at the head of the table, the chair

drawn out by his crabby hands. The old butler had withered to a husk over the past fifteen years. His posture was hunched, his face a patchwork of wrinkles beneath a fuzz of white hair. "Sit you down, Your Grace," he said, helping to push in the chair for him as if Max were still a lad in short coats. "I've saved a nice mushroom broth for your first course, though it's a mite cool by now. Would've been piping hot if only you'd arrived on time."

Max took the scolding with forbearance. It touched him to know that the old retainers still had an unwavering loyalty to him. They had been his closest allies in a youth that had been unsettled by screaming quarrels, fits of hysteria, and slammed doors.

The cavernous house was much more tranquil now. Yet how strange it seemed to occupy his father's chair. Though the dukedom had been his for a decade, Max felt like a usurper within these walls.

He shook off the vague impression and surveyed the rest of the party. The women sat to either side of him, with Pettibone flanking Mrs. Chalmers to the left and Ambrose beside Lady Desmond on the right. They were already halfway through a course of quail and asparagus.

"My dear Rothwell," Elise said, her soft green-gold eyes fixed on him, "though your kindness is to be admired, you mustn't let the staff serve you cold food. The soup should be sent back to the kitchen to be properly heated."

She fluttered a pale hand at the blue-liveried footman, who stopped uncertainly, gripping the large silver tureen.

"Nonsense, I'm not waiting half an hour over so trifling a matter." Max motioned the young man forward, then reached for the ladle to dip the broth into his bowl. "I believed this was to be a cold luncheon, anyway."

"I hope you don't mind," Elise said in her most ingenuous tone, "but I took the liberty of ordering a heartier meal.

I thought you might need more sustenance after your exertions this morning with Goliath."

She had dipped her chin, gazing at him from beneath her lashes, looking for all the world like an adoring wife. The observation stirred uneasiness in Max, and only an ingrained civility induced him to say, "How kind. Though cold ham and chicken would have suited just as well."

"I trust you had a productive session with our champion, eh?" Pettibone said. "How's the old boy's form? Is he keeping up his strength?"

"He's a trifle off his stride, but that's likely due to missing a day of training while we were traveling. Nevertheless, he managed to land his fair share of solid strikes."

Remembering one strike in particular, Max had to force his jaw to relax in order to swallow a spoonful of lukewarm soup. His companions needn't know that he'd been laid out flat, the air knocked from his lungs, all because Abby had distracted him. The alarm on her face as she'd run toward him had served only to hone his ire. Then, as he'd ushered her away, those expressive blue eyes had aroused an entirely different sort of fury in him—the desire to lay *her* flat on the ground in order to ravish her.

Nothing could be more idiotic.

"Goliath's forte is his ability to take plenty of bottom," Ambrose was saying. "Though the amount of punishment he'll face from Wolfman remains to be seen."

"I understand the frontiersman is devilish quick on his feet and faster than lightning," Pettibone commented. "He's reputed to have killed a wolf with his bare hands."

A rapid argument circulated among the men and Mrs. Chalmers, debating the pros and cons of each pugilist, while Elise appeared a trifle bored, nibbling on bits of roasted quail from her mostly untouched plate.

"My money is on Goliath," Max asserted. "And not

only because I've a stake invested in him. The man's an ox and he's deuced hard to cut down. He can outlast any opponent."

"That's why he's the champion," Ambrose agreed. "No backwoodsman from America can beat the best brute in all of Britain. Nevertheless, our man mustn't slack off in his training over the next few days."

"Hear, hear!" Pettibone took a swig of wine. "To England's champ! We're counting on you, Rothwell, to fill our pockets with gold."

"Crabtree is keeping Goliath on a tight regimen," Max replied, naming the trainer he had brought from London. "A brisk five-mile walk after luncheon, then he'll practice his punches on a straw dummy until dinnertime. Beef-steaks, egg yolks, and mutton to build up his strength, a pint of porter, and off to bed with him."

Finchley came to remove the empty soup bowl. "Never fear, Your Grace, you may depend upon Beechy to take excellent care of the monstrous heathen. Why, she's been frying chops for half the morning!"

Elise narrowed her eyes at the butler. Her lips parted as if to object to his unsolicited commentary.

Luckily, Mrs. Chalmers spoke first. "Will Prinny attend the bout?" she asked. "He came to the last one."

"According to the latest gossip column, the Prince is presently in Brighton," Elise said. "It seems the poor man has been laid low with an acute attack of dyspepsia."

"Now there's a stroke of good fortune," Max said, taking a portion of poached fish in wine sauce from the platter Finchley offered. "If Prinny were to attend, I'd doubtless be obliged to offer him accommodations here. Imagine what a disruption that would cause, housing and feeding his entire retinue on short notice. And worse, having to entertain his set of courtly fustians."

"Why, I would be more than happy to help," Elise said, leaning closer and affording him a view of her creamy bosom. "Managing large parties involves hundreds of details, all of which should be handled by one who is skilled in such affairs. You must promise me, my lord duke, that you shall ask for my assistance in any domestic matters that may arise."

He inclined his head in a nod. "Let us hope that will not be necessary."

"There are other ways in which I can offer my support. Perhaps I might review the menus during our stay here. Although the meals have been quite tolerable—"

"Tolerable? They've been delicious," Ambrose said. "I've always found country cooking to be an agreeable respite from the fancier fare of London."

"For a bachelor living in rooms, perhaps," she said archly. "However, His Grace is accustomed to a higher standard. He surely must be missing Gervais and his array of French delicacies."

Finchley brought around a platter of roasted potatoes. "Frenchie grub is fit for frogs," he rasped, "and not proper Englishmen."

"I beg your pardon!" she said, glaring at the butler. "Rothwell, surely you will not allow your servants to continually interrupt us like this."

Max cast a stern look at the old man, who promptly shut his trap, though not without cocking an impertinent eyebrow. "Finchley, pray go and inform Hammond that I'll meet him in my study in half an hour."

"As Your Grace wishes." With an air of injury, Finchley tottered away and gave the party one last baleful glance over his stooped shoulder before vanishing out the doorway.

Max turned back to Elise. He didn't know who had

irked him more, her or the butler, who had fallen into shabby conduct since the time of Max's father. "As to altering the menus, the answer is no. Cook has already taken her instructions from me."

Her eyes widened at the rebuke, and he felt a moment's remorse to have spoken so sharply. The young widow was a vision of loveliness from her golden hair to her shapely figure and kissable mouth. She was the most sought-after temptress in the ton, and everything he desired in a woman. Nevertheless, he felt curiously relieved to have postponed his campaign of seduction. With his sister and aunt in residence, any dalliance must be off-limits until he departed the estate next week.

The necessity of the delay irritated him not just for the most obvious reason of living as a monk, but also because Elise clearly was intent on making herself indispensable to him. She had her eye on the role of duchess, and he needed to put a stop to that notion posthaste. The surest way to thwart her man trap was to establish her in the role of his mistress. Yet he dared not do so just yet. Not after Abby had witnessed that scorching scene in the library the previous afternoon.

His mood souring, he took a swallow of wine. Of all the women in the world, *she* had to be the one who'd forced him to face the recklessness of his actions. The one who had made him realize he hadn't spared a thought for propriety, that he had sunk so low as to engage in depravity when his sister or aunt might have walked into the room.

That event ought to have inspired his gratitude to Abby. She had prevented him from making a dastardly error of judgment. Instead, her presence in his house had caused a knot in his gut that was equal parts antipathy and attraction. Good God, he couldn't still be drawn to Abigail Linton, not after so many years—

". . . Miss Linton."

He was startled to hear her name spoken by Mrs. Chalmers. The woman was looking inquiringly at him, and for one mad moment he feared he had uttered Abby's name aloud. "Pardon?"

"I said that it was a pleasure to meet Miss Linton, Your Grace. She was in the picture gallery this morning as we were touring the house."

"We came upon her admiring the painting of you with your parents," Elise added. "I must say it is a lovely family portrait. How old were you?"

Max gathered his thoughts. "Sixteen, though I haven't viewed the canvas in years. What was Miss Linton doing in the gallery?"

"Watching at the window for your sister's return," Pettibone said. "She made quite the pretty picture herself."

"It's those big blue eyes and the charming blush," Ambrose added with a lecherous waggle of an eyebrow. "In London, she'd put all the ladies to shame."

Max had known these two scoundrels since they'd bonded as boys at Eton, planning pranks while everyone else was asleep, then later, at Oxford, landing themselves in scrapes that generally involved either gambling or the muslin brigade. It made him livid to think of either of them ogling Abby.

"Miss Linton is my employee. You will stay away from her. I trust I make myself clear." Hearing the vehemence in his voice, he made a conscious effort to assume a more affable expression. "There are plenty of other pursuits to keep you occupied—billiards, cards, shooting. Go for a walk or a ride. There used to be a rowboat down by the lake if you care to fish."

"I'm curious," Ambrose persisted, "did you know Miss Linton when you were children? Surely it would be impossible to forget such a charming female living nearly on your doorstep."

Max gave him a cool stare. Though he had never mentioned Abby by name, he'd been a surly beast fifteen years ago. His father had kept him in London for the autumn term, studying with tutors, and when Ambrose had come to express condolences over the duchess's death, Max had let slip an unguarded reference to the thwarted romance.

Now, Ambrose must be speculating that Abby had been that mystery girl. Worse, Elise appeared keenly interested in Max's response, for her speculative gaze was fixed on his face.

Max took a sip of wine before answering. "My father frowned upon me mingling with the locals. So, there is your answer."

"I should guess she was too young for you, anyway," Mrs. Chalmers said. "Miss Linton surely cannot be a day over five-and-twenty."

"She's certainly no ape leader," Pettibone concurred.

"Then I shall be the one to disagree," Elise said, motioning to the footman to remove the plates. "I would put her age on par with Rothwell's. Do tell us, Your Grace, which of us is correct?"

They all looked to Max for confirmation. Finding himself the subject of four pairs of prying eyes did little to improve his disposition.

"Far be it from me to reveal a lady's age," he said. "But she is younger than I am. Beyond that, kindly leave me out of your guessing games."

His testy manner served to put a damper on their speculations, and the conversation turned to other matters for the remainder of the meal. Elise, in particular, seemed intent on making herself agreeable to him, batting her lashes and smiling winsomely. When at last they arose,

Mrs. Chalmers suggested they enjoy the fine weather by taking a tour of the gardens. Elise would have lagged behind with Max, but he put a firm stop to it.

"Go with the others," he said, removing her dainty hand from his arm. "I have estate business to attend to this afternoon."

"But darling, I've scarcely had a moment of your time. Might I not accompany you?"

She stood very close, her soft bosom brushing his upper arm, her lips forming a moue of distress that he should have found enchanting. But today he felt only an impatience to be shed of her, for if he could not seduce the beauteous widow just yet, there was no purpose to enduring her insipid company.

Insipid? When had he begun to think of her in that way?

"A long session with my man of business would bore you to tears," he said. "It cannot be postponed, alas, but I shall see you for drinks before dinner. Now you had better hurry or you'll lose sight of the others."

Max gave her a little nudge toward their friends, who were already far down the corridor. Elise presented him with one last glimpse of her pouty face before she flounced after them, her hips swaying.

He headed in the direction of his study. He was looking forward to the meeting with Hammond. His dealings with the man on estate matters usually were handled by correspondence, and he relished the opportunity to discuss things face-to-face. Then afterward, he had something else to do.

He would ride out to visit Gwen's old governess, an encounter that by necessity must be kept secret.

Chapter 8

As they started down the grand staircase, their footsteps echoing in the vastness of the entrance hall, Lady Gwendolyn cast a nervous glance at Abby. "Are you quite sure that people will like me, Miss Linton?"

The girl had been unnaturally quiet during luncheon in the sitting room where they always took their meals. Now they were heading out to deliver baskets to a number of infirm and needy tenants on Rothwell land. Abby looked forward to the outing, for she had grown up visiting the people of the parish. Yet she could imagine how daunting the task must seem to a girl who had spent her life sheltered in a gilded cage.

She gave Lady Gwendolyn a warm smile. "Of course they'll like you, darling. You're a lovely, warmhearted young lady. In truth, they are far more likely to be worried that *you* won't like *them*."

"Oh my, I wouldn't wish anyone to think such a thing. But what shall I say to them?"

"When at a loss for conversation, the best course is to ask questions. Most people are happy to chat about the things that are of interest to them. You might ask a farmer's wife what type of crops the family is growing, or what the names and ages of her children are. The trick is to ensure that the other person does most of the talking."

"How clever! Yes, I can see where that would be very helpful."

As they neared the bottom of the stairs, Abby noticed that the front door was already open. A footman in blue livery stood at attention while Finchley spoke to a pair of women who stood on the portico. As the old butler stepped aside to allow them entry, a shock of recognition struck Abby.

"Pray excuse me!" she told Lady Gwendolyn, before hastening forward to greet the visitors.

Finchley's squinty eyes gleamed with interest. "Mrs. Rosalind Perkins and Miss Valerie Perkins," he intoned.

"So I see," Abby said, brushing a kiss to her sister's scented cheek. "Rosie, whatever are you doing here?"

"We've come to call, of course! I should think you'd have expected us."

Rosalind looked the picture of fashion in jonquil muslin with a fluted bonnet that sported a trio of egret plumes. Her daughter, Valerie, wore a demure gown of pale Saxon green, a yellow sash tied beneath her bosom. A jaunty straw bonnet crowned her strawberry-blond curls.

Squealing with delight, Valerie hurled herself into her aunt's embrace. "Aunt Abby! I can't believe you're living in such a magnificent house! Why, it's like a palace!"

"Hush, my sweet," Rosalind murmured. "Did I not warn you to mind your manners? It won't do to behave like a hoyden."

"Of course, Mama." Valerie instantly assumed a modest demeanor. She dipped her dainty chin, though her blue eyes sparkled beneath a siren's long lashes. That fetching expression looked as if it had been practiced in front of a mirror.

Abby returned her attention to her older sister. "Surely you must know that I'm not allowed to entertain guests."

"Oh, but we are not *your* guests," Rosalind said. "We're fortunate to see you, but we've actually come to call upon the duke. It's only proper that we should welcome him back to the neighborhood."

Abby choked off a groan. She ought to have realized at once what her ambitious sister desired—for the Duke of Rothwell to fall head over ears in love with seventeen-year-old Valerie. How imprudent of Rosalind! Had she given no thought at all to the awkward position in which she'd placed Abby? Very likely not. Rothwell was bound to be provoked by a request to receive relatives of the governess, no matter how well bred they might be.

Finchley, she noticed, was already disappearing down the long corridor. The ancient butler looked in a hurry to inform the duke of his unexpected visitors. And he was too far away for her to stop him without creating a scene.

Unclenching her teeth, Abby murmured, "Might I remind you, Rosie, you don't live anywhere near this neighborhood any longer. In fact, I would have thought you'd have gone home to Kent already."

"Oh, la! Peter had business in Dorset, so it made more sense for us to await his return before setting out for home together. Clifford invited us to prolong our stay, and Lucille has been very glad for our company since you left her without a companion. How auspicious it was when we heard that His Grace's coach had been sighted in the village yesterday. Why, it is almost as if it were ordained by the fates!"

While speaking, Rosalind was eyeing the gilt and marble appointments of the entrance hall, the high domed ceiling, and the large murals that depicted scenes from *Aesop's Fables,* as if she were imagining her daughter reigning over all this splendor as the Duchess of Rothwell. Meanwhile, Valerie's inquisitive gaze was fastened on Lady Gwendolyn, who hung back shyly by the newel post.

Abby wrestled with the awkward situation. It wasn't her place to introduce Rothwell's sister to anyone without his consent. Yet she could hardly be rude, so she brought her charge forward. "Lady Gwendolyn, may I present my sister, Mrs. Perkins, and her daughter, Valerie."

Both visitors curtsied to the duke's sister, whose lips curved in an uncertain smile. In a hesitant voice, the girl murmured, "It's a pleasure to make your acquaintance."

Her dove-gray eyes flashed to Abby, silently begging for help. "Perhaps," Abby suggested, "you could escort the visitors to the antechamber to await Finchley's return."

Lady Gwendolyn led the way through an arched doorway and into an elegant room with apricot-painted silk on the walls, Sheraton chairs, and porcelain vases on pedestals. Bringing up the rear, Abby prayed that the butler would return swiftly with the news that the duke was not receiving today. How cringeworthy to imagine her sister boasting of Valerie's ladylike accomplishments to Rothwell.

He might be an incorrigible rogue, but that didn't mean she wished to give him ammunition to mock her or her family.

"Oh, I do adore your gown," Valerie told Lady Gwendolyn. "I have been looking for a length of muslin in that very shade of peach. And the ribbons are so pretty, too. Who would have thought to use fawn, but it is absolutely perfect! You must tell me the name of your modiste. I shall turn eighteen in January, so I am to make my bows next spring, and Mama and I are already planning my trousseau. May I tell you about it?"

Lady Gwendolyn looked a trifle bemused by the prattle, but she readily agreed, and the two girls sat down on a chaise near the window. They soon had their heads together in a tête-à-tête, with Valerie doing most of the talking while Lady Gwendolyn smiled and nodded.

"How perfect, they soon will be fast friends," Rosalind confided in a murmur. "It is precisely as I had hoped!"

"Hoped?" Abby said, frowning. "What do you mean? I thought you'd come to charm the duke."

"Half an hour's visit is scarcely adequate. That is why I intend to suggest to His Grace that Valerie would make a suitable companion for his sister. James put the idea in my head when he mentioned that Lady Gwendolyn spends most of her time cooped up in this house with only her aunt and a few servants for company. Do you know how long Rothwell plans on staying?"

As the local vicar, their brother James knew the comings and goings of everyone in the parish, but Abby doubted that he would have suggested such a brazen ruse. No, this had all the earmarks of one of Rosalind's madcap notions. "It's my understanding he'll be in residence for no more than a week, perhaps less," she said dampeningly. "And since you too will be going home to Kent soon, there is scarcely time for a friendship to form. You might as well abandon this scheme."

"Abandon it, bah. When the most eligible man in all of England is right here on our doorstep? Rothwell is past thirty and he must soon be turning his mind to marriage. And why not to my dear girl? Just look at her. Is she not the most taking little thing you've ever seen? Such charm! Such beauty!"

Abby flicked a glance at her niece, who was indeed the essence of the peaches-and-cream young lady. Valerie was personable and lively, and despite her modest portion, she doubtless would attract a great deal of male attention when she made her debut. But she was also a complete widget with little experience of the world.

"Of course she's lovely, but do be reasonable. There must be flocks of girls with grander connections. Besides which, the duke is nearly twice her age and he's a hardened libertine as well. In fact, he has brought several rakes and questionable females here with him—along with a prizefighter out in the stables."

"Oh, la! If Rothwell deems them acceptable company for his sister, then it must be so for Valerie, too. As to marriage, she will have him twined around her pretty little finger in no time. But first, she must have her chance to catch his notice. That is where you can help, Abby."

"Me?" The very notion of being recruited for such mischief appalled her. "I want no part of this scheme. Lady Gwendolyn and I were just on our way out, anyway."

Rosalind frowned. "Where are you going?"

"We're spending the afternoon visiting a number of tenants on the duke's estate." Abby glanced out the window. "I see that our carriage is already waiting outside."

"Ah, I did wonder if someone else had come to call. But you mustn't leave just yet. If Lady Gwendolyn isn't at home, it will ruin everything!"

"All the more reason for us to depart at once. Then I won't have to witness you pitchforking my niece into Rothwell's lap."

As Abby turned away, intending to collect the girl, Rosalind caught hold of her arm. Abby found herself the subject of her sister's sharp brown gaze. "Perhaps there is another reason for your refusal to help," Rosalind whispered. "Is it possible that you still harbor a soft spot for His Grace?"

The question rattled Abby. Rosalind was the only one in the family who knew about that long-ago romance. Abby had been obliged to confide in her sister since there had been no other way to smuggle out letters to Max. It was strictly forbidden for a young girl to correspond with an unrelated male, and so she had not dared to ask her father to frank the letters. Instead, she had sent them to her sister, who was ten years her elder and enjoyed more latitude as a married woman. Since Rosalind had always reveled in clandestine plots, she'd gladly forwarded them to Max.

Now, that inquisitive stare made Abby feel defensive—especially in light of her own disturbing flash of desire at seeing Rothwell stripped to the waist. "Don't be absurd," she said firmly. "That was a mere childhood fancy, and it is long since finished. I can assure you, I've no interest whatsoever in him anymore—nor he in me."

Seeing that Rosalind looked satisfied by the answer, Abby realized belatedly that she ought to have pretended to still carry a torch for him. That might have better served to thwart her sister's plan. But it was too late now.

"I have always envied you for not being of a disposition for marriage," Rosalind said, while checking her reflection in a gilt-framed mirror. "It is quite a trial to fret over one's children, you know, and to always worry that one is doing what is best for them."

"Not of a disposition for marriage?" Abby latched onto that startling statement. Was that how her family viewed her? As a spinster by choice? She'd had no alternative but to spend her youth looking after their parents without ever enjoying a London season. She had loved them dearly and had made the best of matters, yet that didn't mean she had not yearned for more.

"Why, yes, you always seemed so cheerful living with Mama and Papa. It made me glad to see you content to remain at home when none of the rest of us were able to do so. You have always been the kindest and most caring in the family." Rosalind gave her a woebegone look. "Are you certain you cannot find it in your heart to aid your niece on her journey to happiness?"

"I don't understand what it is you expect me to do."

"It's quite simple. I shall seek His Grace's permission to leave Valerie here for the afternoon. Then, when the storm strikes, you must convince him that the roads are a quagmire and beg leave for him to allow Valerie to spend the night."

"Storm?" Abby blinked at the golden beams of sunshine streaming through the windows. "Don't be absurd, there isn't a cloud in the sky."

"Lucille's arthritis kept her abed this morning, and you know how her aches and pains always portend rain. You may be certain the weather will turn foul by nightfall."

It was true, whenever Clifford's wife suffered an attack, it foretold inclement conditions in the near future. But this once, Abby didn't believe it. "Perhaps she's still feeling the effects of yesterday's rain. You surely cannot pin all your plans on such a flimsy hope."

"What I hope is that I may count on you, dearest sister." Rosalind clasped Abby's hands. "Please, if you love Valerie, you must promise to do everything in your power to help her."

Abby hardly knew how to respond. Her sister had placed her in an untenable position. She certainly didn't wish for Valerie to end up a spinster like herself. Yet the mental image of her niece clasped in Rothwell's arms, the subject of his ardent kisses, was simply too much to bear.

Her gaze strayed to the doorway. Good heavens, what was keeping Finchley? If only the butler would return to report that the duke wasn't receiving, then Rosalind would be forced to abandon her scheme and depart.

"It isn't up to me whether to help or not," she said testily. "You must understand, I have no authority whatsoever—"

The words died on her tongue as Rothwell stepped into the antechamber.

Max had been heading into his study to meet his estate agent when a voice from far down the corridor had stopped him.

"Your Grace," Finchley called in a gravelly tone, scurrying forward with the speed of someone half his age. "If I might have a word."

Max turned back to meet the butler. "What is it?"

"You have visitors. Mrs. Rosalind Perkins and Miss Valerie Perkins."

He had no intention of squandering the afternoon in the company of nosy neighbors who would gabble gossip or, worse, thrust their simpering daughters at him. "I don't know anyone by that name. Send them away. Along with whoever else might come knocking."

"If I might be permitted to say, Your Grace, that would be poor manners, indeed. Especially as Miss Abby knows these two very well."

"What has that to do with anything?" Max said impatiently. "She's lived her entire life in the area. I expect she is well acquainted with everyone in and about the village."

"But they're her sister and her niece. Miss Abby and Lady Gwen are with them right now. They happened to be coming down the stairs as I opened the front door."

THE DUKE I ONCE KNEW

The gleam in Finchley's rheumy blue eyes hinted at a certain delight in the situation. Max couldn't imagine what the codger found so amusing. Though he'd wondered if the staff had guessed about his boyhood courtship of the girl on the neighboring estate. Only look at how Beechy had bade him sit with Abby the other day in the kitchen. Perhaps having the two of them living under one roof injected a little unwarranted excitement into the tedium of their everyday lives.

Too bad they'd be disappointed.

"Where are they?"

"I left them in the entrance hall. Shall I show them into the Turkish Saloon? Or perhaps the Gold Drawing Room?"

"No. I'll go downstairs myself. Pray inform Hammond that I'll be a trifle late for our meeting."

Max stalked along the lengthy corridor, his footfalls sharp and clipped. Already, he half regretted the impulse that had spurred him on this detour. He ought to have stuck with his original decision and ordered Finchley to turn them away. There could be no logical reason for him to want a word with any of Abby's relations.

Except curiosity perhaps.

That long-ago summer when they had met nearly every day in their secret glade in the forest, Abby had related many humorous stories about her family members. There had been one about her elder sister Rosalind . . . something about her setting a trap to lure the dashing younger son of a baron into marriage. Max strained to recall the particulars, but the tale was lost to the mists of time.

Not that he wished to remember. Nostalgia served no purpose. Yet he could not deny a certain interest in making the acquaintance of Abby's sister. All four of her siblings had been considerably older than him. Consequently, they'd been married and living elsewhere by the time he and Abby had met. Other than glimpsing them occasionally at London parties, the only one with whom he'd ever had any particular dealings was her brother James Linton, to whom Max had awarded the living at the village church several years ago. The matter had been handled by post based upon a recommendation from the previous vicar.

He'd had only a nodding acquaintance with Abby's parents, too. They'd seemed a devoted couple, though old enough to be her grandparents. He'd seen them in the village from time to time, when he was home on holiday from Eton.

Home. He felt an unwanted catch in his throat to think that Rothwell Court had once been his home. He had lived every day of his life here until age sixteen. His earliest memories were of playing solitary games of pirates, constructing ships out of bedsheets and chairs, and of sometimes escaping the nursery to battle the Spanish or the French amid the shrouded furniture of an unused wing, or to stalk imaginary prey through the jungles of the conservatory, much to Aunt Hester's delight and his nanny's dismay.

Aware he was smiling, Max wiped his expression clean and headed down the grand staircase. The entrance hall was unoccupied save for the footman on duty at the door, but the hum of voices led him across the marble floor to the antechamber. Nearing the doorway, he heard the low pitch of Abby's voice.

"It isn't up to me whether to help or not," she said in a rather distressed tone. "You must understand, I have no authority whatsoever—"

As he stepped inside, she fell silent, those expressive blue eyes widening. What did she mean by having no authority? Judging by the bloom in her cheeks, it must be something she didn't wish for him to know.

He squelched his curiosity. Whatever issue that troubled her did not concern him so long as she performed her duty to his sister and stayed away from his London friends. In particular, he had thoroughly disliked the way Ambrose had salivated over her charms. He found his own attraction to her to be irksome enough, for she was a rustic spinster, too slim and willowy to suit his tastes, and no match for the dainty blond beauty of Lady Desmond.

Nevertheless, Abby had a quiet elegance that was enhanced by her bluish-gray gown, the same one she'd worn while spying on his sparring match with Goliath. He found nothing to praise or criticize in her regular features, yet there was a lively sparkle in her eyes that lit up her expression and set her apart from more practiced flirts. And that luminous look still had the power to twist his gut into knots.

A straw bonnet framed the oval of her face, and he recalled that she'd planned to take Gwen out on a mission of mercy to visit his tenants. That must be why they had been coming down the stairs at the time of her sister's arrival.

He strode forward to greet Abby's sister. A family likeness could be detected in the structure of her cheekbones and the pert chin. With strands of silver in her copper hair, Rosalind Perkins looked to be some ten years older than Abby. The moment she spotted him, her frown transformed into a smile that had the effect of revealing fine lines around her mouth and eyes.

Abby sketched a curtsy. "Pardon me, my lord duke. I was expecting Finchley to return. May I present you to my sister, Mrs. Perkins, and her daughter, Miss Perkins. Rosalind and Valerie, the Duke of Rothwell."

Miss Valerie Perkins sprang up from the chaise where she'd been chatting with his sister, her youthful features alive with coy pleasure. As she and her mother made their genuflections to him, Mrs. Perkins said brightly, "It is a great honor to meet you at last, Your Grace. I trust we are not intruding?"

"I was about to sit down to a meeting with my agent," he said bluntly. "I haven't much time, but since we are neighbors, I did not wish to snub your acquaintance."

"My sister lives in Kent," Abby interjected. "She and her daughter are staying at Linton House for a short visit."

"A prolonged visit," Mrs. Perkins corrected with a side-long look at her sister before turning a smile back to Max. "You see, having grown up here, I've a sentimental attachment to this corner of Hampshire. It's all so charming and tranquil. I do believe my daughter has grown to love the area as much as I do."

"Indeed, I find it ever so beautiful, Your Grace." Miss Perkins made a coquettish peek up at him from beneath a flutter of long lashes. "Most especially here at Rothwell Court. Mama and I greatly enjoyed the drive from the gatehouse with all the lovely trees and the rolling hills. And might I add, the magnificence of the house quite stole my breath away. I daresay there is no finer estate in all of England."

Max hid an unexpected twist of amusement at the gushing tribute. The little minx was barely out of the schoolroom and she thought to beguile him with her kittenish wiles. He intercepted Abby's glance and caught a glint in her eyes as if she'd just had the same thought. For one brief moment, they gazed at each other with a strange sort of kinship. It was as if the past fifteen years had never happened and they were back in their secret glade, sharing a laugh over the absurdities of people.

She blinked and looked away, the warmth of her expression fading into a cool smile. "We mustn't keep His Grace from his business affairs," she told her sister. "And I'm afraid it is past time for Lady Gwendolyn and I to set out on our errands."

"Oh, must they both go?" Gwen piped up, then blushed as everyone turned to look at her. His sister stood rather shyly to the rear of the party, her fingers twined at her waist as she lifted pleading eyes to Max. "That is, I—I wondered if Miss Perkins might come along with me and Miss Linton. Please, Max?"

"But you've only just met."

"That may be true, Your Grace, yet I do believe we are destined to become bosom bows," Valerie Perkins said, slipping her arm through Gwen's. "You see, it has been ever so lonely since all of my friends live in Kent. Lady Gwendolyn has been kind enough to offer to keep me company this week."

"What a marvelous notion," Mrs. Perkins said, gazing fondly at them. "And quite perfect, for you are a mere two years apart in age. Why, I could leave you here in the care of your aunt Abby and send the carriage to fetch you before dinnertime. Provided, of course, that His Grace agrees."

Max had no doubt the plot had been hatched before they'd even set foot on his land. It was patently obvious that she wanted to dangle her pretty daughter in ducal waters in hopes that he would snap at the bait. And little Miss Perkins had ingratiated herself with his sister in order to encourage the scheme.

It isn't up to me whether to help or not. You must understand, I have no authority whatsoever—

Now he understood the distress he'd overheard in Abby's voice. Mrs. Rosalind Perkins must have tried to recruit her assistance, and Abby had balked at the ploy. Not because she still harbored any tendre for him; that was impossible since she'd ignored his numerous letters years ago. Rather, she believed him to be too irredeemable a rake for her innocent niece.

Abby was right. Although the debaucheries of his youth were much exaggerated of late, he had experienced enough sordidness to know himself unfit to wed a mere child, even if he had the slightest interest in marriage, which he did not. His own parents' volatile union had cured him of any such inclination. Nevertheless, the mothers of society continued to parade their naïve daughters in front of him. And nothing irritated him more than to be maneuvered by female tricks.

Max was on the brink of issuing a firm refusal when he looked at his sister. Her soft gray eyes beseeched him, and it struck him suddenly that she had no friends. For most of her life, she had lived in this great pile of a house with only his aunt, a governess, and the servants for company. He had never thought much of it, for Gwen had always been a timid sort, happy to play quietly by herself and shy of speaking to strangers.

But now Max wondered if he'd done her a terrible wrong. Perhaps he ought to have sent her off to finishing school, where she would have met other girls her age. Could he truly deny her this one chance to make a friend?

No. Not even if he had to fend off a budding siren and her ambitious mama.

Smiling at his sister, he said, "It shall be as you wish, then."

Chapter 9

Considering the way in which it had begun, the afternoon turned out to be far more pleasant than Abby had anticipated. She'd fretted that a spirited older girl like Valerie might have a corrupting influence on Lady Gwendolyn. But as they approached their last stop, she had to admit that both girls had behaved admirably.

It had been a tight squeeze for all three of them to fit into the narrow confines of the open carriage. A groom sat on the box ahead of them and kept the pair of horses to a sedate pace over a road that wound through the verdant valley where the tenant farms were located. It was fascinating to watch the last of the corn being harvested, the reapers wielding their scythes with a steady back-and-forth motion while other workers followed in their wake, tying the stalks into sheaves. Flocks of birds fluttered over the shorn fields to peck for stray bits of grain.

They had visited three cottages already, spending time with the residents of each one, including a widow with eight children who'd welcomed a basket of food and clothing, a toothless pensioner requiring broths and possets, and a first-time mother who'd gratefully accepted instruction from Abby in swaddling and calming her colicky infant. Abby had compiled a list of those in need with the help of Mrs. Beech, whose father-in-law lived at this last house. He had wrenched his ankle two days ago, and with all the fancy meals to be prepared for the duke's guests, the cook had been unable to call on him.

The carriage drew to a halt in front of a charming thatch-roofed cottage with pink roses climbing over the doorway. The girls hopped out, first Valerie in a rustle of pale green skirts, then Lady Gwen more cautious and dignified. After stepping down, Abby headed straight to the graybeard who sat on a chair in the shade, his bandaged foot propped on a wooden stool.

His eyes squinted. He drew the pipe from his mouth and tugged his brown cap by way of respect. "Why, 'tis a trio of angels appearing on my doorstep. Ye've not come to carry me up to heaven, have ye?"

The girls giggled. "No, sir," Valerie said very prettily. "Rather, we are here to bring you good cheer."

"'Tis happy I am for visitors. I see there's Miss Abby. She's the finest seraph of them all, that she is."

As he struggled to stand, Abby said, "Pray do remain seated. Mrs. Beech said you must be careful not to cause further harm to your ankle."

"Mustn't disobey the wardress, lest she put me on a diet of bread and water." Sinking back down, he patted his vest, the buttons straining at his stout midsection as he gave a jolly chuckle. "I do believe I might expire of sorrow to be denied her honey cakes."

"I daresay there may be some in the basket she sent," Abby said. "Now, I should like you to meet the duke's sister, Lady Gwendolyn, and my niece, Miss Perkins. Girls, this is Mr. Beech, who is Cook's father-in-law."

"What a pleasure it is to make your acquaintance," Lady Gwen said glowingly. "I have heard Cook mention you."

"Not tellin' tall tales, I trust."

"Certainly not, sir! She has only the greatest fondness for you." The girl bit her lip, then added, "Though I must say, I did not know of your injury. If I may ask, how did you come to hurt yourself?"

Abby was pleased that Lady Gwen had taken her advice to heart. At each cottage, the girl had made an effort to engage the tenants in conversation by asking polite questions. She had not flinched on encountering poor conditions, either. Even when Valerie had wrinkled her nose in disgust, Lady Gwen had held a baby in need of a nappy change, and accepted hugs from grubby children. She had shown herself to be gracious and kind, and in some ways, more mature than Valerie, who was inclined to frivolity.

Mr. Beech regarded his bandaged foot dolefully. "I was fetchin' the kittens out o' the loft when my gumboot slipped on the ladder," he explained. "Just tucked the last one in my pocket when it happened, or she might still be mewlin' alone up there, whilst her mam is off catchin' mice."

"Kittens?" Valerie echoed.

The two girls regarded each other with rounded eyes.

"How old are they, please?" Lady Gwen asked him.

"Oh, 'round about six weeks by now." He waved his pipe. "Gave away some yesterday, but there's two of 'em left. Ye might go and have a peek in yonder stable."

Valerie started to trot away in the direction of a dilapidated structure that looked more like a shed than a stable, but Lady Gwen turned her gaze to Abby. "May we, Miss Linton?"

Abby nodded. "Yes. Only do be careful lest their little claws snag your skirts."

Both girls disappeared through the shadowed doorway.

The groom had taken the basket into the cottage, and now he brought forth two more items that had been lashed to the back of the carriage. They were a matching pair of long sticks, each with a padded crosspiece, which Abby presented to Mr. Beech. "We've brought you a proper set of crutches, for Mrs. Beech said you were making do with only a stout branch as a cane."

His weathered face lit up with a grin. "Such a right fine one she is to think of me comfort. Just like me own daughter. I'll give 'em a try straightaway."

He used one crutch to lever himself up from the chair, while Abby hovered nearby, ready to assist, yet cognizant of the man's pride in doing for himself. He succeeded in standing upright, then tucked a crosspiece beneath each arm before taking a few hobbling steps along the dirt pathway.

"Ah," he said, with a grunt of approval. "That'll be much easier, indeed so."

"Just take your time getting used to them," Abby advised. "There's no need to hurry."

While he practiced walking with the crutches, she glanced around the neat little yard. The climbing pink roses and the purple foxgloves in the garden showed Mrs. Beech's touch. Her late husband, Mr. Beech's only son, had died in a threshing accident before Abby had been born. Shortly thereafter, Mrs. Beech had secured a position in the Rothwell kitchen, returning here whenever she had a free moment to cook and clean for her aging father-in-law. Mr. Beech still farmed the surrounding land, and Abby wondered how he managed alone even when in better health.

As her gaze swept over the shorn fields, she noticed a lone rider cantering down the lane from the direction of a forested area of the estate. She shaded her eyes with the edge of her hand and idly watched him. Suddenly, her heart did a wild flip as she recognized the tall, muscular form of Rothwell astride the big black horse named Brimstone.

He veered straight toward the cottage.

Abby tried to steady the erratic leap of her pulse. She folded her hands at her waist in the hopes of presenting a calm, unruffled façade. But inside, she was a tempest of tension. Had Rothwell followed them here? What purpose could he have? If his meeting with the estate agent was over, why was he not back at the house entertaining his profligate friends?

Why must he come here to disturb the tranquility of their outing?

He swung down from his mount and tied the reins to a post near the garden gate. Brimstone tossed his head and snorted. Abby took an involuntary step backward just as Rothwell glanced at her and raised an eyebrow, as if he found her alarm amusing. The groom who'd driven their carriage sprang forward to help, but the duke waved him away. He murmured softly into Brimstone's perked ears, stroking the animal's glossy mane for a few moments until the horse quieted enough to bend his head down and snuffle the grasses outside the fence.

Abby watched from beneath the shade of an oak tree as Rothwell sauntered up the short path, dwarfing the tiny garden with his presence. He had changed into riding clothes: a dark blue coat, buckskins, and black Hessians, though he wore no hat to protect against the late afternoon sun. His coffee-brown hair lay in attractive dishevelment.

Not that she cared to notice.

He afforded her a brisk nod. "Ah, Miss Linton. I spotted your carriage from the lane. Have you lost your two charges already?"

"They're in the stable looking at some kittens."

His gaze flashed to the derelict structure as a peal of girlish laughter floated on the breeze. Mr. Beech leaned on his crutches, his leathery face wiped clean of its earlier joviality. It struck her that the duke wouldn't even recognize his own tenants since he'd been a boy of sixteen when he'd left.

She stepped forward to perform the introductions. Too late.

He was already reaching out to shake the man's hand. "Rothwell here. You must be Mr. Beech, my cook's father-in-law."

The older man allowed a brief, dutiful handclasp. "Aye, that I am. Though I don't recollect we ever met when ye was a lad. Been gone for a long time, that ye have."

His stiff tone radiated disapproval, and Abby wondered if the duke would take offense. Most of the tenants were diligent farmers who cherished their vocation of working the land. They would be understandably mistrustful of an absentee landlord who showed up out of the blue. Especially an indolent aristocrat who used the profits of their labor to fund his dissolute ways.

Rothwell's mouth curled into a wry smile. "It *has* been too long," he admitted. "However, Hammond has kept me well informed, right down to the last bale of hay and new calf. I am also obliged for his map of the estate showing the location of each farm. That's how I knew this one to be yours."

"Then p'raps ye'll note that I've finished the harvestin'. This leg will be hale again in time for me to sow the winter crop."

Frowning slightly, Rothwell flicked a glance at the bound ankle. "I've not come to discharge you from your land, sir, but merely to make your acquaintance. Might we sit down, then?"

Mr. Beech's inflexible expression eased somewhat and he gingerly lowered himself into his chair with the aid of the crutches. "Just so ye realize, milord. These bones might be old, but a crew helps me bring in the crop."

"Yes, I'm aware that workers travel from farm to farm at harvesttime. I saw them on the ride here. Miss Linton, would you care to join us?"

Rothwell waved at a nearby bench. He looked genial enough, yet his penetrating gray eyes stirred discord within her. Since the last thing Abby desired was to sit right next to him on the narrow seat, she shook her head. "Thank you, but I must go inside and unpack the basket Mrs. Beech sent."

Turning toward the cottage, she couldn't help overhearing the conversation behind her. At least the two men sounded on better terms now. She would never forgive Rothwell if he caused trouble for the country folk she'd known and loved since girlhood.

"I presume you harvested ahead of yesterday's rain?" the duke asked.

"Aye, there's only Digby's farm left to finish today. And best they hurry, afore the storm hits."

"Hmm, I did notice a dark cloud to the north. Would you estimate at least an hour or more before it reaches us?"

"Quite so, milord duke. When the winds start a-blowin' hard, 'tis time ye be on yer way back home."

Abby grimaced. A storm? Good heavens, it mustn't be true. She'd been hoping to avoid the awkward situation of having to ask Rothwell's permission for Valerie to stay the night. That was Rosalind's devious plan, and Abby wanted no part of tossing her coquettish niece into his path.

Entering the tiny cottage, she hastened to a window that faced north. Her heart sank as she peered through the wavy glass panes. Black clouds boiled along the length of the horizon. She prayed they would bring only a sprinkle of rain and wouldn't stop a carriage from transporting Valerie back to Linton House.

She quickly set to work, adding a bit of wood to the fire and pouring water from a pail into the kettle. She tidied the dry sink, put away a few dishes in the small hutch, and then unloaded the basket of food that Mrs. Beech had packed. There was cold chicken and beef, bread and butter, sausages and boiled eggs, enough to feed the cook's father-in-law for several days, along with a generous batch of the honey cakes he loved. While Abby waited for the tea to brew, she peered out the window again to check on the approaching storm. The clouds were looking larger and more ominous by the moment.

Just then, she spied a gig coming at a fast clip along the lane behind the cottage. As the small vehicle rattled by, her eyes sharpened on the lone woman handling the reins.

Miss Herrington?

Abby blinked. No, that was impossible. The former governess had left nearly a fortnight ago, ostensibly due to a family crisis—or perhaps with a secret lover, if Lady Hester was to be believed. Whatever the case, she was supposed to be long gone from this corner of Hampshire.

Yet Abby could swear that it was her. The last time she'd seen the woman in church, the governess had sported the same distinctive bonnet as the one worn by the driver of the gig. It was emerald green with a cluster of cherries and crimson ribbons.

Mystified, Abby dashed outside to see if the men had noticed and found them deep in conversation about the prizefight.

"'Twill be the match of the century, indeed it will," Mr. Beech was saying. "Mayhap better even than any of

James Jackson's. I saw Humphries take on Mendoza back in the day, too, now that was a fight!"

"Then you mustn't miss this one," Rothwell said. "I'll send a groom to drive you there on Friday."

"Ye would do so, milord? But I daren't beg such a grand favor of ye!"

Abby could no longer wait to break in with her news. "Rothwell, do come quickly. You must see the gig that just drove past!"

He frowned slightly, but rose to his feet and excused himself. His movements were too indolent, so she curled her fingers around his arm and hauled him toward the fence, just as the vehicle was disappearing around a bend in the lane.

"There," Abby said urgently, "did you see her? I could swear the driver was Miss Herrington!"

Rothwell flashed Abby a swift, piercing look that oddly appeared more calculating than surprised. Then he cocked an arrogant eyebrow and chuckled. "Nonsense. I received a letter stating that she went to her family in Gloucestershire."

"But did you not notice the woman's bonnet? It's deep green with cherry ribbons, which I myself saw her wear a few weeks ago. Besides which, I caught a glimpse of her blond hair and her pretty features. I don't know how it could *not* have been her."

"Rather, it's mere fancy that is feeding your mistaken notion. I blame it all on my dotty aunt for making you believe the faradiddle that Miss Herrington ran off with a mysterious stranger."

"Then pray mount your horse and ride after her! You'll prove for yourself that it's her!"

"Absolutely not. I won't be sent on a wild-goose chase."

He patted her hand as if she were a child to be placated.

Realizing she was still clutching the hard muscles of his arm, Abby snatched back her fingers. She had never apologized to him for spreading that unseemly gossip, but she wouldn't do so now. At least not until she unraveled the mystery of Miss Herrington's departure.

"Well, I do know who I saw, Your Grace. One would think you'd be concerned that your sister's governess might have lied to you."

"Why? She is no longer in my employ, so it's of no interest to me. Now, I do believe you've forgotten *your* duties." He swept his arm in an authoritative wave for her to precede him down the dirt path.

Abby marched ahead, her arms swinging and her heels kicking up the hem of her gown. His quick denial of her testimony burned in her craw. Only a cad would dismiss the evidence of an eyewitness so readily. Especially when he had at his disposal an easy means of solving the mystery. All he'd needed to do was to leap into the saddle, spur Brimstone to a gallop, and catch up to the gig. The matter could have been settled in the snap of a finger.

Yet it seemed to Abby that Rothwell had been determined from the start to scoff at her word. Did he scorn her so much that he would believe nothing she said? Or was something else at play? Might there be another reason why he had been so swift to refute what she had seen?

She recalled his expression upon first hearing that she'd spotted Miss Herrington. There had been a hint of shrewdness in that sharp look. And he'd shown not even a trace of the surprise that one would expect him to exhibit at the news that a former employee who supposedly had gone away was, in fact, still lurking in the neighborhood.

Abby mulled over the matter. Was it possible that Rothwell already had known Miss Herrington was in the vicinity? The more she weighed the startling thought, the more viable it seemed. But why would he keep it a secret? What could his purpose be?

"Miss Linton! Do come and see this dear little kitten!"

"Look, Aunt Abby, I have one, too!"

Abby realized that both girls were standing near Mr. Beech, and that each cradled a tiny ball of fluff. Lady Gwendolyn held a caramel tabby that was curled fast asleep against her bosom, while Valerie's gray kitten batted at the dangling yellow ribbons of her straw bonnet.

"Please, Miss Linton, may we keep them?" Lady Gwendolyn asked, her eyes shining. "Mr. Beech says they need a good home."

The old man smiled craftily from his chair. "'Twould be a blessin' if I wouldn't have to drown the wee mites."

The girls gasped. "Oh, but you mustn't do so, sir!" Valerie cried. "That would be too cruel! Aunt Abby, pray help us save them!"

"I understand your concern," Abby said soothingly, "but kittens soon grow into cats and I doubt that Mrs. Jeffries will appreciate having two felines prowling the house and sharpening their claws on the silk chairs. Nevertheless, the final decision is up to His Grace."

She turned to look at Rothwell, who stood beside her. A sudden gust ruffled his dark hair so that he looked diabolically handsome. His mouth quirked slightly as he ran a fingertip over the kitten nestled in his sister's hand. Abby watched the stroking motion of that finger and felt her insides contract with an untimely yearning.

"Cats belong outdoors," he said, "and not in the house. They would be welcome as mousers, though, if they were to make their home in the stables."

"The stables!" Lady Gwen said in dismay. "Oh, but they're just babies—"

"Should you object to the arrangement, you may leave

the kittens here. Now, it is time to be off, else we'll be caught out in the storm."

The wind was indeed beginning to blow harder, with a chilly dampness that foretold rain. The sky darkened as the black clouds crept ever closer. Abby fetched the empty basket to use to transport the kittens and informed Mr. Beech that his tea awaited him inside the cottage. They climbed back into the carriage, the girls tucking the covered basket at their feet. Chattering excitedly, they took frequent peeks inside to check on their kittens.

Abby held herself stiffly, for she was keenly conscious of Rothwell riding alongside the carriage. As Brimstone tossed his head, the duke controlled the massive black horse with a deft hand. She didn't know if the tangle of tension inside her was due to her wariness of the horse, or frustration with the way Rothwell's aloof expression masked his thoughts.

Although at one time she had felt perfectly attuned to the workings of his mind, he was now as much an enigma to her as this business with Miss Herrington. If indeed he'd known of the governess's presence in the area, why would he pretend otherwise? Abby remembered how ardently he had defended Miss Herrington in the kitchen the previous day. He had referred to her as *estimable* and then had nearly bitten off Abby's head for repeating gossip that the governess had run off with a lover.

Was it possible that Rothwell was Miss Herrington's lover? That he had embarked upon an illicit relationship with her?

Abby shivered from the chill wind that buffeted the open carriage. The notion seemed utterly implausible. She didn't want to believe that he had sunk so deeply into debauchery. Yet she had always found it odd that he'd employed such a young, pretty woman, for Miss Herrington could be no more than five-and-twenty and she had held the position for at least three years. Given his exalted position, he certainly had the wherewithal to hire an older governess with decades of experience to ensure that his sister had proper guidance.

Another damning fact occurred to Abby. A little while ago, the duke had come riding from the same direction as Miss Herrington, where the lane branched off toward a densely wooded area of the estate. Might he have settled her in a love nest—perhaps a secluded cottage? Was *she* the reason he'd returned to Rothwell Court after so many years—so that he might conduct an illicit affair with her?

The possibility was too monstrous to contemplate. Surely if that were the case, he would have spirited Miss Herrington away to a distant and discreet locale. Unless, of course, the upcoming prizefight had influenced him to keep his latest dalliance close at hand. He wouldn't wish for his sister to learn of his nefarious seduction of her governess, so it would make sense for him to arrange a trysting place away from the house.

Come to think of it, Miss Herrington was fair-haired and petite just like Lady Desmond. Dainty blondes must be the sort of female that appealed to his decadent tastes. In fact, the scoundrel likely kept a string of mistresses scattered hither and yon across England so that he would never be inconvenienced in his wicked pursuits.

Abby gripped her fingers tightly in her lap. Out of the corner of her eye, she could see Rothwell's virile form astride Brimstone. Her quickened heartbeat had to be caused by the twist of wrath that bedeviled her insides. He was no longer the tender young man she had known and loved. How arrogant he had become! How coldhearted to take advantage of the very woman who had been his sister's teacher and companion!

As the carriage arrived at the circular drive in front of Rothwell Court, the wind flung a flurry of fat raindrops that wrested squeals from the girls. Valerie grabbed the basket as she and Lady Gwendolyn hastened up the steps and into the house. Abby knew she ought to go after them, to ensure they took proper care of the kittens. Instead, she waited under the shelter of the portico as the duke dismounted and tossed the reins to a groom.

Frowning slightly, he was looking down at his hands as he stripped off his riding gloves. He appeared lost in thought and barely conscious of Abby's presence. So she stepped into his path and forced him to a halt.

"Rothwell, I must have a word with you."

Chapter 10

Those keen gray eyes sharpened on her. His mouth tightened slightly and his manner exuded imperiousness. He slapped his gloves against his palm. "Tomorrow perhaps. I'm late for drinks with my guests."

When he started to walk past her, she stopped him again, this time blocking the doorway. "I'm sorry, but I really must speak to you immediately. In private."

If she delayed, Abby feared she might lose her nerve. She disliked conflict, not because she lacked strong opinions, but because it was in her nature to create peace and harmony. Her role in the family had always been as the one who'd calmed the troubled waters of discord. Yet now she felt plunged into a sea of turmoil, her mind a tangle of anger and antipathy.

What did it matter what she said to him, anyway, when he had already given her notice? She would not be staying here as governess beyond the end of the week. In the meanwhile, she must do whatever was necessary to protect his sister.

He frowned at her for another moment before giving a curt nod. "My study, then. Come."

As he proceeded through the entrance hall, Abby scurried to keep up with his long strides. The fact that he expected her to trot behind him only fed her ill humor. Who was he to treat her like a dog brought to heel? A mere accident of birth had set his rank above hers. He had no respectable accomplishments in his thirty-one years, only a rotten reputation and a past cluttered with discarded mistresses.

She fumbled with the ribbons tied at her throat and yanked off her bonnet, automatically reaching up to smooth her hair. The long corridor echoed with the sound of their footsteps, his heavy and decisive, hers light and quick. What she needed to say to him would require firm resolve and a determination not to be browbeaten. For Lady Gwendolyn's sake, he must be forced to see the folly of his ways.

As they reached a doorway at the end of the passage, a man strolled around the corner. Lord Ambrose Hood looked like a male fashion plate in a dark rifle-green coat and nankeen trousers, his sandy curls brushing his high shirt collar. In his hand he carried a battledore racket.

"Rothwell! Just the fellow I was hoping to find. We've had to bring our game indoors and we need you to referee—"

"Not now," the duke said, rather curtly. "I need a word with Miss Linton. I'll join you later."

With that, he ushered her into a room rendered dim by the unnatural darkness of the late afternoon sky. Abby had only a glimpse of Lord Ambrose's interested expression before Rothwell promptly shut the door on his friend.

In the short time that it had taken to navigate the passageway, the storm had struck with vicious power. Rain lashed the tall windows and coursed in rivulets down the panes. Trees swayed under the whipping of the wind.

Lightning zigzagged across the dark clouds, chased by rumbles of thunder.

Through the gloom, she could see a spacious, well-appointed study with a mahogany desk as its centerpiece. An account book lay open, and beside it, an assortment of quill pens and a silver ink pot. The wall behind the desk held shelves that displayed leather-bound books interspersed with classical busts.

Rothwell made no move to light a lamp. He merely tossed his gloves onto a wing chair by the fireplace. "It appears we were fortunate to have reached shelter in time."

"I hope Miss Herrington was as lucky to reach wherever she was going."

"Ah. So that's what this is all about." The duke settled himself onto the edge of the desk, folding his arms and fixing Abby with his unnerving gaze. "You're peeved that I wouldn't go gallivanting after a woman in a gig."

She nearly quailed under his scrutiny. But his mocking tone set her teeth on edge and reminded her of her purpose. Gripping the strings of her bonnet, she stated, "Not just any woman. She was Miss Herrington, and well you know it."

"Oh? I barely caught a glimpse of her. And it's rather absurd of you to have expected me to recognize her bonnet. I've met the woman only briefly on holidays when my sister came to visit me."

"Then kindly explain why you didn't appear in the least bit surprised to learn that I'd seen her driving along the lane. In fact, you looked rather secretive. I strongly suspect you already knew she was in the area—and that you wished to hide that fact." Throwing caution to the wind, Abby added, "Because you have recruited her to be one of your—your paramours!"

He stared for a moment while the rain drummed its

staccato beat. Then he threw back his head and laughed. "I see. And how, may I ask, did you arrive at this brilliant conclusion?"

She paced back and forth in front of him, ticking off the reasons on her fingers. "You tried to dissuade me from asking questions about her. You had just ridden from the same direction as she had come, so you must have been visiting her. Yesterday, you nearly skewered me for mentioning a rumor that she'd run off with her lover. Of course, at the time I never dreamed he might be you, Rothwell. And besides which, she is exactly your style!"

"My style."

"Yes, young, beautiful, and fair-haired—just like Lady Desmond. I wonder if *she* knows that you've set up another *chère amie* as her rival. Or is that your typical conduct these days? To flit from one mistress to another as the mood may strike?"

During her tirade, his countenance darkened, and tension crackled in the room like the lightning outside the windows. His lips were thinned, his gaze narrowed, his eyebrows clashing in a frown. "That's quite a burden of sins you've ascribed to me."

"If they are yours, you must own them. I need the truth from you, Rothwell. And for a very good reason!"

"Do tell."

"It is necessary because of my duty to your sister, of course! I must know if I need to be careful that Lady Gwendolyn never encounters Miss Herrington while riding on the estate, for I will not have her exposed to your sordid peccadilloes. And we both know that you can be careless in such matters—only recall your behavior in the library with Lady Desmond."

Abruptly, he straightened up from the desk and advanced on Abby. Her heart thumped wildly within the confines of her corset. For one frightful instant, she feared she had gone too far and that he meant to clamp his hands around her throat and throttle her.

But he merely stalked to a table set against the wall behind her. There, he uncorked a decanter and poured a splash into two crystal glasses. He returned to thrust one of the goblets into her hand.

"Drink this," he ordered.

Abby eyed the dark liquid suspiciously. "What is it?"

"Brandy. You'll need it to recover from the shock."

"Shock?"

"Yes. Given the extent of your delusions, what I have to say will undoubtedly rattle you to the core. I also require your promise that my confession, such as it is, won't go beyond these four walls."

"Only an unscrupulous rogue would demand such a vow when you haven't even told me what it is I'm to conceal! Why should I agree to your terms at all?"

"Because if you don't, then my lips are sealed. And you will forever wonder what secrets I harbor concerning Miss Herrington."

Abby took a swallow from her glass, the liquor burning down her throat. She was conscious of Rothwell watching her. He probably expected her to cough and choke, but she often had sipped brandy with her father in the evenings when Mama had retired early. The two of them could sit for hours discussing some obscure aspect of his historical research about England. If only she could calm her flustered nerves and know such peace again . . .

She scrubbed an untimely nostalgia and focused on her resolve to protect Lady Gwendolyn. "As you insist, then, Your Grace. I promise not to tell anyone—unless of course you've committed an actual crime."

"By gad, you've a low opinion of me," Rothwell growled

before tossing back his drink in one smooth motion. He set the glass down on the desk and gave her an aggrieved stare before adding tersely, "You're right on only one count. I did indeed know the woman in the gig was Miss Herrington."

"So, you were lying to me. I knew it!" Abby stabbed her finger at him, but it somehow got tangled in her bonnet strings, quite ruining the triumphant gesture.

"Don't celebrate too soon. The rest of your assumptions are completely, utterly wrong. So wrong, in fact, that when you leave my employ, you ought to consider making a career of writing Cheltenham tragedies."

She wanted to dash the remainder of her brandy in his too handsome face. Instead, she carefully set the glass down on the desk along with her bonnet, for it wouldn't do to give free rein to the wild emotions only he could stir in her. "Wrong, my lord duke? How so?"

"First of all, Miss Herrington is not and has never been my *chère amie,* as you so indelicately put it. Nor have I ever even considered such an improper arrangement with her. Believe of me what you will, but I won't allow you to besmirch her reputation with your baseless innuendos."

"Then kindly explain why a man of your rank would hire an attractive young lady scarcely out of the schoolroom herself, rather than choosing an older, more qualified governess with impeccable credentials."

Rothwell paced to the rainswept window and combed his fingers through his hair. He stared out at the wild tempest a moment before turning back on his heel to face Abby. "If you must know, I did it as a favor to an old school friend. When William Herrington was killed at Waterloo, his younger sister was left penniless and alone. By chance, Gwen's former governess had decided to retire from service, so I offered the position to Miss Herrington. She was gently bred and I believed she would make an excellent companion for Gwen. There was nothing in the least bit nefarious about it."

In spite of everything, the story touched Abby's heart and left her flummoxed. It was the last thing she'd expected from Rothwell. But could she trust him to tell the unvarnished truth? She tried to picture him in the role of benefactor. Though she could readily believe it of the boy she had once loved and admired, he had broken his vow to her when he'd gone away and never replied to her letters. In the intervening years, he had become an unprincipled rake, the tales of his many exploits having been brought back from London by family members and neighbors.

"Are you saying, then, that Miss Herrington had no relatives whatsoever who might have taken her in?" Abby asked.

"A few distant cousins in Gloucestershire, that is all."

"Then why did you claim that she'd had to leave due to a family crisis? You lied about that, too, for clearly, Gloucestershire is not where she went!"

A flash across the sky cast an eerie light over Rothwell. It made the angles of his face appear hard and sinister and not at all hospitable. "She needed a story to explain her disappearance, that's why. The fact of the matter is that she and her betrothed left to be married in Avon a few weeks ago and returned only yesterday from their honeymoon."

"Married! To whom?"

"A local landowner by the name of Babcock. His parents forbade the match, as Miss Herrington is quite without fortune. When they threatened to disrupt the nuptials, she and her fiancé decided to marry elsewhere. They did not wish to endure the shame of a Gretna Green wedding either, so she applied to me in London for help, and I was able to procure a special license."

Rothwell went to pour himself another drink, then continued, "I might add that I advised the happy couple not to elope, but to stand firm. However, Miss Herrington was adamant, so plans were made to depart in secret and then present the marriage as a fait accompli. Babcock told his parents he was going away to inspect a prize bull to purchase and off he went, with Miss Herrington joining him along the way. Upon their return yesterday, Miss Herrington—or rather, Mrs. Babcock—prevailed upon me to allow them to stay temporarily in an empty cottage in the woods, where I called on them today. Mr. Babcock had already gone alone to break the news to his parents. The new Mrs. Babcock was worried at how long it was taking for him to return, and I can only surmise that's why you saw her driving the gig in the direction of their property."

During this long speech, Abby stood dumbstruck. Now, she flattened the palm of one hand on the smooth surface of the desk in order to hold her wobbly legs upright. "Mr. Babcock . . . and Miss Herrington."

"Yes, I presume you know him?" When she didn't reply, Rothwell strode closer to grasp her shoulders and peer down into her face. "You're pale. Who was he to you?"

"No one! It's just that . . . I never guessed . . ."

She stared mutely over his broad shoulder at the rain weeping down the windows. This past spring, Mr. Babcock had proposed marriage to her, but she had turned him down. He had sworn to ask her again as soon as her year of mourning was completed. Just this morning, while sitting in the portrait gallery, she had decided to accept him. She'd reconciled herself to a future where she would become his wife, bear his children, and hope that in time she might learn to love him.

Instead, he had married Miss Herrington. When had *that* romance blossomed?

Now that Abby thought about it, she'd noticed the couple talking a few times after church, in particular, when the governess had worn that new green bonnet with the cherries. How long had they been meeting in secret? Were they truly so madly in love that they'd felt the urgency to elope? The act seemed contrary to the dull, proper man Abby knew whose conversational ability had been limited to sheep and hops.

She expected a rush of wretched sorrow to immerse her heart. But the truth was, she merely felt deflated and a trifle disappointed. It was dispiriting to contemplate leaving here once Rothwell and his friends departed for London again. Unless she could form another plan for her future, she would have to return to Linton House and settle back into the role of maiden aunt, tending to everyone else's needs and having no husband or children or home to call her own.

"Ah," Rothwell said. "I see that this news has shaken you excessively. Did you perhaps believe Babcock to be *your* beau, hmm?"

Feeling the heaviness of his hands on her shoulders, she jerked up her chin to meet his shadowed gaze. He appeared rather amused, and his ironic tone sparked the white-hot flash of anger she had failed to feel at Mr. Babcock's abandonment.

She stepped back out of his reach. "Never mind him. Rather, I would like to know why you didn't tell me all of this earlier, when I first saw Miss—Mrs. Babcock in the gig."

"It isn't my prerogative to proclaim their news to one and all. Nor is it yours, so I trust you'll honor your promise to keep your lips buttoned until the official announcement is made."

"Of course," she said stiffly. "Though I do think it

would be wise to tell Lady Hester. She is the one who noticed that Miss Herrington was behaving like a woman in love."

"Or in lust, as you would have it."

Abby twined her fingers together and hoped the gloom hid her blush. It was mortifying to face just how far off the mark she'd been. A deep-rooted sense of fairness nudged her to say, "Pray forgive me, Rothwell. I leaped to the wrong conclusion, and I should not have made such a dreadful assumption. It is just that . . ."

"That you are determined to think the worst of me?" He put his fingers under her chin to tilt it up so that she could not look away. "Abby. I wish I knew what it was that turned you so much against me."

The sound of her name on his lips gave her an unwanted thrill, especially when spoken in that low, gravelly tone. She despised the breathlessness he stirred in her, and the host of turbulent feelings that ought to have stayed long buried. "Your libertine ways, of course. I daresay I never really knew you."

He uttered a low chuckle. "Surely you can't still be raking me over the coals for enticing you into a minor indiscretion in the woods all those years ago. Not when I apologized so abjectly in the letters I sent you."

"Letters?" she scoffed. "What letters? You never wrote to me—or answered any of *my* missives, for that matter."

His gaze sharpened. "The devil you say! I watched my father's secretary frank the *billets-doux* that I sent to you— all five of them. I received no replies, no correspondence at all in return. I took it to mean you'd washed your hands of me."

Abby felt a quake inside her. His assertion was too incredible to be believed. Was it true? How could it be possible that neither of them had received the other's notes?

Letters certainly went astray from time to time—but not *all* of them.

Yet why would Rothwell lie to her about the matter? It made no sense. Unless he regretted his sworn vow to marry her once he reached his majority. He surely didn't think she might still try to hold him to it—did he?

"There's no need for you to dissemble," she said stiffly. "I won't appeal to your honor and demand an offer from you. I would never hold you to a promise made when we were practically children."

"Is that what you think this is about? Me, trying to weasel out of that pledge?" He shook his head. "Rather, you negated it when you tossed me over—perhaps for your Mr. Babcock. A pity he never came up to scratch."

Had Abby been one of her little nieces, she'd have stamped her foot. "Don't be absurd. He has nothing whatsoever to do with this. When I wouldn't succumb to your seduction, you headed off to greener pastures. 'I'll seek my comfort elsewhere,' you said. And you very likely pitched my letters into the nearest dustbin."

"Believe what you will, but if *my* letters vanished, it must have been your parents absconding with them. Perhaps they thought you were too young to have a serious beau."

"No one could have done so at Linton House," she asserted. "I checked the mail delivery faithfully, meeting the postman at the door for months on end, to no avail. I finally forgot about you when I became busy caring for Mama after her riding accident."

He frowned rather skeptically. "How did you even manage to write to me, anyway? At the time, I never even considered it, but now I can't imagine your father allowing his adolescent daughter to correspond with an unmarried young man—not even one of high rank."

"I smuggled the letters to Rosalind, who posted them on my behalf. When you didn't respond, I presumed I'd been no more than a summer fancy, easy to forget once you'd sampled the superior amusements of London." Abby paused, then added firmly, "I was disappointed, of course, but it all happened a very long time ago. It isn't important anymore."

Rothwell made no reply, his gaze narrowed on her while the rain continued to fall with no sign of abating. Hail pinged against the windowpanes, but she took little notice. She was too caught up in remembering the excitement of her first romance and then the crushing disillusionment of facing the fact that Max had never meant to return when he came of age, that his vow of eternal love must have been just a trick to convince her to grant him liberties that no decent young lady should allow.

But now it seemed possible that that wasn't entirely true, and they'd been kept apart by forces unknown. If indeed he had written to her, what could have happened to his letters—and hers? She hardly knew what to think.

It was all so very perplexing.

Abby had a hard time thinking, anyway, when he stood so close. It was highly improper for them to be alone together. Especially after she had seen him stripped to the waist in the boxing ring and discovered that she was as weak as any woman when it came to the infamous Duke of Rothwell. It was a galling realization to know that she ached to touch him, to explore the differences between the boy she had known and the man he had become.

She pressed her fingertips into her palms. That would be the height of madness. Not only was he her employer, he was renowned for his expertise in seducing women.

As if he'd read her mind, one corner of his mouth curled into a dangerously attractive half-smile. "So," he mused, "all this time I thought you'd taken a disgust of me for enticing you into misbehaving. But that wasn't the case at all, was it?"

"It can't possibly matter now. The incident is best forgotten. If you'll excuse me, Your Grace, I must return to my duties."

Abby turned away, but Rothwell caught hold of her wrist. "One moment," he commanded. "We aren't done here."

She could scarcely breathe for the swift beating of her heart. It took a concentrated effort to say calmly, "I beg to differ. Neither of us seems to know what happened to those letters. Nor does it appear likely at this late date that we shall ever find out. So, there is nothing more to be said."

"Quite the contrary. I just now confessed that I'd penned a number of groveling apologies to you. But you haven't yet told me what you wrote in *your* letters."

He held on to her, his thumb stroking idly over the inside of her wrist, sending disturbing tingles up her arm. "I'm sure it was just girlish nonsense," she said. "For pity's sake, you can't expect me to recall something I wrote half a lifetime ago. Now do release me, Rothwell."

He continued to lightly caress her tender skin so that she felt flushed and skittish. "I wonder if you made reference to what we enjoyed together. Do you remember, Abby? I certainly do, for you were the first girl I'd ever kissed. We were lying entwined in the grass, and I delved beneath your skirts, ran my hand up your legs, and stroked your—"

"Stop! Only a cad would mention that folly!"

She pulled free and took several steps back, putting her hands to her hot cheeks. How vividly she recalled the intoxicating heat of his kisses, the pressure of his body on

hers, and a touch so shockingly forbidden that it had frightened her into pushing him away.

He settled back onto the edge of the desk, his hands
braced on either side of him. "I suppose you were right to
be angry with me," he admitted rather ruefully. "I was a
randy teenaged boy who didn't know how to control myself. After our quarrel, I went away believing I'd earned
your scorn. So, it really came as no surprise when you
never answered my letters."

His admission of guilt caused a breach in Abby's de-
fenses. Was it possible that he too had suffered pain at their
separation?

Feeling the need to assuage the hurts of the past, she
took a step closer. "Oh, Max, I never hated you. That's
what I wrote to tell you, that I ought to have been more
understanding. You were distraught and in need of comfort. It was the day of your mother's funeral, after all. And
you'd just told me that your father was taking you and your
infant sister to London for good."

He glanced away, his expression turning dark and
brooding. It was as if he were peering into the past. She
did too, remembering how upon hearing the awful news
of his mother's death from childbed fever, she had waited
for Max at the edge of the woods. But he hadn't appeared
for two long days, not until after the private burial when
he'd half dragged Abby through the forest to their secret
glade, where he'd pressed her down onto the grass and proceeded to kiss her with heart-wrenching desperation.

"I also wrote to offer my sympathy and . . . and friendship," she added, leaving out the word *love*. "Our quarrel
wasn't really about seduction, anyway. It was because
you'd shut me out of your private thoughts. I knew you
must be grieving terribly, and I thought if you could just
talk about it to me—"

The sudden grip of his hands around her waist startled
Abby. Without arising from the edge of the desk, he pulled
her forward in one smooth move, placing her in between
his open legs. His eyes glittered silver in a flash of lightning, and she trembled to realize that the brief truce
between them somehow had been shattered.

"Still trying to mend other people's lives, are you,
Abby? Well, some things can never be fixed. It's best to
just lose yourself in pleasure."

His mouth swooped down to capture hers in a stunning,
wholly unexpected kiss. Her lips had been parted to speak,
and his tongue slipped inside to trace her soft inner flesh
with shiver-inducing expertise. The instinct to stop him
brought her hands up between them. Yet even as her fingers spread over the solid wall of his chest, reason and
logic vanished under a torrent of temptation. Desire swept
over her skin, tingling in her bosom and penetrating to the
innermost depths of her body.

The delicious taste of him carried her back in time. It
was as if all those years vanished and they were back in
their secret glade again, clasped to each other in reckless
abandon. She had forgotten the thrill of being held by a
man, of savoring his hard form pressed to her softness, of
inhaling his masculine scent. She had buried those memories because it was too painful to reflect upon what she
could never have with him again.

Yet now he was back and his embrace filled her with
light and color. One of his arms was looped around her
waist, while his other hand cradled the back of her head
as if to keep her firmly locked in his grasp. If only he knew,
she had neither the desire nor the strength to escape, not
when the racing of her heart made her giddy and her legs
felt treacherously unsteady.

Max. He had been the reckless, all-consuming love of

her girlish heart. Yet he was no longer the fumbling boy whose lack of finesse had lent a certain awkwardness to their embrace. Those faded snippets of memory did not do justice to the powerful man he had become. A master of seduction, he kissed her now with an expertise that stirred tremors throughout her body.

The pads of his fingers traced the swells of her breasts through the muslin of her gown. Sweet heaven, when had he shifted his hand to her bosom? She clung to his broad shoulders as he lightly rubbed his thumb over one tip, sparking delightful shock waves that vibrated inside her. *"Max."*

"Shh," he murmured against her lips. "You've a mouth made for kissing."

He demonstrated that statement with enticing sensuality. His teeth gently nipped at her lips, his tongue soothing her sensitive flesh. In his hands, she felt like softened butter, ready to be molded to his will. Nothing in her limited experience had prepared her for this fevered pulse of need. She had only ever known the untutored groping of a boy.

Not the skillful caresses of an inveterate rake.

The thought pierced the haze of her passion. It jarred her back to an awareness of exactly who it was that held her in his arms.

He was not her Max. He was the Duke of Rothwell, a silver-tongued rogue famous for his carnal exploits. He used women for pleasure and then cast them aside. He harbored no love in his heart for any of his conquests.

Least of all her.

Chapter 11

Max was enjoying the kiss far more than he could have imagined. It had started out as a means of distracting Abby from a line of conversation he preferred not to pursue, and then had swiftly intensified into a uniquely gratifying episode. Curious that, for she had not been flirtatious in the least, and he could have sworn she despised him.

Yet any resistance in her had evaporated within moments, and she was kissing him back with willing—if naïve—fervor. Just as startling was his own hot rush of desire for her. He usually avoided virgins like the plague, for their innocence made them either dead bores or giggly flirts. They also angled for a marriage proposal, which he had no intention of ever offering.

But Abby broke all the rules. She not only held his attention, she intrigued and charmed him. It was a delight to discover she was no dried-up spinster. Nor was she the green girl who had once spurned his inexpert caresses. She was a mature woman with unfulfilled needs, and it was a bloody damned shame he couldn't take her straight to his bed—

He felt a hard shove at his chest.

Jolted, he released Abby, and she stepped back out of his reach. Those gorgeous blue eyes glared at him.

"That's quite enough, my lord duke. Kindly recollect that I'm your sister's governess."

Her sudden missishness irked Max as much as having his pleasure so abruptly interrupted. He was accustomed to being the one to decide whether or not to end an erotic encounter. Then again, he should have expected such a quaint reaction since she'd lived all her life in the country, no doubt being courted by dull dogs like Babcock.

Curling his mouth into a smirk, he did a slow survey of her reddened lips, her mussed hair and flushed cheeks. "Come, Abby, don't play the prude. You enjoyed that kiss as much as I did. Your heaving bosom proves it."

"Well, of course I enjoyed it," she candidly admitted. "You're very accomplished at seducing women. It is what you do best."

His grin vanished. He frowned at the sway of her hips as she marched out of the study. She didn't bother to close the door, and the tapping of her footsteps faded into the drumming of the rain.

Acknowledging that he'd been masterfully insulted, Max straightened up from the desk. She had left her bonnet lying there and he grabbed it without thinking. Instantly, he flung it back down again. Fool! He wouldn't go running after her like a lackey.

Instead, he stalked to the window to gaze out into the storm. A steady shower fell from the leaden sky, though the lightning and wind had subsided somewhat. He ought to go and seek out his friends, for he had left them to their own devices for most of the afternoon. But he needed a moment to cool his blood and collect his wits.

You're very accomplished at seducing women. It is what you do best.

From any London lady that would have been a compliment. But not from Abby. She'd implied he'd done nothing of worth in his life, that he was a useless rake. That other people did productive, meaningful things while he was merely concerned with satisfying his own selfish pleasures.

Blast her, he wouldn't be goaded into shame. He had been blessed by birth with a position of power and wealth, and it was his prerogative to decide how he conducted himself. What the devil did she know of his life, anyway? Yes, he'd enjoyed all the leisurely pursuits of a gentleman, including a long string of high-flying mistresses. But he also had hundreds of employees and tenants on his four estates to oversee, a prizefighter to manage, investments to evaluate, a seat in Parliament to fill, and—

Max caught himself. No, he need not justify his existence merely because a governess had dared to rebuke him.

To be fair, though, Abby was not just any governess. She had been his first love—and his last, for she was the girl who had opened his eyes to the idiocy of surrendering one's heart to someone who would poke and pry into his private thoughts. How much better it was to have his choice of women, to relish the white-hot heat of a lusty affair and then have the freedom to move on when boredom set in, as it inevitably did. He could think of nothing more tedious than to spend the rest of his days in the company of one woman.

But would his life have been different had he known back then that Abby had written to him, after all?

He had felt utterly alone in the weeks and months following his mother's death, when his father had fallen into deep despair and had subjected his only son to drunken lectures on the hazards of love matches. Max had desperately craved a reply from Abby in the hopes of finding

sanctuary in her warm and caring nature. But there had
been only silence.

What the devil could have happened to his letters—and
hers? He had a vague suspicion, though it would be impossible to pursue the matter until he returned to London.
Perhaps the situation did warrant further investigation . . .

No. It was all pointless. He liked his life exactly as it
was, dammit. Let the past remain buried. Nothing could
be more abhorrent than the notion of rekindling an ancient
romance with a prickly spinster.

"I wonder what is keeping Rothwell." Elise, Lady Desmond, stood at a gold-draped window in the Turkish
Saloon, peering out at the downpour. "He went for a ride,
if that dreadful butler is to be believed. I do hope he wasn't
caught somewhere in this rain."

"Didn't I tell you? Saw him half an hour ago—whoops!"

Lord Ambrose Hood made a quick lunge to hit the shuttlecock with his battledore, sending the feathered missile
arcing back across the vast room to Pettibone, who dove
over a gilt chair to return fire.

"Huzzah!" Lounging on a chaise, Mrs. Sally Chalmers
let out a cheer. "Good one, Petti!"

Both men were in shirtsleeves, having brought their
lawn game indoors at the first crack of lightning. Like a
pair of rowdy schoolboys, they were now playing amid the
brocaded chairs and baroque furnishings.

Elise should have been amused by their exploits. But
she had felt cross all afternoon, due to being denied the
chance to further her enticement of Rothwell. "Where did
you see him?" she prodded.

Ambrose pinged the shuttlecock back and narrowly
missed toppling a tall vase on a pedestal. "Going into his
study with Miss Linton."

Elise stiffened. She exchanged a telling glance with Sally, who shrugged while idly shuffling a deck of cards. What could Rothwell want with that rustic little baggage? It had better be something proper like a report on his sister's progress in her studies.

"Did he say when he would join us?" Elise inquired.

"Soon."

On that vague reply, Ambrose executed a neat jump shot that sent the shuttlecock sailing toward a gloomy corner. Pettibone lunged and came up short, his paddle striking a figurine on a side table and knocking it onto the fine Turkish carpet.

"Blister it!" the earl cursed. "I concede the round, old boy."

"Not just the round," Ambrose said. "The entire match."

"Ah, well. I'll ring for champagne, then!"

As Pettibone went to tug on the bell rope, Elise minced forward to scoop up the china dog and examine it for chips before replacing it on the table. "You two and your childish games," she scolded. "It's a wonder you didn't shatter half the contents of the room!"

Ambrose grinned slyly at her. "Counting your possessions already, eh? Pray pardon my candor, but I must warn you that Rothwell isn't likely to offer you more than carte blanche."

Elise sent him a cool stare. "Nor is he likely to grant you his sister's hand in marriage. Yet I daresay you still cherish the hope."

"Mea culpa," he said, languidly fanning himself with his paddle. Exertion had mussed his fair hair, making him look as if he'd just risen from bed. "I cannot deny the need to marry an heiress. Of course, that would require sufficient time to romance the girl, when I've yet even to set eyes on her."

"I myself prefer a more mature woman." Pettibone sank down beside Sally and squeezed her knee through her saffron muslin gown. "And our present company happens to be quite delectable."

"Wicked man," Sally said fondly, abandoning the deck of cards in order to control his wandering hands. "Well, I for one must support Ambrose in his quest to marry well. I always say, there's no game worth playing if the stakes aren't high."

"Only look at how you enticed your nabob to the altar," Ambrose said. "Chalmers was as rich as Croesus, as old as Methuselah, and as indulgent as merry King Wenceslaus. Not to mention, he had the good sense to cock up his toes and leave you in sole possession of a mountain of gold."

"Oh, la!" she said with a flutter of her fingers. "I gave Horace a happy few years—and a delightful alternative to his dull account books!"

"Leaving you free now to delight another man, hmm?" Pettibone said, sliding his arm around her waist as he nuzzled her neck.

Elise regarded the lovebirds with a jaded eye. She wanted Rothwell here, making up to her for all the hours of neglect. Instead, he was closeted with that countrified governess. What could he have to say to Miss Linton that would take more than half an hour?

Perhaps the chit meant to entice him. The very notion made Elise fume. When they'd met this morning in the portrait gallery, Miss Linton certainly had displayed airs above her station. She had conversed more like an equal than a servant.

Sally riffled the cards. "What say you to a game of piquet? We shall have a tournament, one couple competing against the other."

Ambrose drew over a small table. "Ten-guinea stakes? I should be happy to relieve you of a portion of that Chalmers gold."

"Sorry, I'm not in a humor to sit," Elise said. "Lord Ambrose, do come and take a turn around the room with me."

Ambrose cast a longing look at the cards, but he offered her his arm and they began to stroll the length of the large chamber. He possessed a handsome physique and a debonair manner, and she might have taken an interest in him, Elise thought, if not for the lamentable fact that he was a mere second son and too often low in the pockets.

"You seem afflicted by a fit of the blue devils today," he observed.

"It is the rain, perhaps. I daresay that bout of measles among Pettibone's staff has dealt us all a raw hand. Had we not been forced to come here, Rothwell would be with us, rather than being drawn hither and yon with estate matters."

Ambrose cast her a cunning look. "Or being closeted in his study with the governess."

"Miss Linton? Bah, she's too long in the tooth to tempt him. She dresses like a servant, her hair is an unseemly red, and her face is far too common."

"Simplicity suits Miss Linton, her hair is a delightful shade of cinnamon brown, and those large sapphire eyes lend a luminous glow to her features." He paused, a little smirk on his lips. "Perhaps the glow comes from living a wholesome life. Alas, neither of us could ever hope to duplicate it."

Elise refused to react to his mischievous jest with anything more than a sniff. It wouldn't do to quarrel with Ambrose when she needed him on her side. She smiled coquettishly at him, saying, "I gather that she and His

Grace are old acquaintances. You knew him at school. Did he ever speak of her when you were young?"

"Rothwell has never been one to kiss and tell. I should warn you, he greatly dislikes anyone prying into his private affairs."

"That is hardly an answer."

He patted her hand. "I'm afraid I must disappoint you then, dear lady, for it is the only one I am able to give."

Men, she thought disparagingly. In certain matters, they would not betray the bonds of comradeship. "I have been pondering, Lord Ambrose, and I believe you and I can assist one another. May I suggest that we form an alliance?"

"How so?"

She stopped by a window at the opposite end of the saloon from where Sally and Pettibone sat playing cards, their raucous laughter and the noise of the rain ensuring that she and Ambrose wouldn't be overheard. "You will help me win Rothwell, and in turn, I shall arrange for you to steal some time with Lady Gwendolyn."

He stared skeptically at her, then laughed. "And just how do you propose to manage that?"

"As a lady, I can seek out her company far easier than you can. I shall go upstairs to visit her in her apartments, drop a good word in her ears, and finagle a way for the two of you to meet."

"And what would I do for you in return?"

"Why, you must charm Miss Linton, of course, so that she dreams of you and not Rothwell."

"Ah, but you forget that it's the young heiress I wish to charm."

"Wherever Miss Linton is, the duke's sister will also be nearby. If you can win the trust of the governess, she will be lulled into believing Lady Gwendolyn is safe with you. I will provide the circumstances, and the rest is up to you."

At that moment, Finchley shuffled into the saloon. The old butler turned a jaundiced gaze on the card players. "Someone rang?"

"Bring us a quantity of your best brandy," Pettibone called over his shoulder. "And champagne for the ladies."

"I fancy a dish of strawberries as well," Sally Chalmers added.

"No strawberries," Finchley said almost gloatingly. "Perhaps Mrs. Beech might've procured some from the greengrocer had we been warned in advance of your arrival. Can't expect her to perform miracles."

While the butler was offering his unsolicited opinions, Elise leaned closer to Ambrose to murmur, "Have we an agreement, then?"

His blue eyes gleamed. "I've always liked playing the long shot. We haven't more than a few days, though."

"Then don your coat, for the game is about to begin."

With that, Elise hastened to catch the butler on his way out the door.

After leaving the duke's study, Abby decided to make a detour to the conservatory rather than head directly upstairs to join Valerie and Lady Gwendolyn. She was too restless to face her duties just yet. The rainstorm would have driven Lady Hester indoors this afternoon, and Abby had a few questions to ask of Max's aunt.

Rothwell's aunt, she corrected herself. She rejected any semblance of friendship with him even though her thoughts were still in a tangle from that kiss. It had been wild and wonderful . . . and deeply disturbing. For many years she had repressed her memories of him, keeping busy fulfilling the needs of her family. But now his embrace had caused an undeniable awakening within her. It had stirred sensations and longings that were best left buried.

Yet she wasn't so naïve as to imagine that Rothwell had any true interest in her. No. The man was a rogue extraordinaire who used his considerable charm and sensual talents to secure whatever he wanted from women.

And what he'd wanted from her was silence.

It had taken only a few moments after leaving his study for that realization to strike Abby. The timing of his kiss could not have been more telling. She had been in the midst of relating the contents of her missing letters to him, how she ought not have quarreled with him because he had been grieving for his mother.

He had chosen that moment to kiss Abby.

Fifteen years ago, he had done the same thing.

Back then, on the day of his mother's funeral, Abby had encouraged him to share his sorrow with her. But he hadn't wanted to talk at all. Instead, he'd drawn her down onto the grass and into his fervent embrace.

He had never liked to discuss his family. Not even when she herself had shared many a tale about her brothers and sisters, her parents, her nieces and nephews. She had told him everything, both good and bad, humorous and painful. In turn, he had spoken only of the servants at Rothwell Court. His reticence about his private life had frustrated her. Now she burned to find out the source of it, once and for all.

Entering the humid warmth of the conservatory, Abby suffered a moment's misgiving. She was now the governess and he was the duke. She ought not to be probing into matters above her station.

But her curiosity proved too strong to resist.

The splatter of the rain on the glass roof masked the sound of her footsteps. An occasional flash of lightning lit the dark clouds. Heading along a path marked by slate tiles, she peered through the dense green foliage. The tall palms and exotic flowers created the illusion of being lost in a jungle.

She reached the area where Lady Hester often worked, but the woman wasn't there. A rough table held a stack of clay pots, a pair of soiled gardening gloves, and an abandoned trowel. Nearby stood a wheelbarrow containing a mound of black loam.

Venturing onward, she passed a large leafy bush and found Rothwell's aunt seated on a wooden bench in front of the glass wall, sipping from a mug and contentedly watching the rain. Upon seeing Abby, her pudgy face brightened with a smile. She patted the place beside her. "Ah, Miss Linton, what a pleasant surprise! Do come and join me."

Abby sketched a curtsy, then sat down on the bench. "I hope I'm not disturbing you, my lady."

"Oh, not at all! Might I offer you a cup of tea? I've brewed a pot on my spirit lamp." Lady Hester sprang up to fetch a mug from a table half hidden behind a rhododendron bush. "Sugar? I fear I've no cream."

"Just a little crumble, thank you."

Swathed in a leaf-green gown that bore smudges of dirt on the skirt, Lady Hester bustled back and handed over the warm mug. She also brought a square tin, placing it in between them on the bench. "I've raspberry biscuits, too. Cook is kind enough to send me a batch every morning." She cheerfully patted her stout middle. "Though I fear I partake of a few too many."

"I'm glad to see you smiling despite the storm keeping you indoors."

"Oh, I don't mind rain a bit! I was just thinking about how happy the trees and plants must be to have a nice, long drink."

They exchanged pleasantries, then Abby said, "I wanted

to speak to you about Miss Herrington, since you mentioned her yesterday."

"How strange that you should bring up her name! You see, I went for a walk this morning, searching for wild thyme. The pink flowers smell especially marvelous early in the day, and I was hoping to uproot a few clumps and grow them in the greenhouse—"

"Er—how does this concern Miss Herrington?"

Lady Hester laughed. "I was just about to tell you that I spied her in the woods on the east end of the estate, though I don't believe she saw me. She was in the company of a local man, a Mr. Babcock. I do hope he isn't leading her astray, for he has been most kind in the past, allowing me to hunt for marsh orchids along the riverbank on his property. There is a rare variety that I'm hoping to find, you see."

Before Lady Hester could veer off on another tangent, Abby said quickly, "You'll be pleased to know that Miss Herrington is now Mrs. Babcock. I have it from Rothwell that they married in secret and have just returned from their honeymoon. They are to make an announcement soon, but until then, we are obliged to keep mum."

"My gracious! I *knew* I recognized the look of a woman in love." She peered owlishly at Abby as if searching for some sign in her face, too.

Discomfited, Abby shifted her gaze outside to the drenched landscape while she sipped her tea. She hoped to goodness that her appearance betrayed nothing of the passionate kiss that she and Rothwell had shared. She was certainly *not* in love. Far from it!

She quickly changed the topic. "I imagine you've wandered every square inch of this estate. You've lived your entire life here, have you not?"

"Indeed! Ah, the grasslands and the water meadows and

the forests, all with their many delights of flora and fauna. I especially enjoy the changing of the seasons, watching tiny plants grow and mature." She reached over to pat Abby's arm. "But why am I telling you this? You grew up nearby, too, so you know how beautiful it is."

"Yes, I loved to roam the woods on my family's property. May I make a confession? When I was a girl, and the old duke and duchess were in residence, I would sometimes sneak onto Rothwell land whenever there were balls just so that I could hear the lovely music."

A misty melancholy touched Lady Hester's face as she glanced out at the rain. "Cordelia did enjoy entertaining large parties, often with fifty guests or more. The rooms were full of laughter and conviviality . . . at least for a time."

"I never had the honor of meeting the duchess," Abby said. "Though once when I was a child I saw her clad in an elegant sky-blue gown, riding through the village on a white horse. With her blond hair and delicate form, I fancied her to be a fairy princess."

"As did Bertrand when first they met, only look how mistaken he was. Such a tragedy! I did try to warn him . . ." Lady Hester blinked, glancing over at Abby as if just recalling her presence. "Oh, fiddle, here I am blathering about the past when I ought to be fertilizing my moth orchids. It is necessary once a week to keep them in bloom, and I'm already a day overdue. You will excuse me, won't you?"

She hopped up from the bench, and Abby had no choice but to set down her mug and take her leave. It was clear that Lady Hester would offer no more insights. Strange that, for she had seemed in a reminiscing mood.

As did Bertrand when first they met, only look how mistaken he was. Such a tragedy! I did try to warn him . . .

Bertrand had been the name of Max's father, Abby recalled. Why had Lady Hester said he had been mistaken about the duchess? Was the tragedy her untimely death? And about what had Lady Hester tried to warn him?

Heading upstairs, Abby felt as if she'd been given a tantalizing glimpse into the past, only to have the curtains closed in her face. More than ever, she had the distinct impression that all had not been well within the walls of this grand house. There must have been some sort of strife between the old duke and duchess. If only Max would have confided in her!

Ah well, it was time for her to don the mantle of governess again. She had abandoned her duties for more than an hour already. Heaven only knew into what sort of mischief Valerie might have lured Lady Gwendolyn. And the kittens! Abby had forgotten all about them. She could only hope they had not climbed the draperies or shredded the silk coverlet on the bed.

But when she opened the door and stepped through the antechamber into the large white-and-gold bedchamber, it was to discover the rooms were uninhabited. Their shawls and bonnets were strewn on the bed, but both girls—and the kittens—had vanished.

Chapter 12

Abby made a quick search of the nearby bedchambers. The floor was deserted, for Rothwell's guests were housed in the west wing. Hastening back downstairs, she tried to think of where the girls might have gone. Had they taken the kittens to the stable in accordance with the duke's command?

Surely not in the midst of a downpour.

She pursed her lips. What if they'd encountered Rothwell's dissolute friends? He had expressly ordered Abby to keep his sister sequestered in this area of the house. Although Lady Gwendolyn was too well mannered to disobey, Valerie was another story. Abby's niece had always been a lively sort, prone to seeking out adventure, especially when she had a younger accomplice who looked to her for guidance.

This was all Abby's fault. She ought not to have made a detour to the conservatory and pried into private matters that were none of her concern.

Reaching the bottom of the marble steps, she hurried past the newel post and spied reinforcements halfway down the long corridor. Mrs. Jeffries and Finchley stood with their gray heads together in whispered conversation. Neither appeared to be happy; the housekeeper had a sour expression on her bony features and the butler's grizzled brows clashed in a frown.

Mrs. Jeffries turned, the ring of keys jangling at her waist. "Miss Abby, thank goodness you're here. There is a terrible situation! Finchley and I are at our wit's end."

"It could've been avoided," Finchley groused, "if I'd had the sense to lead that Jezebel up to the garret and lock her in. Thought of it too late, more's the pity."

Abby didn't even have to ask to whom he referred. "Why would you take Lady Desmond to the attic?"

"She bade me show her to Lady Gwen's rooms, that's why. I refused, but the bit o' muslin claimed to have an urgent message from the master meant for his sister's ears alone. Then, when I led her upstairs, she pushed right past me and slammed the door in my face. Nearly snapped off my nose!" He rubbed the sharp beak as if to make certain it was still there.

"But I was just upstairs and Lady Gwendolyn wasn't anywhere to be found—nor was Miss Perkins."

"'Tis what I was about to tell you," the butler went on. "I skulked in the passage, and not five minutes later, Lady Trollop came prancing out with both young misses following like ducklings, one of 'em toting a basket."

"The kittens," Abby said. "They're from Mr. Beech's farm."

"Eh? Well, I followed the lot of 'em downstairs and they went into the Turkish Saloon where there's all manner of card playing and gambling in progress. I would've stood guard by the door, but they ordered me out." He shook a knobby finger. "That lot has an orgy planned, you mark my words!"

"Where is His Grace? Surely he can be depended upon to protect his sister from harm."

"He rang for his valet, so he must've gone upstairs to change from his riding clothes," Finchley said. "Meanwhile, only the good Lord God knows what is happening in that den of iniquity!"

"The strumpet sent me away, too, when I offered to chaperone," Mrs. Jeffries added, fairly quivering with outrage. "Oh, Miss Abby, I fear that our sweet Lady Gwen will be caught in the snares of one of those brutal ravishers!"

Abby hoped the situation was not quite *that* dire, though her insides were knotted with worry. Both girls were far too young and inexperienced to be left unguarded in the company of worldly-wise aristocrats of dubious moral character. Especially when one of them was Rothwell's current mistress.

"Pray show me there at once," she said, a militant expression on her face. "I vow, they will not dare to eject *me*."

Gripping her skirts, she followed the old butler through a maze of corridors until he delivered her to a great arched doorway. From inside came the trill of girlish merriment mingled with the unmistakable voices of Rothwell's guests, though she could not quite make out their words. She gave Finchley a reassuring nod before proceeding into the room.

Her anxious gaze swept the large chamber with its gold brocade wallpaper, the crimson Turkish rugs, and the rich gilt furnishings. Spotting the small party of people gathered near one of a pair of fireplaces, she schooled her face into an expression of cool civility and marched toward the group.

Lady Desmond was the first to see her. Clad in dainty, blossom-pink muslin, she was standing a little apart from the others as if she'd been watching the doorway. "Ah, Miss Linton. Do come and join us."

The friendly invitation made Abby instantly wary. What mischief was Rothwell's paramour up to now? On the two other occasions they'd met, yesterday in the library and this morning in the picture gallery, the woman had been nothing short of snooty.

Then Abby's attention was drawn to the scene in front of the hearth. Lady Gwendolyn and Valerie knelt on the floor, laughing at the antics of the kittens. Opposite them, Lord Ambrose crouched on one knee. He had tied a string to a feathered shuttlecock and slowly dragged it along the rug for the tiny felines to stalk. The gray ball of fluff was the first to pounce, batting at the shuttlecock while the caramel tabby attacked from the other side. The resulting battle sent the girls into gales of giggles.

"Little Graybeard wins again," Lord Pettibone crowed, as he and Mrs. Chalmers watched from a nearby chaise. "He has pluck, just as I predicted."

Valerie glanced up, her face glowing. "Look, Aunt Abby! Aren't they just the most precious little creatures? Lord Ambrose has fashioned a toy for them to play with."

"It was very clever of him," Lady Gwendolyn said. She looked especially charming today in her peach gown, with her soft chestnut curls and large, dove-gray eyes. She stole a shy glance at the handsome rake, who regarded her with entirely too much interest.

Mindful of her subordinate status, Abby curtsied to the group even though she was seething inside. A nearby table held a deck of scattered cards as if a game had been interrupted. "I'm sorry if the girls have intruded on your pastimes. They really oughtn't to have come here."

"Nonsense," Lord Pettibone drawled, holding up his quizzing glass to observe the felines playing on the rug.

"We have been very entertained by the match. I've already won eleven guineas from Mrs. Chalmers in guessing which kitten would strike first. The gray has more spirit."

"The tabby has more heart," Mrs. Chalmers said, her brown eyes sparkling with laughter. "Look at how fiercely she fights."

"There, you see, the girls aren't troubling us in the least," Lady Desmond purred. "It has been quite pleasant to have two such lovely additions to our party. That's why I invited them to join us."

The woman's brashness incensed Abby. "If I might have a word, my lady."

They stepped a short distance away while the others cheered on the kittens, and Abby said in an undertone, "You ought never to have brought them here, Lady Desmond. Surely you're aware that it's highly improper for underage girls to be present when there is gambling going on!"

"Nonsense, we're only having a bit of lighthearted fun. The strict rules of London drawing rooms needn't apply in the country, anyway."

"I must beg to differ. His Grace specifically told me to keep his sister cloistered from his guests. Had he wished for Lady Gwendolyn to meet you and the others, he would have arranged the introductions himself."

Lady Desmond arched a delicate brow, a trace of cunning on her face. "A pity you weren't around, then, to pass along his warning. If I may say, I was terribly distressed to discover that Lady Gwendolyn and your niece had been left to their own devices, without the governess anywhere to be found. Where exactly were you, Miss Linton?"

Under the scrutiny of those green-gold eyes, Abby had to fight the rise of a blush. Did Lady Desmond know about that kiss? Had she guessed?

Surely not.

It seemed likely, though, that Lord Ambrose had mentioned seeing Abby and Rothwell going into the study. If Lady Desmond was the jealous sort, perhaps she intended to make trouble for Abby by pinning the blame for this fiasco on her.

"His Grace knew my whereabouts," Abby hedged. "That is all that matters." Ignoring Lady Desmond's frown, she returned to her charges. "Young ladies, I'm afraid it's time to go. If you will gather up your kittens, please."

"Must we?" Valerie said, pouting a little. "But they're having so much fun—and so are we! Wouldn't you agree, Gwen?"

Lady Gwendolyn nodded. She looked equally downcast, though she obediently reached for the caramel tabby. It settled into her hands and immediately yawned. "Perhaps it's time for their naps. And we must fetch them a dish of cream from the kitchen."

"Oh, all right," Valerie said grudgingly, rising to her feet. "We still need to decide on names, too. Forgive me, Lord Pettibone, but I cannot really care for Graybeard. Hmm. Perhaps Cloud since we found him just before the storm. No, I'm not sure that's right, either."

She picked up the gray ball of fluff and cuddled it to her bosom. Unfortunately, the shuttlecock had become entangled in its tiny claws. The kitten mewed, trying to disengage itself from the feathers.

Lord Ambrose leaped up to assist. "Allow me, Miss Perkins. It will take just a moment . . . there, we have the little one free now."

"Thank you, sir." Valerie lowered her chin and fluttered her lashes at him. "You are so very kind."

Lord Ambrose looked rather taken by her coquettish

manner. He ran one finger over the tiny gray cat. "Scamp," he murmured. "Now that would be a fine name, I believe."

"Scamp! I do like that! It seems I am in your debt, sir."

The little exchange alarmed Abby. Valerie's behavior was much too forward for a seventeen-year-old and she was far too inexperienced to be flirting with a London rake nearly twice her age. The last thing Abby needed was for her niece to be swept up in dreams of romance. She herself knew from painful experience how quickly adolescent girls could form an intense infatuation. Lord Ambrose seemed the sort who flirted with anyone in a skirt, for he had been making eyes at Lady Gwen at first, and now at Valerie.

Beckoning, Abby turned toward the doorway. "Do come along, girls."

Before she could take more than two steps, disaster appeared in the form of Rothwell entering the saloon. Her heart jumped to her throat. It was absurd for her knees to weaken at the mere sight of him. Certainly, he looked as handsome as sin in a charcoal-gray coat and white cravat, but he was also her employer. For that reason, she must prepare herself to face his wrath.

He came to a dead halt, his gaze locking with hers. For a moment, it was as if they were the only two people in existence. The intensity of his eyes blazed into her. Assailed by a sudden shortness of breath, she felt giddy and flustered. Especially when his gaze flicked to her mouth and she knew that he too was remembering their passionate kiss.

How shocking it was to feel so starved for another taste of him. Not that it would ever happen again. No. She wouldn't permit herself to yearn for a dissolute rogue. He hadn't kissed her out of love or tenderness, anyway, but for the purpose of distracting her from probing into his private past.

Then he turned his attention to his sister. An expression of surprised displeasure came over his face. "Gwen?"

Lady Desmond glided forward to loop her arm through his. She tilted a flirtatious smile up at him. "Why, Rothwell, what a pleasure it is to see you. I trust you've completed all of your dreary business at last?"

"Yes." He kept his gaze on his sister. "Gwen, please come forward. I would like to know why you're here."

Shamefaced, Lady Gwendolyn trudged toward him, clutching the sleepy tabby to her bosom. She could barely meet his eyes. "We only wanted to show everyone our kittens. Oh, Max, pray don't be angry with me."

"I expect you to know better than to introduce yourself to any guests without my permission. However, it isn't *you* that I fault."

His gaze flashed back to Abby. Those steely eyes bored into her. This time, they were devoid of any warmth at all.

She drew a breath to speak, but what could she say? It *was* her fault. If she had gone straight back to Lady Gwendolyn's chamber, instead of stopping to question his aunt in the conservatory, none of this would have happened. She would have been present to stop Lady Desmond from luring his sister downstairs.

Yet if she voiced the truth, he might perceive it as tattling on one of his guests. "I'm sorry, Your Grace," she said. "Perhaps I was too long delayed in your study."

"Perhaps you were," he said.

The faintly caressing note to his voice again brought to mind their torrid embrace, and a thrill shimmied over her skin. He surely couldn't have been as affected as she had been. Rothwell plied his skills on women all the time. It wouldn't mean anything to him except a momentary episode of self-indulgence.

"You mustn't scold Aunt Abby, Your Grace," Valerie piped up. "It was Lady Desmond who invited us to join the party."

Rothwell turned to Lady Desmond. "Is this true?"

"I'm afraid so," she admitted, tilting her head back to regard him through the screen of her lashes. "It is I you should hold to blame, Rothwell. You see, I'd hoped to do your sister a good turn."

Abby stared in surprise. She'd fully expected the woman to deny her role, and this abrupt switch in tactics was baffling. What was she up to now?

The duke frowned at his *chère amie,* whose pretty face wore a look of contrition. "A good turn."

"Yes, you see, it struck me that Lady Gwendolyn spends all of her time here at Rothwell Court with only a governess for company. How will she ever develop the skills necessary to navigate society? Why, she'll be overwhelmed, never knowing what is suitable and what is not. How much wiser it would be for her to mingle with us, to learn how to converse with a few select members of the ton—here in the safety of your home."

Rothwell glanced at his sister. He appeared struck by the notion that he had somehow failed her. "Gwen's debut won't be for three years yet."

"It is best to begin such training early. Joining our company for a few days surely cannot harm her, especially under your watchful eye." Lady Desmond smiled engagingly at him. "Perhaps it will even induce you to spend more time with us."

Rothwell seemed taken by her persuasiveness, gazing down at her as she clung to his arm. With her fair curls and womanly curves, she was the essence of English beauty and the dream of every blue-blooded rake.

Abby unclenched her teeth to say, "I must respectfully object to this notion. Innocent girls should never be privy to improper behavior like gambling."

"Ah," Lady Desmond murmured, "but there can be nothing improper so long as you, Miss Linton, are present to chaperone the duke's sister."

Those kittenish eyes held a gleam of artfulness, Abby thought. She couldn't quite fathom why Lady Desmond would welcome the company of a sheltered fifteen-year-old, for they surely could have nothing in common. Her purpose couldn't be wicked, though, if Rothwell was present.

A possibility wormed its way into her mind. Was Lady Desmond angling for a marriage offer from him? Did she wish to ingratiate herself with the duke's sister in the hopes of winning his heart?

With considerable distaste, Abby mulled the thought. Now, that explanation made sense. The widow must be hoping to demonstrate her worthiness as the perfect wife for him.

Lord Ambrose strolled into the group. "Max, you old dog, I'll consider it an insult if you dare to suggest your sister or her lovely friend are in any danger from us. Especially as we shall be on our very best behavior."

"That isn't saying much," he remarked dryly. "Nevertheless, I'll take the matter under consideration."

"We shan't be here long, so why wait?" Lord Ambrose said. "Perhaps the young ladies would care to dine with us this evening."

"What a splendid notion," Valerie chirped, looking charming as she cuddled her kitten. Then her lips formed a little moue. "Oh! But I'm afraid Mama is expecting me to return home. Though it seems to be still pouring rain in buckets. Do you suppose the roads are safe to travel? I should not wish to be drenched or, worse, stuck in the mud somewhere."

She regarded Rothwell with innocent expectancy.

It wasn't only her niece's kitten that was a scamp, Abby thought. With those bright blue eyes, Valerie appeared utterly disarming, as if Rosalind had not coached her daughter on how to finagle an invitation to stay. But at least this had spared Abby the embarrassment of broaching the topic with Rothwell.

Lady Gwendolyn stepped closer to her brother. "Please, Max, we mustn't send Valerie out into the storm. Might she not spend the night here? I'd be happy to lend her whatever she may need."

Rothwell cocked an eyebrow. He looked lordly and forbidding, the master of the household. Then abruptly he smiled, shaking his head in good humor. "As you wish, then. I surrender. She may stay for as long as her aunt will allow."

Chapter 13

After leaving the kittens in the kitchen under the watchful eyes of a footman, the girls had a delightful time trying on gowns in Lady Gwendolyn's dressing room. The young maidservant who was assisting them seemed to be having as much fun as they were, so Abby slipped out to go to her own bedchamber directly across the corridor.

The pretty room had pale yellow walls, rosewood furnishings, and sky-blue chintz hangings on the canopy bed. With the rain clouds bringing an early twilight, a lighted candle lamp had been left on a table by a servant. Abby had been surprised at first to be assigned such grand accommodations, rather than an austere cubicle near the other servants. But this had been Miss Herrington's room. And now that she knew the former governess was the sister of one of Rothwell's old friends, it all made sense.

Abby winced at the memory of her wrongful assumption. She had thought the worst of him when the truth had been quite the opposite. The duke might be a hardened rake, but he was to be commended for his kindness in giving Miss Herrington a position after the death of her brother in battle. And for securing the special license for her elopement, too.

The fact that Miss Herrington had wed Mr. Babcock left Abby feeling out of sorts. Like Rothwell, the man had broken his promise to her. How could this have happened to her a second time? Yet when she searched herself for anguish, she found only a trifling sense of relief. In all honesty, she'd never developed a strong affection for Mr. Babcock; he had merely been a way to escape the role of the maiden aunt, dependent upon the largess of her siblings.

Pondering her future, she picked up the candle and went into the dressing room. She balked at the notion of returning to Linton House to live with Clifford and his wife, Lucille. Though she loved her family dearly, she yearned for something more. Something of her own choosing.

If only it were possible for her to stay in the role of governess to Lady Gwendolyn! But she doubted Rothwell would change his mind. Too much acrimony remained between them.

Abby opened the wardrobe to examine its modest contents. Having seldom had occasion to attend fancy events, she possessed little that was suitable for dinner at a duke's table. But there was an indigo-blue silk that she'd worn to the village Christmas ball the year before her parents had died. The gown might not be in the latest stare of fashion, but its classically simple elegance had always pleased her.

While dressing, she settled on a plan. She would accept Rosalind's request to help with the preparations for Valerie's debut. Then she would accompany them to London in the spring, so that she might finally see the city that her siblings had described in glowing detail. She would partake in the dancing and parties and sightseeing that she'd missed while caring for her infirm parents. Perhaps it wasn't too late to meet a gentleman who would court a spinster of her advanced years. Barring that, she could apply to an employment agency to seek a position as a governess or companion.

A world of possibilities lay ahead of her.

Feeling greatly cheered, she finished her toilette and then turned to and fro in front of the pier glass. She'd left off her cap and pinned up her hair in a softly becoming style. The mirror showed a tall, slender lady, bright-eyed and smiling, and still attractive enough to catch male attention.

What would Rothwell think of her transformation?

Against all good sense, the memory of his embrace washed her in warmth. Abby closed her eyes and fancied his arms around her again. She felt the pressure of his hard body, the caress of his skillful hands on her bosom. The mere act of reflection made her breath quicken and her insides burn.

How she yearned to discover the mysteries of physical love. That experience, however, would never be with the duke. He was so jaded a scoundrel that he couldn't be faithful even to his current mistress.

He had caught Abby off guard. It must never happen again.

"Ah, the Three Graces have arrived. Be still, my heart!"

As Lord Ambrose swept a deep bow, Valerie and Lady Gwendolyn giggled with delight. Abby merely smiled at his exaggerated manners, especially when he made a show of kissing their hands in turn. He had met them at the door to the drawing room just now when they had come down for dinner.

"Good evening, Lord Ambrose," she said, extracting her hand from his. "I'm sure you've had ample experience in charming ladies. Girls, let this be a lesson to beware of gentlemen who pay you compliments that are far too extravagant."

"Oh, Aunt Abby, we *know* it is just a flirtation," Valerie said, looking adorably sweet in an aqua-blue gown. "I'm sure Lord Ambrose is the perfect gentleman. Isn't that so, Gwen?"

Lady Gwendolyn merely nodded, her eyes modestly downcast, a blush tinting her cheeks. It was clear she felt a bit shy conversing with one of her brother's friends without the kittens around to serve as a distraction.

Catching him eyeing the girl's coltish form outlined in primrose sarcenet, Abby said quickly, "My niece will be launched in the spring, Lord Ambrose. Perhaps you might tell her a bit about what to expect from the London season."

He turned his gallant attention to the older of the two girls. "Endless entertainments, of course. During the day, you'll have your fill of shopping and visiting all the attractions, and at night there's the theater, the opera, concerts, and more balls and rout parties than any girl could ever imagine. If truth be told, Miss Perkins, you will scarcely find time to catch your breath."

"Oh, it all sounds perfectly wonderful. I can scarcely wait." Valerie batted her lashes at him. "Dare I hope to look forward to encountering *you* in town, sir?"

"Valerie!" Abby chided in an undertone. "That is entirely too forward. He will think you a gazetted flirt before you've even made your bows."

"Nonsense," he said, an attractive half-smile on his lips. "I find your niece to be quite refreshing. Though I daresay I won't be able to squeeze through the crush of suitors who will undoubtedly surround her."

Valerie chirped a reply, but Abby didn't quite hear it.

Rothwell had appeared at her side. The air took on a sudden sparkle as every particle of her awareness sprang to attention. A whiff of his spicy masculine scent sent a flurry of warmth throughout her body. In his fine evening clothes, he looked every inch the master of the house.

He must have come from somewhere behind her. Lord Ambrose had met them at the door, so she had not walked all the way into the drawing room.

"Good evening, ladies," he said, giving them a nod.

His gaze lingered on Abby, roaming over the slim-fitting blue gown and the softened style of her hair. She found herself hoping that the slight upturn at one corner of his mouth indicated appreciation. Surely it could not be wrong to desire his admiration. Any woman would feel flattered to have earned a second glance from a handsome duke.

Even one who was notorious for his many conquests.

Abby glanced over at the girls, pretending an interest in their curtsies, when in reality, she strove to calm the wild fluttering of her heart. She was no longer a green girl, she reminded herself. Though it was natural to be attracted to him, she must retain a firm hold on good sense.

Lady Desmond strolled into view, a vision in amber crepe with a demitrain that Abby privately thought too fancy for a country dinner. Diamonds glinted at her throat and ears, including a dainty feathered aigrette tucked into her blond curls. She slipped her hand into the crook of Rothwell's arm, and he acknowledged her presence with a cool smile.

"Perhaps Lady Gwendolyn and Miss Perkins would join us for a drink," she said to him. "A glass of ratafia for the young ladies would not be amiss."

Rothwell turned his attention to Abby. "What is your verdict, Miss Linton? Will the governess permit her niece and my sister to drink spirits?"

The glint in those gray eyes caused a treacherous heat in her. She realized two things in quick succession. First, that his manner held a hint of playfulness. Second, that it was far easier to resist his allure when he was harsh and aloof. "I believe a small glass would be perfectly proper."

"Excellent. I shall see to the pouring at once."

As he strolled away, Abby drew a deep breath in an effort to collect her scattered senses. That one moment of being the subject of his warm attention had had a ruinous effect on her equilibrium. His initial coldness toward her seemed to have been mitigated by the discovery that neither of them had received each other's letters.

"Do come along, girls," Lady Desmond said. "We shall enjoy a nice chat before dinner."

She looped her arms through Lady Gwen's and Valerie's, but before they walked off, she aimed a keen look at Lord Ambrose. Abby wondered at its purpose. Were those two conspiring in some manner?

Whatever it was, she doubted it could be respectable.

Lord Ambrose swept his hand toward a pair of chairs apart from the rest of the party. "Miss Linton, will you do me the honor of sitting with me? I find large groups to be intrusive when one is in the company of a lovely lady."

"More flattery, sir? You seem adept at honeyed words."

As they seated themselves, he gave her an amused frown. "If we were in a London drawing room, I would presume that you were being coy. But you truly don't seem to be aware of your own beauty."

"I am far too advanced in years to expect such praise— or to believe it."

"Advanced in years, bah! Max is one-and-thirty, and I know you to be younger than him."

Was he guessing, or had Rothwell been discussing her with his friends?

She glanced across the room to see the duke handing out wineglasses to Valerie and Gwen, who were perched side by side on a chaise. Abby was pleased to see that Lady Hester had joined them tonight, and was talking amiably with the girls, along with Mrs. Chalmers and Lord Pettibone. Rothwell took a seat close to Lady Desmond and smiled at something she said to him.

Abby aimed her own smile at Lord Ambrose. "*Am* I younger than the duke? A lady never reveals her age."

"Ah, so you're mysterious as well as beautiful. I know so little about you, only that you grew up on the neighboring estate. I believe you said your brother resides at Linton House?"

"Yes, Clifford and my sister-in-law, Lucille, are alone now that their four children have married. I lived with them until recently."

His keen gaze flitted to the others. "How does the lovely Miss Perkins fit into the family?"

"She's the daughter of my middle sister, Rosalind, who lives in Kent. They came for an extended visit when my brother James's youngest was christened a fortnight ago. James is our local vicar."

"A genteel family, to be sure, yet you've sought employment as a governess. Dare I be indiscreet and inquire as to why you're obliged to earn your bread?"

"Not obliged, sir. Rather, it is by choice." Abby decided it wouldn't hurt to reveal a bit of her circumstances, since he looked rather startled by her admission. "You see, I felt the need for a change after nursing my parents for many years and playing maiden aunt to all the children of my brothers and sisters. My family objected, of course, but they've come to accept my decision."

Lord Ambrose raised an eyebrow. "I've never known a lady who would *choose* to labor for a living."

"I like to keep busy. And teaching one sweet, well-behaved young lady is hardly work. Rather, it's a joy."

"Why not marry instead? In London, you'd have your pick of gentlemen." He winked at her. "Even at your advanced age."

"Perhaps," she hedged, unwilling to reveal her hope to accompany her sister and niece for the coming season. "But enough about me. If I were to go to London, what would people tell me about *you*?"

"That I'm a lovable rogue with a deft hand at cards, and I'm a dyed-in-the-wool member of Rothwell's raffish set." He leaned closer, taking her hand and raising it to his lips. "But perhaps I'm of an age to reform my wicked ways should I meet that one perfect woman . . . a dazzling nonpareil like you, Miss Linton."

Lord Ambrose must be very popular with the ladies, Abby thought in wry amusement. With his sandy hair and blue eyes, he exuded an air of boyish charm. She extracted her hand from his. "What fustian. Forgive me, sir, but that is pure humbug."

"You wound me, dear lady. Or perhaps that is the sharp pierce of Cupid's arrow that I suffer."

Abby laughed. She couldn't help herself. "Enough of your romantic nonsense. You must promise me that you won't use such flattery on Lady Gwendolyn or my niece. They are far too young to see through a man of your vast experience."

"Then I shall flirt only with you, Miss Linton."

"You're incorrigible. I do wish you would be serious for once."

He placed his hand over his heart. "I can be as solemn as a judge."

"Then pray try to see my point. It is my duty to protect Lady Gwendolyn from harm. I only wish . . ."

She glanced over at the party to see Lady Desmond lean close to whisper something in Rothwell's ear. All of a sudden, the duke looked straight at Abby and fixed her with a cool stare. The brief teasing warmth he'd exhibited toward her earlier seemed to have vanished. Did he dislike seeing her in conversation with one of his friends? Had Lady Desmond remarked upon it to him?

"Wish?" Lord Ambrose prompted.

Abby decided to be frank. "I only wish the duke had not brought his paramour to this house. He should have known better than to risk a situation where his innocent sister would meet such an unsuitable female."

"Don't blame him, blame the spots."

"Spots?"

"Our original plan was to stay at Pettibone's estate in Surrey, but when we arrived, it was to find that his entire staff had come down with the measles. Imagine that! With the prizefight looming, Rothwell couldn't chance Goliath falling ill, so we decided to come here instead. It was all very spur-of-the-moment, I assure you."

"I see." That did explain quite a lot, yet Abby still felt uneasy with the circumstances. "Nevertheless, I cannot approve of him permitting his sister to associate with his mistress—even if it is far from the London gossips."

"Perhaps I should let you in on a little secret, then."

"Secret?"

"I wouldn't be so certain that Lady Desmond *is* Rothwell's mistress."

"But I—" Abby stopped herself in time to keep from admitting that she'd caught the two of them *in flagrante delicto* in the library. The mere memory of that scene filled her with heated indignation. "I assumed it must be true. They do seem very partial to one another."

"Partiality can also mean courtship. As I am certainly

partial to you, Miss Linton." He caught her hand and kissed it, then let her go. "Ah, there's that batty old butler now, come to summon us to the table. And just in time, before you should wrest an offer from this hardened bachelor!"

Chapter 14

The next morning, Valerie and Lady Gwendolyn walked arm in arm toward the stables. Listening to their chatter, Abby smiled, for one would never guess they'd met for the first time less than a day ago. Valerie was every bit as horse mad as Lady Gwen and once they'd decided on an early-morning ride, it had been impossible to dissuade them. The paths might be damp, the puddles many, but the girls were keen for a canter nonetheless.

Valerie glanced over her shoulder while continuing down the path. "Are you *quite* sure we can't attend the prizefight, Aunt Abby?"

That topic, regrettably, had come up at dinner. Abby would rather they'd never learned of it, for her niece was too often drawn to the forbidden. "No, you most certainly may not. It isn't a proper place for ladies."

"But Lady Desmond and Mrs. Chalmers are going."

"*Young* ladies, then. And pray do not badger me, for His Grace has said *no* most emphatically, and I concur with his decision."

"We do have the picnic tomorrow to look forward to," Lady Gwendolyn pointed out.

"Yes, indeed!" Valerie's face brightened. "I'm so happy Lord Ambrose suggested it. It shall be so much fun. On our ride, we must keep a watch to find the perfect spot."

Holding the heavy skirts of their riding habits, they skipped ahead while Abby followed at a more sedate pace. It was a joy to see them so exuberant. Especially Lady Gwendolyn, who had blossomed simply by having a friend close to herself in age.

Even so, she was the quieter half of the pair. At dinner the previous evening, she had been demure and well behaved, listening wide-eyed to the swirl of conversation and speaking only when someone directed a comment or question at her. Valerie, on the other hand, had chattered vivaciously with everyone, in particular Lord Ambrose, who had been seated beside her. At bedtime, Abby had been obliged to have a talk with her niece about the importance of allowing other people to get a word in edgewise.

She'd also taken care to warn them both again that Lord Ambrose was an outrageous flirt and they mustn't take his compliments too seriously. Abby herself had been the recipient of several teasing smiles and winks from him during dinner. She would never admit it to the girls, but of all Rothwell's friends, Lord Ambrose was the one she liked the best. He was a charming man with a ready wit and an engaging smile. Like the duke, he'd no doubt left a trail of broken hearts over the years.

At the moment, though, she needn't worry about him beguiling her two adolescent charges. It was not quite nine and too early for any of the London party to be awake.

Except . . .

Her steps faltered as she spied Rothwell riding in the paddock.

As irksome as a bad rash, he sat astride Brimstone, putting the massive black stallion through his paces. They were a sight to behold. Broad-shouldered and fit, the duke appeared to be at one with the horse as they soared over rails set as obstacles at regular intervals.

As Valerie and Lady Gwen drew near, he reined in his mount alongside the white fence. They chatted for a moment; then the girls disappeared into the stable. Abby was relieved that her niece seemed more interested in the ride than in flirting with him, despite Rosalind's scheme to acquire a duke as a son-in-law. He was much too seasoned a rogue for a mere schoolgirl. How embarrassing it would be if her niece made a cake of herself over him.

It was awkward enough to face him after the scorching kiss they'd shared the previous afternoon. They'd been surrounded by people at dinner. He'd sat at the head of the table, too distant for private conversation, though several times she'd caught him looking intently at her, his expression inscrutable.

Now, Abby was tempted to beat a swift retreat. But she forced herself to continue walking toward the stables. It was her duty to see the girls safely off, and she would not give him any cause to chastise her.

Besides, she'd had enough with being lily-livered. She hadn't stood up to her family and left home only to turn coward now.

As she approached, Rothwell waited for her by the fence. Meltingly attractive in a blue coat, buckskins, and gleaming black boots, he sat straight in the saddle, the morning sun gilding his coffee-brown hair. The horse tossed its mane and snorted, but he controlled the beast with effortless ease.

Was it true, as Lord Ambrose had suggested, that Lady Desmond was not the duke's paramour?

At dinner, Rothwell certainly had been attentive to the delicate blond beauty. He had seated her in the honored spot to his right. His manner had been well bred and sociable as he'd chatted with her and his other friends. Abby had caught only snippets of their conversation, which had centered around people and events in London, subjects as far out of the realm of her experience as the moon. It remained a mystery as to whether he was courting Lady Desmond for the purpose of marriage or a sordid liaison.

Abby paused to sketch a curtsy. "Good morning, Your Grace."

When he inclined his head in a nod, she continued walking along the path toward the open doors of the stable. She hadn't taken more than three steps when his commanding voice halted her.

"Running off so quickly, Miss Linton?"

Her fingers twined in the lavender muslin of her skirt, Abby spun toward him. The sun was bright in her eyes, the golden rays limning his masculine form. "Pardon me, but I really must go and check on the girls."

"The groom is there to help them mount. I doubt you would be of much assistance."

"It is my duty, nonetheless."

"Then I absolve you of it. Come closer now."

She took several steps and stopped again, her cautious gaze flicking to Brimstone. Clearly displeased to be kept on a firm rein, the horse bucked its head against the bit. "Was there something you wished to discuss, Your Grace?"

"Yes. Pray walk over here to the fence."

"Why? I can hear you perfectly well."

"Come," he ordered, though not without a hint of amused exasperation. "Surely you will not allow an irrational fear to control you."

How dare he taunt her. Yet he was right. And hadn't she just been lauding her own bravery, anyway?

Teeth clenched, she forced herself to pace forward,

keeping a close watch on the colossal horse. Befitting his
name, Brimstone appeared to have sprung from the fiery
depths of Hades. His dark eyes were wild, his manner restive, a front hoof pawing the dirt.

The strong odor of the horse pervaded the air. Her
breathing came in shallow spurts and her palms felt
clammy. It was all she could do to stand her ground.
"There, Rothwell . . . you have had your way. Now . . . say
what you will and be done with it."

As she glanced up at him, he didn't look annoyed in the
least by her impertinence. Not that she would have cared,
anyway. She was too busy wrestling against the urge to
flee. All that stopped her was the determination not to disgrace herself by acting like a ninny.

Just as he parted his lips to answer, however, the clop-
ping of hooves came from the direction of the stable. She
jerked her head around to observe the approach of Lady
Gwendolyn mounted on Pixie, her gray mare, and Valerie
on a chestnut. The middle-aged groom named Dawkins
rode behind them on a large bay.

Abby stood very still, her feet rooted to the ground. She
felt trapped in the midst of too much horseflesh with nowhere to run. There was no need to worry, she assured herself. Only a simpleton would feel such trepidation over so
commonplace a sight as people on horseback. Yet her
mouth felt as dry as dust, and a light-headed sensation
made her teeter on the verge of a swoon.

"We plan to ride all the way around the lake," Lady
Gwendolyn called out. "Are you certain you won't go with
us, Max?"

"We would greatly welcome your company," Valerie
added with a flirtatious fluttering of her lashes. "On such
a fine horse, Your Grace, you must be quite the brilliant
rider."

"Perhaps another time," he said, tempering his refusal with a smile.

The girls appeared too excited by their impending ride to be disappointed by his rejection. The party set out along the dirt path with Lady Gwendolyn in the lead.

As they rode past, Abby pressed her palm to her bosom. Her heart thumped so hard that it seemed necessary to trap it inside her rib cage. She took several quick breaths before glancing up to see Rothwell watching not them, but her. His look was intent yet unfathomable, and she couldn't help feeling defensive under his scrutiny.

Striving for coolness, Abby gathered her shattered nerves. "You really ought to go with them. Your sister sees so little of you."

"I have other plans for the morning."

"Ah, yes, your prizefighter, Goliath. Well. Don't let me keep you."

She started to sidle away when he said, "I haven't dismissed you. Come back here at once."

"Why?"

"Because it is my wish. Please."

Abby disliked that he had authority over her. Yet when he spoke in that silky, confident tone, she felt compelled to obey even though disquiet gnawed at her insides. Keeping a wary eye on Brimstone, she edged closer to the fence.

Rothwell leaned down slightly, the saddle creaking. "Look at me, Abby."

He spoke her name like a caress, lending an intimacy to his words. With great reluctance, she tore her gaze away from the great black beast. Their eyes met, and his were deep and steady, radiating warmth.

"I am in complete control of Brimstone," he said. "It is impossible for him to hurt you in any way. You are perfectly safe with me. Do you understand that?"

The certainty in his manner seemed to shrink the dread inside her. It was as if he'd thrown her a lifeline that channeled support and strength into her. She could feel the flow of that reassurance into every pore of her body, wrapping her in comfort and protection. When he regarded her with such conviction, she felt an irresistible desire to believe whatever he said.

Ever so slowly, she nodded.

"I want you to step up onto the fence now," he said.

The knot of her fear expanded again. "No!"

"I'd like for you to stroke his mane, that's all. You need to do this, Abby. For your own peace of mind."

"That isn't necessary!"

"Yes it is. There'll be a fence in between you and Brimstone at all times. Remember, I shan't allow him to hurt you. Now, put your foot on the bottom rung of the fence. There's a good girl. Look at me, not at him. You can trust me, Abby."

She gazed up into his warm gray eyes and glimpsed the boy she'd once loved. Max. Heaven help her, he was handsome with that lock of dark hair fallen onto his brow and the charming curve to his lips. He had grown into a fine-looking man, so much so that she felt a different sort of agitation assail her insides.

Under the influence of his encouraging voice, her anxiety ebbed and somehow, without conscious thought, she found her fingers grasping the top of the fence while the toes of her shoes sought the bottommost slat. She drew herself up and clung there, her pulse hammering at the nearness of the horse. To distract herself, she concentrated on Rothwell's leg, the buckskin breeches molded to his powerful thigh, the glossy black boot with its pair of tassels. He could control his mount with his knees, she reminded herself, and he surely had a secure hold on the reins . . .

"Give me your hand," he urged softly.

She had a clawed grip on the fence. Though a splinter had poked into her forefinger, she scarcely noticed the prick. He kept talking to her in that soothing tone until she uncurled her fingers so that he could grasp her wrist.

Warm and large, his hand swallowed hers, leading it inexorably upward until her bare palm settled over the long strands of the mane. Brimstone shied slightly and she sucked in her breath with a shudder.

"Easy now," Rothwell said, though whether to the horse or to her, Abby didn't know. Nor did she care.

She was too focused on the warmth of the animal's neck against her skin, the rough silk of its mane. Childhood memories pushed into her mind to ease the stranglehold of her dread. She had ridden often before her mother's terrible tumble all those years ago. She remembered loving the freedom of cantering through the meadow, the sun on her face and the wind in her hair . . .

"Climb a bit higher so you may reach him more easily," he murmured.

Abby hesitated, then inched up another rung. She could not deny that his presence lent her confidence. It was impossible to imagine doing this all by herself. Emboldened, she leaned farther over the fence, the better to stroke that glossy mane.

"There, you see," he said, "it isn't so very difficult to overcome one's fears. You always loved riding. We'll soon have you on horseback again."

Her startled gaze flashed to his. "No! Absolutely not! Don't even think to talk me into that. It will never happen!"

His brow furrowed slightly, and she had the shameful

sense of having spoken like a coward. Uncomfortable beneath his penetrating eyes, she looked down at her hand,
still resting on Brimstone's neck. There was no need to feel
embarrassed. Surely she had accomplished enough already
just by summoning the nerve to *touch* a horse . . .

It was then that it happened.

In a blur of motion, Rothwell bent down and locked his
arm around her waist, scooping her up in front of him on
the horse. She landed sideways against his chest, the hard
leather of the saddle pressing into her bottom. But that minor discomfort vanished beneath a rush of terror.

Brimstone reared. The world tilted dizzyingly. Into her
mind flashed the image of her mother being thrown in the
air, then landing with a hard thud on the ground. Crying
out, Abby grabbed hold of Rothwell and clung for dear life.

Lady Desmond stood at the window in her dressing
chamber. Her fingers clutched the ivory brocade drapery
as she stared out at the distant scene near the stables. Having excellent eyesight, she could discern the duke's fine
figure astride his black horse inside a paddock. He was
leaning down and talking to Miss Linton, who came to the
white fence and then climbed up onto it. He seemed to be
coaxing her, for he took hold of her hand and encouraged
her to stroke the horse's mane.

Elise compressed her lips. What was that rustic saying
to him, to hold his attention like that? It had been difficult
to find out much about their past, but she was certain those
two did share a history. Max had been exceedingly close-
mouthed about the matter, despite her subtle inquiries. But
she could see the truth in the way his eyes tracked Abigail
Linton whenever he thought no one was looking.

He was entirely too interested in the drab governess.

Then Elise's gaze widened in astonishment to see Max

pull the woman up into the saddle with him. Sitting sideways, she flung her arms around his neck in a brazen embrace. Why, that little minx—!

The crash of splintering glass rent the air. Elise spun
around to see her maid staring in horror at a shattered fla-
con lying on the marble top of the dressing table. Liquid
dripped onto the carpet, and the overpowering odor of
roses filled the room.

Elise surged forward to cuff Monique's ear. "Clumsy
oaf! That was my favorite perfume!"

"I—I'm so very sorry, milady." In her rattled state,
Monique had forgotten her self-styled French accent. "It
slipped out of me hand."

"It was the only bottle I brought with me. So tell me
now, what am I to wear for the remainder of this trip?"

"With your ladyship's permission, I might run down to
the village shop—"

"You would have me stink of an inferior scent? Oh,
never mind. Just clean up this mess at once before I choke
on the smell."

Elise hastened back to the window and opened the casement, gulping in fresh air. To add icing to her irritation,
the duke and the governess had vanished from sight. She
scanned the surrounding woods, but saw no sign of them.
Had Max put Miss Linton down? Or had he ridden away
with her? Did he intend to engage in a tryst—while he
neglected Elise?

Fuming, she considered the situation. She was still in
her dressing gown, so she could hardly rush out to find
them. It wouldn't do, anyway, to act in anger. Men didn't
care for nagging, sharp-tongued females.

One thing was certain. She would not allow herself to
be usurped by a rustic who was thirty if she was a day. Not
when Elise had schemed for months to catch Rothwell's

eye. Not when she needed his considerable wealth to pay off her mounting debts. Old Desmond had left her nearly penniless when he'd keeled over on their honeymoon. The bulk of his estate had gone to his snooty son who'd wanted nothing to do with his father's second wife.

Especially one who had been plucked from the stage at a Covent Garden theater.

Conscious of her inferior antecedents, Elise craved respectability as much as she did affluence. It had not been enough to marry a mere baronet. Many of the upper crust still regarded her with nose-in-the-air disdain.

She knew, however, that Max would not be as easy to maneuver into marriage as Desmond had been. The duke had made it clear he desired her only as his mistress. And now it seemed there was an old flame to distract his attention even from that.

But Elise had faced worse odds. Henceforth, she would not let Max out of her sight. She must prod Lord Ambrose into keeping his side of their bargain by distracting the governess.

Nothing and no one must prevent the former Elise Gumbleton from becoming the Duchess of Rothwell.

Chapter 15

Max concentrated on controlling Brimstone, using the reins and his knees and a sharp word of reprimand. The stallion quickly settled, though still tossing his head and snorting his angry displeasure.

It wasn't nearly as easy to calm an armful of frightened female.

Abby was jammed against him, her hands clamped around his neck in a death grip. Except for the softness of her bosom against his chest, her body felt rigid and stiff. She buried her face in his cravat, her breath coming in short gasps.

Blast it, he had only made matters worse. He had not intended to grab her like that. But her declaration about never riding again had troubled him greatly, as had seeing her shrink from something she'd once enjoyed. An intense desire to help her had spurred him to act.

He'd surprised even himself. Despite his bad reputation, he was usually a man who thought things through and weighed the consequences. That was why he'd never gambled away his fortune like so many others in his circle.

Yet somehow Abby had breached his natural caution.

She had always had that effect on him. A case in point was their kiss the previous day, when he hadn't harbored any designs on her, yet he had ended up with his lips on hers and his hands roaming all over her luscious body.

Keeping one arm securely locked around her waist, he urged Brimstone toward the open gate of the paddock. He needed to make haste before Abby yelped again and brought one of the stable lads running. The last thing he wanted was for someone to see the master abducting the governess, especially with her skirts flung up to her knees to reveal a pair of very shapely, stocking-clad calves.

Luckily, most of the grooms had found one excuse or another to linger at the rear of the stable complex so they could watch Goliath engage in a sparring session with his trainer, Crabtree. That was where Max had intended to spend his morning—if only he hadn't acted so impulsively.

He set Brimstone on a path heading deep into the woods, away from the lake. Now that he was committed to this course of action, he was damn well going to see it through. It was the only way to persuade Abby to conquer her illogical fear. Exactly why that mattered so much to him was something he didn't care to examine—

Her fist lashed out to strike his chest. "Put me down, Rothwell! This instant!"

Brimstone broke stride and danced to the side of the path. Max set the horse right with a flick of the reins while concentrating on the spirited woman in his arms. "Hush. Don't fight me. You're perfectly safe."

"No, I'm not. I want to be standing on the ground." Her voice rose. "Let me go! I mean it!"

She squirmed against his hold, which only spurred Brimstone into a more restive and agitated state. Max knew he had to stop her struggling before the stallion took a mind to rear again and landed them both flat in the dirt.

"If you don't wish to be tossed," he said firmly, "you'll stop wriggling and keep still. Brimstone feels your fear. Horses can sense emotions. You know that. If you calm down, then so will he."

The fight went out of Abby, though her slim body still felt taut and resistant. She took several shuddery breaths and he knew his message had reached her. Ever so slowly, she eased her head into the crook of his neck, so that her lace cap brushed against his jaw. The fingers of one hand clutched the lapel of his coat in a white-knuckled grip.

He was far too keenly aware of her feminine curves. One of her hips was pressed against his groin and he fought the rise of heat. God help him if she noticed the hardness there. It was not a reaction that a countrified spinster ought to inspire in him. He preferred his women to be lush and eager and skilled in the art of lovemaking.

Nevertheless, he acknowledged an undeniable tug of attraction to Abby. He enjoyed sparring with her, making her blush. There was a comfortable sense of familiarity in her presence, too, a vitality that he'd experienced with no other woman. The faint lilac scent of her skin invoked powerful memories of his youth, when they'd lain in the grass together. She had been the first girl he'd ever kissed. How soft and sweet she had been . . .

Abby hissed out air between her teeth. "There, I'm perfectly still. Now, rein in this horse and let me down."

"You're still nervous and Brimstone senses it. That's why he's being so skittish. If I try to dismount now, he might rear again." Max felt confident that he could handle the temperamental animal, but he hoped to accustom Abby to being on horseback again. If he released her too soon, all would be for naught. "You might as well relax and enjoy the ride. It's in your best interest to do so. The last thing you want is to act as prickly as a bramble."

He frowned ahead at the trail that meandered through the woods. That last phrase had emerged from the depths of the past. Maybe she wouldn't remember such a silly detail. He scarcely recalled it himself. A long time ago, he'd locked away all memories of that particular summer.

"A prickly bramble," she said, stealing a glance up at him. "That's what you used to call me whenever we disagreed."

"Did I? I suppose you're right."

"Of course I'm right. It was because of the way we met. I came to my secret glade one summer afternoon, only to find *you* there, stretched out in the grass with your nose in a book. *Gulliver's Travels,* I seem to remember."

He had been so engrossed in a description of the giants of Brobdingnag that he hadn't even heard the approach of her footsteps. "It wasn't your glade, but mine. It is located on Rothwell land, after all."

"No, it's on the edge of Linton property, and well you know it," she said rather indignantly. "I'd been going to the glade for years, ever since my brother James took me fishing there."

"You were trespassing. If you like, I can show you the survey that confirms the border of my estate. The stream marks the western boundary."

"Well! I daresay you misread those papers, for James swore it was our land. He's six years older than you *and* he's the vicar, so I should think you ought to trust his word."

Ownership of the glade had always been a favorite dispute of theirs and it still was now, much to his amusement. He was also pleased that the little exchange seemed to have distracted Abby sufficiently that she was no longer so tense. She rested against him, her face tilted up, a challenging glint in her blue eyes. If reminiscing about the past could diminish her fears, then he was more than willing to continue with the tactic.

"Never mind James," Max said. "We were speaking of brambles. You brought it all on yourself, as I recall. Instead of greeting me politely, you stomped toward me in a fit of pique without looking where you were going. It's no wonder you tripped and fell into a bramble patch."

"I beg your pardon! I did *not* trip. You leaped up suddenly and gave me a terrible fright. It was *your* fault that I stumbled."

He chuckled. "A gentleman always stands in the presence of a lady, so don't look daggers at me, Miss Bramble. And a lady should thank her rescuer—especially when he is kind enough to pluck a number of thorns out of her tender hide."

"There were only two, and they were stuck in my arm. I could have managed well enough on my own."

She unclenched her tight grip on his coat and startled him by slipping the tip of her forefinger between her lips and sucking on it. Despite his resolve to remain insensible to her charms, Max felt pierced by an arrow of heat. He couldn't take his eyes from the sight of those soft lips or turn his mind from the fantasy of feeling her hot mouth on a certain portion of his anatomy.

With any other woman he would have known her action to be intentionally arousing. But not Abby. She knew nothing of the erotic games played by the more daring ladies of the ton.

Frustrated by desire, he snapped, "Is something wrong with your finger?"

She instantly removed it, curling her fingers into her palm. "No."

"Hmm. I could always tell when you were fibbing."

"I never fibbed to you about anything!"

"Oh? What about the time when we were playing ducks and drakes, and you claimed your stone skipped seven times when it was really only six?"

Tilting back her head, she released a burble of laughter. "Fifteen years and you're still sulking because I beat you fair and square."

Max found himself smiling back, dazzled by the luster of beauty that lit up her face. "Bramble! I always loved the way your eyes sparkle when you laugh."

Her mouth softened, the luminous glow diminishing until only the merest trace remained. Yet he knew it was there, waiting to be coaxed out again by some man other than himself. That thought laid him low even though he knew they were not right for one another. Abby was made for marriage, while he had sworn to avoid the institution.

As such, he deemed it wise to put space between them. "Brace yourself," he said. "We're stopping here, and you'll finally have your chance to get down."

Here turned out to be a place familiar to both of them, Max realized with a start as he reined in Brimstone and surveyed the wooded area. He had not intentionally come to the secret glade. It must have been an unconscious inclination that had guided him.

An outcropping of rock formed a natural shelter around part of the clearing, almost like welcoming arms. A swift-flowing stream made a boundary on one side, while tall oaks spread out leafy limbs in a canopy. The previous day's torrential rain had flattened the plants, leaving the ground damp and the air cool. A brown toad on a rock warmed itself in a patch of sunlight. Nearby, a dragonfly flitted along the surface of the water.

"Down you go," Max encouraged, when Abby hesitated. Despite her earlier demands, now she seemed almost reluctant to dismount. "Be quick about it. I assure you, I have a grip on the reins."

Biting her lip, she gave a little nod. Then, with his aid, she slid out of the saddle and landed lightly on the ground. She stepped away as he swung off the horse and tied the reins to a bush. Brimstone tossed his head once, as if to establish who was in charge, then set to work trimming a patch of grass.

Abby stood watching from beside the massive trunk of an old oak. The lavender gown skimmed her slender form, and their tussle on horseback had loosened a few wavy reddish-brown strands from her lace cap. Max experienced another unwanted twist of desire. She brought to mind a nymph of the forest, ready to take flight at the first glimmer of danger.

With Brimstone safely secured, she turned to survey the area. A look of wonder widened her eyes. She stepped past a boulder and into the clearing with its lush carpet of grass. "The glade! Why, I haven't been here in years."

Nor had he, Max thought. Why had he stayed away so long? He had returned to his ducal seat only once in the past fifteen years, and that had been a brief, overnight visit a decade ago to bury his father in the family chapel where all the Dukes of Rothwell were laid to rest. It had been a private ceremony with only the old rector and the household staff in attendance, along with five-year-old Gwen and Aunt Hester. At his father's last request, none of the villagers or neighbors had been invited.

What if he had sought out Abby back then? Would he have learned about the mix-up with the letters? Would his life have turned out differently?

Max dismissed the thought. There was no point in re-hashing the past when he possessed the wealth and status that allowed him to do exactly as he pleased. He was perfectly satisfied with the state of his affairs.

He strolled to join Abby. "The place looks the same, though the bramble bush has grown. Perhaps you had better stay close to me so you don't stumble into it."

"Bah," Abby said, ignoring the arm he offered. "I'll be perfectly fine so long as you don't startle me again. You have a particular talent for doing so."

"Ah, I presume you're still irked that I took you up onto Brimstone."

She wrinkled her nose at him. "*Irked* is too mild a word for it. But I cannot say I'm sorry to visit this spot again."

With that, she walked to the edge of the brook, bending at the waist to look into the water. Max was hard-pressed not to stare at the way her gown molded to her feminine form, or to think about smoothing his hand over the curve of her derriere and then drawing her into his arms to taste her lips again. To be honest, he wanted far more than that. He wanted to lay her down in the grass and finish what they'd started all those years ago, when he had been too unskilled to know how to please a woman.

But she deserved better than an act of reckless depravity.

"I see a fish," she said, glancing over her shoulder at him, her face alight with excitement. "It's a big one, hiding over there in the reeds."

He came beside her to observe the water with its rocky bottom and melodic babbling. Spying the sleek shape gliding through the shadows, he said, "A pity we don't have a rod and reel. Between the two of us, we used to catch quite a few trout here."

An interest in the sport of angling was how he'd explained his frequent absences to his strict father. It had provided Max with an excuse to escape the oppressive atmosphere of the Court. Here, he had found peace and an unexpected friend in Abby.

Though he had noticed her in the village from time to time—especially once she'd developed a figure—he had never spoken to her. His father had been a stickler for proper behavior in the heir to the dukedom. He had insisted that Max maintain a distance from the locals as befitting his exalted rank. It wasn't an issue most of the year when he had been away at school. There, he'd had a wide circle of friendships with boys from the best families. But during the holidays, he'd been often lonely and left to his own devices.

Until he had met Abby.

She flashed a wistful half-smile at him. "It was fun, wasn't it, meeting here in secret? That was my last summer of freedom before Mama suffered her accident and needed my constant help."

She was absently rubbing her forefinger, the same one she'd suckled. He caught her hand and inspected it, seeing a reddened streak on the tip of her forefinger. "So that's what it is. You've a splinter."

"From the paddock fence. It's nothing."

She tried to tug her hand free, but he took hold of her elbow and guided her to the flattened boulder that they'd sometimes used as a table for picnics or to play a game of spillikins with sticks they'd gathered. The surface looked dry, washed clean by the hard rain.

"Have a seat," he said. "That sliver needs to come out."

She plopped down, tugging at her skirts with a flouncing shake that conveyed impatience. "You needn't fuss, Rothwell. I'll get it out myself later. I've done so a hundred times for my nieces and nephews."

"You hurt yourself on my fence," he said, examining

her finger more closely. "Surely you would not deny me the chance to make amends."

"How so? I hope you don't mean to try to squeeze it out. It'll just break into tinier pieces." Again, she tried to twist at his grip.

"Hold still, Bramble. I need to determine which direction it went in."

Looking a trifle anxious, she peered downward, too. "You see? It's gone completely under the skin. There's nothing to be done until I can fetch a needle from my sewing box."

He grinned. "Oh, ye of little faith."

One of her eyebrows hitched upward as he drew the pearl stickpin from the folds of his cravat. Placing her hand palm up on his knee, Max employed the sharp end of the stickpin to gently pierce the top layer of skin over the bit of wood. It was a slow task, and her light, elusive scent wreaked havoc with his concentration. So did the feel of her delicate hand lying so trustingly in his.

To distract himself, he said, "You did quite well on Brimstone."

"I had little choice in the matter. Had I known your intention, I'd never have come anywhere near the fence."

"Or any horse, either. At least now you're over that hurdle."

"Hmph. Being forced to ride isn't the same as choosing to do so. And I don't see what difference my private qualms are to you, anyway."

Max didn't want to get into his reason when he didn't entirely understand it himself, so he deflected. "You'd never have agreed had I asked politely. And tell the truth now, it wasn't so very frightful, was it?"

"Of course it was!" She released a breath. "At least at first, I was scared witless. But it helped when you talked to me. Then . . . well, I didn't think about it quite so much after a while."

Having exposed the little splinter, he used the utmost care to nudge it free, bit by tiny bit. "The best way to conquer fear is to face it head-on. Tell me, what made you so afraid of horses, anyway? You used to be an avid rider. The other day, you mentioned something about your mother taking a tumble."

"Her hip was badly fractured and it never healed properly. She was housebound from then on. She needed crutches—and my help—in order to hobble from room to room."

"But you weren't the one who was thrown. So why would her accident cause such terror in you?"

"I witnessed it, for one. Mama persuaded me to accompany her on a jaunt through the meadow. Although she didn't ride much anymore, she thought it might . . . cheer me." Her troubled gaze met his, then flitted away.

According to what she'd told him earlier, the accident had happened shortly after their quarrel. Did that mean Abby had been melancholy over him? Max didn't want to ask. "Tell me exactly what happened."

"We were taking a shortcut through the woods when Buttercup caught her hoof in a rabbit hole and stumbled. Mama was tossed through the air and hit the ground with a dreadful thud. She lay utterly still. For a moment, I thought . . . I thought she was dead."

The horror in her voice disturbed him, so he changed the focus. "Buttercup was the bay mare you used to ride."

"Yes, though Mama was on her that day. I don't remember why exactly." Her teeth sank into her lower lip. "But she wasn't the only one with a fracture. Buttercup's leg was broken . . . she had to be put down. Oh, Max, it was awful. I—I can't even begin to describe it."

Ah. That explained so much. He could imagine the trauma of that scene and Abby in a panic, desperate to ease her mother's pain, agonized over what to do for the injured horse, then having to leave them in order to go for help.

"I'm sorry, Abby." He wished he could think of something more eloquent to say. His friends would mock him, for he was known as a silver-tongued devil.

But Abby didn't seem to notice. "In the weeks and months afterward, Mama was nervous at the thought of me riding, so I gave it up. The very notion made me anxious, too, and I found myself avoiding horses. As the years passed, my dread became more and more ingrained." She gave him a self-deprecating smile. "So you see, Rothwell, I am officially a coward. The girl who once raced you on horseback is gone. I have lost all my pluck."

Max felt the powerful urge to take Abby in his arms, to hold her close and offer her reassurance. But that was no longer his right. They each led their own lives now. Things were exactly as they should be. So why could he not shake this sense of a bond between them?

"Nonsense," he declared. "It is simply a matter of reacquainting yourself with horses. The more you're around them, the more your fear will subside."

"Do you really think so?" she said doubtfully.

"Absolutely. In fact, I suggest you visit the stables every day. Gwen will be ecstatic at the chance to accompany you. And should you ever wish to try your hand at the saddle again, feel free to borrow one of my horses. I'll instruct my grooms to offer you any necessary assistance."

One corner of her mouth lifted in wry humor. "For what little time I have left at Rothwell Court, that is."

On that first day in the library, he'd dismissed her from his employ. Abby was to depart after the prizefight. Now Max was in the uncomfortable position of regretting his hasty decision. On the one hand, she had deceived his aunt into granting her the post without his permission; on the other, Gwen seemed to adore her new governess.

So did he. Far too much. And if he kept her on, he would be forever encountering her on holidays whenever he saw his sister. Nothing could be more dangerous than to invite such temptation into his ordered life.

He changed the subject. "Look, the splinter is finally out and with nary a whimper from you. So you cannot be so very fainthearted."

Examining her finger, she uttered a small laugh. "Oh, I never thought myself so spineless as to quail over something *that* small."

"Nevertheless," he said, replacing the pin in his cravat, "you now have the distinction of being the only woman in the world to be doctored with a pearl stickpin once owned by Queen Anne. She gave it to my great-grandfather more than a hundred years ago."

"I *am* impressed, then!"

They shared a smile. For a moment it was as if no time at all had passed, and they were still fast friends. Yet he was very aware, too, that he desired to know her in the present. To learn all of her private thoughts and opinions, to tease her into laughing, to spend time in her company for the pure enjoyment of it. But that would be madness.

Max turned his gaze downward to break the spell. He drew out his folded handkerchief and wrapped the linen around her finger. "Hold that in place until you can put a proper dressing on it."

Abby was silent a moment as she touched his monogram embroidered on a corner of the makeshift bandage, an *R* bracketed by tiny strawberry leaves. Then she aimed a guarded stare at him. "Why are you being so nice to me, Rothwell? You were cold and haughty at first."

"After we quarreled all those years ago, I believed you'd come to despise me. Naturally, I was less than pleased to see you in my house. It wasn't until yesterday, when you said you'd never received my letters, that I realized I'd drawn the wrong conclusion."

"I thought *you* despised *me*. So I suppose we're both guilty of making assumptions."

"Then we needn't behave like two combatants in a prizefight. Truce?"

He held out his hand, and after a hesitation, she placed hers in his, careful not to disturb the improvised bandage. How soft and warm she felt, how kissable her lips looked. One small tug, and she could be in his arms . . .

As if sensing the lusty direction of his thoughts, Abby extracted her hand. She drew up her legs beneath her skirt and hooked her arms around her knees. It was the way she'd often sat talking to him. "What do you suppose happened to the letters?" she asked.

He had a suspicion, but it couldn't be explored until he returned to London. "Who knows? They went astray somehow."

"All of them?" She shook her head. "No, someone must have taken them, and it certainly wasn't my parents. Mama could scarcely hobble and Papa was usually in the library, absorbed in a book. I always fetched the post for them. So it had to have been *your* father."

"Perhaps."

"You never spoke much about him. What was he like?"

Frowning, Max glanced away to watch the brown toad on the rock catch a fly with a flick of its tongue. "Proud, stately. A stickler for propriety."

"He took you and Lady Gwen away after the funeral. Why did he never bring you back here? Was he so terribly distraught over your mother's death?"

His muscles tensed. Her direct gaze seemed to peer into his very soul, so he lowered his eyes to her mouth. "Forget about the past," he growled. "I can think of a better way to occupy our time."

He leaned closer, his hand cupping her silken cheek. He craved to lose himself in the simple pleasure of tasting her mouth again. The little catch in her breathing told him she wanted that, too. Her lashes were lowered slightly, her expression softened, her lips parted to receive his kiss . . .

Abby thrust up a hand to shove him away. "Don't *do* that. You're trying to distract me. It happens every time I ask you about your family."

Was that true? Caught off guard, he dissembled. "Perhaps I just like kissing pretty women."

She gave him a skeptical look. "Be honest, now. You're evading my questions."

He ran his fingers through his hair. Maybe if he gave her a brief summary, she would cease her badgering. "If you must know, my childhood was filled with loud quarrels, fits of weepy hysteria, interspersed with chilly silences. My father was a strict disciplinarian and my mother temperamental. They were utterly unsuited and should never have married."

"Then why did they?"

"Why does anyone wed? She was a beautiful woman and he was a nobleman in need of an heir. He was infatuated with her, even though she drove him mad with her dramatic demands and extravagant whims—"

He cut it off there. That was all Abby would wrest out of him. His father had made him swear a solemn oath never to reveal the family secrets—and he'd already confessed more to her than to any other living soul.

Sympathy warmed her face. "Oh, Max. It can't have

been easy for you. Do you suppose they loved each other at least a little?"

"Love. It's merely a romanticized term for lust."

"That's not true! My parents loved each other very much. They were devoted friends, laughing together, sharing meals, discussing everything under the sun. *I* think love is the most important part of a marriage."

That glow was in her eyes again, lighting up her whole face and seducing his senses. Wispy curls of cinnamon hair framed features that might be deemed commonplace if not for the radiance of her spirit. If she'd ever had a season, Miss Abigail Linton would have been besieged by suitors.

And he would have been jealous as sin.

He leaned closer. "Enough about me. I confess to being curious, Abby, how did you end up as a governess?"

"I cared for my parents until they both passed away of influenza last autumn. Then I decided to leave home for a change." She lifted her chin. "I daresay becoming a governess seems a paltry adventure to you, but not to me."

"It seems a travesty of justice, that's what. Couldn't your sisters and brothers have helped out with your parents?"

"They were all married with children. Anyway, I'm the youngest by seven years, so the task fell to me. But you mustn't think it was a trial, for I loved Mama and Papa dearly. They were very precious to me."

Max felt a twist of anger nonetheless. He was beginning to size up the situation, and to develop a disgust for her siblings, who had denied Abby the chance to wed. In particular, he had a nodding acquaintance with her eldest brother, a pompous fellow more than twenty years her senior, whom he had encountered from time to time in London.

"Clifford Linton is head of your family now, is he not?

Surely he's capable of providing for you so that you needn't labor for a living."

"Of course! In fact, he insisted that I remain at Linton House. But I wanted something . . . more."

She deserved a husband and children of her own. Instead, with all those sisters and brothers, nieces and nephews, she must have been treated as an unpaid servant. Little wonder she preferred to teach just one well-behaved girl.

"You should be married. Were you disappointed that Mr. Babcock didn't offer for you?"

She reared back, her cheeks pink. "How impertinent a question!"

"I'm merely stating the obvious. There must be a dearth of suitable gentlemen in this rural neighborhood."

"If you must know," she said stiffly, "I consider myself to be quite firmly on the shelf."

Feeling unaccountably angry, he glowered at her. "You don't feel like an old maid, though, do you, Abby? You still have hopes and desires. Last evening, you didn't appear spinsterish in the least when you were laughing and flirting with Ambrose before dinner."

"We were merely talking."

"Oh? You two seemed quite cozy. If you've any aspirations in that direction, I would advise you to think again. He's too hardened a libertine to propose marriage."

Her lips tightened. Releasing her knees, she scrambled off the boulder. "Pray be assured, Your Grace, I do not regard every bachelor I meet as a potential husband. Far from it! Now, if you'll excuse me, I've lessons to prepare."

He rose to his feet. "I'll take you back."

"Don't bother yourself. I would rather walk."

Abby marched off in high dudgeon. To her credit, she didn't so much as falter while passing Brimstone. She headed down the narrow dirt path until her slim form vanished into the forest. He wasn't worried that she'd lose her way, for she knew these woods as well as he did.

But he *was* exasperated with himself. Why the devil had he brought up Ambrose? Now she would know that he'd been watching her the previous evening—though at least he hadn't been fool enough to confess to a burning desire to grab his best friend by the lapels, haul him out of the chair, and plant him a facer for daring to trifle with her.

Max stalked to Brimstone and untied the reins. He'd had no right to prose on about marriage, either. What she did with her life was none of his concern. Who was he to render advice on wedded bliss, anyway?

He had no interest in the institution.

Yet his thoughts remained on Abby. Damn, why had he given up so easily all those years ago? When he hadn't received any response to his letters, why hadn't he returned here and confronted her? Instead, he had convinced himself it was irrational to pine after a country girl when there were countless more sophisticated women who fawned over him.

You're very accomplished at seducing women. It is what you do best.

Max swung into the saddle. Her condemnation of him after their kiss the previous day still smarted. Perhaps because there was a degree of truth in her assessment of him. He *had* allowed himself to while away his life in the idle pursuit of pleasure. It was a hard fact to face. And it stirred in him the need to achieve something greater.

Perhaps the answer lay right here.

He turned Brimstone toward the farms that lay to the south. He would visit a few of his tenants before returning to the house. In a very short time here, he had discovered a great satisfaction in riding over his land, in knowing that everything, as far as the eye could see, belonged to him. Having grown up at Rothwell Court, he knew every square inch of the estate. Yet he had a nagging awareness that he'd neglected his farmers, the servants, and the villagers who depended upon him. He must take a more personal interest in the future, rather than merely reviewing account ledgers sent to him by his estate manager.

At the moment, however, he felt pulled in too many different directions. He had Goliath to prepare for the upcoming prizefight. He needed to spend more time with his sister. He also had a duty to see to the entertainment of his guests.

Max experienced a guilty start. He had been neglecting Elise in particular. In fact, until this moment, he hadn't thought of her even once today. He had best pay her heed, or he would lose his chance to seduce the loveliest plum of the ton.

Nevertheless, as he rode onward through the forest, his thoughts kept returning to Abby.

Chapter 16

The moment she stepped through a side door and into the house, Abby heard the distant sound of upraised voices coming from somewhere along the marble corridor. She paused only long enough to remove her dirty shoes before hurrying in stocking feet to investigate.

It had taken her the better part of an hour to walk back to Rothwell Court. She had marched fast at first, her steps driven by a tempest of roiling emotions. But after muddying herself by splashing through several puddles, she had slowed to a more measured pace while ruminating on the unsettling encounter with Max.

He had been alternately talkative and tight-lipped, kind and meddlesome, gentle and forceful. He had badgered her about marrying, poked into her private hopes and dreams, while granting her only an abbreviated glimpse of his family upbringing. Worst of all, despite his own tarnished reputation, he'd had the temerity to chide *her* for flirting with Lord Ambrose!

Yet, in retrospect, she was glad that he'd hauled her up onto Brimstone without warning. His technique might have been infuriating, but his intent had been worthy. She likely never would have mounted a horse on her own. And now that she had ridden again, even if she didn't feel entirely cured of her fear, at least the experience had bolstered her confidence.

In the doing, though, he had wreaked havoc with her peace of mind. She had forgotten how wonderful it felt to be held by a man. Once having overcome her initial shock, Abby had felt perfectly at home in the saddle with his arm firmly clasped around her waist. Her thoughts lingered on the memory of his muscled form, his masculine scent, his enticing body heat. It was not an experience that would be easy to forget.

Yet forget it she must.

Max was her employer, not her suitor. And if she could no longer bring herself to think of him as Rothwell, that was her own cross to bear. She must not be fooled by his concern for her fears, his attentiveness in removing the splinter, his interest in conversing with her. He was a man who used women for one thing and one thing only.

Or was he? Why could she not rid herself of the notion that there was more to him than met the eye? Why did she yearn to spend more time in his company, to discover everything about him?

Abby longed for a few moments of solitude in which to unravel the tangle of feelings inside her. But after a lifetime of settling family squabbles, she felt duty-bound to seek out the source of the quarreling voices.

Heading through a doorway, she found herself in a sitting room with gilt-framed paintings of flowers on the sunny yellow walls. The remains of breakfast lay on a round table by one of the windows overlooking the rose garden.

Across the spacious room, Lady Desmond and Lord Ambrose stood arguing—or rather, Lady Desmond seemed to be doing most of the talking. Their attention was trained on the gargantuan man who was crouched on all fours, peering beneath a large rosewood bureau. Nearby, Finchley observed the proceedings with a smirk on his wrinkled face.

"You're taking too long for such a simple task," Lady Desmond scolded Goliath. "Whatever is the problem? Just seize the creature and begone!"

"Problem is," the prizefighter grunted, tilting his battered face up at her, "ye're scarin' the wee mite with all yer squawkin'. Ye're worse than a yowlin' molly cat callin' fer her tom."

"I beg your pardon! Ambrose, will you just stand there and allow that brute to insult me?"

Lord Ambrose gave her a droll look. "Seeing as how he's England's boxing champion, I should think it wiser for *us* to refrain from insulting *him*."

As she huffed out a breath, Finchley swung his withered fists at an imaginary opponent. "Have a care lest he catch you with his famous left hook," the butler said with a rusty cackle. "*Bam,* and he's darkened your daylights."

"You stay out of this," Lady Desmond groused. "Servants are to be seen and not heard."

Abby cleared her throat. "Excuse me. May I ask what is amiss?"

They turned to watch her approach. Lord Ambrose grinned, his bold gaze flicking up and down her form. Lady Desmond merely curled her lips in distaste. Abby could only imagine how untidy and windblown she appeared, her hem dirty, the mud-caked shoes dangling from one hand.

"Ah, reinforcements have arrived," Lord Ambrose said, affording her a courtly bow. "Elise and I were enjoying a cup of tea when one of the kittens darted into the room.

He dashed beneath the bureau and now refuses to come out. It's Scamp, the gray one belonging to your niece."

"It's all the fault of that big bruiser," Lady Desmond snapped. "He should know he's forbidden to enter this house. He belongs out in the stables!"

"'Ey!" Goliath protested. He sat back on his massive thighs to glower at Lady Desmond. "I told ye the tiny feller slipped in when Mr. Finchley opened the back door. Weren't me fault 'e ran in 'ere—or that ye screeched like a banshee and scared 'im."

Seeing anger smolder in the woman's eyes, Abby said quickly, "Whatever were you doing with one of the kittens, sir?"

"They was followin' me along the path to the kitchen, is all. So I picked 'em up. Scrappy little things, ain't they?"

It was then that she realized the other kitten was peeking out of the pocket of his green checkered coat. It was the golden-brown tabby that Lady Gwendolyn had named Caramel. Stroking its tiny head with his massive paw, Goliath wore a soppy expression on his battle-scarred features. It was so incongruously sweet a sight that Abby found herself smiling.

At that moment, a streak of gray lit out from beneath the bureau and raced across the fine carpet. The boxer reacted half a second too late, grabbing for the kitten and missing.

Pandemonium ensued as Scamp dashed in between Lord Ambrose's boots, then attempted to run behind Lady Desmond. She yelped and tried to step away, confusing the kitten, who made a flying leap up onto her skirt, where it clung with its tiny claws, a dab of gray against her rose-pink gown.

"Eek! Shoo! Get it off!"

Lord Ambrose went down on one knee to disengage the

feisty kitten. Abby dropped her shoes and hastened to help. He was chuckling as he handed over the wriggling fur ball to her. "There you go," he said, "and no harm done."

"No harm?" Lady Desmond wailed. "Why, my gown is ruined!"

"I was referring to the kitten," he said, attempting a sober expression though laughter still danced in his blue eyes. "As to your skirt, why, the damage is scarcely noticeable."

Cuddling the squirmy bundle to her bosom, Abby leaned down to peer at the fabric. "I must concur. There are only a few pinprick holes that your maid can easily repair."

Lady Desmond twitched her skirts away. "Pray keep your distance, Miss Linton. I don't wish to get mud on myself, too. You should never have allowed Lady Gwendolyn and your niece to adopt such wild animals."

"Actually, the decision wasn't mine. Rothwell approved it. And you did seem to like the kittens yesterday."

Lady Desmond sniffed. It was clear she didn't wish to be reminded of her ploy to introduce Lady Gwendolyn to the London group. "Where is His Grace, by the by?"

Abby's heart lurched at the sharpness of the woman's stare. She handed the kitten to Goliath, who had clambered to his feet. Had she and Max been seen when he'd carried her away on horseback? Why else would Lady Desmond ask such a question of her?

"I wouldn't know his whereabouts, my lady," Abby said truthfully, for she had no idea whether or not he'd remained at the glade. "Though I did see him in the paddock quite a while ago, when I walked down there with Lady Gwen and Valerie for their morning ride."

"Ah, so that's where the young ladies went," Lord Ambrose said. "A pity, for I was hoping to consult with them on the plans for tomorrow's picnic."

"They should be back very soon," Abby replied.

"They were intending to look near the lake for a suitable location."

"You needn't have a care for the victuals," Finchley advised. "Mrs. Beech is already cooking up beefsteaks and chickens and all manner of jellies and cakes. Mrs. Jeffries is gathering the linens, and the footmen hauled down a heap of baskets from the attic."

Lady Desmond turned her ire on him. "Shouldn't you be assisting the effort by polishing the silver instead of offering unsolicited reports?"

"Aye, milady. I'll see our champ out, then." Looking unperturbed by her rudeness, Finchley motioned to Goliath, saying, "I thought you was naught but a monstrous heathen at first, but 'tis plain you're a true Englishman—better'n some I can say."

The age-shrunken butler had to crane his neck to look up at the young giant, who cradled both kittens in one oversized paw. As they left the room, Abby wondered in amusement if Max knew that his ruthless champion had a soft spot for baby animals.

She turned back around to see that Lady Desmond was picking up a scrap of white cloth from the floor. Abby's good humor vanished in an instant. She glanced in chagrin at her bare hand. Of all the luck, the handkerchief that Max had wrapped around her injured finger must have slipped off while she was chasing the kitten.

Any hope that Lady Desmond might not realize it belonged to him died a swift death. Turning it over in her dainty hands, the woman arched an eyebrow as she spied the embroidered ducal monogram. Instead of confronting Abby, however, she merely gave her a dark look as she tucked the square of linen into a pocket of her gown.

"My dear Ambrose," she purred, "why don't you accompany Miss Linton to the stables? As governess, it is her duty to be present when Lady Gwendolyn returns from her ride."

"A capital notion." He smiled winningly at Abby. "If Miss Linton doesn't object to my paltry company, that is?"

"I'm rather muddy from my walk in the woods. I was hoping to tidy up a bit."

"You look dazzling to me," Lord Ambrose said with characteristic gallantry. He cast a downward glance at her stockinged toes peeking out from beneath the hem of her gown. "Although if we are to venture outdoors, it would be advisable for you to don your shoes."

Abby wanted nothing more than to escape to her bed-chamber, to ponder the tumultuous emotions Max had stirred in her. But she mustn't allow Lord Ambrose to go to the stables alone. Her first priority was to chaperone the girls, not to indulge her own wishes.

Accepting his arm, she intercepted Lady Desmond's sly look and suspected this was an attempt to distract her from the duke. If only the woman knew, Max had no interest whatsoever in rekindling a childhood romance. He had made that abundantly clear this morning when he had prodded Abby to find a husband.

That had been the moment when a dismaying realiza-tion had struck her. The moment when she'd faced the truth that had lurked in her heart from the instant she set eyes on him again.

For better or for worse, she was still head over heels in love with him.

On the day of the picnic, Max dismounted from Brimstone and handed the reins to a groom. He was looking forward to spending time with his sister. Between the entertain-ment of his guests and the impending prizefight, he had seen Gwen mostly from afar. The anticipation of finding

Abby with his sister should not be a consideration, yet it energized him nonetheless.

As a pair of footmen set up tables in the shade, he spotted his sister chatting excitedly with Valerie Perkins near the drooping branches of a willow. Pretty in pink, Gwen stepped forward to say rather timidly, "Attention, please!"

Valerie clapped her hands. "Come, gather around," she called to the scattered group. "We have a surprise for you."

The others had traveled by carriage to this idyllic spot at the far end of the lake. Lord Pettibone sauntered toward the girls with Mrs. Chalmers on one arm and Lady Desmond on the other.

Max cast only a cursory glance at the trio. He scanned the scene until he spotted a couple talking near the water's edge. His gut tightened. Blast it, Abby should not be in Ambrose's company.

Especially when Max had advised her to beware of that scoundrel.

Ambrose appeared entirely too smitten with her. And no wonder. In a simple lilac gown that was exceptionally becoming to her tall, slender form, she would not have been out of place strolling with the ton in Hyde Park. A straw bonnet tied with lilac ribbons framed her lively features. As they turned to join the others, Ambrose placed her hand on his arm. He bent his fair head closer to say something to her, and she laughed in response. Her face took on the radiant glow that set her apart from all other women.

The sight incensed Max.

He stalked toward them. As her employer, he was responsible for her welfare, and he must not allow her to fall under the spell of a charming rake. Especially not one whose foibles he knew too well.

A hand on his arm brought him to a halt. He looked

over to see Lady Desmond smiling fetchingly at him. An extravagant leaf-green bonnet brought out the green-gold of her eyes and the peaches-and-cream hue of her skin. "Your Grace, I'm so very pleased you've arrived. I must say, that brutish prizefighter is taking up entirely too much of your attention. But at least you're in time to be on my team."

"Team?"

"We're dividing into pairs for a scavenger hunt." Her full bosom pressing into his arm, she gazed soulfully up at him. "I haven't the foggiest notion where to look for anything on the list, so please do say you'll be my partner."

Max controlled a twist of vexation at the prospect of enduring her company. Which was preposterous considering he'd invited her along on this trip for the sole purpose of wooing her into his bed.

At least that had been the plan before their detour here to Rothwell Court, where his sister's presence prohibited any such dalliance. And where Gwen's new governess had proved to be an unexpected distraction.

Bound by rules of civility, he could hardly refuse Elise's request. They joined the others to find Abby accepting a small basket from his sister and setting off arm in arm with Ambrose toward a patch of woods. Pettibone and Mrs. Chalmers strolled along the path that followed the shoreline of the lake.

Max seldom suffered puritanical impulses, but he was tempted to put an immediate halt to this scavenger hunt on the grounds that it was improper for unmarried couples to go off together. However, Gwen looked so animated and excited as she handed him a collection basket that he lacked the heart to ruin her fun.

"Here's the list, Max," she said, thrusting a paper into

his hand. "Be as quick as you can! There's a prize for the winning team!"

Chattering like a pair of magpies, she and Valerie hastened off toward a gentle grassy slope beyond the end of the lake.

Max set his sights on the route that Abby and Ambrose had taken, intending to keep a watch on the two of them. But Evelyn held back, playfully tapping his coat with her folded fan.

"Now, that would be cheating, Your Grace! Each team must take a different direction, and someone has already gone that way. Come, we shall do better to walk toward that spinney."

He grimly acceded to her wishes and let himself be steered toward the thicket of trees. As they walked, he scanned the dozen or so items on list. An acorn, a mushroom, a yellow wildflower. None of it seemed particularly difficult to find, thank God, because the sooner they finished this nonsense, the better.

It was a fine day in late summer, sunny and warm, with nary a cloud in the sky. The air grew pleasantly cooler among the trees, yet Max couldn't enjoy the sylvan surroundings. He was too distracted by the thought of Abby alone with Ambrose. To make matters worse, he was tramping through the woods with a prissy female who squealed at the sight of caterpillars and played dumb in their search for the objects on the list. That was for Max to do, she said while batting her lashes, for he had a much sharper eye than a mere female.

What rot. He was morbidly certain that Abby was enjoying the hunt. She had always liked the outdoors. In their younger days, she wouldn't hesitate to pick up a worm or a frog or whatever else caught her fancy.

After looking for what felt like an hour, he had found only a conifer cone and a bird's feather. It didn't help that Elise kept up a continuous brainless chatter in his ears, so that he couldn't enjoy a moment's peace. Or that she kept trying in that gratingly sultry tone to convince him to stop and rest when it was obvious she was angling for a kiss. Refusing to think about why the prospect held such little appeal, he forged relentlessly onward.

Max was striding along, peering up into the branches to see if he could locate an abandoned bird's nest, when Elise tripped over something. She let out a squeaky yelp and her fingers dug into his arm. Since he was holding the basket in one hand and she was pulling on his other arm, he was unable to grab her in time. Momentum carried him down to the ground with her.

They landed in a grassy patch with Elise sprawled over his chest. She opened her eyes wide. "Oh! Forgive me, Your Grace, there must have been a rock in the path. I daresay you saved my life!"

As she flapped her lashes in coquettish distress, Max suspected he'd been hoodwinked. Especially since he could spot no large rocks in the vicinity, and she had contrived to fall on him in such a way as to preserve her gown from being soiled. It took a prodigious effort for him to reply in a civil tone.

"I sincerely doubt your life was in danger, my lady. Now, do allow me to help you to your feet."

He made a move to arise, but she looped her arms around his neck and moved sinuously against him. "There's no need for haste, is there, darling? I believe I owe you a kiss at the very least."

She pressed her lips to his, her tongue flicking out with a practiced sensuality that would have enticed him only a few days ago. But he was already disgruntled at being maneuvered, there were twigs sticking into his back, and—well—she simply did not arouse as before.

That realization was so galling that he decisively ended the kiss.

Catching hold of her waist, Max lifted her out of the way so that he could spring to his feet. He brought her up with him, then released her at once. Elise straightened her skirts while peeping at him from the screen of her lashes. She resembled a pouty little girl, but then, she'd been a stage actress when old Desmond had wed her, and luckily for her, he'd keeled over dead on their honeymoon.

"Have I displeased you, Your Grace? Truly, I didn't mean to be so clumsy. Pray accept my apologies."

Max forced himself to smile. It would be foolish to engage in a disagreeable quarrel when he had no desire to endure her crocodile tears. "It's entirely my fault for not watching the path. I am the one who must beg forgiveness, my lady. Now, we had better return before a search party is sent out to look for us."

He brushed a few grass blades off his clothes before picking up the basket with its pitifully incomplete contents. On the walk back, he strove to keep up his end of the conversation. Elise continued to flatter and cajole him, and he did not wish to alienate her in the midst of a house party, nor to cause trouble when the prizefight was looming in a mere two days' time. Better he should contrive to keep her at arm's length until they returned to the city, where he could safely cut the connection.

She uttered some inanity, and his debonair smile hid the fact that her wiles no longer had the slightest effect on him. It was a shocking admission for a man of his lusty reputation to make, that he felt repelled by the most gorgeous, sought-after woman of the ton.

Instead, he had developed an unbearable passion for a certain spinster governess. To make matters worse, Miss Abigail Linton was the one woman whom he must never, ever seduce.

Chapter 17

On the morning of her birthday, Abby awakened before dawn from a restless sleep. A faint gray light seeped past the curtains and cast a pale luminosity over the bedchamber. The covers lay in a tangle at her feet. Her nightdress, too, was twisted as if she'd tossed and turned. Despite the coolness of the air, she felt damp and overheated.

She had been dreaming of Max.

Of that she was certain, for she could still detect his presence as if he'd lain right here in the bed with her. She had a vague memory of his hands sliding over her body and the breathless sense of being drawn toward something irresistibly thrilling. The very thought of it brought a flush to her skin. Closing her eyes, she sought to hold on to the last wisps of sleep in an effort to recapture the dream.

But it slipped away into nothingness.

Leaning on her elbow, Abby glanced at the softly ticking clock on the bedside table and then plopped back down again. It was only six ten, which meant she had over two hours before joining the girls for breakfast at half past eight. There was no need to arise just yet.

Hugging the feather pillow, she rolled onto her side.

After a few minutes, she shifted position again, but to no avail. She had been too disturbed by that erotic dream to slumber any longer.

With a sigh, she slipped from the bed and padded barefoot to the window. She drew apart the curtains and opened the casement. Pressing her palms to the stone sill, she inhaled a deep draught of fresh morning air. The aroma of recently cut grass and the chirping of birds invigorated her spirits. A rosy tinge on the horizon heralded the approach of sunrise, gleaming faintly on the quiet dark surface of the lake in the distance.

Today was her thirtieth birthday, Abby realized with a start. The fateful day that she'd so long dreaded had arrived at last. She smiled wryly, for she certainly didn't feel any older or wiser. The only discernible difference in her was the longing she felt for Max, heart and body and soul.

Yet he could never be hers.

That fact had been reinforced at the picnic the previous day. The girls had organized a scavenger hunt in which Abby had been paired with Lord Ambrose. He'd proven to have a competitive streak that matched her own, and they'd scurried hither and yon to locate all the items on the list. The first ones to return to the picnic site, they had still been laughing over the silly prize of matching flower crowns when Max and Lady Desmond finally had straggled back in last place, having collected less than half of their list.

Nevertheless, the woman had looked as satisfied as a cat that had lapped an entire dish of cream. By their slightly disheveled appearance, it appeared as though they'd spent their time engaged in amorous activities. Max's expression had been oddly contrite as he'd sent a penetrating look at Abby. Not that that excused him. Had she not been a peacemaker at heart, she'd have been sorely tempted to hurl a plate of Mrs. Beech's lemon tarts at the two of them.

Releasing a sigh, Abby stared out at the lake. She mustn't let herself believe he could change his basic nature, even though he'd helped her overcome her dread of horses and had doctored her injured finger—not to mention employed Miss Herrington after the death of her brother.

No, the Duke of Rothwell was still an incurable rake renowned for his harem of mistresses. If he had once been a sweet, gawky youth, no one would guess it now.

But Abby knew. Perhaps that was why she could not crush this foolish longing for him. Her emotions were still tangled up in the past. How ridiculous that a thirty-year-old spinster should pine for a dashing nobleman who could have any woman he wanted at one snap of his fingers!

Love. It's merely a romanticized term for lust.

He had told her that on the day they'd gone to the glade, and she would do well to take him at his word. He had grown too cynical, too hard-hearted from a life of dissipation. There could never be anything between them, and that was that.

The serene waters of the lake beckoned to her. She would not waste another thought on Max. Instead, she would celebrate this milestone birthday by doing something bold and improper and forbidden for a modest governess. Something she had not done since girlhood.

She would wash away her troubles with a swim.

There was something about being in the country that invigorated him, Max reflected, as he pulled on a pair of breeches in the shadowy confines of his dressing room. In London, it was not uncommon for him to fall into bed at dawn and sleep past noon. Society balls often lasted into the wee hours, gaming clubs thrived in the middle of the night, and of course, there was always the demimonde to keep a man awake and entertained. But here, he'd taken up the habit of retiring early on the excuse that he needed to oversee the training of Goliath each morning.

The truth of the matter was, he'd found himself rather bored by the endless rounds of cards and dice with his friends. The gossip and storytelling that had amused him in the city now seemed tedious and sometimes even cruel. And when Elise played the toadying coquette, he found himself unfavorably comparing her to a prickly bramble of a governess who would sooner scold than fawn over him.

It was an unsettling thing for a man to question the state of his life. Especially when only a few days ago, he'd found it to be perfectly satisfactory.

Standing at the washstand, he grimaced as he splashed cold water onto his face. The footman had not yet brought a pitcher of hot water. Toweling off, Max rubbed his raspy jaw and decided that a shave could wait until later. He was in no humor for company, and his valet was too fussy and talkative for any reasonable human being to endure before the sun was even up.

He grabbed a shirt at random from the drawer and pulled it over his head. Carrying the candle back into the predawn darkness of the bedchamber, he set it down on a table. Then he bent over to touch his bare toes a few times to get his blood moving. The ducal apartment was cavernous enough for him to perform cartwheels if he so desired, although there was a stiff formality to the décor of green brocade hangings and heavy mahogany furniture that precluded any such frivolity. The room looked exactly as it had in the time of his father's reign, a fact that disturbed Max on a visceral level.

If he stayed here for any length of time, he would order Mrs. Jeffries to redecorate . . .

He stopped himself in mid-thought. Stayed? This was to be a brief visit, nothing more. A prolonged sojourn had never been in his plans. Yet the notion held an indisputable appeal. Perhaps he had avoided this house and its unhappy memories for too long. He certainly would relish the opportunity to gain more firsthand knowledge about the workings of the estate.

And to have the chance to kiss Abby again.

Max gave an impatient shake of his head. No. He was far too dangerously attracted to her, and a liaison with his sister's governess was out of the question. Long ago, he'd learned to avoid all but the most casual flirtations with respectable single ladies. A careless dalliance could result in being leg-shackled, and marriage was a state he had forsworn after witnessing the tragic end to his parents' union.

Love didn't enrich a man; it made him wretched and weak.

His belief on the matter had not changed simply because he had swept Abby up onto Brimstone and ridden with her to their secret glade. Or because he had enjoyed every moment of their conversation. They weren't children anymore. Although as a youth he'd wanted to wed her, he'd long since acknowledged the value of freedom from emotional entanglements. How much better to be in the enviable position of having any woman he desired!

Except for the virtuous ones like Abby.

He stalked to the bedside table and picked up a book. Nothing was more guaranteed to distract his mind than reading about techniques of animal husbandry. Better he should focus on breeding than brooding.

He carried the tome to a leather chair by the bank of

tall windows, where he'd already drawn back the curtains. Over the past few days, it had become his habit to watch dawn spread over the vast expanse of his land. There was something fascinating about the gradual lifting of the darkness. In the city, he'd never even noticed the beauty of the morning sky, perhaps because it was too often obscured by coal smoke or fog. But here, no buildings blocked the sunrise, no gardeners or grooms disturbed the landscape just yet. The quiet was broken only by the trill of birdsong . . .

He caught sight of someone walking down the path to the lake. It was a slender woman in a pale dress.

Abandoning his book, he threw open the window and leaned out to study her in the grayness of predawn. There was something familiar in the way she moved, the proud set of her shoulders, and the briskness of her heels kicking up the hem of her gown. The sight stirred his blood more than any calisthenics could do.

Abby.

Where the devil was she going?

All prior caution flew out of his head. Here was his opportunity to speak to her away from the nosy eyes of his friends. He'd been wanting to do so ever since the picnic the previous day, when he and Elise had returned late from the scavenger hunt. The cool censure on Abby's face had disturbed him. He knew she had assumed the wrong idea, and he didn't owe her an explanation, yet he felt compelled to get back into her good graces nonetheless.

Striding into the dressing room, Max shoved his bare feet into a pair of shoes, not bothering with cravat or coat. Urgency beat in his veins. He had the strange notion that she would melt into the mist if he didn't make haste.

He flew down a side staircase, his footsteps echoing hollowly on the marble. Not a soul roamed the corridors;

not even the servants were about their duties yet. There was just enough illumination from the windows for him to see his way through the gloomy house.

Emerging onto the terrace, he cut through the formal gardens, where the scent of late-blooming roses perfumed the dewy air. Then he proceeded at a smart pace along the path that meandered to the lake. In the ten minutes or so that it took for him to reach the surrounding trees, the barest glimmer of sunshine was beginning to creep over the hills.

Yet he caught no glimpse of Abby.

Nor did he see her upon reaching the water's edge near the small Greek temple, a folly commissioned by his grandfather to beautify the view. Max glanced quickly around, but detected no sign of movement on the nature trail that encircled the lake. With the lightening of the sky, he ought to be able to spot her. Where could she have gone?

Gentle ripples disturbed the glassy surface of the lake. The sound of splashing caught his attention. It was then that he noticed her dark wet head, and the rhythmic stroking of her pale arms as she propelled herself through the water a short distance out from shore.

By God, she was swimming.

Max stared. Given the prim woman she had become, it was the last thing he'd have expected of Abby. She'd clearly presumed her privacy would not be compromised at this early hour. He ought to depart at once and spare her the embarrassment of discovering she was not alone.

Instead, he was sorely tempted to peel off his clothes and join her.

Quelling the mad impulse, he retreated into the gloom of the trees and leaned against the rough bark of an oak. He watched for a time as her slim body glided through the water. She was wearing some sort of white garment, a shift perhaps. Her strokes were rather inexpert, yet graceful nonetheless.

Much like Abby herself.

The lake had to be cold. With the approach of autumn, the days were beginning to grow shorter. The morning air had a slight chill, for it was already the first of September.

The first of September.

Awareness jolted him. Today was Abby's birthday. Long ago, they had celebrated it in the glade with one of Mrs. Beech's honey cakes. That had been their last happy afternoon together before the death of his mother.

Max banished the bittersweet memory. It was no use wishing he could turn back the hands of time and alter what had happened. No use wondering if he might have made better decisions. What was done was done. Damn it, he liked his life exactly the way it was.

Abby stopped swimming. She tilted her head back to watch a large heron fly over the water; then she paddled in place for a few minutes before starting toward the shore.

The time had come for him to leave. He should return to the house and pretend he'd never been here. There could be absolutely no excuse to linger.

Yet his feet felt rooted to the earth. He could not tear his gaze from her.

Upon reaching the shallows, she stood up, emerging from the water like Venus rising from a seashell. The filmy garment she wore barely reached her knees. The dawn light painted her with a rosy glow, and the wet cloth clung like a second skin to her womanly curves.

Dripping, she lifted her arms and squeezed the water from her long hair. All the breath left his lungs. Her graceful action only served to draw attention to the beauty of her form. The damp shift might as well have been transparent, for he could see the dusky points of her nipples and the enticing shadow at the top of her long legs.

In that moment, Max knew his fate was struck. He could no more resist that fate than he could resist breathing. He craved Abby. No other woman would do. She was the one he'd dreamed about for too long, the one against whom every other woman had been measured and found wanting.

His heart pounding, he started toward her.

Chapter 18

The first plunge into the chilly lake made Abby instantly regret her decision to go for a swim. It was madness to have come here when she might still be snuggled in the warmth of her bed. She also ought not have convinced herself to run into the water without first acclimating herself by degrees. It was shockingly cold. Had her face not been submerged, she might have shrieked loudly enough to awaken every living creature on the estate.

Her head broke the surface and she gasped for air. Paddling furiously in place, she blinked the droplets from her lashes. Despite the jolt to her senses, the icy water felt as smooth as silk against her skin.

Exercise would warm her up, she knew. In childhood, she'd swum with her nieces and nephews in the spring-fed pond on her family's land. They had been all nearly the same age. It was one of the oddities of having much older siblings who were already married with children at the time she had been born. Of course, many years had passed since then, and Abby hoped she remembered what to do.

She stayed close to the shore where it was deep enough to swim, yet her toes could almost touch bottom. Practicing the strokes, she choked on several gulps of water before mastering the rhythm of coordinating her arms and legs. It took mental as well as physical effort to concentrate on her movements. As her confidence grew, she made a number of forays back and forth. The water swished in her ears, and a pleasant warmth began to pervade her muscles. Despite her momentary doubts, she felt grateful now to have awakened early enough to enjoy this rare gift of freedom.

At last she stopped, scissoring her legs in place to catch her breath after all the exertion. She watched, awestruck, as a heron flew low over the water with great beats of its broad wings. Across the lake, a deer ventured out of the woods to lower its head and drink. The brushstrokes of dawn painted the scene with a softly luminous quality.

If only Max were here to see this beauty, perhaps he'd never leave.

The thought invaded her peace of mind. How imprudent of her to feel a bone-deep yearning for him to stay on at Rothwell Court when it would only cause her heartache. And it was a moot point, anyway. She couldn't imagine him ever giving up the refined amusements of London in order to rusticate in the country, no matter how close to heaven his estate might be. The past fifteen years had changed him into a man of the city. It would be wise to remember he was no longer the callow youth who had once roamed these woods with her.

Yet she didn't want to be wise, not today of all days. Wisdom meant growing old, and she wasn't quite ready for that. Tomorrow would be soon enough to don the drab mantle of spinsterhood.

Tomorrow was also the day of the prizefight, and after that the duke and his friends would depart. Her short stint as governess would be over, and she would take Rosalind up on the offer to help with Valerie's debut.

But leaving here was too gloomy to contemplate on this fine morning. As a birthday gift to herself, she would forget the future and enjoy what little time she had left with Max. Yesterday, Lady Gwen had begged him to join their party on a visit to the village this afternoon, and he had accepted. With Lady Desmond always on the prowl, there might not be a chance to enjoy a precious few moments alone with him, but one could always hope.

Cheered by the prospect, Abby paddled toward the shore. The house would be stirring soon. If she hoped to steal back into her bedchamber without being seen, it was necessary to put an end to this interlude.

In the shallows, she stood up and let the water roll off her body. The early morning air felt almost warm after the chill of the lake. Nevertheless, her wet state raised gooseflesh on her skin. She must hurry and don her dry clothes.

Lifting her arms, she squeezed the excess water out of her heavy tresses. The swim had left her feeling refreshed and relaxed. There was something sinfully hedonistic about being outdoors in a state of undress. It brought back an echo of that erotic dream she'd had of Max . . .

Oh, Lord, she mustn't think such thoughts when an overheated state had been the reason why she'd come to the lake in the first place. Wouldn't that be a lark if she needed another cold plunge! Laughing at herself, she darted to the pile of folded garments lying on the steps of the Greek temple. Just as she reached down to grab the linen towel on top, a noise startled her.

The crack of a twig. The scrape of a footstep.

Someone was coming!

Gasping, Abby straightened up at once. The towel clutched to her bosom, she spun toward the direction of the sound. A man was walking out of the shadows of the forest. He came straight toward her, his strides purposeful.

Max.

She stared wide-eyed in the throes of shock. It seemed for an instant that her dreams had conjured him out of the ether. That fleeting notion vanished as the crunch of his footsteps on the stone path assured her that he was no phantom lover, but a flesh-and-blood man.

He had left off the trappings of the elegant gentleman this morning. A white cambric shirt outlined the powerful muscles of his shoulders and chest, and a pair of fawn breeches hugged his long legs. His dark hair was tousled, a lock falling onto his brow. An air of wildness seemed to emanate from him, as if he'd abandoned all pretense of polite manners. The piercing intensity of his gray eyes caused a lurch within her depths. The sensation was half alarm and half allure, causing an emotional tug-of-war that rendered her speechless.

He stopped directly in front of her. Her senses sharpened, she could hear the pounding of her heart as she caught a trace of his appealing male scent. He was unshaven, as if he'd just arisen from bed, and his bristly jaw enhanced the uncivilized aura about him. But he made no attempt to touch her, keeping his hands gripped at his sides.

"Abby," he murmured.

The soft caress of his voice resonated inside of her. His gaze roved downward over the sodden shift that adhered to her body. She had been chilled, but now his bold stare suffused her in the heat of a blush. She could only imagine the scandalous eyeful he must be getting, for the garment was nearly transparent. Her only sop to modesty was the small linen towel that she clasped to her bosom.

She might as well be standing naked in front of him.

Questions tumbled through her agitated mind. What was she to do? Where had he come from? Had he been watching her swim? What must he think of his sister's governess behaving like a hoyden?

Despite the embarrassing impropriety of the situation, she found herself aching for the warmth of his arms. If only he would hold her close and never let go. On the day when he had taken her up on Brimstone and ridden with her to their secret glade, she had seen glimpses of the tender boy that she'd loved with all her heart—the man she still loved in spite of the wicked reputation he had acquired since then. A keen yearning for him threatened to crumble her self-discipline. It was imperative for her to escape before she did something reckless and downright idiotic.

Abby edged toward her clothing. "You oughtn't be here, Max . . . I mean, my lord duke. Nor should I. If you'll excuse me . . ."

He took a step to block her path. A suggestive smile tipped one corner of his mouth. Reaching out, he brushed his fingers over her cheek, leaving a trail of sparks. "I'm exactly where I want to be. Aren't you?"

She swallowed. "I—I hardly think—"

"For once, darling, don't think." He plucked the towel from her nerveless fingers and flung it away. "Just *feel*."

Pulling her flush against him, he brought his mouth down over hers in a deep, drowning kiss. A marvelous flow of delight filled her as if she'd taken an intoxicating swig of champagne. At the touch of his tongue, she parted her lips to allow him to explore her more thoroughly. She clasped her arms around his neck and stood on tiptoe, the better to feel his closeness. His hold on her tightened as if he too experienced a profound need in his soul.

Darling. Was she really his darling? It seemed impossible to be true. Yet with every beat of her heart, she wanted to believe that Max cared as intensely for her as she did for him.

In his embrace, Abby felt the joy of homecoming, of being in the place where she belonged. The heat of his solid form warmed all the coldness inside of her. With so little clothing to separate them, she was acutely aware of the broadness of his chest and the strength of his muscles. Her skin tingled all over as he caressed her face, her back, her bosom.

Oh my, being kissed by Max was heaven. He gently nibbled at her lips, murmuring sweet nothings until she felt on the verge of a swoon. Surely no other experience in life could even come close to this. The rules of proper behavior no longer seemed important. Being held by him felt right and perfect. It stirred in her the irresistible desire to surrender herself into his keeping.

If temptation had a face, it belonged to the Duke of Rothwell.

The thought disturbed the fullness of her pleasure. No wonder so many women flocked to him. Max was amazingly skilled at kissing—and other erotic acts, according to gossip. Was she truly willing to become just another one of his conquests?

Abby drew back slightly, although she was unable to bring herself to separate their bodies. Instead, she rested her palms on his chest to keep a measure of distance from him. Maybe she could convince *him* to walk away. "Max . . . we're outside. Someone might see us here."

"Mm." He nuzzled her neck, his tongue flicking out to taste the hollow of her throat. "It's far too early in the morning."

"But . . . I'm *soaked*. I'm getting *you* all wet."

"A simple matter to fix."

He yanked the cambric shirt over his head, dropping it onto the grass and affording her a spectacular view of his bare chest. Her rapt gaze followed the dusting of black hair that narrowed to a line, trailing downward across his flat belly to disappear inside his breeches. He looked every inch the wicked rake that young ladies were warned to avoid.

Thirty-year-old spinsters ought to know better, too.

Aware that she was ogling, she lifted her gaze to his. "Why are you here, Max? Don't you think Lady Desmond might object?"

"It's no concern of hers." He drew Abby close again, tracing his fingertip along the scooped neck of her shift. "In fact, when I spied you from my window, I had to follow. I was hoping for the chance to explain something."

"Yes?"

He cocked a dark eyebrow. "I believe you may have made a wrongful assumption yesterday at the picnic."

The progress of his fingers distracted her. Now they were swirling lightly over the wet cloth covering her bosom. "How so?"

"If Lady Desmond looked rather disheveled after the scavenger hunt, it was due to her stumbling over a rock and falling. Nothing of note happened between us. She is not my lover—nor has she ever been."

Abby scanned his handsome face for deception and found none. Lord Ambrose had been telling the truth, then. Yet she could not forget that scorching scene in the library when she'd caught Max romancing the blond vixen. "I see. So it is merely a commonplace event for you to kiss women senseless and to reach underneath their skirts."

His lips tilted in a boyish grin. "Only if they're willing."

"I daresay many are eager to win the attentions of a wealthy duke."

"How lowering you are to a man's pride, Miss Bramble. All this time, I thought it was my scintillating companionship they sought."

His wandering fingers on her bosom made Abby struggle to keep her mind on the conversation. Honesty made her concede, "I cannot deny that's part of it. You're a very charming man, and— Oh!"

She inhaled a sharp breath. Now he was gently massaging her nipple between his forefinger and thumb. The action ignited a filament of fire that burned down to the very depths of her womb. Rational thought fled as wanton heat spread through every part of her body.

Her legs melting, she leaned into him, clinging to his strong shoulders for support. "Max! What do you think you're *doing*?"

He brought his head down to feather his mouth over hers. "I'm giving you the gift of pleasure. Today is your birthday, is it not?"

The tender nip of his teeth on her lower lip caused another quake inside of her, even as his words struck her with surprise. "You remembered!"

His air of lighthearted banter vanished, and he gazed deeply into her eyes. His hand cradled her cheek as if she were precious to him. "I may have been gone for years, Abby, but I've never forgotten anything about you. Nor have I ever stopped desiring you."

The huskiness to his tone made her heart take wing. Was it possible that he too felt a bond between them that had survived the test of time? She wanted desperately to believe that. Even more, she craved for Max to show her the mysteries of lovemaking.

In that moment, Abby knew beyond the shadow of a doubt that she didn't wish to be a dried-up spinster who had never experienced a dalliance with a man. The Duke of Rothwell might be a rogue incapable of fidelity, he might leave her tomorrow and never return, yet she wanted to learn everything that he could teach her. He was right, she could think of nowhere else in the world she preferred to be but here in his arms.

Her fingers sought the roughness of stubble on his jaw. "Oh, Max, I want you, too. I want all the pleasure that you can give me. Here. *Now.*"

His eyes darkened with that same fierce look he'd worn when he'd walked out of the woods. "Then you shall have it."

Thrusting his fingers into the tangle of her damp hair, he subjected her to a kiss of unleashed ferocity. His other hand roamed boldly over the curves of her body. A glorious yearning swept through her, making her heart race and her insides curl. She could not get enough of him, the magic of his mouth, the silkiness of his hair, the heat of his skin. Hunger built in her, the craving to let him do with her whatever he willed. She cared nothing for the past or the future, only that she might know the joy of being with him in the present.

His wildness gradually eased into a softer kiss that was no less thrilling to her senses. He worked his hand inside her shift to cup her bosom in his big palm. Then he proceeded to play with her, lightly and teasingly. The tingling heat provoked by those slow caresses wrested a moan from her as she moved sinuously against him. "Max. *Oh, Max.*"

"I want to see all of you," he whispered against her ear.

With that, he peeled the loose undergarment off her shoulders. Any trace of shyness she felt was overshadowed by the greater need to feel her flesh pressed to his. The desire to join their bodies seemed inevitable, she marveled, a natural component of her love for him.

And she did love him, even if he could not return the

sentiment. She drew a breath to ease the ache in her chest. Tomorrow would be soon enough to think about that. For now he was hers, and nothing else mattered.

Under his guiding hand, the damp shift slithered downward over the mounds of her breasts and lower, until it fell into a pool at her feet. All the while, the brush of his fingers sent sparks over her bare skin to feed fuel to the feverish ache inside of her.

He placed his hands on her shoulders while his admiring gaze roved over her nudity. "You reminded me of a nymph when you came out of the water. How beautiful you are, Abby."

Under his scrutiny, she felt more like a brazen wanton than a lady of strict moral upbringing. But she wouldn't trade this moment even if it brought her a lifetime of censure. The hot intensity in his eyes made her feel young and vibrant and desirable. It was passion that radiated from him, and the same desperate longing bedeviled her, too.

Abby slid her palms over the sculpted muscles of his chest. Standing on tiptoe, she tenderly kissed his mouth. She didn't quite know how to articulate what she wanted, only that she wished he would do it. *"Please."*

Max seemed to understand, for he made a feral sound in his chest. He caught her in his arms and pressed her down onto the grassy verge beside the temple so that she lay beneath him. Then he proceeded to engage her in a series of soul-stirring kisses. When he stroked her bare breasts, kneading the fullness and stimulating her skin, a flush of pleasure suffused her entire body. It felt utterly natural to be lying with him like this, reveling in the enjoyment of his unhurried caresses.

She adored the heavy weight of him. Her own hands learned every inch of his torso, though further exploration was foiled by the fact that he still wore his breeches. Nevertheless, she was keenly aware of the most private part of him, a thick hardness that pressed into her thigh and made her quiver with unladylike curiosity.

His lips left hers to lay a necklace of kisses over her throat. He shifted his attention lower to draw the sensitive peak of her breast into his mouth, and the stroking of his tongue caused a shocking rush of pleasure. Unprepared for it, she gasped. "Oh!"

He paused to look at her. His eyes were vigilant, his breathing weighted, as if he fought to control himself. He tenderly brushed back a strand of damp hair from her cheek. "Are you afraid, nymph? You needn't be."

He was referring to that time long ago, she thought, when his clumsy attempt at seduction had caused her to withdraw in alarm. What would have happened had she allowed him to complete the act? If they had not quarreled, instead? Would he have kept his promise to return and marry her, in spite of the mishap with their letters?

Abby banished the memory. None of that signified anymore. There was only the here and now.

She traced his damp lips with her fingertip. "I could never be frightened of you. Not anymore."

Catching hold of her hand, he nuzzled the sensitive hollow of her palm. "If you wish me to stop at any time, you've only to tell me and I shall."

"Oh, Max. I believe I might die if you stop."

One corner of his mouth quirked in a strained smile that bespoke his own intense desires. They kissed again with an insatiable passion that left her soft and willing in his capable hands. As birds twittered in the branches overhead, Abby felt like a creature of nature, uninhibited and set free of restraints.

Driven by feverish urgency, she slipped her fingers into

the waistband of his breeches and gave a little tug. "Will you—? Will we—?"

"Patience, darling. I'll have your pleasure first."

"But I *am* pleased. Very much so!"

A rakish glint lit his eyes. "We'll see about that."

He said no more, merely sliding the palm of his hand downward over the flatness of her belly, where it lay warm and heavy and possessive while he kissed her again. Then, with torturous deliberation, his fingers strayed southward until one of them slipped inside the nest of her womanhood.

Abby cried out in startled wonder as his touch unleashed a flood of decadent sensations. All of her awareness focused on his fingertip as he swirled it around her throbbing center. His caress felt so sinfully alluring that she instinctively parted her legs to encourage him. While he played with her, his mouth strewed leisurely kisses over her breasts, her belly, and . . . lower.

An inkling of his intent penetrated the fog of her passion. Gazing down at his dark head, she was unable to articulate a protest, for a quivery excitement swelled within her. When at last he parted her folds and blew softly on her wetness, it was fuel to the blaze of her desires.

All modesty fled at the first lap of his tongue. The divine sensation was half pleasure, half torment. Abby tried to lie still, but it proved impossible not to move her hips in an effort to assuage the scorching rise of excitement.

Tilting her head back on the grass, she threaded her trembling fingers into his hair, craving something beyond her perception. Desperate need encompassed her entire existence; soft cries of frustration eddied from her throat. At the very instant when she could bear no more, the tension broke and she tumbled headlong into a sea of blissful release.

As the waves of euphoria began to recede, she felt Max's weight leave her. She lifted heavy eyelids to watch in a happy daze as he unfastened his breeches and stepped out of them. Magnificent in his nakedness, he stood in the dawn light against the backdrop of the white marble temple like a Greek god descended from the heavens.

The sight stirred an impassioned ache of anticipation in her. He was all muscle and sinew, the broad span of his chest tapering down to a lean waist and hips. His jutting member was as splendidly large as the rest of him. Her gaze skittered over that portion of his anatomy, then flashed upward to see him watching her with a rather fierce half-smile.

The hungry promise in his stare made her shiver, not from maidenly fear, but from a resurgence of readiness. There was more to come, she knew, and she desired it all.

Smiling up at him, she lifted her hand in invitation. He took hold of it, his warm fingers gripping hers. His possessive gaze flicked over her as she lay indolently in the grass, before he brought himself onto her again, drawing her over onto her side to face him.

She sighed in contentment at the warm, solid feel of him. Even in her dreams she had not imagined this joy of lying naked with a man. No, not just any man. Max, whom she had loved forever.

She kissed his stubbled jaw. "I begin to fathom your wicked reputation. You've made me a very happy woman."

A smile flirted with the corners of his mouth. "We're far from finished."

"Mm. Have I mentioned how glad I am that you followed me here today?"

His gray eyes studied her with a penetrating intensity. He brushed back a lock of her hair from her cheek. "When

I saw you swimming, I ought to have gone away. But I couldn't stop watching you, Abby. Or stop craving you."

Pleased by his infatuated tone, she undulated her hips and his manhood twitched, hot and heavy against her thigh. "Perhaps you should have joined me in the water."

He sucked in a breath between his teeth, then lightly slapped her bare bottom. "Nymph. And to think I stayed away from you all these years."

Because you don't love me.

The unwelcome thought flitted into her head as he pressed her back against the grass to kiss her throat and breasts. Abby arched her neck, wanting to lose herself in the heated haze of desire. She was glad that he hadn't expected a reply. The last thing she needed was to spill out her heart to an experienced rake. The love that dwelled within her must remain a secret. Let him return to the city none the wiser.

Winding her arms around his neck, she kissed him back with all the fervor that she dared not put into words. The world slipped away, leaving only the two of them, entwined in passion. Timeless moments passed in which they explored each other's bodies. He knew a dozen ways to make her moan with pleasure, a dozen more to enhance the mounting tide of her fervor. His hand slid down between them to caress the place that burned so exquisitely for his touch. Now that she knew what awaited her, she rolled her hips against his in an effort to quench the fire.

When the tip of him probed her center, a shiver of keen readiness rippled through her. Yet still he teased her with kisses and caresses until her skin felt slick and hot and she lay panting beneath him. Only then did he enter her with a smooth, inexorable thrust.

A twinge of pain made her stiffen, her nails raking

down his back. Surely he was too large, too thick. But any discomfort swiftly faded away into a superb sense of fullness. Nothing in her experience could match the marvel of feeling him embedded so deeply inside herself. She closed her eyes and sighed, the better to savor the perfection of their joined bodies.

When she opened them again, Max was braced over her, his muscles taut as if to hold his passions in check. His eyes were dark, his lashes half lowered as he stared down at her. He bent his head to brush a warm, almost reverent kiss to her brow. *"Abby . . ."*

A fierce tenderness vibrated in his voice. Awash with emotion, she reached up to trace his beloved features. She couldn't have spoken at that moment, for her throat felt too taut. He completed her; they were meant to be together like this. It felt gloriously right to be ravished by him, as if this were the moment for which she had waited her entire life.

He began to move inside of her, drawing back slowly to her entrance, only to press inwardly again. The deep, steady friction of his actions carried her to breathless heights. All the while, he scattered kisses over her face and whispered rough endearments about her beauty, her perfection. His every utterance enhanced the mounting fire of her passion.

She arched her hips, finding the rhythm of his thrusts until it seemed they were one person, caught up in wild harmony. The enticing torment chased away all coherent thought. Instinctively, she wrapped her legs around his waist in an effort to become ever closer to him.

Uttering a low growl in his chest, he quickened his movements to a frenzied pace, driving into her harder, faster. Her breath came in labored gasps and his skin felt hot against hers, slick with sweat. Each thrust transported her higher on the climb to that indescribable pleasure . . .

And then she was there, falling into heaven, released into the radiant waves of paradise. In the midst of the ecstatic glow, she was aware of Max lunging into her one final time before his powerful body shuddered from the vigor of his release. Groaning her name, he settled over her and buried his face in the crook of her neck.

They lay entwined for a time as their breathing eased and their heartbeats returned to normal. Awash in pure happiness, she savored the feel of him still inside of her, though he was not as fully engorged as before. He seemed as if he'd fallen into a doze, and she could think of no more wonderful gift than to hold him like this.

By slow degrees, Abby grew aware of the chirping of the birds and the lapping of water. The whisper of a cool breeze against her exposed skin tugged her back to an awareness of their surroundings.

Her eyes snapped open. The dawn sky had brightened considerably. She could see leafy branches swaying overhead and the sunlit luster of the marble temple. The hard ground felt cold beneath her back.

Heaven help her. She and Max were sprawled naked in the grass by the lake. Outside in the open where anyone might come upon them.

Chapter 19

He drifted in a fog between wakefulness and slumber, too drained of strength to move or think. His every breath held the alluring scent of woman. And not just any woman. *Abby.*

His semiconscious state rejected any more lucid thought than that. It was so much finer to luxuriate in the feel of her body beneath him, to relish the pillow of soft breasts and the cradle of feminine hips. Those long legs had been wrapped around his waist in the throes of passion. Who would have thought she could be so damned seductive as to make him lose his mind? Or that such an amazingly sensual woman could be hidden beneath prickly primness—

Her hands rudely shook his shoulders. "Max! Get up! We mustn't tarry here any longer."

Yanked from his reverie, he raised his head and his chest clenched at the sight of Abby. Damp cinnamon hair feathered around her face and flowed downward to coil around her bare breasts. Her flushed skin and reddened lips gave testament to her well-satisfied state. Those expressive blue eyes stared up at him in urgent supplication.

In an effort to rise, she was squirming rather delightfully beneath him. Despite his sluggish state, his body made a valiant attempt to revive. It was surely impossible, yet he craved her again. That was when he noticed a fact that jerked him fully awake.

He had not withdrawn. He had spilled his seed inside of her. It was a reckless mistake he hadn't committed in years, not since he was a callow youth, and a courtesan had taught him that means of preventing the siring of illegitimate offspring.

"Max, are you even listening? Pray, move off me at once. We must hurry and get dressed."

He stared starkly at her for another instant before springing to his feet. He ran one hand through his mussed hair, while extending the other to pull her upright. She arose nimbly, a wealth of untidy locks cascading around her shoulders and down to her slender waist. Her wide-eyed gaze flicked over his naked body, then lowered demurely as she hastened around him, going to the neat pile of her clothing on the steps of the temple.

Realizing the source of her agitation, he found himself unexpectedly amused. "Why so shy all of a sudden? We're no different than Adam and Eve."

"Don't be absurd. Anyone might come upon us."

"Bah. It's just after dawn. The gardeners are still at their breakfast."

"Well, we had better not take that chance."

Watching her bend down to snatch the top garment, Max was certain he had never seen a lovelier sight. The early light painted her feminine curves with a pearly glow. As she straightened up to shake the wrinkles out of a spare shift, her shapely body held his attention. He mourned the prospect of her covering it again.

Several long strides took him straight to her. Reaching

underneath the curtain of her hair, he skimmed his hand down the smoothness of her spine and over the pert curve of her bottom.

She started, whirling around to face him. "Do stop! Really, Max, there's no time for us to . . . to . . ."

"Make love again?" Grinning, he dangled a dry oak leaf in front of her face. "You'll be pleased to know I was merely brushing off a few leaves and blades of grass."

A blush tinged her cheeks. "Oh. Thank you, then."

He found himself both charmed and irked by her reversion to modesty. Watching her pivot away to don the shift, he crumbled the dry leaf between his fingers. She wasn't like other women, who tended to spout praise for his prowess or tried to wheedle gifts out of him. He was exceedingly glad of that. He didn't need gushing commentary to know that Abby had enjoyed their coupling every bit as much as he had.

Yet she wasn't truly going to end this affair without making any demands on him, was she?

At the very least, he expected recriminations for stealing her maidenhood, perhaps tearful accusations that he'd seduced her, then a plea for the immediate posting of their wedding banns. But she didn't even seem inclined to scold him for tempting her into sin.

The fact of the matter was, he didn't know what the devil she was thinking at all. She had closed him out. It was as if now that she'd experienced the joys of sex, Abby no longer needed him.

She tugged a pale blue gown over her head, thrusting her arms through the cap sleeves and letting the hem fall to her feet, then discreetly adjusted the fabric over her bosom. Her hasty manner disgruntled him. Clearly, she couldn't wait to don the trappings of civilization and make her escape.

Smoothing her hands over the skirt, she frowned at him. "Max, for heaven's sake, your *clothes*," she said in a stern governess tone. "If we're found here like this, you'll be obliged to . . ."

"To offer for you, Abby?"

Her eyes fixed on him for a moment. They were big and blue and eloquent, and he cursed himself for bringing up the topic of matrimony. Why had he done so? He surely couldn't be considering . . .

She gave a brisk nod. "Yes, so do make haste. Not even the Duke of Rothwell could escape a leg shackle under such circumstances. My brothers would force you to the altar with a fowling piece loaded with buckshot. I'm quite certain that is the last predicament in which *you* would wish to find yourself!"

Her emphasis on the word *you* rubbed Max the wrong way.

Scowling, he snatched up his breeches, yanked them on, and buttoned the placket. He could have done without her unvarnished denunciation of his character. Especially since she had already told him a few days ago that his greatest accomplishment in life was seducing women. Did she really think him such a cad that he would abandon her?

Obviously, she did.

He shrugged away the fact that his dissolute reputation had never given her any reason to think otherwise. She ought to know he'd been racking his brain to find a way out of this dilemma. He hadn't, after all, *planned* to make love to her. For a man who prided himself on levelheadedness, this was new territory for him. What *was* he supposed to do now? He knew how to handle actresses and opera singers, randy widows and courtesans and a host of other experienced women. But never before had he seduced a virginal lady, let alone one whose past was so entangled with his.

Seeing Abby strain to fasten the back of her gown, he went to lend assistance. He pushed aside the silken heaviness of her hair, still damp from her swim, and started at the bottom of the long row of buttons.

"You needn't bother," she said over her shoulder. "I've done without a maid before, so I've become quite adept at buttoning myself."

His fingers paused on one of the tiny white buttons. "I see," he snapped. "You're so independent you'll refuse my help even with this?"

She halfway turned her head to give him a contrite look. "Oh, Max, I'm sorry. That was terribly abrupt, wasn't it? I only meant that you'll be wanting to start back to the house. It won't do for us to be seen walking in together."

Instead of mollifying him, her apology only further abraded his temper. He focused his attention on the buttons. As his fingers brushed the lovely curve of her waist, he found himself brooding over the prospect of never again having the right to touch her.

"It doesn't matter if we're seen together," he said testily. "I intend to marry you, of course."

The words slipped from his tongue. Max hadn't made a conscious decision to voice them. He hadn't thought ahead to the consequences of his actions at all. From the moment he'd spied her from the window, his brain had been addled by desire for her. Now, he suffered a moment's panic before he used logic to cudgel his emotions back into a box.

The fact was, he *had* to make her his wife. It was the only honorable choice of action for a gentleman in such a situation.

Abby stood motionless, her fingers frozen on the top

button of her gown. Then she slowly lowered her arms and turned to stare at him, one eyebrow lifted in a graceful arch. "You'll marry me *of course*? If that was a proposal, it was shoddily done."

"Forgive me, but surely you can see that wedlock is the only answer." He glided the backs of his fingers over the soft skin of her cheek. "I've ruined you, Abby. I owe you restitution for that."

Pursing her lips, she regarded him inscrutably, and he had the uneasy sense that he was handling this all wrong. Then she combed her fingers through her tangled hair and began to wind it into a loose coil atop her head. "You are prepared to give up all your other women, then?"

Her cool question knocked him off kilter. It was something he'd never even considered with any other female. Which was perhaps why he'd never spared a single thought for the topic of fidelity. In society, wives generally looked the other way when their husbands took mistresses.

"I see," she said, before he could articulate a reply. "Your hesitation tells me my answer. Well, I refuse your dictate. I believe that wedding vows are to be taken very seriously, and if you cannot promise to do the same, then we've nothing more to say on the matter."

Leaving his side, Abby glided to the steps of the temple. She leaned down to pick up a few pins, pushing them one by one into her hair to anchor the soft curls in place. In profile, she appeared serene and unruffled in contrast to his own agitated state.

Feeling as if he'd been poked by one of those pins, Max snatched up his shirt and dragged it over his head. She had rejected him, by God. She would not be his wife, after all. He ought to be relieved at his close escape, yet his gut churned, making him feel on the verge of exploding.

He stomped toward her. "You aren't thinking this

through," he said aggressively, stuffing his shirttails into the waistband of his breeches. "You can't just walk away and pretend that nothing happened between us."

"I'm not pretending any such thing. I enjoyed what we did together, Max. Very much so. It was truly a wonderful experience." Her eyes glowed in such a way that his heart leaped; then the light died as she glanced toward the path to the house. "But I mustn't linger here any longer. Your sister will be expecting me to breakfast with her."

"Not yet. We haven't settled certain . . . matters."

"Matters?" She cocked her head, her eyes narrowing. "I do hope you don't think to persuade me to continue our dalliance. That's impossible, you know."

"Of course I know! You needn't lecture me on how to treat a lady."

"Then what?"

She looked genuinely puzzled, and he thrust his fingers through his hair again. It was difficult for him to force out the words. "You're forgetting that there may be consequences. I might have impregnated you, Abby."

She caught her breath. Softness shone in her eyes as she slipped her hand down over her midsection. Then the radiance of emotion faded and she shook her head. "No. No, I don't believe that's very likely."

"How can you be certain?"

"Because . . ." Her cheeks turned a becoming shade of pink. "I've heard my sisters observe that a woman seems most likely to conceive at the midpoint between her monthly courses and, well, mine have just ended."

He certainly hoped she was right. Or did he? There was something curiously appealing about the fantasy of Abby suckling his son or daughter at her breast. He had to firm his jaw against a soppy smile.

Good God, had he gone completely mad?

Frowning moodily, he watched Abby lift her hem to slide her bare feet into a pair of dainty leather shoes. Even that simple action fascinated him. The sweet curve of her neck looked tempting enough to kiss. Now that he knew how beautiful and responsive she was underneath all those clothes, he wanted to turn back the clock and make love to her all over again.

But she was right, blast her. They must not indulge their lust anymore. Not ever again. It was over.

Unless she *was* with child. Would she marry him, then?

He caught hold of her shoulders. "You will promise to tell me at once if you do find yourself in a delicate condition."

"Yes," she murmured, "of course."

Time seemed suspended as they gazed at each other. He felt the need to say something profound. But the glib phrases he usually employed on parting from other women seemed all wrong. He couldn't think of how to frame the words to express his impossible wish to prolong their liaison.

All of a sudden, she smiled at him with heartfelt warmth. Arching up on tiptoe, she brushed a butterfly kiss over his lips. "Thank you, Max, for the finest birthday gift anyone has ever given me."

With that, Abby pulled away from him. She collected her wet towel and shift, then darted lightly up the path that led through the trees. Though he watched until she vanished into the woods, she did not look back.

A knot stuck in his throat as he paced to and fro along the shore of the lake. He felt obliged to allow her a head start of at least ten minutes. After all, she had been adamant about them not being seen together.

Max took umbrage at the thought. He was accustomed to being the one to walk away, the one to make the decisions and issue the orders. First and foremost, she ought to have accepted his proposal. Then he wouldn't have been left with this bedeviling sense of guilt and loss.

Maybe he'd handled the matter all wrong. Maybe she'd have been more receptive if he had dropped to one knee, clapped his hand to his heart, and declared—what? Undying love?

Not Abby. Surely not. She was too sensible, too mature, too prim to expect mawkish romance—though she'd been none of those things today. In his arms, she had become a giving, sensual, passionate woman.

Love is the most important part of a marriage.

Max stopped pacing. She'd said that to him two days ago, when they'd ridden to the glade. Was that the real reason she'd refused him, then? Because she believed him capable of feeling only lust for her?

Of course she would think so. She had judged him by his wicked reputation and expected nothing better of him. She scorned him as a man who would carry on affairs even while married. If only she knew, he could think of no other woman but her. He was obsessed with her, consumed by a hunger that transcended carnal passion.

It wasn't love, though. No. It couldn't be. He had put all that starry-eyed nonsense behind him long ago, after witnessing the destruction that love had wreaked on his father, a robust man who had ended up weak and broken.

Max sank down on one of the marble steps of the temple. Scrubbing his hands over his whiskered face, he sought a logical explanation for his inner turmoil. He was infatuated with Abby, certainly. He felt an uncommonly strong fondness for her because of their shared past.

That was all there was to it.

Yet, as he stared out over the lake, the truth dug its claws into his mind and refused to let go. Oh, hell, why deny it? He *was* in love with Abby.

And nothing in his life had ever shaken him so much.

Chapter 20

When the party set out after luncheon to visit the village of Rothcommon, Abby had a mask of serenity firmly in place. She smiled graciously, spoke only when addressed, and in general, adopted the modest demeanor expected of a governess. Tranquility was second nature to her, although today it was an act designed to hide the havoc in her heart.

The ducal coach conveyed the women, while the three gentlemen followed on horseback. Clad in their London finery, Lady Desmond and Mrs. Chalmers occupied the seat opposite Abby and the girls. Valerie kept up an exuberant chatter, exclaiming over their bonnets and gowns, soliciting fashion advice, and asking their recommendations about the best shops in London.

"I predict your debut season shall be a triumph," Mrs. Chalmers said with a good-humored smile. "Yours, too, Lady Gwendolyn, in a few years' time. You are both such lovely ladies that all the eligible young bachelors are bound to be vying for your attention."

Lady Gwen's eyes sparkled. "You must promise to write and tell me all about it, Valerie."

"Of course!" Valerie sighed dreamily, clasping her

hands to the bosom of her sage-green gown. "Oh, I can scarcely wait. How thrilling to think about being courted. Imagine if two gentlemen actually fought a duel over me!"

"Duels are outlawed," Lady Desmond said dampeningly. "Anyway, it would be of no use to you if one of your suitors was dead and the other forced to flee to the Continent."

"Well, I daresay it would be very exciting, anyway," Valerie asserted. "And extremely romantic, too! Don't you agree, Aunt Abby?"

"Perhaps that's a bit—"

"Oh, I shouldn't take the advice of your aunt on this matter," Lady Desmond cut in. "She is hardly an expert on London society. After all, she never even had a season."

Valerie's blue eyes widened. "Mama never told me that. Is it true, Aunt Abby? But why did you not make your debut?"

Conscious of being the subject of everyone's stare, Abby clasped her fingers in her lap. "I was busy caring for your grandmama and grandpapa, that's why. Sometimes, there are things in life more important than balls and parties."

"Hear, hear," Mrs. Chalmers murmured in a kindly tone. "You are to be commended for your devotion, Miss Linton."

Lady Desmond pursed her lips, and that sour expression spoiled the incomparable beauty of her face. A straw bonnet with cream ribbons covered her gold curls and framed her flawless features. The pale lilac crepe of her gown lent her an air of elegant refinement that made Abby feel drab in a sky-blue muslin that was three years outmoded.

It was a relief when the conversation turned to other matters. She disliked being the center of attention, especially today, when it was a struggle to keep an untroubled expression on her face. Lady Desmond had been particularly contrary, and Abby had intercepted more than one speculative glance from her.

She hoped that the intimate episode with Max wasn't somehow evident in her appearance. Having scrutinized her reflection in the mirror before departing, the only outward sign she had been able to discern was a faint pinkness to her cheeks left by his unshaven jaw.

Deep inside, however, Abby felt utterly changed, as if she'd been awakened after a long sleep. A vibrant glow suffused her body, although her heart was another matter entirely. She had known from the start that Max didn't love her, and she had encouraged his seduction without the slightest intention of coercing him to the altar. Nevertheless, when he had made his offer, his palpable reluctance had cut into her soul. It would have been better if he'd not been chivalrous at all, if he'd just gone on his merry way like the rogue that he was. Instead, the proposal had been issued in dictatorial fashion, his voice stern and detached.

I intend to marry you, of course.

For one weak moment, Abby had been sorely tempted to accept him. Max, whom she had loved forever, could finally be her husband. She could share his life, bear his children, enjoy that wonderful intimacy with him again. Unfortunately, it would also mean tolerating his penchant for other women. She would have to look the other way when he took mistresses. She would sleep alone on nights when he was out satisfying his lust elsewhere.

That repellent prospect had given her the strength to refuse him—and to hide her hurt behind an unruffled façade. At least she could be thankful she'd had the presence of mind not to turn maudlin on him. The very last response she wished to inspire in him was pity.

The coach drew to a stop in Rothcommon and the pas-

sengers stepped out onto the village green with its medieval stone cross covered in moss. Nearby, ducks swam in
a small pond beneath the spreading branches of an ancient
oak.

Abby strove not to stare as the gentlemen dismounted,
leaving their horses with a groom. From the corner of her
eye, she spied Max conversing with Lord Pettibone and
Lord Ambrose. Though she could not discern his words,
the mere sound of his deep baritone made her skin tingle.
He chuckled at something one of the others said as if he
hadn't a care in the world.

When the men ambled toward the group, she felt breathless from the wish that he would seek her out. They had
parted on good terms by the lake—she had made certain of that in order to prevent any awkwardness between
them.

Her heart fluttered as he glanced in her direction. Their
gazes met and held for an eloquent moment, and the buoy-
ancy of anticipation swelled within her bosom. He
stepped away from his friends as if to walk toward her.

Lady Desmond glided forward to catch his arm and
steal his attention. As she smiled winsomely at him, Max
returned the smile. They made a handsome couple, he so
tall and dashing and she so dainty and stylish. He leaned
down to murmur something that made Lady Desmond coo
and preen.

Abby's heart plummeted. For a man who had declared
the widow wasn't his mistress, he appeared perfectly enraptured by her company. There wasn't the least sign of
reluctance or aversion in his manner.

Perhaps it was nothing unusual for him to make love
to one woman in the morning and then flirt with another
in the afternoon. He must be relieved that Abby had let
him off the marital hook. And why should he prefer her

company, anyway? She was, after all, merely his sister's governess.

The party began to stroll along the high street, where the array of small shops included a haberdashery, a linen draper's, and the Fox and Hound Inn. On any other occasion, she would have enjoyed visiting with the merchants, all of whom she'd known practically since birth, including her friend Lizzie, who assisted at the bookshop owned by her scholarly husband.

At the moment, however, Abby felt a strong need to escape. Though it was her duty to chaperone Lady Gwen, Max was present to serve as a deterrent to any mischief. Surely she would not be missed for a short time.

She drew Valerie aside. "I intend to call on your uncle James and aunt Daphne at the parsonage. Would you care to accompany me?"

"Oh, no! I would vastly prefer to stay with Gwen. I promised to show her a length of mulberry ribbon that Mama and I spied at the draper's last week."

"Well, mind you don't chatter too much. I won't have His Grace thinking you poorly brought up."

"You needn't worry, Aunt Abby, I'll be perfectly well behaved. Nor shall I flirt with the duke as Mama wishes. He's far too *old*. Besides, he already has a particular liking for Lady Desmond." With that, Valerie skipped ahead to join Lord Ambrose and Lady Gwen.

Abby blew out a sigh. At least that was one benefit to Max's interest in the comely young widow. She could feel reasonably assured that her niece wouldn't make a cake of herself over him.

She turned her back on the others and went in the opposite direction, heading toward the other end of the village, where the spire of St. John the Baptist Church could be glimpsed through the trees. She hurried on past the stone roundhouse and the apothecary's cottage with its fragrant herb garden.

When she reached her destination, the iron gate squeaked beneath a push of her hand. The parsonage was a square edifice built of honey-colored stone and covered in ivy. A stand of leafy elm trees separated it from the ancient Norman church.

Going up the flagstone path, she could hear the shouts and squeals of children from the open windows. The familiar sounds were a balm to her battered heart. She had come here for the purpose of notifying her family that she would be returning home in a few days' time.

It was impossible for her to remain at the Court. As much as she'd grown to love Lady Gwendolyn, Abby could never continue as governess, knowing she would be obliged to see Max from time to time. Although she'd toyed earlier with the notion of convincing him to let her stay on, she knew now that he wouldn't relent. Not after the intimacy that they had shared. A man of his stature would never leave his innocent young sister in the care of a ruined woman.

It was simply not done.

Strangely, though, Abby didn't *feel* ruined. Far from it. Their remarkable union had made her feel whole for the first time in her life, as if she had finally found a missing part of herself. For that reason, she could never feel a particle of regret. She was fiercely glad to have shared such closeness with Max, even if it had left her now with a sense of loss. The melancholy that lodged in her heart would subside eventually, once he returned to London and she was spared the pain of seeing him anymore.

On that resolute thought, she raised her hand to knock on the front door. Before her knuckles could strike the white panel, however, the squeak of the garden gate sounded behind her. It was too early for the afternoon post. Perhaps a parishioner had come to see her brother in his capacity as vicar.

Curious, Abby glanced back over her shoulder. She froze, her hand in the air and her heart pounding, as she spied the man who strode briskly up the walk.

Max was the consummate gentleman in a coat of coffee-brown superfine and biscuit-colored breeches with glossy black boots. An immaculate white cravat set off his dark handsomeness to perfection. Her errant mind produced the carnal image of what he looked like beneath all that clothing, and it sparked a spontaneous flare of desire.

He swept off his beaver hat and inclined his head in a nod. "Abby," he said. "You're quite the fast walker. It's a wonder I caught up to you."

Aware that she was still poised to knock, Abby lowered her arm. Her legs felt so shaky that she deemed it best to skip the obligatory curtsy. Afraid he might guess her weakness for him, she put up her chin. "I expect you've come to scold me for shirking my duties."

"Not at all."

"Then why did you follow me?"

"Your niece said you were coming here to the parsonage. And it occurred to me that I've never met your brother James. When I granted him the living several years ago, the matter was handled by correspondence. I was hoping you would be kind enough to introduce us."

"I'm surprised you could pry yourself away from Lady Desmond's side."

"Ambrose was good enough to distract her on my behalf." In a featherlight touch, he ran the backs of his fingers down her cheek. "You're not jealous, are you? I told you she means nothing to me."

Scalded by his touch, Abby took a step backward. She

parted her lips to utter a tart denial, then realized that she *was* behaving like a woman scorned. But it wouldn't do to reveal the ravages of her heart. She had sworn to conduct herself in a calm, dignified manner around him. It was the only way for her to survive these next few days until he departed for good.

But sweet heaven, it was difficult to feign indifference when his gaze flicked to her mouth and he stood so close that a whiff of his male cologne brought back the exhilarating memory of lying naked in his arms. A pulse of longing throbbed in the place where they had been joined only a few short hours ago. The intensity in his gray eyes told her that he too remembered that rapturous pleasure.

Why, oh why, had he come after her? Did he truly wish to meet James, or was that just a flimsy excuse to pursue her for his own amusement? Max was, after all, a rogue. Perhaps he thought that she could be enticed into continuing their illicit flirtation.

She glanced up at the open window, where the peals of childish laughter rang out. "Jealousy has nothing to do with this," she said in a hushed tone. "Rather, I'm reminded of your fondness for a variety of women. And it seems I must reaffirm that there shall be no further . . . congress between us."

"You made that quite clear this morning."

"I warn you, when we are in the presence of my family, you must not make even the slightest reference to our . . . our . . ."

"Lovemaking?"

In spite of her resolve, she felt her cheeks heat. "Yes, and our past, too. Only my sister Rosalind knows of that, and I swore her to secrecy."

"I'll endeavor to be on my best behavior, then." Max leaned over Abby and rapped hard on the door. At the same time, he brought his head closer and murmured into her ear, "You may depend upon me, nymph."

The hint of teasing in his tone inspired a host of lascivious longings in Abby. Desire spiraled through her body and fizzed beneath her skin. She had been right to suspect him of trifling with her! And she mustn't feel so thrilled about it, either, for this was just an idle game to a man of his ilk.

But when she frowned up at him, he appeared aloof and haughty as befitting his exalted station. There was not so much as a twitch at the corner of his mouth or a gleam in those iron-gray eyes. He might have been a sober-minded judge who had never once strayed from the path of virtue.

She was still framing a suitable retort when the door swung open a crack. A small, ginger-haired boy with his shirt untucked stood in the narrow slit, a smear of what looked like plum jam on his freckled face. He craned his neck to gawk at Max before shifting his attention to her. A gap-toothed grin spread over his face.

"Aunt Abby!"

As he threw out his arms for a hug, she managed to turn his head to the side before the jam was transferred to her gown. She sank down to his level to rub at the sticky spot with her thumb. "My goodness, Bertie! I believe you've grown an inch this past fortnight."

"Nurse measured us, and I'm almost as tall as Prissy!" he bragged, naming his sister Priscilla, who was two years his senior.

"Indeed? That *is* remarkable. Now do stop wiggling."

Max handed Abby a folded handkerchief, which she accepted gratefully, using it to finish cleaning the boy's face. Arising, she glanced at Max and wondered what he would think of her family—or why it should even matter to her.

"Your Grace, if I may introduce my nephew, Herbert Linton, second oldest of my brother's four children. Bertie, kindly make your bow to the Duke of Rothwell."

Bertie bent over at the waist, one arm at his back, the other in front as Abby had drilled him. But she had never instructed him to thrust out his hand as he did now.

"I'm six. How old are you, sir?"

"Bertie! It isn't polite to ask someone their age."

"Why not? People are always asking *me*."

"A logical point," Max said as he leaned down to shake the boy's grubby paw. "I daresay some adults may not like it, though, so it's best to do as your aunt says. I, however, will admit to being one-and-thirty."

"Oh. Papa is seventy-three, and that's a great deal more, I think."

"Rather, your papa is seven-and-thirty," Abby corrected with a smile. "Now, the proper thing to do is to invite us inside. Then you must inform your papa and mama that they have visitors. And pray, do not run in the house."

Having thrown open the door and dashed off, Bertie checked himself in mid-scamper. He proceeded at a more sedate pace and vanished through a doorway. As Abby stepped into the foyer, she heard him shout for his mother.

"Well," she said on a laugh as Max closed the door and set his hat on a table, "it seems I must apologize for his manners."

"Don't be absurd, I was once a little rascal, too. Besides, he isn't your responsibility."

Abby parted her lips to object. But Max had a point. Though she loved her nieces and nephews as dearly as if they were her own, Bertie belonged to James and Daphne.

It struck her anew that she was unlikely ever to have children. She had refused the only marriage offer that she'd ever wanted. Perhaps if she accompanied her sister and

niece to London in the spring, she might meet someone
else . . .

Her tender heart rebelled at the notion. It was far too
soon to think of wedding another man after sharing such
intimacy with Max. The flame of longing for him burned
too deeply inside her. She couldn't imagine loving anyone
but him. Yet succumbing to the temptation to relent served
no purpose. Her decision was firm. She would not subject
herself to the pain and humiliation of a philandering husband.

She held out the slightly soiled handkerchief to him. "I
believe this is yours."

Taking her hand, he curled her fingers around the square
of linen. "Keep it. You always seem to be without one at
critical moments."

His tender grip beguiled her. So did the warmth in his
gray eyes. He did not release her, only gazed down at her
intently while her pulse skittered and her breath quickened.
Oh, heavens, she knew precisely how he'd charmed so
many women into his bed. She herself felt caught in the
throes of a powerful enchantment cast by the allure of his
masculinity.

In a gruff tone, he murmured, "Abby, I wish—"

The click of approaching footsteps shattered the spell.
Flustered, she stuffed the handkerchief into the pocket of
her gown. Untying the ribbons beneath her chin, she hung
her bonnet on the row of hooks on the wall just as her
sister-in-law hurried into the foyer.

Unlike the typical vicar's wife, Daphne dressed stylishly since her father owned the local draper's shop, and
she seemed always anxious to hide her common birth, as
well. Today she wore a gown of yellow-sprigged muslin
with a Belgian-lace cap on her sable hair. Her manner was
unusually frazzled, her brow furrowed.

"Abby, thank goodness you're here!" she said, rushing forward to offer a quick embrace. "Clifford and Lucille and Rosalind have come to call, Nurse is ill with a cold, and I am at my wit's end with the children! I was just now trying to shoo them outside to play in the garden, but they refuse to listen to me! Perhaps you'd be a dear and have a word with them, for they always heed what you say— *Oh!*" Her eyes widened on Max, who had been standing to one side, but now had stepped into her view. "Forgive me, sir, my son neglected to mention there was another visitor."

Abby performed the introductions and was amused to see her talkative sister-in-law stunned speechless for a moment. Daphne dropped into a curtsy worthy of obeisance to a king. "Your Grace, this is such an honor!"

As she arose, he offered his hand to assist her. "The honor is all mine, Mrs. Linton. And I must beg forgiveness for having arrived unannounced."

An explanation seemed in order, so Abby said, "A party of us came into the village for the afternoon, and the duke expressed a wish to meet James, so here we are. I'm afraid it was rather spur-of-the-moment."

"Perhaps this is a bad time for you?" Max asked their hostess, his manner perfectly correct, as if she were not goggling enraptured at him as women were wont to do. "I wouldn't wish to impose upon your hospitality."

Daphne recovered herself. "Impose? Why, certainly not, Your Grace! I'm sure that my husband will be anxious to make his bow to you. Do come with me."

Chapter 21

Following her sister-in-law down the narrow passage, Abby was intensely aware of Max's presence close behind her. She rued his intrusion on this visit when she had hoped to find comfort in the bosom of her family. At the same time, her mind was preoccupied with wondering what he had meant to say to her before Daphne's arrival had interrupted him.

Abby, I wish—

I wish I could kiss you senseless again.

I wish I could devote myself to you, and you alone.

I wish that you would change your mind and marry me.

Oh, botheration. It was best that she not speculate on his meaning. No doubt it had been just another charming bit of nonsense that would have tempted her excessively when she needed to remain strong.

They entered a parlor containing a clutter of comfortable old furnishings along with framed biblical scenes on the walls. Abby had always liked the informality of the small chamber, though she feared Max would find it sorely lacking compared to the splendor of Rothwell Court.

Nothing in his handsome features betrayed so much as

a smidgen of scorn, however, as Daphne blurted out his identity to the four people gathered in a cozy chat. "The Duke of Rothwell has come to call!"

Since her sister-in-law still looked bedazzled, Abby did the honors. "Your Grace, if I may present my brothers, Clifford and James, along with Clifford's wife, Lucille. I believe you've already made the acquaintance of my sister Rosalind, when she brought Valerie to visit Lady Gwendolyn."

Max was all charm and courtesy as he greeted the two gentlemen and two ladies. Clifford and James bowed before shaking Max's hand in turn, while the women curtsied to him. Rosalind and Lucille came forward to kiss Abby's cheek, though their admiring attention remained on the duke.

"It is indeed a pleasure, Your Grace," Clifford said jovially, as if he had not just been denouncing the Duke of Rothwell as an infamous libertine only a fortnight ago while forbidding Abby to work in his house. "I realize our acquaintance is only slight, but I have often considered our situation as close neighbors to be a singular honor."

"I'm afraid I've been an absentee landlord these past fifteen years," Max said. "I'm hoping to rectify that in the near future."

The bottom dropped out of Abby's stomach. Was he truly intending to spend more time at Rothwell Court? "You can't really mean that," she blurted out, then flushed as everyone turned to stare at her.

"Why would you question the word of our guest?" Clifford chided. "Pray, beg His Grace's pardon at once."

"That isn't necessary," Max said, his smile amiable. "One can hardly blame Miss Linton for being surprised. After all, I've been away for so long that most of the villagers wouldn't even recognize me. Perhaps, sir, you wouldn't mind if sometime I were to observe your methods of animal husbandry."

"It would be my pleasure," Clifford said, sufficiently distracted to cease glowering at Abby.

While the men talked, she gathered the shreds of her composure. The prospect of encountering Max in the village from time to time was both dismaying and appealing. But surely he was only making polite conversation since he was a man who craved the vices of the city.

Wasn't he?

"Perhaps you would join us in a glass of elder wine, Your Grace." James turned to add, "Abby, would you be so kind as to ask Nettie for another glass—or two, if you would like some?"

She dutifully went to the kitchen and procured the items from the harried maid, who was peeling carrots for dinner. Upon Abby's return, she found the men still chatting in a group. Max frowned slightly as she handed the wineglasses to her brother, and Abby wondered what had displeased him.

There was no opportunity to find out.

Just then, a dark-haired young girl came dashing into the room. She was screeching with laughter as Bertie chased after her with a wooden sword. Three-year-old Sarah brought up the rear, riding on a stick horse. They weaved around the chairs and tables, making such a racket that a sudden wailing issued from the cradle in a darkened corner of the room.

"Oh, no," Daphne moaned, rushing to the infant's side. "Freddie had just dropped off to sleep."

"Children!" James said sternly, pointing at the door. "Go out to the garden at once."

"But, Papa, I'm a knight hunting for dragons inside the

castle," Bertie protested. "If I leave, Princess Prissy will die!"

"It seems that you are trying to slay the princess, not the dragon," Abby observed. "Perhaps Prissy would be wise to go outside where there is more room for her to run from you."

Max strolled to the window and peered out at the walled garden. "The arbor would make a stout fortress, especially as it is surrounded by a moat of thorny rosebushes."

Eight-year-old Prissy appeared enchanted by the notion. "I claim the fortress as *mine*!" She dashed out the door with her dragon-slaying retinue trailing close at her heels.

Abby blinked at Max. A moat of thorny rosebushes? Where had a disreputable duke learned just how to appeal to a child's imagination? Even more puzzling, why had he bestirred himself to do so?

As he returned from the window to rejoin the others, she burned to ask him, but hesitated lest she betray any hint of familiarity with him in front of her family. Especially in light of her earlier outburst. Then Lucille spoke up, her eyes bright in her plump face. "I must compliment you, my lord duke, on your remarkable skill with children."

Max gave her a wry smile. "I grew up an only child until the age of sixteen. When I was very young, I would entertain myself with games of make-believe."

Ah, Abby thought, so that explained it. She felt a sudden softness to picture him as a little boy, playing all by himself in that great house. Why had he never told her about that? Although she'd encouraged him to talk when they were youths, he had always been reticent about his life at the Court.

Clifford waved everyone into seats, offering the best chair to their noble guest. He cast a grimace at the cradle in the corner, where Daphne was attempting to rock the fussy baby back to sleep. "Such a bothersome hue and cry!" he said. "I beg forgiveness, Your Grace, on behalf of my brother."

An anxious look drew down James's thin features as he poured the wine and handed a glass to Max. "Rather, I must be allowed to make my own apologies for the disruption, Your Grace. You see, Nurse awakened with a sore throat this morning, so I brought the cradle downstairs from the nursery. Poor Daphne has been contriving to keep the children entertained."

"Pray, do not concern yourself over such a trifling matter," Max said, his expression good-natured as he settled into his chair. "Especially as Miss Linton and I arrived in so unexpected a manner. However, I must inquire, can your maid not help out?"

"Unfortunately not," Daphne said from her stool beside the cradle. "You see, Nettie is far too clumsy a girl to trust with our dear Freddie."

"That is the trouble with servants," Rosalind added, looking smart in a gown of striped jonquil muslin, the few silver strands in her copper hair betraying her forty years. "They are either inept, or are forever falling ill at the most inconvenient times. I daresay Abby is the lucky one, not to have the headache of running a household or worrying about one's children."

"Yet our youngest sister has always had an uncanny way with infants," Clifford said. "Abby, do see if you might calm Freddie, so that His Grace need not be subjected to such incessant whimpering."

Daphne hopped up, barely hiding her relief to be set free from duty, and went to join the others, while Abby set down her wineglass and went to the corner. Instead of sitting, however, she picked up her crying nephew from his cradle. She cuddled his tiny swaddled form against her shoulder and gently patted his back.

As she walked to and fro to soothe him, his fretting began to subside. She had always loved the sweetness of a baby's face tucked into the curve of her neck. It never seemed a burden to comfort her nieces and nephews, for it was a gift to hold them close.

She was conscious of Max's keen glance at her as he discussed parish matters with James. "If there is anything that wants repair either here at the parsonage or at the church, you must not hesitate to send word to my man of business."

"That is most kind of you," James said with a grateful smile. "There is a matter of deathwatch beetles in the choir loft, but I'd hesitated to impose on you for such an expense."

"It's no trouble whatsoever. The church is under my jurisdiction, after all. I would be remiss in not funding its upkeep."

How was it that Max could speak in such a perfectly agreeable tone with her family, while looking askance at her from time to time? She didn't think that trace of disapproval was evident to anyone else, but she knew him well enough to notice it. Beneath all that civility, something seemed to be bothering him, and she could feel his censure as if he were glowering outright at her.

Of course, a woman holding a baby must be a novel sight to him. This morning, he'd appeared unnerved by the possibility that he might have gotten her with child. Perhaps his usual strumpets had some sort of illicit method of preventing pregnancy, and he disliked being reminded of Abby's lack of experience.

Well, she did not have to heed him. On the pretext of soothing Freddie, she went out into the corridor and proceeded into the small dining chamber with its cream walls and the russet draperies framing the open windows. She walked around the old-fashioned oak table in an effort to regain a sense of peace in holding the now-slumbering baby.

The quiet reprieve didn't last long, for Rosalind hurried through the doorway. "Where is Valerie?" she whispered.

"Visiting the shops with Lady Gwendolyn," Abby replied in the same hushed tone.

"Hmm. Could you not have contrived for her to accompany His Grace here? I've been counting on you to encourage a courtship between them."

"I warned you, Rosie, I would not participate in such a scheme. And Valerie agrees. She confessed to me today that she finds him to be too old."

Her niece also had noted his partiality to Lady Desmond. But Abby didn't care to mention that.

"Oh, rubbish," Rosalind murmured with feeling. "Many girls marry older gentlemen. She'll realize that when she has her come-out next spring."

"Perhaps, but I rather doubt it will matter. She seemed quite taken by the notion of entertaining a host of suitors closer to herself in age."

Rosalind gave her sister an assessing look. "I wonder if perhaps you yourself have designs on the duke."

Fighting a blush, Abby glanced down at the sleeping baby. "Designs? Don't be absurd."

"I noticed His Grace watching you just now. It was covert, to be sure, but I've been in society long enough to recognize these things. So tell me the truth, has he rekindled the romance you two shared years ago?"

Abby hesitated, then decided it would be best not to deny it. Especially as she had a burning question to ask Rosalind. "Yes, though I very much doubt it will come to anything. But I was wondering about something. Are you quite certain that you forwarded the letters that I wrote to him all those years ago?"

"Absolutely! I myself made sure they were properly franked. They were addressed to Rothwell House in Grosvenor Square." Rosalind's eyebrows arched in curiosity. "Do you mean to say that he never received them?"

"I'm afraid he did not."

"Abby, I'm so very sorry! But it wasn't my fault, I assure you! What do you suppose could have happened? Might his father have taken them?"

"I don't know—and likely will never know. But his letters to me vanished as well, and so we each thought the other had lost interest. Oh, you needn't look so tragic, Rosie. It happened a very long time ago."

"But it *is* tragic. If you'd kept up the correspondence, Rothwell might have offered for you when he came of age." The warmth of sincerity on her face, Rosalind stepped closer to place her hand on Abby's shoulder. "I know I've pinned my hopes on Valerie, but believe me, dear sister, I never would have done so had I known you still harbored feelings for him. And I would be every bit as happy if *you* were to marry him!"

Abby's eyes misted. There was no support as comforting as a sister's when one's spirits were low. But she could only imagine Rosalind's shock if she were to learn that only a few hours ago, Abby had turned down the chance to become the Duchess of Rothwell. That must remain her secret.

"He's a rakehell who has no true interest in matrimony," she said firmly. "Nor have I any interest in having a libertine as a husband."

"Oh, bosh. Many gentlemen sow their wild oats, then settle down when they fall in love. My Peter certainly did.

Now, perhaps we should rejoin the others, for we must not deny Rothwell his chance to steal admiring glances at you. I do believe he might be more than a little in love with you already!"

Abby had to smile at that outrageous statement. She didn't have the heart to tell her sister that Max viewed *love* as a romanticized term for lust.

He stood up as they entered the parlor. "Ah, here are your sisters. And just in time for a toast."

Clifford and James rose to their feet, too, though they appeared mystified by his intention. James made haste to refill everyone's glasses, while Abby went to place Freddie back in his cradle. The infant stirred a little and wiggled his bottom before settling back into slumber.

When she turned around, the others were waiting, their inquisitive eyes on Max. He commanded attention by his very presence, she noted, for he had an air of authority that put people in awe of him. She could not help but admire the change from his awkward, sometimes sullen youth. In the intervening years, he had acquired a cool self-possession as befitting his exalted rank, and she felt a bit in awe herself.

A slight smile on his lips, he lifted his glass. "I wish to propose a toast to your sister, Miss Abigail Linton, on this occasion of her birthday."

The room fell quiet except for the sounds of childish laughter drifting from the garden. Abby stood motionless as everyone's attention shifted to her. It was eminently clear that the significance of the calendar date had come as a surprise to them.

She had never expected them to remember. As the youngest, she hadn't had the opportunity to celebrate many birthdays with her much older brothers and sisters. For most of her youth, they had been grown and gone, living elsewhere with families of their own. In recent years, the day had been observed quietly with only her parents.

The faces of her siblings and their spouses reflected a series of emotions: consternation, chagrin, guilt. Then a babble of comments spilled forth.

"You might have said something," Clifford blustered.

"How dreadful that it slipped my mind," Rosalind said.

"We should have planned a party for you," Lucille fretted.

"Pray forgive us, dear sister," James added.

Their manner apologetic, they crowded around Abby to kiss her cheek, to offer a hug, to wish her all the happiness in the world. She knew they loved her, and so she accepted their remorse with a certain discomfiture. She would never have chosen to mortify them over such a trifling matter.

This was Max's doing.

Her gaze flashed to him as he stood by the hearth. He looked smugly pleased by the upheaval he'd wrought. As if he had just done her a great favor instead of causing distress to those who were most dear to her in all the world.

As they left the parsonage, Max tried to fathom Abby's coolness toward him. He could see that she was in high dudgeon. Her chin was elevated, her lips firmed, her brow slightly furrowed. She hadn't approved of him toasting her birthday, and it baffled him as to why.

Until that moment, her family had been taking advantage of her good nature, begging her to discipline their children, dispatching her to the kitchen to fetch wineglasses, ordering her to soothe the baby. As if it were her duty to serve their demands. She had done it all with admirable serenity, while he had bitten his tongue to keep from rebuking the lot of them in no uncertain terms.

The birthday reminder had been a civil way to accomplish his purpose.

The wrought-iron gate squeaked as he opened it. He let her pass through ahead of him, and as he stepped out beside her, Max offered his arm. She hesitated, glancing up at him rather irritably, her eyes big and blue.

"I realize you're angry with me," he said, "but I hope not so much that you'll refuse even a simple courtesy."

Abby slipped her hand into the crook of his elbow. As they began strolling down the street, she said, "I'm irked, yes. You ought not to have embarrassed my family like that."

"They deserve to be ashamed. They were fawning over me, while chiding you like a child and expecting you to attend to their every need. You're not their servant, Abby."

"Of course I'm not! I was helping out as I always do. Perhaps you can't understand it, but I enjoy taking care of my nieces and nephews. We're family, and that is what family members do for one another."

"I saw no one doing anything for you, though, not even on your birthday. They didn't even remember the date. You should have been visiting with the rest of us instead of shouldering someone else's responsibilities."

She bristled. "Daphne was at her wit's end. Would you have me refuse to lend assistance?"

"Not necessarily. However, Rosalind or Lucille might have offered their services, too. Especially as you have been separated from your family this past fortnight and would have enjoyed the opportunity to talk with everyone."

"That's precisely why I *didn't* mind. I haven't had the chance to hold Freddie in weeks!"

Seeking to smooth her ruffled feathers, he placed his hand firmly over hers. "Assure me, then, that you've never felt misused. That they've never assumed you to be at their beck and call." When her gaze faltered, he took a stab in the dark. "Isn't that the real reason why you left home to become a governess? Because you felt ill-treated and un-appreciated?"

Within the frame of her straw bonnet, her eyes glinted with strong emotion. Her lips parted as if to hurl an invec-tive at him. Then she huffed out a breath and glanced away for a moment. "If you must know, then yes. The last straw was at Freddie's christening . . ."

They had reached the village green. Max stopped be-neath the shade of an oak tree and turned her to face him. He wanted badly to caress her cheek, pull her into his arms, and kiss away her troubles, but he didn't dare do so out in the open where anyone might see them.

He held her hand instead, contenting himself with rub-bing his thumb over her palm. "Will you tell me about it?"

Gazing at him, she nodded. "On that day, they were dis-agreeing about where I should live now that Mama and Papa were gone. Clifford wanted me to remain at Linton House as a companion for Lucille and to be close enough to help James and Daphne. Rosalind requested that I accompany her back to Kent to prepare for Valerie's de-but, and Mary—my oldest sister—wished to claim my ser-vices in Suffolk, to watch her twin grandsons while their parents traveled abroad."

"I would venture to guess they didn't ask your opinion on where *you* preferred to live."

She rewarded him with a wry smile. "No, and I had a strong aversion to becoming the old maiden aunt, shuttled from household to household. I'd heard that Miss Her-rington had left unexpectedly, so I told them that I in-tended to apply for the post of governess. They tried to talk me out of it, but I was determined to make a life of my own choosing."

His chest tightened with the fierce desire for her to choose him. "Abby, I won't apologize for having made that toast today. I wanted to right a wrong. To see you celebrated as you richly deserve."

"Yes, I realize now that you meant well." Her eyes were soft with a luminosity that lit up her whole face and made it difficult for him to breathe. Yet the radiance faded as swiftly as it had appeared. "Nevertheless, you must understand, Max, that it really isn't your place to look after me."

Her words gutted him. They were a galling reminder that Abby had refused his offer of marriage. She would sooner be her family's unpaid servant than take her place at his side as his duchess. How could he blame her? He was the one with the hedonistic past, the one who hadn't known in an instant whether or not he could remain faithful to wedding vows.

Now that it was too late, Max knew he'd renounce every vice if only she would love him. He'd never look at another woman for as long as he lived. Yet he could see no way, short of joining a monastery, to convince her of that.

What was he to do now?

It chilled him to imagine ending up a broken man like his father, weeping over a woman who had crushed his soul. God Almighty! No wonder he'd avoided entanglements for so many years.

All love accomplished was to tie a man into knots.

Chapter 22

By design, Abby was nearly tardy for dinner that evening. She reached the drawing room just as Finchley arrived to summon everyone to the table. Max subjected her to a brooding glance, but there was no time for conversation. He already had Lady Desmond on his arm as they led the way, followed by Lord Pettibone and Mrs. Chalmers. Lord Ambrose gave Abby a rueful grin as he escorted Valerie on one arm and Lady Gwen on the other.

Since Lady Hester also hurried in late, Abby joined Max's aunt. She was perfectly content to take up the rear. It was part of her plan to survive the next few days with her heart intact.

At dinner, she played the role of the modest governess and kept her attention on the courses of braised chicken pie, roasted pheasant, and raspberry cream cake. Out of the corner of her eye, she saw Max look in her direction a number of times, but she pretended not to notice. To have unburdened herself to him about her family had felt good, yet it could not alter the fact that it was a dangerous folly to love a man to whom fidelity was a foreign concept.

Despite his claim that he had no interest in Lady

Desmond, he spent ample time in her company. She sat in the honored spot to his right and monopolized his attention. And if he appeared to be somewhat grim of feature tonight, well, Abby refused to speculate on the source of his ill humor.

The conversation centered around the prizefight scheduled for midday on the morrow. The London party had a lively discussion about the strengths of Goliath in comparison to those they'd heard about his celebrated opponent from the wilderness of America, Wolfman. The ladies appeared to anticipate the brutal spectacle as avidly as the men.

The girls listened with wide-eyed interest. Seated side by side, they whispered to each other. Then Valerie said on a sigh, "How exciting it all sounds! Perhaps Gwen and I might attend if we watch from the rear and Lord Ambrose agrees to protect us."

Lord Ambrose chuckled. "Oho, don't pull me into your scheme, minx."

His face stern, Max set down his wine goblet. "I've already made it clear that such a mill is no place for young ladies. There will be a throng of unsavory ruffians and rowdy gentlemen, none of whom are suitable company for a pair of sheltered girls."

"What if we promise to be very discreet?" Lady Gwen said earnestly.

"No. It's out of the question. You and Miss Perkins shall remain here with Miss Linton, and that is final."

The girls lapsed into crestfallen silence, though it didn't seem to dampen their spirits overall. Once dinner was over, and the men remained to drink their port while the ladies withdrew to the drawing room, Valerie and Lady Gwen retreated to a private corner to giggle and murmur together.

Abby tried to keep her mind on the chatter between the other two women. Lady Desmond engaged Mrs. Chalmers with a stream of titillating gossip about people in society that Abby didn't know. She felt like a bumpkin, and judging by the sly looks from Lady Desmond, that appeared to be the intent. It was a blatant reminder that Abby was not one of the haute ton.

Nevertheless, she prevailed with a resolute smile that didn't falter even when Max returned with the other gentlemen. The intimate joy they'd shared that morning seemed now like only a lovely dream. As he veered toward Abby, Lady Desmond intervened, tugging him into the group of his London friends.

It was all for the best, Abby told herself. Nothing could be more foolish than to pine for him. Holding firm to her resolve, she informed the girls it was time for the three of them to retire for the evening.

As they left the drawing room, her wayward gaze sought out Max, only to find him watching her. The burning intensity in his eyes seemed to touch her very soul. And her imprudent heart fell in love with him all over again.

The following morning, Abby and her two charges trooped down to the stable yard to watch the party set out for the prizefight. Garbed in elegant finery, Lady Desmond and Mrs. Chalmers rode in an open curricle, with Lord Ambrose and Lord Pettibone beside them on horseback. Max, Goliath, and the trainer climbed into the black ducal coach, presumably to talk strategy during the twelve-mile drive to the site of the match.

It was a blessing that Max would be gone for most of the day, Abby reflected. She could not so much as look at him without hungering to feel his arms around her and his lips on hers. His mere presence was enough to weaken her decision to put an end to their illicit romance.

Valerie and Lady Gwen waved a wistful good-bye, heaving dramatic sighs as the party disappeared from sight. "I'm sorry you weren't allowed to accompany them," Abby said. "I know it must be a disappointment."

"We shall be fine, Auntie," Valerie said nobly. "You are not to worry about us. We'll recover by going for a very long ride."

"The longer, the better," Lady Gwen added, "for it will distract our minds from our anguish."

The girls didn't look particularly anguished, however, as they exchanged a bright-eyed glance before dashing into the stables to fetch their mounts. They were soon on their way with a groom following close behind.

Left to her own company, Abby strolled down a wooded path, as she'd fallen into the habit of doing each morning. She would never have admitted it aloud, but she felt as cheated as the girls at being denied the chance to participate in the exciting event. What an adventure it might have been, to view such a contest! Well, to be honest with herself, perhaps it was not so much the bare-knuckle boxing that lured her as it was the chance to have a glimpse into Max's world. She had a great curiosity to see him in his element, and it was frustrating to be forced to miss the opportunity.

When she returned from her walk over an hour later, the stables had a deserted air. No shouts or cheers came from the area behind the buildings where Goliath had been training for the past week. No one was exercising horses in the paddock, either, for Max had required most of the grooms to accompany his party to the fight.

Seeing that Valerie's gray kitten was stalking a butterfly, Abby picked up the ball of fluff for a quick cuddle before releasing him again. Scamp darted off into the grasses to chase Caramel, and the two kittens engaged in a friendly tussle.

Abby rested her arms on the paddock fence and gazed out over the expanse of green lawn toward the lake. She usually relished having time to herself, for idleness had been a rare commodity in her life. But today nothing could settle her restless mind. She felt caught in a thorny tangle of doubts.

Had she made the right choice in refusing Max? Should she have accepted his offer, despite the reluctance with which it had been issued, and been grateful for whatever crumbs of affection he threw her way? He might never truly love her, but it was clear that he was fond of her at least. He would not have followed her to the parsonage otherwise. Nor would he have shown an interest in her family—or made that toast in honor of her birthday.

Yet when they'd rejoined the others in the village yesterday, he had gravitated toward Lady Desmond. The woman had been miffed by his abandonment, and Abby wanted to believe he'd only been trying to avert a scene. But why fool herself? She had given him a set-down, telling him in no uncertain terms that it wasn't his duty to look after her. She mustn't regret it, either. There could never be a future for them. He had a weakness for seducing women, and that was the one foible she could not abide.

Her gaze strayed to the splendor of Rothwell Court with its honey-stone walls and tall windows, the slate roof and many chimneys gleaming in the sunlight. It struck Abby that she might have been mistress of this magnificent house. Yet she would trade it all for a thatch-roofed cottage if only Max could love her—and her alone.

Just then, she spied a man leading a horse over a low rise beyond the gardens. She recognized his bandy-legged gait. It was Dawkins, the groom who had ridden out with Lady Gwen and Valerie.

He was alone now.

Struck by alarm, Abby clutched her skirts and hastened toward him. Something had to be wrong. Upon drawing closer, she noticed that the big bay was limping.

"What's happened? Where are the young ladies?"

Pulling off his cap, Dawkins bobbed his balding head, his lined face drawn with shame. He could barely meet her eyes. "Gone, miss. I tried t' chase after 'em, but me horse went lame."

"Gone? What do you mean?"

"Miss Perkins said they was havin' a race, an' I mustn't try t' follow 'em. As if I'd disobey the duke's order t' watch her ladyship! But when I galloped in pursuit, Sultan threw a shoe. I hollered fer 'em t' stop, but they mustn't have heard me." Dawkins added gloomily, "His Grace'll have me head fer this."

"In which direction were they going?"

Dawkins jerked his thumb behind him. "East, miss. Near the Haslemere road."

Her thoughts in a whirl, Abby walked alongside him as he led Sultan toward the stables. A race, indeed! Valerie would earn herself a severe scolding for such an act of recklessness! Or was it perhaps more than just an irresponsible prank?

She didn't want to even consider the shocking notion that sprang into her mind. But the moment it entered her head, she feared with a sinking certainty that it was true.

The best riding paths on the estate went around the lake and through the woods to the west, where her family's lands lay. There could be no reason for Valerie and Lady Gwen to head toward the east.

Unless they intended to sneak into the prizefight.

In escalating dismay, Abby pieced together the scraps of memory. Their keen interest at dinner the previous evening in attending the match. Their whispered conversations in the drawing room, and again this morning, when they'd stopped talking the moment she'd stepped into Lady Gwendolyn's bedchamber. The animated glances they'd exchanged while bidding farewell to the London party.

It all seemed so obvious now. Valerie had even had the audacity to warn Abby that they were going on a very long ride and she was not to worry.

A sick sensation squeezed her stomach. Dear God, her niece must have dreamed up this foolhardy scheme. Lady Gwen was too well behaved to disobey Max of her own accord. And the real fault, Abby knew, lay with herself. If she hadn't been so preoccupied with her romantic troubles, she might have noticed their conspiratorial air.

Max would be furious that Valerie had led his sister astray. He would be entirely justified in his wrath, too. If Lady Gwen came to harm, Abby would never forgive herself. Even if they didn't fall into the clutches of some ruffian, an innocent young lady could taint her reputation simply by being seen at such a raucous event.

Her mind in a flurry, she watched as Dawkins led the bay into the paddock. Was there any chance that she could catch up to the girls before Max found out? She had to try at least. But the only feasible way to do so was on horseback.

A chill prickled her spine, but she didn't give herself time to think. "Will you be so kind as to saddle the fastest horse for me? I intend to go after Lady Gwen and Miss Perkins."

"Ain't none left, miss, what w' the Londoners, the young ladies gone, and now Sultan turnin' lame. I might've harnessed the gig fer ye, but the duke sent it t' Mr. Beech this mornin'." Shaking his head, Dawkins heaved a mournful sigh. "Back in the old duke's day, every stall here was filled. A fine stable he kept, never less than a dozen o' the best hunters! As well, there was the prettiest set of dapple-gray steppers fer the duchess's carriage—"

"You can't mean to say there isn't a single horse left in the entire stable!"

"Well, now, there's Brimstone. But he's a big un and only the master rides him."

Her legs quivered. Her palms turned icy. But the consequences of doing nothing were so dire that Abby swallowed hard and said, "Pray saddle him for me at once."

"Beggin' yer pardon, miss, but I'll do no such thing! He's too spry fer a lady. Ye'll break yer neck. An' then the duke'll break mine!"

She lifted her chin. "You may set your mind at ease on the matter. I've ridden Brimstone before. I did so with Rothwell's permission, too. So you will do as I say, or upon the duke's return he will be most displeased to learn that you stopped me from finding his sister!"

Dawkins goggled at her for a moment; then he hastened to the tack room to fetch the saddle. She breathed a prayer of thanks that the groom had swallowed that outrageous half-truth. He needn't know that Max had hauled her up onto the great black horse entirely against her will. Or that she'd needed the duke's close proximity to ward off her fears.

In short order, Dawkins had the saddle on Brimstone. Abby had been pacing, and as he led the restive beast to the mounting block, it took all of her fortitude just to walk the few steps to the horse. When she stroked the animal's silken mane, he tossed his head in displeasure.

"He ain't used t' the sidesaddle," the groom warned, giving Abby a worried frown. "Mind ye keep a firm hand on him, miss. Give him half an inch, and he'll send ye flyin'."

Memory thrust her backward in time to see her mother tumbling off Buttercup with a hard thud and then lying on the grass. The scene was so vivid that her resolve very nearly withered. She blinked the awful vision away and clenched her teeth to keep them from chattering.

Gripping the pommel, Abby hoisted herself into the saddle. She owned no riding habit, but she was too intent on leashing her fears to trifle over the shocking display of her stockinged legs revealed from mid-calf downward.

Brimstone shied and danced at the unfamiliar weight of her. No sooner had she gripped the reins than she caught one last glimpse of Dawkins's anxious face before the animal took off at a trot with nary a signal from her.

Unprepared for the quick start, she hung on for dear life. The paddock streamed past and then Brimstone was cantering down the path toward the lake, huffing and snorting like a fiend from the depths of Hades.

A dizzying panic paralyzed Abby. Her heart thudded as fast as the horse's hoofbeats. What had she been thinking? This was madness. Death surely would strike her at any moment!

Then the animal slowed and his powerful muscles bunched beneath her. As she realized his intention, a cry lodged in her throat. She had a split second in which to brace herself before he reared, his front legs pawing the air.

By some miracle, she managed to maintain her seat. In the midst of the fog of fright, instinct took control of her reactions. She drew firmly on the reins to let him know who was in charge.

With a thud, his hooves hit the ground again. He took off like a shot with her still clinging to the saddle. All of the equine knowledge that she had repressed for so many years came flooding back into her mind. She knew intuitively how to get him under control with a deft tug of the leather ribbons. He was heading the wrong way, and she decisively turned him in an easterly direction.

Max had reminded her that horses could sense a rider's emotions, and she took several deep breaths to calm her wild heartbeat. Brimstone was still chomping at the bit. Perceiving that a neck-or-nothing gallop across the meadow would allow him to release his pent-up energy, she leaned low over his neck and gave the animal his head. After a mile or so of sprinting, he began to slow considerably, settling into a steady canter.

Her tension began to abate as she rediscovered the pleasure of riding. Relaxation permeated her limbs. For the first time in many years, Abby enjoyed the rush of the wind against her face. A long-lost sense of freedom eddied through her, and she found her confidence building and her spirits brightening. She could scarcely wait to tell Max that he'd been right to encourage her to overcome her nervousness.

Not that he would offer praise.

Today, he was far more likely to flay her with a severe tongue-lashing. He'd be furious that she'd ridden Brimstone. Worse, he'd never forgive her for failing to notice that his sister was being lured into danger by Abby's niece. The sobering prospect made her spur Brimstone onward.

Drawing on her knowledge of the countryside, she took a shortcut through a spinney that would pare a few minutes off the journey. Within half an hour, she arrived in the village where the match was to be fought. It proved easy to locate the site. She simply followed the large number of country folk pouring over hedges and ditches to a large, open field.

An enormous canvas tent had been erected near a stand of ancient oaks.

The surrounding area was jammed with carriages, carts, and gigs. Grooms lounged here and there, and a few were trying to peek under the canvas, only to be chased away by officials. A rumble of excited voices emanated from inside the tent.

Leery of testing Brimstone's reaction to the crowd, she reined to a halt beyond the outer fringes of the gathering. She gingerly slid down and secured the reins to a stout sapling. The hard ride had settled Brimstone. After a few desultory tosses of his glossy black mane, he lowered his head to crop a patch of grass.

Grateful to have arrived in one piece, Abby shook out her crumpled gown and stuffed a few wind-whipped strands of hair back into her bonnet. Then she made haste toward the tent, zigzagging a path through the congestion of vehicles.

Never in her life had she prayed more fervently that she was wrong. That the girls had not come here, after all. That they had merely gone for a ride and she had leaped to the wrong conclusion. In such an instance, she would be extremely happy to return to Rothwell Court with no one the wiser.

Just then, however, she noticed a pair of horses tethered to a tree. One was Lady Gwendolyn's gray mare, Pixie. The other was Valerie's chestnut gelding.

Chapter 23

When Abby approached the flap of the tent, a hulking brute barred her way. He had the build of a fighter beneath his rough garb, and a hard-nosed face with beady black eyes. "Shilling," he said, thrusting out a grubby paw.

She blinked at him in consternation. It had never occurred to her that there might be an entry fee. "I'm afraid I haven't any money."

"Then away wid ye."

He reached past her to snatch a coin from the man behind her, who quickly ducked into the tent. Other late arrivals crowded her from the rear, shoving and grumbling at her to move out of the way, that the match was about to begin.

She would not allow herself to be turned off. Not after that bruising ride. And certainly not with Valerie and Lady Gwen somewhere inside, mingling with the boisterous crowd.

Lifting her chin, Abby fixed the man with a regal glare. "I've come from His Grace of Rothwell's house with an urgent message. The duke will be extremely displeased if you prevent me from delivering it."

The brute's flinty expression eased in a twinkling. He bobbed his head in a respectful bow. "Ah, well! Ye might've said so! Go on in!"

In a moment, Abby found herself ensnared in a mass of teeming, catcalling, shouting humanity. The rowdy eagerness of the mob was palpable in the close air. Mostly men, they were farmers and merchants and gentlemen intermingling with shadier characters. The few females she spotted were the bawdy sort with whom no lady would associate.

The task she faced was daunting. How was she ever to find the girls in this swarm?

Deciding to make a circuit of the tent, Abby squeezed her way through the throng, earning herself a few elbows and trying not to breathe too deeply of the scent of unwashed bodies. Luckily, no one paid any heed to her. Everyone's attention was trained on the ring in the center of the tent.

All of a sudden, a great cheer arose from the horde. The wave of sound nearly deafened her. Peering through the shifting sea of people, Abby caught sight of Goliath stepping into the ring.

A huge greatcoat swathed his hulking form. With a dramatic flair, he flung off the garment to reveal his massive, bare chest. Wearing only a pair of breeches, he flexed his bulging muscles, strutting around the ring like a cock of the walk. Another thunderous ovation swept the tent. Men clapped and stomped their feet for England's champion.

The roar died down as his opponent came into view, and Abby had her first sight of an American frontiersman. In stark contrast to Goliath's theatrical manner, Wolfman made no attempt to engage the crowd. He merely dropped his fur cloak into the arms of a handler in a corner of the ring. His face was impassive. Although taller than his

opponent, he was not quite as broad of chest, yet he radiated a lithe, sinewy strength.

Riveted, Abby had to tear her gaze away in order to resume the hunt. It wouldn't do to let herself be distracted
when time was of the essence. Better she should search for
Lady Gwen's sky-blue riding habit, and Valerie in burgundy. But neither of those colors could be seen in the
masses of people.

Hoping to gain a clearer view near the front, she edged
her way through the tightly packed gathering. She lost
count of the number of times she said *pardon me* with an
ingrained politeness that was lost to the noise inside the
tent. When at last she wriggled her way closer to the open
center, she spied the London party.

A rope had been strung between four stakes to mark off
the dirt-packed arena. Beyond it, on the far side, a special
viewing area was occupied by members of the gentry,
mostly dapper gentlemen. Abby didn't recognize any of
them except for Lord Pettibone and Lord Ambrose, who
were in the company of Mrs. Chalmers and Lady Desmond. They were laughing and chatting while waiting for
the fight to begin.

A short distance away, Max stood in his shirtsleeves in
a corner of the ring. He didn't appear to notice his friends
or the surrounding multitudes. His entire attention was focused on the pugilists. Lifting his hand, he signaled to
another man, who promptly rang a bell.

The two rivals stepped to a line scratched down the center and shook hands. Without further ado, Goliath flew at
his adversary in a flurry of blows. The frontiersman leaped
to the side and landed a hard hit to Goliath's jaw that
sent him staggering backward. The champion caught his
balance and barreled forward again like a raging bull.
Wolfman was soon bleeding down one side of his face,

while drawing blood himself with lightning strikes on Goliath that inspired a series of collective gasps from the onlookers.

Abby took advantage of everyone's preoccupation to steal closer and scan the assemblage. It was then that she spotted the girls.

They were standing behind the gentry and near the back wall of the tent. They seemed to be quarreling. Abby's niece was trying to pull Lady Gwen's arm, but the girl emphatically shook her head. Her face looked pale and scared. Valerie then moved forward alone, as if determined to work her way up to the front where Max's friends stood.

Of all the reckless nonsense!

Abby plunged through the horde in an effort to reach the other side of the ring before it was too late. Crude curses rang in her ears. Men growled and snapped at her, but most let her through. She had to catch Valerie before any of the London party spotted her. Then there might yet be a chance to spirit her and Lady Gwen out of the tent before Max caught sight of them.

Luckily, his full attention was concentrated on the boxers. Goliath was swinging his fists like twin sledgehammers. All of a sudden, he landed a blow that sent Wolfman crumpling to the ground. The crowd let out loud bellows of delight.

Max strode forward to count over the fallen man, who seemed a lifeless lump of flesh and bone. Yet in the next moment, he sat up and sprang lightly to his feet again, and the fight resumed with as much ferocity as before.

In that moment of distraction, Abby lost sight of her quarry. She couldn't see Valerie anymore, and could only surmise that the tight cluster of cheering gentlemen barred her from view.

Abby inched her way forward until she had nearly

reached Max's friends. Thankfully, their avid attention was on the match, giving her time to scan the throng behind them. It was critical to escape detection. By keeping her face averted, she hoped the brim of her bonnet would hide her features.

She had ventured so close to the ring that the thud of every blow assaulted her ears. The grunts of the combatants underlay the roar of the assembly. Suddenly, her heart leaped.

There!

She spied Valerie squeezing between two gentlemen who were shouting with great gusto at the boxers. They stepped aside upon seeing the young lady, ogling her for a moment before returning their attention to the ring.

Her niece's strawberry-blond curls and pert features were framed by a bonnet of chip straw with a cluster of burgundy flowers. The girl froze in place. Her blue eyes rounded on her aunt.

Then Abby suffered a shock that pulled her attention away from her niece. Lady Elise had appeared directly beside her.

"You!" the woman snapped. "What are *you* doing here?"

Abby drew a sharp breath. Her stupefied mind scrambled for a reason to explain her presence at the prizefight. If only Valerie had the sense to make a quick retreat, there might yet be a faint chance . . .

"I've brought a message for Max," she blurted out.

Even as the words left her mouth, Abby realized her mistake. She should have referred to him as duke or Rothwell or His Grace. A proper governess would never dare to use her master's given name.

"Max, is it? *Max?*"

If looks could kill, Lady Elise's face was a lethal

weapon. Malice twisted the beauty of those dainty features. Her green-gold eyes were narrowed, the rosebud lips curled in contempt.

In the next instant, Abby felt a hard shove against her spine that sent her lurching forward. It happened so fast she was unable to stop herself from tripping over the rope and tumbling straight into the ring.

She glimpsed Max's stark gaze on her, then the boxers locked in mortal combat. Momentum hurled her against a hard body. A sharp elbow clipped her in the side of the head.

With the swiftness of a candle winking out, the world went dark.

A drumbeat pounded inside her skull. The incessant thrum of it made her head hurt abominably. Striving to escape the barrage of pain, she fidgeted weakly and moaned.

Something cool and damp came over her brow, and the throbbing subsided to a dull ache. A cloth. The comfort of it helped to pull her out of the dark depths and into feeble awareness. So did the sharp scent of hartshorn, and she irritably batted away the hand holding it to her nose.

Her eyelids fluttered open. The light stabbed like daggers and as she blinked against it, a familiar face swam into view. He was leaning close, peering down at her. She knew those hazy gray eyes. They could be cold as granite, though at the moment they shone warm with concern.

His image abruptly split apart into twin copies. The oddity of it muddled her mind.

"Max?" she said, her voice a mere croak. "Why are there two of you?"

"Hush, don't try to talk. We'll be home very soon."

Home. Not Linton House. He meant Rothwell Court. A

faint longing stirred in the midst of her pain. Oh, how she wished it were her home, too.

Her perception slowly sorted through various sensations. She was reclining in his lap with her head on a pillow. Her bonnet had somehow vanished. That gentle rocking motion must be his coach. But how she had come to be here eluded her comprehension.

"What . . . happened?"

"You fell into the ring at the prizefight and suffered a knock on the head."

Disjointed memories flitted through her mind. One in particular caught her attention. "Brimstone! I left him . . ."

"I surmised as much," Max said rather dryly. "One of the grooms will bring him home."

"And the girls . . . ?"

"We're right here, Aunt Abby."

Valerie's subdued voice came from somewhere nearby. Abby cautiously turned her sore head and saw their fuzzy forms occupying the opposite seat. She blinked in a vain attempt to bring them into focus. "Oh . . . thank goodness you're safe. I was so afraid . . ."

Lady Gwendolyn burst into tears, and Valerie passed her a handkerchief. "Shh," she whispered. "I want to cry too but we mustn't. It will only make her feel worse."

As Gwen's weeping diminished to sniffles, another faint memory eddied through Abby's mind. "Dawkins . . ."

"We tricked him," Valerie admitted in a low, quivery voice that sounded entirely unlike her usual intrepid self. "We pretended to be having a race, and then left him behind in the dust. Please, Your Grace, don't blame him—or Gwen, either. The plan was entirely my notion."

"That isn't *entirely* true," Lady Gwen protested. "I—"

"Enough," Max said. "We will speak of this matter later."

At his imperious tone, Abby lifted her head slightly. "There's something else I must explain . . . about Dawkins . . ."

The mere act of tilting her neck caused her vision to spin dizzyingly. The words that had sat on the tip of her tongue scattered in all directions. The clanging in her brain resumed, and she collapsed back onto the pillow.

His fingers lightly stroked her cheek. "Not another syllable from you, Abby. Whatever it is, there will be time enough later to tell me."

Despite her recent bid for independence, she felt content to let him make the decisions. Especially since at the moment she couldn't seem to string two thoughts together. Sighing, she shut her eyes and drifted back into the peace of nothingness.

Chapter 24

As Max lifted Abby out of the coach, she barely stirred in his arms. A goose egg marred the tangle of cinnamon hair on the side of her head. With her eyes closed, she looked young and vulnerable, and her pale stillness caused a clutch of fear in his chest.

He carried her up to the portico, where a footman threw open the door and admitted them into the entrance hall. The servant gawked at Max's burden, then thrust out his arms. "Your Grace! If I may assist—"

Max aimed a black look at him. The fellow shrank back and deferred to Finchley for direction.

The butler's grizzled brows arched in alarm. "What's this? I knew that demon beast would toss her when Dawkins said she'd gone out on Brimstone! 'Tis just the same as what happened to her mother!"

"It wasn't Brimstone," Max growled. "Send someone to fetch Mrs. Jeffries. And show the doctor up to Miss Linton's chamber at once."

The man had driven his gig closely behind the ducal coach. Max always engaged a top-notch London physician to attend these prizefights. Inevitably, there were injuries that required immediate treatment, stitching wounds, applying ointments, bandaging limbs.

England's champion deserved cosseting. But today, Max hadn't spared a thought for Goliath's welfare—especially as he'd been the culprit who'd bashed Abby in the side of the head with his elbow, accidental though it had been.

His footsteps echoing sharply on the marble, he mounted the grand staircase, while Gwen and Miss Perkins trudged after him with all the enthusiasm of condemned prisoners on their way to the gallows. Let them stew. If not for their misbehavior, Abby wouldn't be in such a predicament.

Her niece dashed ahead to fling open the door to Abby's chamber, which was located directly across the corridor from his sister's suite of rooms. He waited a moment while Gwen pulled back the coverlet of the four-poster. Ever so gently, he laid his precious burden down on the bed and arranged a feather pillow beneath her head.

Unable to resist, he cupped her face. "Abby."

Her lashes fluttered open. Confusion hazed those blue eyes, and she rubbed her cheek against his hand like a kitten seeking a cuddle. "Max? Why are you in my bedchamber? You know that we mustn't—"

He hastened to put his finger over those beautiful lips. Good God, speaking of cats, she'd almost let one out of the bag. Gwen and Miss Perkins already had been staring goggle-eyed at the two of them in the coach. He could only imagine what they must be thinking to see him on such intimate terms with the governess.

"Ah, here's the physician," he said in relief. "Come in, Dr. Woodhull. I'm afraid Miss Linton doesn't look any better."

A middle-aged man with an air of quiet competence, Woodhull carried a leather satchel, which he placed on a table. "That's only to be expected after the jostling of the coach. Now that she's snug in bed, we should see an improvement—at least by tomorrow." Middling in stature, he came to peer up into Max's face. "You'll want to put a slab of raw beefsteak on that eye, Your Grace. It's beginning to blacken and swell."

Max had completely forgotten the injury he'd sustained while snatching Abby from the jaws of death. "Never mind me. Miss Linton was babbling nonsense just now."

"A bit of befuddlement is normal in these cases. I'll examine her again just to be certain. But chances are, she'll be right as rain within a week or two."

"A week or two!" Miss Perkins blurted out. "Oh, no! Is it that bad, then?"

"Time is the best healer for knocks on the head," Woodhull advised. "The brain has been jolted, and it can be dangerous to rush the recovery."

Miss Perkins parted her lips as if to ask more questions, and his sister appeared on the verge of tears again, so Max hustled them both out of the bedchamber. "Go," he ordered. "I'll speak to you two shortly."

Shamefaced, they disappeared into Gwen's rooms. Not a minute later, Mrs. Jeffries came scurrying down the corridor, the ring of keys jangling at her waist. Flustered, she bobbed a curtsy. "Your Grace! I came as soon as I heard! How is Miss Abby?"

"Go in and see for yourself. The doctor is examining her now."

The door closed behind her, leaving Max alone to pace like a caged lion out in the ornate corridor. He wanted nothing more than to stride into the bedroom, to hear any diagnosis the instant it was rendered, and to learn what treatments were ordered. And why shouldn't he? This was his house, by God!

His fingers were actually curling around the knob when sanity restored his good sense. He had no right. Abby was his servant, not his wife. Though he would change her status in an instant if only he had the power to convince her of his constancy.

Stalking down to the end of the passage and back, he relived the nightmarish scene of watching her tumble into the ring. Nothing had ever struck such terror into his heart. Such accidents did occur from time to time as the spectators surged against the ropes. They usually happened on the edge of the arena, though, and the fellow could scramble out safely.

Never before had Max seen someone pitched straight in between the two combatants. And certainly not a woman!

The time it had taken him to reach Abby had seemed an eternity, though it couldn't have been more than a second or two. He recalled shouting, then plunging into the midst of flailing limbs, even as the pugilists belatedly sprang apart. Unfortunately, the damage had already been done.

He gingerly touched his swollen eye. Would that he might change places with her and be the one with the brain injury!

A footman came trotting down the corridor with a collection of jars and bottles rattling on a silver tray. "Your Grace, Mrs. Jeffries requested me to deliver her balms and medications."

Max rapped on the door. As the servant was admitted, Max craned his neck for a glimpse into the sickroom. But the doctor was on his way out and blocked any such view.

Leather bag in hand, Woodhull quietly shut the door. "You'll be pleased to know that our patient responded well to my tests of cognitive function. Mrs. Jeffries has offered to sit with her." He chuckled. "Such a fussbudget the woman is, but that is to be expected, I suppose! I would venture to guess that Miss Linton is a great favorite with the staff."

"She'll recover, then?"

"I've no reason to believe otherwise. It's nothing that a week or two of rest and a light diet won't cure. I've left a tonic to rebuild her strength, and it seems Mrs. Jeffries already has a supply of her own restoratives."

"You'll stay the night," Max commanded.

"Shall I not return to the arena, then?"

"No. Goliath will be brought back here. You may tend him later."

Woodhull bowed. "As you wish, Your Grace. Now, if you might direct me to a place where I shall await your summons."

He was dispatched to a downstairs parlor with the footman as guide.

Max lingered for a moment outside Abby's closed door. He was sorely tempted to keep watch at her bedside and damn anyone who questioned his right to do so. But that would cast an aspersion on her character, and he'd blacken his other eye before he would cause her further harm.

Besides, there were other matters that must be settled.

He rapped sharply on his sister's door, and Gwen peeped out. Her eyes were red-rimmed and watery, but he steeled himself against sympathy. "You and Miss Perkins will accompany me to my study at once."

She gulped and nodded, disappearing for a few moments before emerging with Abby's niece in tow. Both girls looked suitably downcast. Knowing that his silence would intensify their dire imaginings of the ghastly fate that awaited them, he didn't speak another word while leading the way along the corridor and down a side staircase.

Upon reaching the ground floor, he heard the approach of voices. The party of his friends came around a corner, a dispirited air clinging to them.

Ambrose called out, "Ho, there, Rothwell. Of all the ill luck, Goliath has lost the match!"

"It happened not ten minutes after you departed," Pettibone added, escorting Mrs. Chalmers. "England's champ went down with a thud like the fall of a mighty oak. We all lost a tidy bundle on him."

Preoccupied with thoughts of Abby, Max took the news with forbearance. "He was set off his stride by the accident, perhaps. Though I'm inclined to think Wolfman was the better fighter and deserved to win the purse."

Elise rushed forward to clutch at Max's arm. "My lord duke, your poor eye! It is turned a most putrid shade of black. You must be in horrid pain!"

"Bah, he's made of sterner stuff than that," Ambrose said. "The real question is, how does Miss Linton fare? I've been in a torment over it!"

Recalling Ambrose's flirtation with her, Max frowned balefully at his friend. "She should recover fully, although the doctor prescribed a week or more of bedrest. You won't be seeing her again before we leave here."

"Come with me, dear Rothwell," Elise coaxed. "I'll ring for a cold compress for your eye."

Valerie stepped out from behind him. "How cool you are, Lady Desmond, when you know full well that the duke would be perfectly unharmed if not for your treachery. And my aunt would not now be lying upon her sickbed!"

Max swung toward Abby's niece. "What do you mean?"

"I saw her push Aunt Abby. Lady Desmond deliberately shoved her into the arena!"

"Oh, hush, you little brat," Elise told Valerie. "You're trying to divert Rothwell from his anger at your own misbehavior!"

"I am not! I will gladly endure my punishment, whatever it may be! But you won't get away with hurting my aunt. She's worth ten of you."

White-hot anger seared Max. Judging by the way Abby had been propelled into the ring, it made perfect sense that she'd been pushed. He had assumed it to be accidental, though. Now, he could well imagine Elise perpetrating such a vile trick, for she had undoubtedly observed his partiality toward Abby.

Yet he also knew this accusation had earned Valerie an enemy. An accomplished gossip, Elise could cause trouble for the girl when she made her debut next spring. A few whispers in certain ears impugning Valerie for her shabby conduct in attending the prizefight could result in her being shunned by polite society.

He would not see Abby in despair over her niece being ostracized. Not when it was within his power to prevent it.

Leashing his fury, he addressed Valerie. "I will hear nothing more of this wild talk. Lady Desmond is my guest, and you will apologize to her at once."

"I won't!"

"You will, for you have promised to endure my punishment. Now make good on your vow."

The mulish look remained on her pretty features. But she drew a breath and said grudgingly, "I spoke out of turn, your ladyship. I beg your pardon."

Elise nodded with spiteful satisfaction. "See that you never tell such a falsehood about me again."

Noting that Valerie looked about to explode, Max decided to postpone his stern lecture. "Girls, return upstairs and do not disturb Miss Linton. The rest of us shall repair to the drawing room for refreshments."

The party had no sooner seated themselves and rung for a bottle of burgundy than Finchley appeared in the doorway to inquire if the duke would receive Mr. Clifford Linton and Mrs. Rosalind Perkins. The coincidence of their arrival surprised Max; he'd only just intended to sit down at the writing desk to dash off a note informing them of Abby's injury.

In short order, the butler ushered Abby's brother and sister into the drawing room. Clifford grimly strode forward to make his bow to Max, frowned at the bruised eye, then said without preamble, "Where is my sister? How badly was she injured?"

"Pray tell us," Rosalind said, her face drawn with worry. "We have been terribly distraught!"

"She suffered a bump on her head, but she will make a full recovery. One of the best doctors in London has assured me of that."

"I suppose you hired him for the prizefight," Clifford said bitterly. "Pardon me, Your Grace, but I must question your judgment in allowing my sister to attend such an unseemly event!"

Though bristling at being castigated like a naughty child, Max made allowances for the man's distress. "She wasn't there at my invitation, sir. Rather, she went to rescue my sister and Miss Perkins, who, by the way, disobeyed my orders and lured Lady Gwen to the match."

Rosalind gasped. "Are you certain of that?"

"Quite. Your daughter has admitted as much."

"I insist that Valerie and Abby be fetched at once," Clifford intoned. "They must both return home to my care."

"I'm happy to summon your niece, but I'm afraid the

doctor ordered that Miss Linton not be moved. I assure you, she's being given every possible attention."

"There's nothing like a sister's care, though," Rosalind said. "May I see her?"

"She's resting. You may return on the morrow."

Max would not budge on the matter, so a footman was sent to fetch Valerie, who entered the drawing room with obvious trepidation. She looked woeful upon being told that her visit had come to an end, but seeing the stern scowls of her uncle and mother, uttered no complaint.

His friends spoke their good-byes to her, and Lord Ambrose bowed over her hand. "I beg leave to call upon you next spring in London, Miss Perkins. Perhaps you will consent to stand up with me for a dance."

A hint of spirit returned to Valerie in the form of a wobbly smile. "I would be honored, sir."

Max escorted them downstairs to the entrance hall in order to make an inquiry out of earshot of his friends. "May I ask how you discovered so swiftly that your sister had been injured?"

"Why, a groom rode straight from the match to notify us," Rosalind said. "We believed that you had sent him."

Watching them depart in their carriage, Max had a strong suspicion that Elise had dispatched that messenger. She had shoved Abby into the ring. Then, guessing that Abby's family would insist on her returning home, Elise had seized the chance to oust her from his house.

He clenched his jaw. Elise soon would discover that she herself was the one banished from his sight. He intended to make certain that she would never trouble Abby again.

Yet he could not escape a measure of guilt himself. He had invited into his home a woman so spiteful and devious that she had nearly killed Abby. And for that he could not readily forgive himself.

Chapter 25

By the next morning, Abby felt improved enough to sit up in bed. She still needed the curtains drawn, for the sunlight hurt her eyes. But at least the throbbing in her head had diminished to a minor ache.

"One more spoonful, Miss Linton," Lady Gwen begged. "Then you will have finished the bowl."

Abby refrained from voicing her aversion to thin gruel. She dutifully allowed the girl to administer the serving, knowing that it would benefit Gwen as much as herself.

Mrs. Jeffries bustled over to claim the empty dish. "Mrs. Beech will be very pleased. She's keeping a potful simmering for later."

"Perhaps I might have some toast, too?" Abby said hopefully.

"I'm afraid Dr. Woodhull ordered a strict diet for today. It is my duty to see that you follow his instructions to the letter."

Abby meekly submitted to this benevolent bullying. The housekeeper meant well and it served no purpose to argue, anyway. She was determined to fill the role of mother hen, and Lady Gwen was so anxious to atone for her misconduct that Abby didn't have the heart to refuse their help. Being used to activity, however, she felt restless at being confined to bed.

A knock sounded on the door, and when Mrs. Jeffries opened it, Abby quivered at the sound of that familiar, deep voice. She longed to see Max—yet she hoped the housekeeper would have the good sense to turn him away.

He stepped into the bedchamber. She caught only his handsome profile as he turned to speak to Mrs. Jeffries. His impeccable garb of dark blue coat, riding breeches, and black knee boots only made Abby more aware of her own state of dishabille. She was clad in nightdress and wrapper, her hair a tangle due to the awkwardness of having a bandage wrapped around her head.

"Miss Linton," he said, affording her a formal bow. "I've come to check on your progress."

"You'll be happy to hear that I'm seeing only one of you today." Then, as he stepped to the foot of the bed, she gawked at his bruised face. "Oh, your eye!"

"It's nothing."

"He dashed straight between the boxers," Lady Gwen said in worshipful awe. "I saw him snatch you up and carry you to safety!"

"A sight you never would have witnessed had you remained home where you belong," he sternly reminded her. "You'll have ample time to reflect on that since you're forbidden to ride for the next month. Nor will you be allowed any communication with Miss Perkins during that time."

The girl miserably met his gaze. "You're right to punish me, Max, for I wasn't merely following Valerie. I was every bit as much to blame as she was."

This noble confession touched Abby's heart. "It's important to learn from your mistakes, dearest. I know that you never meant for me to come to harm."

"Oh, Miss Linton, I swear I didn't." She hastened to the bed to squeeze Abby's hand. "I confess, it was the worst moment of my life!"

Max came to steer her away. "Gwen, Mrs. Jeffries, if you will kindly leave us, I'd like a word alone with Miss Linton before I leave for London."

The announcement of his imminent departure struck Abby with a knell of dismay. Her already fretful spirits sank even lower. She had hoped he might linger for a day or two longer. It had been a comfort just knowing he was present in the house. The time for her to remove from Rothwell Court forever also loomed, and as much as she loved them, it was disheartening to contemplate returning to her family.

"This is most improper!" the housekeeper scolded. "Master, you cannot mean to be alone with an unmarried lady in her bedchamber."

"You may wait outside in the passage if you like, and leave the door open a crack. Then you can hear Miss Linton scream in the event that I should take advantage of her weakened state and attempt to ravish her."

He made it sound so ridiculous that Mrs. Jeffries unbent enough to smile sheepishly at him. She and Gwen disappeared, leaving Abby alone with Max.

As he turned toward her again, the sight of his blackened eye wrung her heart anew. Yet his slight smile had vanished, and he looked so aloof that she felt shy in his presence. Wondering at his coolness, she could only surmise that now that he was going away, he saw no purpose to continuing his flirtation with her. Worse, she feared he held her to blame, at least in part, for what had happened the previous day. What must he think of her for having allowed her niece and his sister to run wild?

There were so many things she wanted to say to him.

Yet one in particular sprang to the forefront of her mind. "Dawkins! My memory is hazy, but it seems I meant to tell you something important about him yesterday—"

"You needn't explain. I've already blistered him for believing that faradiddle about me having allowed you to ride Brimstone."

"He *did* try to dissuade me," she said in the groom's defense. "I trust you can see that I had no choice but to go after the girls."

"Not at the risk of your own neck! And certainly not when you were terrified of horses. Better that Dawkins had gone in your place."

Max frowned at her from the foot of the bed. He might at least have praised her for overcoming her fear! "Pray forgive me for trying to protect your sister from scandal," she said stiffly. "Though I must also apologize for my niece being a corrupting influence on her. No matter what Lady Gwen might say, she'd never have dreamed up such a scheme on her own."

"No, she would not," he said in a milder tone. "Though perhaps I should be pleased that she misbehaved for once in her life."

"She *has* been sheltered here," Abby ventured. "Despite what happened yesterday, it's been greatly beneficial for her to have the company of more than just a governess and an aunt who spends most of her time gardening."

"I intend to rectify that henceforth."

He had expressed a desire to spend more time here at his ducal seat, and now he watched her keenly as if awaiting her reaction. Yet she didn't dare let it raise her hopes. "Max, why did you not come back until now? What has kept you away from the Court all these years?"

"Shall I say it was you, Abby?"

Nettled by uncertainty, she said hotly, "No! Rather, I've

long suspected it had something to do with your family upbringing. But I don't know the truth because you always dissemble whenever I ask you about it. So what is it? Do you leave Gwen here because you blame her for your mother's death?"

He had begun pacing while she spoke, but gave a start of surprise at that last remark. "Gwen? Certainly not, why would I?"

"Your mother died of childbed fever soon after your sister was born. I thought perhaps Gwen reminded you of that unhappy time. It would explain why you've stayed away."

"You're speaking of things you know nothing about!"

"Then enlighten me. Or I shall go on thinking the worst."

"It's far from the worst. The worst is that—" He bit off his words and ran his fingers through his hair, turning the neatly combed strands into an attractive tousle. When he glanced in her direction, it was as if he were seeing not her, but some long-ago horror. "The worst is that childbed fever was just a falsehood my father put about to cover up the truth. The truth is that . . . my mother took her own life."

Abby gazed at him in stark disbelief. "Oh, Max, no. How? Why?"

"Mama was a capricious woman who could be merry and whimsical for weeks on end, the most adorable companion any child could ever hope to have. But she was also prone to long bouts of melancholy and fits of hysteria. She would snap at my father, slam doors, smash things." He resumed his pacing. "One of those episodes occurred after Gwen was born. It was more dire than the others, and I remember my mother weeping in bed for days on end. She hid the laudanum prescribed by the doctor until she had accumulated enough for her purpose. Then she swallowed all of it down at once."

Abby was horrified by the revelation of the shock and anguish he must have suffered. And it had happened during the time when they'd known each other! She had not seen him until after the funeral, when he had refused to talk about his grief, desiring only to make love to Abby, which had led to their quarrel. Now she could see that it had been her well-meaning attempt to coax him to speak of his mother that had caused him to storm off in anger.

Watching him pace now, she wanted nothing more than to comfort him. But the grimness of his mood felt like a veil of ice between them. Quietly she asked, "Why didn't you tell me any of this back then?"

"My father swore me to a strict vow of secrecy. He would not have her name besmirched. Not even Gwen knows." He laughed rather harshly. "Now you see how good I am at keeping promises, for I have just broken one."

"Silence was a terrible burden for him to have set upon you," she said, indignant not at Max but at the old duke. "But I imagine he was gripped by pain. He loved your mother very much, did he not? You said so once before."

"He worshipped the ground she walked upon. You would have, too, had you known her in her happier times, when she was all charm and liveliness."

Grim-faced, he frowned into the distance. What a volatile childhood he'd had in comparison to her own. If only he had told her about it before now! She couldn't help but think that sharing the burden might have eased his torment.

"So that's why your father took you and Gwen away right after the funeral. He could no longer bear to live here at the Court, where there were so many memories. Nor could you."

He looked at her, his lips twisted into a strange half-smile. "Perhaps it's time to chase away the ghosts. Would you not agree, Miss Linton?"

His formality stung, and she hid the hurt by answering in kind. "I would say that it is none of my concern, Your Grace. I shall be departing here as soon as I am recovered."

"So you will leave my sister."

"It's inevitable," she said, showing him a tranquil expression. "You told me from the start that I must go when you do. Besides, I cannot imagine you would wish for a ruined woman to continue in the role of governess."

He stared at her for a moment, his granite-gray eyes concealing his thoughts. Then he came forward and pressed a warm kiss to her hand, his fingers tight around hers. "I trust you'll stay at least until I can hire a suitable replacement in London. Will you promise me that?"

She prayed he couldn't tell how swiftly her heart was beating. Or how much she wished he could love her as she loved him. "Of course."

He gripped her hand for a moment longer. She held her breath in reckless hope for some word of affection from him. But it never came. Releasing her, he strode from the bedchamber without a backward glance.

Mrs. Jeffries came bustling back into the room. She was armed with a pewter mug. "This posset is straight from the kitchen. I've added a dollop of Dr. Woodhull's tonic to it."

Abby dutifully drank the warm milky brew without even tasting it, then persuaded the housekeeper to withdraw on the excuse that her patient was in sore need of a nap.

As soon as the door closed, however, Abby pushed back the covers and arose from the bed. She felt a trifle wobbly on her feet, and the mere act of standing made her head throb. Nevertheless, she managed to walk to the windows that overlooked the front drive.

Twitching back the draperies, she peered outside. The sunlight hurt her eyes, but she was driven by the acute desire to have one last glimpse of Max. Heaven alone knew if he would fulfill his stated intention to return, and even if he did, she would not be here at Rothwell Court to welcome him.

His black traveling coach was parked below by the covered portico. The coachman sat atop the high seat and a footman stood at rigid attention, holding open the door of the vehicle. Lord Pettibone handed Mrs. Chalmers into the conveyance before entering it himself.

As Max's tall form came into view, Abby caught her breath. Sunlight gleamed on his dark hair, still mussed from when he'd run his fingers through it. She wanted to fling open the window and call out to him, just so that he would look up at her.

In the next instant, she realized that Lady Desmond had a proprietary hold on his arm as they walked to the coach. From above, the dainty widow looked like a vision in rose-pink with an egret plume stylishly decorating her silk bonnet.

Abby released the curtain and stepped back. She oughtn't feel such a stab in her heart. She had seen those two together many times before, and of course they would be traveling to London together. They moved in the same select circles, after all.

Yet it was a harsh reminder that Max was returning to his old life. He might speak offhandedly about coming back here, but it was far more likely that the pleasures of the city would beguile him too much. How foolish she'd been to dream he might mend his wicked ways for her sake!

Tears overflowing her eyes, she sank back onto the bed and buried her face in her hands. It was best to face the truth. Maxwell Bryce, the Duke of Rothwell, did not love her. Nor would he ever.

He would always be an incorrigible rake.

Chapter 26

A fortnight passed before Mrs. Jeffries deemed Abby to be in the pink of health. Lady Gwendolyn immediately proposed an excursion to the village. She and Abby had been cooped up for too long, she declared, and it would do them both wonders to venture out of the house.

Abby required no persuading. Ever since that bout of weeping on the day of Max's departure, she had drifted in a gray, lethargic state. She obediently drank the restoratives prepared by Mrs. Jeffries. She thanked Lady Hester for the vases of flowers. She strove to listen when Lady Gwen read books aloud to her and to smile when the kittens were brought for a visit.

Inside, though, she felt empty and colorless. But she knew that Gwen wanted to cheer her up, so she made the effort. The girl needed a friend now that Valerie had returned to Kent with Rosalind.

Abby had promised her sister she'd go to London in the spring for her niece's debut. Surely by then her spirits would be mended sufficiently that she might enjoy her first sojourn to the city. Perhaps she might even meet a gentleman who would court a lady of her advanced years. And if she encountered Max at a society party, well, she'd smile serenely as she always did.

As they strolled down the high street, the chill wind brought a nip of autumn. Lady Gwen wished to see if there were any new goods in stock at the draper's, so they headed there first. A young woman was coming out of the shop, and she stopped short. A smile bloomed on her pretty features within the emerald-green bonnet with its crimson ribbons and the cluster of cherries.

Lady Gwen hastened to wrap her in an exuberant embrace. "Miss Herrington! You're back!"

"I'm Mrs. Babcock now and living at Meadowcroft Farm. Oh, it's so good to see you again, Lady Gwen. And you, too, Miss Linton. I understand you're the new governess."

"Only for a short time," Abby said. "My family needs me back home. I'll be leaving when the new governess comes from London."

Miss Thackery was due to arrive on the morrow, according to a letter Lady Gwen had received from the duke. Dawkins was to drive Abby back to Linton House then. She assured herself that her spirits would perk up once she was back in the bosom of her beloved family.

"I've told His Grace how very grateful I am for his assistance," Mrs. Babcock was saying. "He's helped me twice in my time of need. I don't know what I'd have done without his kind support."

"Oh, I'm so glad to hear it," Lady Gwendolyn enthused. "A nicer and more considerate gentleman is nowhere to be found!"

Ever since getting his note two days ago, hand-delivered by a messenger from London, the girl had been singing her brother's praises at every turn, and it had driven Abby deeper into the blue devils. What a shock it would be to

Lady Gwen if ever she learned of his dissolute ways. Even if he couldn't reform for Abby, he might do so for his sister's sake!

As Mrs. Babcock took her leave and they entered the small shop, Abby cast a desultory eye over the displays of cloth and rolls of ribbons. She exchanged cordial greetings with the shopkeeper, who was the father of her sister-in-law, Daphne. She helped Lady Gwen pick out a length of Honiton lace to trim one of her gowns.

But all the while, she could think only of how glowingly Mrs. Babcock had spoken of Max. The former Miss Herrington was the sister of his school friend who had died in battle and left her destitute. Max had provided her a position in his household. Later, when Mr. Babcock's parents had opposed the marriage, Max had obtained a special license for the happy couple to wed in secret. He had reluctantly revealed that story to Abby only when she had accused him of having nefarious designs on the former governess.

Abby would rather not have been reminded that Max had any shred of decency. Certainly, he had helped her to overcome a fear of horses. He had doctored the splinter in her finger. He had snatched her out of the boxing ring and carried her to safety. But in the end, the Duke of Rothwell had gone back to his debauched life in London.

By the time they finished their shopping and were being driven home in the carriage, Abby had worked up a certain antipathy toward him. At least resentment felt better than sinking deeper into that awful morass. No doubt, at this very moment, he was lying in Lady Desmond's scented embrace, for he was no longer required to resist the woman's charms now that he had gone away from his sister's company.

". . . after what Lady Desmond did," Lady Gwen said.

Nonplussed, Abby stared at the girl. "Pardon?"

"I was talking about what an eventful month this has been," Lady Gwen said. "I enjoyed meeting Max's friends, except for that dreadful woman. I'll never forgive her for pushing you!"

"Pushing me?"

"Yes, at the prizefight. Valerie saw her shove you into the ring. Surely you felt her ladyship's hand at your back!"

Searching her memory, Abby had a vague recollection of a brief, angry exchange with Lady Desmond—then the sense of a hard thrust. After that, everything went blank. But she had never made the connection. And now, she felt sickened to think that someone could despise her so much.

"I'm afraid that day is still something of a blur to me."

"My brother was furious when Valerie accused Lady Desmond," the girl confided. "He made Valerie apologize. It seemed terribly unfair, but he explained to us later that he feared her ladyship might make trouble."

"He *knew* she'd pushed me?"

Her dove-gray eyes grew larger. "Perhaps I oughtn't have said anything. But I thought you'd remembered, Miss Linton. Oh, please don't be angry at Max. He meant well, I'm sure!"

"It's all right, darling. I doubt I shall ever see your brother again."

Abby was too caught up in her own dark reflections to do more than peripherally notice the sparkle that came into Lady Gwen's expression. The girl parted her lips as if to reply. Then she apparently thought better of it and turned to gaze out the window.

The revelation had yanked Abby fully out of the doldrums and stirred her to a wintry wrath. The gall of Max, to know the malicious trick that Lady Desmond had perpetrated and then to go off with the woman as if it were

nothing at all! Maybe in his unprincipled world, people behaved with such wicked treachery, but not in hers!

Abby fairly itched for a quill and paper to write him a
censorious letter. Oh, it would be a more blighting epistle
than any he had ever received! Every frosty word would
numb that flirtatious charm of his and freeze his ducal ar-
rogance. Her mind was busily composing the biting missive when Lady Gwen's voice broke into her icy musings.

"Oh, look, Miss Linton! The ducal coach is behind us.
I can see the Rothwell crest on the side!"

Abby's heart careened against her corset. Max! He had
come back.

Disbelieving, she leaned over Lady Gwen's shoulder to
peer outside. As the carriage followed the winding curves
of the drive through the estate, she could indeed see the
coach trailing them.

She sat back, gripping her gloved fingers in her lap.
It took a moment to collect her disordered thoughts and
assume a pose of glacial dignity. Well! So much the better.
Instead of writing that note, she would have the chance to
give the duke a severe reproach in person.

She remained in a state of rigid control as the carriage
drew up before the portico and a footman handed them out
onto the graveled drive. A moment later, the coach came
to a stop as well.

Abby braced herself to be poised and cool, to request
an interview with His Grace at the earliest possible con-
venience. She would not even have to bide her tongue, for
she needn't be constrained by the fear of losing her post.

When the coach door opened, however, out came a
middle-aged woman in sober garb, her figure tending to
plumpness. No other passenger emerged. A footman re-
trieved a portmanteau from the boot before the coachman
continued toward the stables.

Realizing that Lady Gwen was gliding toward the visitor, Abby belatedly followed. "Welcome to Rothwell Court," the girl said. "I'm Lady Gwendolyn Bryce. May I presume you're Miss Thackery, my new governess?"

The woman smiled as they shook hands. She had plain, pleasant features and an air of quiet, aristocratic competence. "If I may be so bold, you're every bit as engaging as His Grace described. And I must add, it was kind of him to allow me the use of his traveling coach."

"Very thoughtful, indeed! You're a day earlier than expected, but I daresay I simply misread his note. I'm pleased to meet you, though. Miss Linton recently suffered an accident, and she wishes to go home to her family."

As they entered the house, Miss Thackery clucked over Abby without being so indiscreet as to press for details of the injury. Abby kept mum about the prizefight and so did Lady Gwen. Luckily, the new governess turned her interest to the great hall with its frescoes of classical scenes.

"It's a large house, but you'll soon learn your way around," Lady Gwen told the woman as they started toward the grand staircase. "Perhaps once you've had some refreshment, you might allow me to take you on a tour."

A lump formed in Abby's throat. She ought to be glad the two appeared to be getting along so well. With newfound confidence, the girl had matured in only a few short weeks. Her timidity had transformed into a ladylike graciousness. It had helped tremendously to have Valerie as her companion and to mingle with Max's friends. Abby liked to think she herself had played a part, too, by taking the girl out to visit the tenant farms.

They were starting up the stairs when Lady Gwen turned back. "Oh, I nearly forgot! Miss Linton, would you mind fetching a book of poetry from the library so that I might read to you tonight? Edmund Spenser, perhaps."

"There's no need since my head doesn't hurt anymore," Abby said. "And with Miss Thackery here, I should pack the last of my things and depart."

"Oh, but you mustn't! We won't have time for a proper farewell! Please, Miss Linton, say you'll stay for one more night."

Abby found her hands clutched in earnest entreaty. The girl looked so despondent that Abby's resolve weakened. "As you wish, then. I'll return home in the morning."

In a twinkling, a bright smile replaced the wretched sadness. "And you will promise to go straight to the library for the book?"

"Yes."

Wondering at the girl's insistence, Abby peeled off her gloves as she headed down a long corridor. She had a fleeting sense of having been maneuvered. But unable to discern any reason for it, she let her mind drift to the matter of her own exodus. It was daunting to have the moment cast upon her so swiftly. One more night, that was all she had left here. How quickly this grand palace with its stately rooms had come to feel like home to her!

To distract herself from melancholy, she considered the scathing letter she meant to write to the duke. With Lady Gwen in the capable hands of Miss Thackery, now was the perfect opportunity. There would be paper and pen in the desk in the library.

She tried out different phrases in her mind. *Your unscrupulous associations . . . escorting that venomous vixen . . . a disgrace to the nobility . . .*

By the time she entered the library, Abby had worked herself into a fine fettle. There could be no more wicked lord in all of England than the Duke of Rothwell, who had brushed off a cruel act committed by his latest *chère amie* as if it were nothing worse than a child's prank, and then he had continued to keep that perfidious peahen close at his side—

She halted in her tracks. The force of her fury had conjured Max from thin air. Yet when she attempted to blink away his image, he remained very much a solid, flesh-and-blood man.

He stood a short distance away with his hands braced on a library table. He was frowning down at some papers on the mahogany surface as if they contained the secrets of the universe. A pulse of errant desire began to beat in her depths. How elegant he appeared in a charcoal-gray coat with a white cravat that set off the handsomeness of his features. He might have looked utterly haughty and unapproachable if not for the fact that his hair was delightfully mussed as if he'd combed it with his fingers.

He seemed unaware of her presence. She could quietly retrace her steps, retreat from the manor, and flee through the woods to Linton House.

But she wasn't a coward, not anymore. She had quite the withering speech prepared for him—if only her wayward heart would cease pestering her with the urge to fling herself into his arms.

Abby glided purposefully forward. "Good afternoon, Your Grace. How fortunate is your return! You are precisely the person I wished to see."

Chapter 27

He straightened up at once, his gaze locking with hers. All trace of his blackened eye had vanished, she noted. A strange sort of caution seemed to edge his expression, along with a lack of his usual assurance.

It was then that she realized this was no chance encounter. He had been waiting here for her. And he had recruited his sister as his accomplice.

"Abby," he said, a charming smile forming on his lips. "It's good to see you looking so well. How are you feeling?"

"I'm perfectly fine, as you already know. Lady Gwen will have kept you apprised of the state of my health." Gripping her gloves, she took a step closer. "Your being here isn't happenstance, either. You instructed your sister to invent an excuse to lure me to the library."

"I wasn't certain if you would receive me."

On that cryptic statement, Max approached, and Abby thought for a moment that he meant to sweep her into his arms and kiss her senseless. She must repulse him, of course—even if her breathing was erratic and her heart was beating so fast that a swoon seemed imminent.

She caught an alluring whiff of his masculine cologne as he walked past her and closed the door. When he turned back, he wore a grave expression. Did he appear paler? If so, it was not out of pining for her, but merely an effect of his libertine ways.

Realizing he awaited her reply, she said, "I'm quite happy to receive you, my lord duke, for you've saved me the trouble of putting pen to paper. I was just now intending to compose a letter to you."

"A letter. For what reason?"

That arrogant cocking of his eyebrow was a small thing, but it set her over the edge. She flung her gloves onto the nearest chair. The carefully constructed phrases deserted her as anger poured out in a torrent. "To rake you over the coals, that's why. You *knew* Lady Desmond deliberately pushed me into the ring, yet you drove off to London with her as if nothing whatsoever had happened!"

"No, I most certainly did not."

"Don't deny it, sir! I myself saw you with that venomous vixen. You were climbing into your coach with her!"

"A wretched spy you would make! If you'd kept watching—from your window, I presume—you'd have seen me mount Brimstone as soon as I'd handed her inside. That was the last time I saw her."

Torn between elation and disbelief, she stuttered, "But—but she's so beautiful. I knew you hadn't made her your mistress here, but I was sure you must have been consorting with her in London this past fortnight."

"Do you truly believe that I could make love to a woman—*a venomous vixen*—who had done such a vile deed to you, Abby? What sort of monster do you take me for?"

Abby saw the whiteness of anger around his firmed mouth. In that moment, she realized how terribly mistaken she had been, how she had once again leaped to the wrong conclusion about him. It was like a veil being lifted so that she could see him clearly again.

Hardly daring to hope, she started toward him, then stopped, unsure of herself. "Oh, Max, forgive me. I—I don't really think that. It's just that I was—well—*envious* that she had gone away with you. Especially since you were so—so cold and aloof toward me when last we met."

During her speech, his expression had eased, and he came to put his hands on her shoulders. "Abby, if I was cold, it was from the guilt that was lashing at me. *I* was the one who'd put you in danger by allowing that woman under my roof. I should have realized her malice and sent her away." One corner of his mouth twisted. "Then later, when I told you about my mother, I feared you had taken a disgust of me. All you could speak about was your eagerness to leave my house and return to your brother's."

She cupped his jaw in her palms. "Oh, no! I was glad you'd finally told me the truth. I could never think badly of *you* for the actions of your parents. If that's why you've stayed away this past fortnight . . ."

"Actually, I was on a mission. Come."

She let him take her hand. His imperious manner was back, but Abby no longer minded. She was too gratified to know that he seemed to have returned to Rothwell Court specifically to see her.

And pleased to learn he had not been with that woman, after all.

He took her over to the table where he'd been standing when she'd walked into the library. There, he drew back a chair and invited her to sit while he himself settled onto the edge of the table.

"Let me say that I've spent very little of the past two weeks in London. Mostly, I've been chasing all over

England trying to locate my father's former secretary. Bucklesby retired to a village in Staffordshire, but when I rode there, he'd gone to Tunbridge Wells to take the waters. The man was devilish hard to find, he wasn't registered at any of the inns, but I finally tracked him down to a private house where he was staying with a relative."

Abby had been staring at Max, wondering at his purpose in telling her all this, when it struck her. "The missing letters!"

His mouth curved. "Indeed. I thought if anyone would know what had happened to them, it would be Bucklesby. He's a magpie who dreads nothing more than to toss the least scrap of paper. As it turns out, my hunch was correct. It was Bucklesby whom my father had instructed to dispose of the letters, and Bucklesby who had not been able to bring himself to do so. He'd even smuggled the letters out of the house on the chance that I might someday ask for them."

On that astounding statement, Max turned to pick up the papers that he'd been staring at upon her entry. It was a stack of slender letters.

Abby reverently took the little pile from him. The topmost missive bore her own neat penmanship with his Grosvenor Square address, and when she turned it over, a small wafer of wax still sealed the tightly folded paper.

Clutching the packet to her bosom, she lifted her gaze to him. "You haven't read them?"

"No. I deemed it something we ought to do together."

Anxiety dampened her rising spirits. Was that why he'd come back, then? Just to show her these letters? Was this to be only a moment of nostalgia among old friends?

He surprised her out of those morbid reflections by sinking to one knee beside her chair and taking her hand. "Abby, I must explain how this came about. After my mother's death, my father was a broken man. He spent the last few years of his life in a haze of drink, morose and weeping for her. And he warned me time and again never to commit the folly of falling in love."

What awful advice to give to his son! Especially when Max had been wounded himself. Her little flare of indignation melted into understanding. "I expect that's why he took the letters, then. He wanted to protect you from being hurt, from suffering the pain that he was suffering."

"You're kinder to him than I can ever be," Max said, his voice vibrating with anger. "My father caused the rift between us, and you must allow me to apologize for that."

"Apology refused. No one can take the blame for someone else's deed, Max. It wasn't *your* fault that neither of us received the other's letters."

"Nevertheless, I ought to have honored my promise to court you when I came of age. But by that time, I was convinced that love makes a man miserable and wretched." He paused before adding huskily, "As indeed it can do."

He was gazing at her in a tender way that set her heart to soaring. Was he saying that he loved her? Was it even possible? Oh, she prayed so!

She went willingly when he rose to his feet and pulled her up into his arms. He attempted to lay a string of kisses over her face, only to be foiled by the brim of her bonnet. "Blast this dratted thing," he said with flattering impatience, untying the ribbons and hurling the offending hat to the floor.

"That's my best bonnet, I'll have you know!"

"I'll buy you a dozen finer ones, then."

On that, his lips came down over hers with enough warmth and devotion to kindle a fire in her. Abby wrapped her arms around his neck and returned the kiss with all the love in her heart. She wanted so badly to believe that he could love her, and only her. But did she dare hope that he had changed his wicked ways?

Keeping a little of herself reserved, she drew back to regard him. "You seem to have an affinity for seducing ladies in the library, my lord duke."

"Oh, sometimes I prefer the lakeside."

Ah, he did know how to conjure up delicious memories! And he was taking full advantage, nuzzling her throat and nipping at her ear, reminding her of his expertise in the art of pleasure.

Resisting his provocative lips, she murmured, "It's enjoyable to have a fling in the arms of a practiced rogue. But life isn't all hot kisses and dizzying embraces, at least not for us ordinary mortals."

"You're a nymph, not a mortal, and I love you most desperately. I was hoping—*praying*—you might put me out of my wretched misery." He looked at her with a dazed sort of intensity. "What say you?"

She melted against him. "That I love you, Max, with all my heart. I would never have *made* love without being *in* love." Despite that impassioned declaration, a remnant of prudence prodded her to add, "I'm not like you."

He touched his forehead to hers in a penitent way. "Abby, I swear to you by all that's holy, I will never look at another woman so long as I live."

"That may prove difficult. There's Lady Gwen and Mrs. Jeffries and Beechy and all the other female servants. Not to mention my sisters and my nieces and—"

"Bramble!" he said, chuckling. "You know what I mean! I intend to take my wedding vows very seriously."

Though her heart rejoiced, she gave him a stern look. "If that was a marriage proposal, it was shoddily done."

His mouth twisted in chagrin. "Ah, my darling! I did flub it again, didn't I? I had it all planned out . . . we would read the letters together. Or rather, you'd read mine . . ." He crouched down to collect the *billets* where they had fluttered to the floor. Looking up, he added rather plaintively, "Then, when you came to the part where I'd reiterated my wish to marry you, I would have . . . Oh, devil take it!"

The last of her fears vanished as she saw her silver-tongued duke flounder for words. The knowledge that his flirtatious charm had deserted him at such a time could only mean that his feelings for her ran deep and true.

Still kneeling, he tightly grasped her hand. "Abigail Linton, will you do me the great honor of becoming my wife?"

For one golden moment, her heart felt too full for words. She marveled that the infamous Duke of Rothwell could give up his freedom for a thirty-year-old spinster who had never traveled farther than twenty miles from home. And she could see in him both the polished man he was now and the gawky youth she'd once known. They were one and same.

"Yes, Max. Oh, yes, I'll marry you."

The letters went flying again as he sprang up for another kiss, this one rich with promise and rife with love. When they were both giddy with happiness, she murmured against his lips, "Now, what would you have done if I'd said no?"

Holding her close, he cocked an eyebrow in that insufferable manner. "I'd have taken you to the stables and showed you the fine cream mare that I purchased at Tattersall's yesterday. And I'd have said there could be no bride gift without a bride."

"Max! Truly?" She hid her sparkling interest in the

mare behind a chiding look. "Ah, I see. You're not only arrogant, but unscrupulous. You think I can be bribed."

He lifted her hand to his lips, kissing it with fervent tenderness. "What I think, nymph, is that if falling in love is folly, I'll gladly be the most foolish man in England."

Coming soon . . .

Look for the next novel in Olivia Drake's
Unlikely Duchesses series

FOREVER
AND A DUKE

Available in January 2020
from St. Martin's Paperbacks